Books in THE HARDY BOYS CASEFILES™ Series

Available from ARCHWAY Paperbacks

THE
HARDY
BOYS

CASEFILES™
COLLECTOR'S EDITION

FRANKLIN W. DIXON

AN ARCHWAY PAPERBACK
Published by POCKET BOOKS
New York London Toronto Sydney Tokyo Singapore

This book is a work of fiction. Names, characters, places and incidents are products of the author's imagination or are used fictitiously. Any resemblance to actual events or locales or persons, living or dead, is entirely coincidental.

AN ARCHWAY PAPERBACK *Original*

An Archway Paperback published by
POCKET BOOKS, a division of Simon & Schuster Inc.
1230 Avenue of the Americas, New York, NY 10020

Rock 'n' Revenge copyright © 1991 by Simon & Schuster Inc.
Choke Hold copyright © 1991 by Simon & Schuster Inc.
Uncivil War copyright © 1991 by Simon & Schuster Inc.
Produced by Mega-Books, Inc.

ISBN: 0-671-02034-X

First Archway Paperback printing September 1998

10 9 8 7 6 5 4 3 2 1

THE HARDY BOYS, AN ARCHWAY PAPERBACK and colophon are registered trademarks of Simon & Schuster Inc.

THE HARDY BOYS CASEFILES is a trademark of Simon & Schuster Inc.

Cover design by Jim Lebbad

Printed in the U.S.A.

IL 6+

THE
HARDY
BOYS

CASEFILES™
COLLECTOR'S EDITION

ROCK 'N' REVENGE

Chapter

1

"CANCELED? WHAT DO YOU MEAN, the ski trip's been canceled?" Joe Hardy shouted into the receiver.

He listened for a few moments and then slammed down the phone. "Rats!" Joe's blue eyes flashed angrily.

"What's the matter, Joe?" asked his older brother, Frank.

Joe glanced over at Frank, who was filling a camera bag at the far end of the kitchen. Frank had a long telephoto lens in one hand and the camera body in the other.

Frank Hardy's dark, lean form contrasted with Joe's muscular body and blond hair. The two brothers' personalities were as different as their looks. Frank was the calm, logical brother, while Joe often acted impulsively. Yet it was these very differences that made the pair such a successful team of detectives.

"That was Mr. Abrams, the ski club advisor," Joe said, disappointed. "He says the spring break ski trip's been canceled."

"What happened?"

"A warm front melted all the powder off the slopes, and no one's making snow because it's too warm."

"Why not come to the sports arena with Callie and me, then, and watch them set up for the Buddy Death concert?"

"Buddy Death?" Joe said scornfully. "He stinks!"

Frank shrugged and picked up the camera bag. "Suit yourself. I'm going to pick up Callie and head over there now."

Frank walked toward the back door, whistling slightly off-key. Joe watched him go, still sulking. Spring break was his last chance that year to ski at Snow Valley. He'd been looking forward to tackling Suicide Slide one more time that season.

The kitchen door slammed, snapping Joe out of his reverie. "Hey, Frank! Wait up!" he called.

"The place seems kind of empty with Mom and Aunt Gertrude away," he admitted, joining his brother in their black customized van.

"Even Buddy Death has to be more fun than hanging around the kitchen by myself."

Frank grinned as he started the van's engine and pulled out of the driveway. He was glad to see Joe acting like himself again. "Yeah. Who knows when Dad'll be back from San Francisco."

Joe sighed and nodded. Fenton Hardy was a well-known private detective whose work often took him away from Bayport.

After a short drive they pulled up at the house of Frank's steady girlfriend, Callie Shaw. Frank tapped the horn twice, and the front door quickly opened. Callie waved and ran out to the van, her pretty face glowing with excitement.

"Hi, Joe!" Callie said. "I wasn't expecting to see you today."

"My plans got canceled. Guess it's your lucky day," Joe kidded.

"It sure is!" Callie said. "Doing this piece on Buddy Death is my big chance with the Bayport *Times*. If I do a good job, the features editor promised me regular work, which shouldn't be a problem with Frank Hardy, ace photographer, at my side."

Frank laughed and threw the van into gear. "What kind of background stuff did you dig up on Buddy Death?" he asked as he stepped on the accelerator.

"Not much. He hasn't been on the heavy

metal scene that long, and, of course, this is his first national tour.''

"I don't get what all the fuss is about," Joe said. "You know heavy metal's my music, but I think Buddy stinks."

"Buddy's last LP shot up to number one and never came down. He's got an enormous following," said Frank. "I'm not really into heavy metal, but he's okay."

The van topped the next hill, and the oval-shaped Bayport Sports Arena, its white dome gleaming, seemed to fill the horizon.

As they pulled into the parking lot Joe noticed several helicopters circling overhead. On their sides were the emblems of three major TV networks. "What are they looking at?" Joe asked.

"That," said Callie. She pointed at the main entrance to the arena. It was jam-packed with teenagers in ripped-up clothes, heavy make-up, and brightly colored hair. They milled about excitedly, chanting Buddy's name. One fan was playing Buddy's music on a gigantic boom box while others danced in frantic circles to the wild, angry beat.

"The concert's not for two days, and they're already camped out," said Frank. "I told you, Joe. Buddy has the Midas touch."

After parking the van, the trio checked in with arena security and were allowed into one of the four wide, high-ceilinged access tunnels that led directly onto the huge floor of the arena.

"Wow. This *is* major," Joe said as they cleared the tunnel. A huge stage had already been partly erected across the north end of the space. A crew of roadies was speedily assembling a network of steel crossbeams and pillars to support the apron of the stage, which extended in a half circle into the audience.

"Look up there," said Frank.

Joe raised his eyes and spotted members of the lighting crew moving along narrow catwalks that stretched across the center of the enormous dome and ran along the edges.

"What are those towers for?" Callie pointed to the tall steel structures on either side of the stage. "They look like giant Tinkertoys."

"They support the speakers," Joe told her. "For a concert this size they'll need enough speakers to knock down the back wall." Joe watched the crew, impressed by the way each person moved thirty feet above the ground, supported only by a small harness.

"The tour must cost a fortune," said Callie.

"You kids don't know the half of it." Joe turned to see a short, bald, middle-aged man in gray slacks, a yellow- and red-striped sweater, and dark sunglasses lounging beside a pile of equipment.

He walked over to Callie and the Hardys.

"You kids got a pass? This shindig's not open to the public."

"I'm Callie Shaw from the Bayport *Times,*" Callie said.

"Oh. That's different. I'm Syd Schacht. I'm the promoter of this tour." He gave Callie a toothy smile and shook her hand. "Who're your friends?"

"I'm Frank Hardy, Mr. Schacht. I'm Callie's photographer."

"And I'm Joe Hardy. I'm just along for the ride. I hope that's okay."

"Sure!" Schacht replied. "Just stay out of everyone's way." Then he frowned and muttered to himself, "Hardy, Hardy—why does that name sound familiar?"

"Maybe you've heard of their dad," said Callie. "Fenton Hardy, the detective?"

"Oh, yeah!" Schacht grinned from behind the sunglasses. "He did an investigation for a friend of mine a few years ago. Saved him a pile of money. Well, it's good to know we've got friends in high places." He laughed loudly and slapped Frank on the back.

"Frank and Joe are detectives, too," Callie said. Schacht just nodded.

"Is Buddy around yet?" Callie asked.

Schacht pointed to a shiny black motor home parked near access tunnel C at the opposite end of the arena. Joe was surprised to see a motor home inside the dome, but he realized

6

that the access tunnel they had come through had ceilings high enough to accommodate even big equipment trucks.

"He's in there with his manager, Bobby Mellor," said Schacht. "Poor guy spent all morning doing interviews, and he's feeling out of it. Maybe you should talk to the rest of the band first. Come on, I'll introduce you."

Frank and Callie followed Schacht toward the stage. "I'll catch you later, Frank," Joe said. "I want to check out this operation."

"Keep your head up, kid," said Schacht. "There's a lot of steel flying through the air today."

Joe waved in acknowledgment and turned toward one of the sound towers, where a team of twenty roadies was passing six-foot lengths of steel pipe upward in a human chain. Joe was intrigued by the way the roadies assembled each level of the tower from the corners, bolting the diagonal supports to the corner posts.

After a few minutes Joe wandered over to look at Buddy Death's black motor home. Stylized white skulls with the initials BDB on the forehead—the logo for the Buddy Death Band—were painted on both sides of the motor home. Another one decorated the hood.

Suddenly Joe grew aware of the sound of someone singing and playing an acoustic guitar. It was a beautiful sound—high and clear.

7

Nothing like the sound of Buddy Death's band members.

Curious, Joe followed the sound through access tunnel C to a side door and peeked outside. He spotted the singer immediately.

She was a tall, slender girl with auburn hair that fell in waves past her shoulders. She was dressed in a white cotton blouse and a colorful peasant skirt even though it was still wintry. She was so intent on her playing that she didn't notice Joe approach.

"Hi," he said, flashing her a friendly grin as she noticed him and stopped singing. "Don't stop on my account. You play beautifully."

The auburn-haired girl blushed and lowered her eyes. "Thanks," she said.

"What song was that?" Joe asked. "It sounded kind of familiar."

Suddenly his face cleared, and he snapped his fingers. "I know! It's that new Buddy Death song. Boy, talk about different styles, though!"

He laughed out loud, not noticing that the girl's expression had grown cold. Abruptly she slung her guitar over her shoulder, turned, and stalked off.

"Hey! What'd I say?" Joe called, bewildered. The girl kept walking, her fists clenched and her back straight.

"Oh, well. Win some, lose some." With a shrug Joe let the door swing shut and headed

8

back down the tunnel to find Frank and Callie. As he walked past Buddy Death's motor home he heard angry shouting.

Through a gap in the curtains covering a window Joe could see two men arguing. Joe recognized Buddy Death. He was tall and lanky with pale white skin and long, snarled black hair. The other man, a head shorter than Buddy, was slim, dark-haired, and deeply tanned.

Joe moved closer to the window. Though the men were yelling loudly, he couldn't make out any words.

Just then the door swung open and the short, dark man stormed out. He checked around, probably to see if anyone had heard the commotion, and then disappeared down tunnel C. Joe, who stood in the shadows behind the motor home, relaxed. The man hadn't seen him. Nor had he noticed the fat blue-jeaned roadie who had walked up behind Joe to watch the show.

"I wonder what that was about," Joe said to the roadie, whose grim expression was almost hidden behind a drooping mustache.

"Just Bobby and Buddy goin' at it as usual," the fat man drawled. "Bobby is Buddy's manager. They fight so much it's a wonder they get any work done." The roadie ambled off.

Nothing was happening there, so Joe continued toward the stage, where Callie, Frank, and Schacht had joined the other members of Buddy Death's band.

"There you are, Joe," said Callie as he joined them. "Just in time to meet the one and only Skeezer Bodine, Buddy's bass player." Joe shook hands with Skeezer, a small, elfin man with thinning blond hair. Then Callie introduced him to Sammy Shine, the drummer. Sammy was a rail-thin nineteen-year-old with a mop of bright red hair that hung down almost to his waist.

"Nice to meet you, man," Sammy said enthusiastically as he pumped Joe's hand. "And this here's our lead guitarist, Eric Holiday." Joe was reaching over to shake hands with the bearish guitar player when a loud bang startled everyone.

"Uh-oh," said Holiday.

Joe followed Holiday's gaze toward the black motor home. Buddy Death had kicked open the door and was stalking toward the stage. The heavy metal musician wore mirrored sunglasses, but still his expression wasn't hard to read. His mouth formed a tight, angry line.

He stomped up the stairs to the stage. "Syd!" he screamed. "Are we ready for lighting rehearsal or not?"

"Sure, Buddy." Schacht hurried over to

Buddy's side. "We were just waiting for our star."

"All right! Let's get this show on the road!" Buddy yelled.

Skeezer and the others immediately moved into place on several large Xs chalked on the stage.

Buddy strode up to center stage, then stood looking around in bewilderment. "Hey, where's my mike stand?" he demanded.

Schacht turned pale. "It won't be here till tonight. The sound truck had a flat."

"I need my stand, man!"

Schacht turned to the fat roadie Joe had talked to earlier. "Tex, dig up a mike stand."

Just then Joe heard a screech of metal overhead. He glanced up at the network of catwalks and supports that hung over the front of the stage. A giant spotlight suspended directly over Buddy's head had partially broken away from its support batten and was swinging by only one bolt. Joe made a dash up the steps and onto the stage.

"Watch out!" he yelled. But he was too late. The spotlight broke loose, falling straight for Buddy!

Chapter

2

BUDDY WAS ROOTED to his spot by fear, his mouth hanging open as he stared up at the plummeting spotlight.

Before Frank had time to react he saw a flash of movement from out of the corner of his eye.

It was Joe diving at lightning speed for Buddy.

A split second before the giant light reached Buddy, Joe had plowed into him at waist level, sending both of them flying several feet from the impact area.

The spotlight tore through the stage with a thunderous impact and finally came to rest on the mangled network of steel struts under the stage. One corner of it stuck up out of the stage floor at a crazy angle.

Everyone onstage clustered around Joe and Buddy. Frank and Callie started to help Joe up from where he lay sprawled.

"Are you okay, Joe?" Callie asked anxiously.

Joe didn't reply immediately, which worried Frank for a moment until Joe mimed that he was all right and had just had the wind knocked out of him.

Just then there was a frantic shout from the stands. Frank turned to see a skinny figure in a black motorcycle jacket waving his arms in the air.

"What's that kid doing here?" Schacht pulled a walkie-talkie from his back pocket. "Security! There's an unauthorized person in the arena! I want him apprehended and brought to me!"

Skeezer, who had helped Buddy to sit up, was anxiously asking him, "Buddy, you all right?"

Meanwhile Frank and Callie had helped Joe up, too.

"That was close!" Joe said shakily, running a hand through his hair.

"Yeah, too close!" Frank said as he picked up his camera. Using his camera's telephoto lens, he aimed it up at the bracket where the spotlight had hung. "They'd better have some pictures for the police."

While Frank was taking pictures a potbellied security guard dragged the struggling teenager in the motorcycle jacket up the stairs and onto the stage. The teenager had a scared expression on his pale, undernourished face. He struggled to escape the guard's grip.

"Here he is, Mr. Schacht," the guard announced. "I got the little weasel."

"Okay, kid, what are you doing here?" Schacht asked angrily.

"N-nothing," the skinny boy stammered. He tossed his mop of dark, greasy hair. "I just wanted to hear Buddy practice, I swear!"

"How'd you get past the security guards?" Joe asked curiously.

The potbellied guard frowned. "Why don't you butt out, sonny?" he growled at Joe. "Leave the interrogating to professionals."

"I didn't do anything!" the teenager squealed.

"Shut up, kid!" The guard jerked the boy's arm roughly for emphasis. "Let's see what's in your pockets."

A quick search turned up a set of motorcycle keys, six crumpled dollar bills, a package of chewing gum, an adjustable crescent wrench, and a small knife.

"This wrench could've loosened the bolts on the spotlight," Joe said.

The teen's eyes grew round. "Hey, wait a minute! I had nothing to do with that light. I

14

was just watching Buddy. I wasn't anywhere near it, I swear!"

"Let the kid go." Sammy Shine spoke up from where he sat on an equipment case. "He couldn't have gotten up to or down from the catwalks without somebody seeing him."

"What's everybody waiting for? Call the cops!" Buddy demanded. "This guy tried to kill me!"

"Now, Buddy, let's not jump to any conclusions," Schacht said quickly. "We don't need that kind of publicity right at the start of the tour. What if it gives some nut the idea to do a copycat crime at a later gig?"

"Then arrest him for trespassing!"

"I don't think so." He turned to the frightened boy. "What's your name, son?"

"D-David Pauling, sir."

Schacht nodded and turned to the guard. "Take him back to security and question him. If he seems clean, let him go."

The guard's mouth fell open in astonishment, but he knew it was no use arguing. "Come back to my office, Pauling," he ordered, and he led the boy down the stairs and toward his office.

Joe went over to his brother, who had put the viewfinder of his camera to his eye and was searching the catwalks.

"Frank, don't you want to be there when they question that kid?" Joe asked impatiently.

15

"Nope," Frank replied. "This is none of our business, or had you forgotten?"

Suddenly Frank noticed a flicker of movement among the struts surrounding the fallen spotlight. With a twist of his wrist he changed the focus on the lens. A figure dressed in black from head to toe emerged from the background. The black-clad figure was down on one knee, and it appeared that he was tying something shiny onto one of the struts. As soon as he brought him into focus Frank snapped a picture. As the auto-rewind whirred and Frank pressed the shutter again the figure glanced down and noticed him. Instantly the black-clad person moved behind a cluster of pin spots and scuttled into the shadows.

"Hey! There's somebody up there!" Frank shouted as he snapped half a dozen more photos in rapid succession. He thrust his camera bag and camera at Callie.

"Frank, what—"

"No time to explain!" Frank sprinted to the ladder at stage left that led to the jungle of catwalks, cables, and spotlights above the stage. "Joe—go up the ladder stage right. See if we can trap that guy!" Frank called over his shoulder.

Frank leapt from the ladder to the nearest catwalk and moved along it as fast as he dared. By the time he reached the hole where the spotlight had been there was no sign of the stranger.

Frank checked down the catwalk that curved around the sides of the arena dome for any sign of movement. As far as Frank could tell it was empty, as were the catwalks that ran across the width of the dome and the one that stretched from the north end of the arena all the way to the south end.

He peered into the tangle of spotlights, cables, and supports over the stage but couldn't make out any movement there.

This is weird, Frank thought, edging out on the narrow catwalk toward the center of the dome. The guy vanished into thin air—

Frank's thoughts were cut short as he tripped and stumbled forward.

"Help!" Frank shouted as his feet fell out from under him. His arms windmilled frantically as he tried to grab on to anything for support. Just as he totally lost his balance one hand grabbed a guy wire that steadied the catwalk. Frank's body slipped off the catwalk, and the thin wire cut into his palm with searing pain. But he hung on grimly.

"Help! Somebody come quick!" Frank's body hung from the single wire. The arena's concrete floor was a full thirty feet below. "Help! I'm falling!"

Chapter 3

"HANG ON, FRANK!" Joe yelled, climbing onto Frank's catwalk and running toward his brother.

Just then Frank heard a shout from above. "Okay, kid—I've got you!"

Frank turned his head up as far as he dared and spotted a muscular, bearded man perched on the steel supports just under the top of the dome. To Frank's astonishment, the big roadie seemed to be falling toward him.

He jerked to a stop right beside Frank, suspended from a nylon safety line attached to his harness. He grabbed and held on to Frank, who noticed the roadie's many tattoos. His left shoulder bore the emblem of the navy's elite SEAL unit with a black dagger through it. His right forearm bore a blue lightning bolt.

Joe helped pull Frank onto the catwalk, then gave the big man a hand.

Frank also extended his hand to the roadie, then winced as the man's iron grip crushed his injured palm.

"Thanks, mist—" Frank began, his words turning to a yelp of pain.

"Forget it, kid," the roadie growled with a Brooklyn accent. "All in a day's work."

"I'm Frank Hardy, and this is my brother, Joe."

"I'm Kong," the roadie growled.

"You sure are," Joe joked, still shaken. "It sure was lucky you were close enough to help Frank."

The big man's expression grew stern. "If you're gonna be working up here, you wear safety harnesses! It's not safe to go stumbling around."

"I didn't stumble. I was tripped," Frank corrected him.

"What tripped you?" Joe cut in.

"I'm not sure, but it left a nasty welt on my shin."

"Here's what did it—piano wire!" Joe cried. He pointed to a piece of silver wire that lay flattened across the catwalk. "Looks like whoever you saw up here wasn't eager to be followed."

19

"What I want now is a closer look at the bracket that spotlight fell from," Frank said.

"Who are you guys, anyway? What were you doing up here?" Kong demanded, an angry edge to his voice.

Ignoring him, Frank moved carefully out to the bracket so he could examine it closely.

"I knew it!" he said triumphantly. Four bolts dangled loosely from the back of the bracket. Frank examined them for wear and saw that they were all new and shiny. There was no sign of breakage or torn metal.

"That spotlight didn't tear loose," Frank called over to his brother. "It was deliberately dropped."

"Are you sure?" Joe asked as Frank made his way back to Joe's catwalk.

"Positive. The heads of the bolts aren't even scarred, so whatever did it had the right kind of tools for the job."

"Man, Frank, you are one lucky guy that Kong was right there." Joe led the way back to the ladder. Kong, scowling, followed a short distance behind.

"Maybe it wasn't just luck that he happened to be there," Frank muttered as soon as Kong was out of hearing range.

"What do you mean?" Joe muttered back.

"That piano wire was a professional booby trap, Joe. And I just noticed Kong had a tattoo from the navy's SEALs, their guerrilla outfit.''

"You think Kong—''

"I don't want to talk about it right now,'' Frank whispered, glancing behind them at Kong.

As soon as the brothers hit the stage Callie ran to Frank and wrapped her arms around him. "You scared me to death,'' she said. "Don't ever do that again!''

Frank started to reply, but just then he heard a shout from the far end of the arena. "Syd!'' yelled a tall, dark-haired, barrel-chested man dressed in denim overalls and a tie-dyed shirt. He hurried toward the stage, waving a sheet of paper. His blue eyes shone with grim urgency under dark, bushy eyebrows.

"Where were you, Jake?'' Kong boomed at him. "Somebody tried to squash His Majesty with a spotlight.''

"Huh? What're you talking about?'' Jake stopped in confusion.

"A spotlight came loose over the stage. It almost crushed Buddy,'' Schacht told him.

"And when I went up to investigate,'' Frank added, "I fell over a trip wire the joker left behind. It almost killed me.''

"Who are you?'' Jake asked Frank belligerently.

"Take it easy, Jake,'' Schacht said in a low voice. "These kids are Frank and Joe

21

Hardy. They came in with a reporter.'' Schacht turned to the Hardys. ''Boys, this is Jake Williams, my road boss and special effects supervisor. Now, what's that paper you're waving around, Jake?''

Jake handed it to him without a word. While Schacht scanned it Joe looked over his shoulder. The note was printed in pencil in block letters.

Buddy Death is too evil to live. He will not perform in Bayport or anywhere else, for he'll soon be dead.

Blade

''Where did you find this?'' Joe asked.

Jake looked at him quizzically, then replied, ''It was pinned on the door of the office that Schacht's using with this.'' He produced a slim, deadly looking dagger from the side pocket of his overalls.

''Looks like a standard-issue U.S. combat knife,'' Frank said. ''They give them to the army and marines, but the prankster could have bought one at a surplus store.''

Schacht looked at the Hardys with increased interest. ''Jake, will you excuse us a minute?'' he said.

He led Frank and Joe to the rear of the stage and made sure they were alone before speaking.

22

"What's going—" Joe began before Schacht cut him off impatiently.

"I just had a brainstorm," he explained. "I'm worried about what's going on here, but if it gets into the papers that there's some killer after Buddy, this concert's going to be dead for sure. I've got to stop this guy, but I can't afford to call in the cops."

He hesitated. "How'd you kids like to help Buddy and me out?" he said. "Sniff around, see what you come up with. I can give you jobs in the crew as cover."

Joe looked at his brother and grinned. "You don't have to ask us twice," he said eagerly.

"Great." Schacht seemed to be a little relieved.

"Where do you want us to start?" Frank asked.

"How about with your girlfriend?" Schacht indicated Callie, who stood talking with Eric, Sammy, and Skeezer. "She's got to keep quiet about this if we want to nab the guy."

"Mr. Schacht, if you're asking me to put a gag order on Callie's story, the answer is no," Frank replied firmly.

"Who said anything about a gag order?" Schacht replied. "I just want her to hold off on filing the story about the spotlight until you catch Blade."

"I don't know," said Frank.

"Look," Schacht offered, "I'll make you a

deal. You get her to wait twenty-four hours, and I'll make sure it's exclusive."

Frank frowned. "If it means that much to you, I'll give it my best shot. But no guarantees."

As Frank walked out of the wings Schacht told Joe Kong's legal name. Joe looked up and noticed that Jake Williams and Kong were standing to one side of the stage, watching them.

"Uh, there's Callie. You coming, Joe?" asked Frank.

"No way!" Joe shook his head. "Sweet-talking Callie is your department."

Joe watched with amusement as Frank led Callie away from Eric, Skeezer, and Sammy. Callie's smile faded as she listened to what Frank had to say, and the stubborn expression Joe knew so well appeared in its place.

"Oh, well. It's not my problem," he told himself, wandering toward the back of the stage. Schacht, too, hurried away, and the roadies went back to work. Joe wondered where the musicians had gone. He guessed the light rehearsal had been postponed until after the spotlight was replaced.

Just then Joe heard Buddy's voice from somewhere backstage. He peered into the darkness and finally spotted Buddy standing in the shadow of some wooden crates, talking heatedly with someone he couldn't see. Joe moved in closer to listen in on the rock star's conversation.

"I told you over and over again—I don't want you around, Clare! Are you stupid or what?"

"How can you be so mean to me after what we've been through?" said a tearful female voice.

"It's over, Clare. Just accept it and move on like I have," Buddy shouted.

Joe moved back into the shadows as Buddy turned and started stalking away from the unseen woman. Then he heard the woman begin to sob behind the crates.

Instinctively Joe moved toward her. As he did he stepped on a thin piece of wood that broke with a loud crack. Buddy froze in the wings, turned, and glared at Joe. Then without a word he marched off.

Joe immediately rounded the corner of the crate and saw the auburn-haired girl he'd met earlier. She stared up at him, wiping her eyes, and frowned.

"Hi," Joe said nervously. "Listen, I'm sorry if I offended you this afternoon." He took a step toward her.

"It's all right." She looked him in the eye for the first time. "You didn't know any better. Music is just a touchy subject with me." She pulled out a tissue and blew her nose.

"My name's Joe Hardy. I just joined the road crew." Joe stuck out his hand.

The girl smiled and shook Joe's hand briefly. "I'm Clare. Clare Williams. My brother Jake's the road boss for Buddy's group."

"Yeah, I met him," Joe said. "Listen, I couldn't help overhearing you just now," he went on. "Buddy was pretty rough on you."

Clare's smile disappeared instantly, and the angry, sullen scowl Joe had seen before reappeared. "What do you know about it?" she snapped. "Why don't you just mind your own business?"

"I was just trying to help," said Joe.

"Nosy's more like it. If I need your help, I'll ask for it!" Furious, Clare pushed past a stunned Joe Hardy and ran off into the darkness.

"Okay already!" Joe stared after her and shook his head. "Boy, that girl sure is touchy."

He wandered back onstage and found Frank and Callie both smiling. Frank must have offered to keep Callie posted on the progress of their investigation, he realized. Callie enjoyed a good mystery almost as much as a great scoop.

"Hi," Joe called as he approached them. "Everything work out all right?"

Frank nodded. "We—came to an understanding."

Suddenly they heard someone shouting from

the other end of the stage. Joe turned to see Buddy pointing at him.

"Hey, punk!" Buddy yelled. "What're you doing on my stage? I saw you spying on me, you little creep!" He marched over to Joe, his green eyes flashing dangerously. The nearby crew members backed away out of danger.

"I wasn't spying on you. I just happened to be walking by when you were yelling at that poor girl," Joe said evenly.

"You shut up!" Buddy screamed. He was shaking with fear and anger. "I want you out of here, or there's going to be trouble!" He pushed Joe in the chest.

"Stop it," Joe said quietly, anger flashing in his eyes.

"Take it easy, man," he heard Frank say. "What's the matter with you?"

"I want both of you out of here!" Buddy shouted. Snarling with rage, he reached for a nearby pile of scrap lumber and grabbed a two-by-four. Brandishing it like a baseball bat, he advanced on the Hardys.

"What are you doing?" Callie screamed. "Watch out, Joe! He's going to kill you!"

Chapter

4

JOE DUCKED as Buddy swung the two-by-four. Frank saw it miss his head by a fraction of an inch. He dived onto the stage and rolled to his left, coming up in a fighting crouch several steps from Buddy.

Seeing that Joe was out of reach, Buddy turned on Frank and ran toward him, swinging the plank.

"Callie—get out of here!" Frank yelled.

As Buddy swung the board Frank grabbed the end of it with both hands, yanking it from Buddy's grasp.

Buddy stumbled past Frank, then turned and charged him again.

Frank agilely sidestepped Buddy's charge and tripped him, sending him sprawling.

"What's going on here?" Schacht shouted angrily as he ran across the stage.

"Your star tried to crown us," Joe said, barely containing his temper.

"Take it easy, Buddy. What's the problem here?" Schacht asked soothingly.

"I don't want strangers hanging around here, Syd! I told you that!" Buddy yelled.

"They aren't strangers. I hired them for your road crew."

Buddy glared at Frank and Joe. "How do I know one of them's not Blade?" he demanded.

"Buddy, baby, I promise. Joe saved your life just a few minutes ago. Why would he rig a light to fall and then risk his neck saving you? Also I know their dad personally! We'll get Blade, but he ain't going to be one of these two."

At these words Buddy calmed down, but he still scowled doubtfully at the brothers. "It better not be," he grumbled at last. "I don't like strangers around me, Syd, You keep these guys out of my hair!"

Frank watched Buddy stalk off. "All right, I accept your apology," he quipped. Joe added, "Thanks for the thank-you for saving your life."

"The kid's on edge," Schacht tried to explain. "Heavy metal bands have been taking enough flak in the media already. Now he's got to worry about people staying away

29

from his concerts because they think they're unsafe. Not to mention the question of his own survival."

"Yeah, okay," Joe said impatiently. "Just give us a place to start with this."

Schacht motioned for Frank and Joe to come nearer. "Work closely with the roadies," he whispered. "See what the word of mouth is on this Blade character."

"Was today the first time anything like this has happened?" Frank asked.

Schacht hesitated. Then he shrugged. "Okay, you might as well know everything," he said. "We got another note two days ago. Same block printing, same signature."

"Why didn't you tell us this before?" Joe wanted to know.

"Bobby Mellor and I agreed not to talk about it. We figured it was just a crank letter. Buddy's already nervous enough about this tour. We've got the note back at our hotel."

"Does Buddy get a lot of crank letters?" Frank asked.

"A few. Mostly they're from parents who don't like his music. Blade's letters were the only serious threats."

"We'll need to do some background checks on the people around Buddy right away," Frank decided.

Schacht nodded. "Okay. I'll tell Jake and

Bobby that you're running errands for me. How's that?"

"Good," Joe replied. "This shouldn't take more than a few hours."

After returning to the Hardy home Frank, Joe, and Callie held a quick planning session in the kitchen.

"Since I've already dug up some info on Buddy, I can finish snooping into his past," Callie volunteered.

"Good." Frank smiled at her. "See if you can find evidence that Buddy was threatened before."

"While she's doing that, Frank, I'll dig around for info on Bobby Mellor and the guys on the crew," Joe suggested.

"Good," Frank agreed. "I'll see what I can come up with from that law enforcement data net Dad uses."

As soon as Callie left to go to the library to read old newspapers and Joe went to work in Fenton Hardy's office, Frank began searching the law enforcement data bank on his computer, using his father's access code. Soon Kong's complete military history appeared on the screen. "Wow," Frank said, scrolling down the list of information. Not only had Kong spent five years in the navy, two of them in the elite SEAL commando unit, but he also had a lengthy criminal record since being dishonorably discharged from the navy.

"All right. A lead at last," Frank said to himself. He instructed his computer to print up a hard copy of Kong's military record and rap sheet and then moved on to the other suspects.

Hours later a rumble in Frank's stomach reminded him how many hours had passed since breakfast. He went downstairs to the kitchen and found Joe already there, munching on their Aunt Gertrude's chocolate-chip cookies.

"Just in time," Joe said as Frank seated himself across the table and snagged a handful of cookies. "I found something interesting in Mellor's credit records."

"Don't tell me, let me guess," Frank replied with a smile. "All his credit records go back only five years. So do all his other records, according to the data net."

"What do you make of that?" Joe asked.

"I'd say we have two choices—he's in a witness protection program or he's hiding out from creditors or something. I also checked out that crazy fan, David Pauling. His rap sheet consists of one traffic ticket. The address he gave the police officer is a vacant lot in the waterfront district. And there's more," Frank added.

Just then Callie appeared at the kitchen

door, and Frank stopped talking to open the door for her.

"Hi, guys," she said. "Not much hot stuff on Buddy, but I photocopied everything, anyway. I thought if we went over it together, you might turn up something I missed. What did you get?" she asked Frank.

"I was just about to tell Joe that both Jake and Kong were in the service," Frank said, handing Callie a cookie. "Jake was in the Army Corps of Engineers until about five years ago, specializing in demolition. Kong was in the navy, and both guys were stationed in Japan at the same time."

"Maybe that's where they met," Callie speculated.

Frank nodded his head. "Now, here's the really interesting part, folks. Kong was in the elite navy SEAL unit. He was in the brig several times in the service and finally got booted out of the SEALs. He's been in and out of jail since he got out of the navy."

"For what?" Joe asked.

"He had multiple raps for assault, illegal weapons possession, one for illegal possession of dynamite, and two for burglary." Frank sat back with a satisfied expression.

Concern showed in Callie's face. "I want you to be careful around Kong. I don't trust him."

"Don't worry, Callie. We'll be careful around

everybody until we know for sure who Blade is."

"We should probably head back to the arena," Joe said, "before our absence looks suspicious."

As soon as they entered the arena Frank saw the security guard who had taken Pauling away striding toward the stage.

"Excuse me, Mr. Schacht," the guard said loudly. "I want to make my report before I go home."

Schacht waved the man over. "Sure. I want you to meet the newest members of my security team," he added in a low voice. "They're working undercover. Boys, this is Captain Hubbard."

Hubbard looked surprised and not very pleased at the news, but he shook hands with the boys, aware that Syd Schacht was watching.

"Now," said Schacht, "what did you learn from that kid in the motorcycle jacket?"

Hubbard squared his shoulders and began giving his report in a crisp voice. "His name's David Pauling. He's sixteen, a high school dropout, and unemployed. He's a big heavy metal fan, and if you ask me, he's obsessed with Buddy Death."

Schacht frowned. "You think he had anything to do with that spotlight falling?"

Before Hubbard could answer, Joe jumped in.

"We examined that spotlight bracket right after the light fell. The bolts looked like they were deliberately loosened. Pauling would have had to move pretty fast to loosen the bolts and then be down on the arena floor when it crashed."

Hubbard looked annoyed at the interruption, but Schacht seemed pleased at Joe's analysis.

"Anyway," Hubbard continued, "I let him go. I don't think he's dangerous, and I couldn't hold him for the knife he had on him because he has a clean record with the Bayport police."

"Would you mind giving us a look at your notes on Pauling so we can do a follow-up?" Frank asked.

Hubbard seemed reluctant, but Schacht prodded him.

"All right," Hubbard said. "Come back to my office."

As Hubbard turned to leave Kong came lumbering into view from the rear of the stage. "Sound truck's here, Mr. Schacht," he reported. Then, turning to Frank and Joe, he said, "Jake wants you down at the tunnel entrance ASAP, Hardys."

"We'll be there in a few minutes," said Frank.

"Jake wants you there now," Kong insisted.

"But—" Joe objected, and Kong planted himself menacingly in Joe's path.

"Don't worry, boys," Schacht said with a wink. "I'll take care of your errand myself."

"Let's go, Joe," Frank said to his brother. "No point in stirring up any more trouble."

Joe gave Kong a hard look before he followed his brother toward the stairs.

"Go through tunnel A," Kong instructed. "Jake's got everyone unloading so the sound crew can set up tonight."

"Tonight?" Frank said in surprise.

"What's the matter, you wimps afraid you'll miss your bedtime?" Kong taunted.

"Listen, mister, my brother and I can keep up with anybody on your road crew, including you," Joe retorted, his temper flaring.

Kong laughed. It was not a nice laugh.

"We'll see about that," he said.

A few minutes later sweat was pouring down Frank's face as he and Joe pushed big wheeled cases down a ramp from a semitrailer parked outside the arena at the mouth of access tunnel A. Jake stood near the bottom of the ramp with a clipboard, directing the roadies, while Kong supervised the unpacking of the cases with Manny Sterns, the head of the sound crew.

It seemed to Frank that he, Joe, and the other roadies had been unloading for hours without making a dent in the pile of equipment.

While they were working Frank saw Bobby Mellor arrive. He heard the manager ask Kong and Jake to climb into the equipment trailer, saying, "I need you to help me go over these equipment manifests."

Joe had stopped working to get a drink from a nearby water cooler.

"Quitting already, huh, punk?" Kong growled behind him.

"No. I just stopped for a drink of water, if that's okay with you, 'boss,'" Joe said sarcastically.

"Okay, you got your drink. Get back to work. There's still lots to do."

Frank saw what had happened and went over to his brother. "Take it easy, Joe. Let's just concentrate on the case."

As the Hardys started unloading equipment at the base of the ramp Frank heard a low rumbling sound. Instinctively he turned his head toward the noise. A dark shape was hurtling down the equipment ramp.

Frank glanced over his shoulder and saw that Joe was bending over a small crate, his back to the ramp. He seemed oblivious to the massive equipment case that was only seconds away from crushing him!

Chapter

5

"JOE!" FRANK SHOUTED.

Joe whipped around to see the case hurtling toward him. He threw himself backward. Beside him the big case roared down the ramp and smashed into Joe's crate, splintering it on impact.

"Joe, are you all right?" Frank peered anxiously into his brother's face.

"I'm okay, I guess," he replied, wincing as he got to his feet. "It's just my back. And my elbows. And my tailbone."

"What's going on out there?" an angry voice yelled from inside the truck. Joe and Frank turned to see Bobby Mellor striding over to the crate that the equipment case had smashed. Mellor's face was dark with anger.

"Five hundred bucks worth of equipment!" Mellor screamed, pointing at Joe. "You were unloading the stuff! It's your fault!"

"Hey, wait a second," Joe said angrily. "I didn't even touch the case!"

"Kong!" Mellor shouted. "Jake!"

Kong appeared in the doorway of the trailer and trotted over to where Mellor stood.

"These two morons smashed up a whole box of equipment! Get rid of them! Now!" he shouted, pointing at Frank and Joe.

Jake Williams suddenly jumped down from the trailer. "Let's all take it easy," he said quietly.

The group turned to look at the barrel-chested road manager. "Good idea," Frank agreed. "Look, we were just standing at the bottom of the ramp, and it came rolling down on us!"

"Okay," Mellor said, disgusted. "We've already wasted too much time. I want all this stuff in place for a sound and light check by midnight."

"All right, you heard the man," Jake shouted at the roadies who had crowded around the splintered crate. "Let's get on it, people! Frank, find Manny and ask what you can help with. Joe, you stay here with the rest of the crew."

Before Frank left, Joe pulled him aside for a quick conference. "That was no accident,

39

Frank. Could Blade already be on to us?" he asked in a low voice.

"Who knows?" Frank commented, adding, "But it's funny how Mellor appeared just before you nearly got flattened."

"I'll keep an eye on him," Joe replied.

"We shouldn't forget Kong and Jake were in there, too," Frank said. "Maybe one of them pushed it."

"The only thing we know for sure is that we can't rule anybody out," Joe replied.

The rest of the unloading went smoothly. When the semi was empty Joe helped to move the enormous speakers into the arena on wheeled carts. He watched as the speakers were hoisted up into the air by a small crane and bolted to the sound towers and the framework above the stage.

To Joe's surprise, it was only nine o'clock when he was told he could go home. He found Frank up in the catwalks helping Manny Sterns, a plump, pony-tailed man, to secure one of the speakers to a support. Joe pitched in, and the speaker was soon tightly bolted to its bracket.

"How much longer do you think you'll be working?" Joe asked his brother.

"That's up to Manny here."

"You can go," Manny told him. "Just be back here at six tomorrow morning."

"See you then," Frank said. He and Joe

climbed down from the catwalk and headed for the arena's parking lot.

Joe yawned as he and Frank walked up to their van. "Boy, I'm beat," he confessed. "I never realized being a roadie was such hard work."

"I have some more work to do before we turn in tonight," Frank replied. "I want to develop those photos I took."

Joe glanced at his watch. "Speedy Photo closed a few minutes ago."

"Ah, but I have a secret weapon," Frank said with a crafty smile. "Duke Wampler from my calculus class works there, and he owes me a favor. Let's hope he stayed late. I'll drop you off at Mr. Pizza. Order us a large pie with the works. I'll meet you there in twenty minutes."

Joe noticed his brother's disappointed expression the minute Frank appeared in Mr. Pizza. He quickly understood why after scanning the prints. They were hopelessly blurred, showing just the back of an indistinct figure in black on the catwalks above the stage. Even magnified, the photos were only slightly clearer.

"This is it?" Joe asked in disbelief.

Frank nodded. "Yep. That last picture is the best Duke could do with the enlarger. It shows where the guy's shirt had pulled out of his pants. See, there's some kind of intricate design on his T-shirt underneath."

"Where does that leave us?" Joe asked.

"Back at square one, I guess." Frank reached for a slice of pizza.

"Then let's eat this pie and get out of here." Joe shoved the photos back into the envelope. "We have to be up at the crack of dawn tomorrow."

When Joe awoke the next morning he found Frank standing over him already dressed.

"Hurry up, Joe. We only have half an hour to get to the arena."

"What about breakfast?" Joe mumbled.

"Jake said they always feed the crews on these arena jobs."

Joe nodded sleepily and reached for the jeans draped over the chair next to his bed. "I knew there had to be *some* reason people took this job," he said.

When they walked into the arena Joe saw that most of the roadies were already there, clustered around tables set up on the arena floor beside the stage. The tables were laden with pastries, fruit, cereal, bacon, and scrambled eggs.

At the sight of food Joe felt himself perking up. His stomach rumbled as he made a beeline for the trays of pastries. After loading his plate with sweet rolls and doughnuts Joe searched for Frank and saw him sitting with some of the sound crew, a plate full of fruit balanced on his lap.

The one thing that still puzzled Joe was why anyone would want to kill Buddy Death. Now, he figured, was as good a time as any to see what he could find out about the rock star from the people who worked for him.

Spotting the fat, mustached roadie named Tex sitting on a crate, Joe went over and joined him.

"Hi," Joe said. "Mind if I sit here?"

"Naw, go ahead," Tex twanged.

"Thanks," Joe replied. "Sure is nice to have a hot breakfast, huh?"

"Yeah," Tex agreed. "We're going to need it with the day we got ahead of us."

"They sure work us hard," Joe commented.

"Well, I don't mind working hard, but I wish we were working for some other band, man."

"Why's that?" Joe asked. "Don't you like working for Buddy?"

"Nope," Tex replied. "I think he's a jerk."

"Why?" Joe inquired.

"Because he hassles his road crew. But I guess a no-talent punk like Buddy doesn't know any better. He's made a lot of enemies already."

"Oh, yeah? Like who?"

"Like Kong, for instance," Tex said, sipping his coffee. " 'Course, Kong's been ticked off at Buddy for years. Even before working on this tour."

"How come?" Joe asked in surprise.

" 'Cause of Clare Williams. She and Buddy were a real item a few years back. But when Buddy started heading for the big time he dumped her. She was never the same after that."

"Hmm," Joe said thoughtfully. Now there was some information that might turn into a good lead, he thought. "But what's that got to do with Kong?"

Tex just shook his head. "Kong and Jake, Clare's brother, are old friends from way back. Kong always thought the sun rose and set on Clare. When Buddy dumped her Kong got really mad."

"Interesting," Joe muttered to himself. He excused himself and casually sauntered over to Frank. "Hey, Frank," Joe said quietly, "can we talk?"

Frank looked up and grinned at him. "You read my mind, Joe. Let's go somewhere we can talk privately."

Joe led his brother over behind a stack of empty packing boxes, where they were out of sight from the rest of the crew.

"You've got that look in your eye, Joe. What'd you pick up?" Frank said eagerly.

"A motive, maybe. Did you know Kong hates Buddy's guts?"

Frank nodded. "Yeah. Some of the guys were telling me all about how Buddy dumped Jake's sister. And that she's been following the tour around ever since."

"But if it's Jake's sister who got dumped, what's Jake's attitude?" Joe wondered.

Frank looked thoughtful. "Jake doesn't seem to care. He hired on to do this tour after Buddy dumped Clare, and the roadies say all he's ever done is tell Clare to go home."

"What about Bobby Mellor?" Joe put in. "I saw him having a major screaming match with Buddy in his motor home. And I still want to know what he was doing *six* years ago."

Frank started to reply but was interrupted by the sudden arrival of Buddy's limo through access tunnel B. It screeched to a stop near the food tables, startling several roadies into dropping their plates.

"Why's he here so early?" Joe asked Frank.

"I heard he's an early-morning nut," Frank answered.

"All right, breakfast's over! Time to get to work!" Buddy announced as his limo door flew open.

Kong separated himself from one group and

45

went over to stand in front of Buddy, glowering at him.

"We go to work when Jake tells us to, not you," Kong growled.

"I don't want any of your lip, ugly," Buddy told him. "I'm the star here. I could have you fired any time."

"Oh, yeah? You fire me, and Jake and half the crew'll walk. And then where will you be, Mr. High-and-Mighty Rock Star?" Kong shouted, taking a step toward Buddy.

Joe saw Buddy flinch, then stand his ground.

"You're crazy if you think I'm afraid of you, you big goon," Buddy said, turning a shade paler than usual.

But before the confrontation went any further Jake and Bobby Mellor emerged from the nearest access tunnel.

"Okay, breakfast's over. Let's get it on, people!" Jake bellowed. "How about a little hustle, gang? There's a big press conference tonight, and I want all the special effects ready to go."

Joe drained his juice, and then he and Frank went over to Jake, who was reading the roadies' assignments off a clipboard. Frank was again assigned to work with the sound crew, while Jake told Joe to get a safety harness from Kong and gave him his assignment. "Joe, I want you to climb the right sound tower and make sure all the speakers are hooked up. Start at the top and work your way down. Ordinarily I'd have one of the sound crew check it, but they're spread pretty thin today."

"You got it," Joe replied. Then he went to find Kong. Kong gave Joe the tools he'd need and a nylon harness.

Joe then went over to the tower and began climbing. The scaffolding was easy to scale, but it creaked ominously as Joe went higher. As he neared the top the tower began swaying. This gives me the creeps, Joe said to himself, but when he looked down he saw Kong watching his progress. He thinks I'm going to wimp out, Joe thought angrily. His anger made him move up the stack faster.

As Joe kept climbing the swaying of the tower grew more pronounced. When he reached the top he hooked his safety line to a beam just above the topmost cluster of speakers.

The swaying motion, which had seemed gentle at first, had become a violent swinging from side to side. Joe's right foot slipped from the crossbeam on which he was standing. He scrambled desperately for a hold.

He heard a loud, high-pitched screeching of bending metal, and then the tower shuddered forward.

Joe clung to the corner as the tower fell, thinking about the thousands of pounds of steel that seemed determined to crush him.

Chapter

6

"LOOK OUT! THE TOWER'S FALLING!" Frank shrieked from the overhead catwalk as the sound tower pitched forward with Joe hooked to its underside. Joe will be crushed, he thought, frustrated by his own helplessness.

Then, at the very last moment, Joe unhooked his safety line and leapt free of the tower. His arms and legs windmilled frantically as he lunged out for the edge of the fabric canopy that was stretched over the apron and the front half of the stage.

When he saw Joe catch the edge of the canopy Frank felt himself breathe again.

The sound tower crashed to the arena floor a second later with a *clonk* of hollow metal on concrete, just missing the edge of the stage.

Bent support struts and crossbeams flew in all directions, causing roadies to dive behind any available cover.

Frank barely noticed these things as he scrambled along the catwalk. Below him, at stage right, Frank saw with vast relief that Tex and Benny, another roadie who had been working in the lighting grid over the stage, were pulling Joe up from the edge of the canopy.

"Joe, are you hurt?" Tex asked as he pulled him onto the catwalk.

"I'm all right," Joe replied.

Frank saw that his brother was descending the stage-right ladder.

"That was a close one," Frank said after descending a ladder and meeting his brother on the stage.

"Courtesy of our pal Blade, I bet," said Joe.

"That tower falling did seem a little too convenient to be an accident," Frank agreed.

"Let's have a look at it," said Joe.

Frank jumped down from the edge of the stage to examine the twisted struts from the tower as Buddy emerged from his motor home. He kicked the side door open with a bang.

"Now what's gone wrong?" he shouted as he stomped toward the wreckage of the sound tower.

49

Benny told Buddy what had happened, pointing at Joe as he told him. Buddy fixed Joe with a look of rage and strode over to him.

"Man, everything you touch you destroy!" Buddy yelled at Joe. "My stage may not be ready for tonight's press conference! You're history! Finito!"

"Joe was on top of the tower and was lucky to get down in one piece. He didn't have anything to do with it falling down. Maybe you should try to find out why that tower fell before you have them clear away the wreckage," Frank suggested.

Mellor looked at Frank with an impatient expression, then snapped, "I don't care why it's down. I just want to see it up again. And fast!"

That's a funny attitude to take, Frank thought.

Roadies moved in from every corner of the arena to start picking up the pieces. Joe held them off for a few minutes while he examined the wreckage of the tower.

"You sound like you don't care whether or not Blade gets Buddy," Frank ventured.

Mellor gave him a speculative look before answering.

"Sometimes I wish I'd never found that creep. When I discovered Buddy he was fronting for some nothing bar band in New York City. I recognized his potential and created his image. You'd think he'd be grateful, but not him!" Mellor's voice rose to a high pitch, and Frank noticed that his face was turning a deep shade of red.

Mellor sighed heavily and then seemed to get control of himself. With a shake of his head he smoothed his hair back. "Sorry if I went off there for a second. It's just hard for me, knowing that as soon as I help make Buddy a star he's going to tear up his management contract with me and split."

"You sound pretty certain of that," Frank observed.

"Are you kidding me?" Mellor said bitterly. "That creep has stabbed every friend he ever had in the back. All he cares about is making it to the top of the rock biz. As soon as he thinks he's used me up, I'm history."

Abruptly, as if sensing he'd said too much, Mellor ended his conversation and turned away.

"Better get to work. I've got a lot to do," he muttered as he walked out.

Frank looked at the tower wreckage on the arena floor and saw Joe beckoning him to come over.

"What did you find, Joe?" he asked.

Joe held up a metal standard, one of the corner supports that the horizontal cross-beams and diagonal support struts were bolted to.

51

Puzzled, Frank examined it but didn't see what was wrong with it. "I don't get it, Joe," he said, handing it back.

"It looks like somebody deliberately sabotaged it by removing the locking pins from the corner support," Joe told him, pointing at the empty slots where the cotter pins went.

"Maybe the pins got dislodged when the tower fell."

Joe shook his head. "Not likely. I examined all the other standards. The locking pins were bent, but they were all in place," he said firmly.

Over Joe's shoulder Frank spotted Jake Williams trotting out of access tunnel A. Jake looked sweaty and anxious as he surveyed the wreckage.

"Oh, great! Another disaster! I better order the steel for another tower now if we're going to be ready for the rehearsal," Jake muttered as he trotted down the tunnel he'd come out of.

"This has got to be Blade's work, but who is Blade?" Joe asked.

Frank shrugged his shoulders. "It could be Mellor, or Kong, or even Jake. Blade has to be working from the inside. One of the roadies or even you and I would have noticed a stranger moving around here. What do you think?"

"I don't know why," Joe told him, "but

I've got a gut feeling that Mellor might be Blade. He looked mad enough to kill when he was talking to me about Buddy."

"That doesn't make sense, Joe. I don't think Mellor would knock off the man who was his bread and butter."

"Mellor doesn't strike me as the most stable guy in the world," Joe insisted stubbornly. "He may be so eaten up with resentment that he's not thinking rationally. Besides, think about this: Mellor's been right there every time Blade caused an accident."

"There were a lot of people around after the accidents. Kong and Jake were usually around, too," Frank retorted.

"But think about it, Frank. Mellor was the only one around after all three accidents Blade arranged. And there is still the question of all those missing years."

Frank paused and reflected on what Joe was saying and had to admit that he was right. But a little voice in the back of his head told him not to jump to any hasty conclusions.

"Come on, Joe, you know we have to have solid evidence before we can make any accusations. We don't have anything at all like that. Besides, Kong and Jake still seem to have stronger motives because of Jake's sister."

"Well, all we can do is keep on digging," Joe replied.

As Joe stood up the other roadies began

clearing away the sound tower and loading it on wheeled carts that Kong and Tex had pushed up beside the wreckage.

Looking up from his work a couple of hours later, Frank saw Schacht emerge from Buddy's motor home and mop his brow with a brightly colored handkerchief.

"How'd it go with Buddy, Mr. Schacht?" Joe asked as Schacht walked past the roadies up to the stage.

Schacht shook his head. "One of these days I'm going to smack that little weasel right in the kisser," he said. "But at least I got him calmed down enough to rehearse."

"Where's the rest of the band?" Frank asked.

"They travel in a separate limo," Schacht replied. "Speaking of which, where are those guys?"

"Here we are, Syd," Skeezer Bodine called cheerfully from the wings. "We came in the back way."

Turning, Frank saw Skeezer, Sammy, and Eric amble onstage, talking and laughing. Sammy wore a wild yellow suede outfit with fringe on the legs and arms, while Skeezer and Eric wore T-shirts and torn jeans. Kong and two other roadies followed them and set up microphone stands, Sammy's elaborate drum kit with a big bass drum bearing the Buddy Death Band logo, a V-shaped array of electronic drums, his cymbals and a rack of congas, and assorted percussion instruments. It took Kong only a few minutes to put up Buddy's mike stand and lay out Eric's guitars and Skeezer's electric bass, all bearing the black and white BDB logo.

Despite all the accidents that had plagued the gig so far, Frank thought the band members were in good spirits, especially Sammy and Skeezer. Skeezer had taken his electric bass from its stand and was doing a duckwalk across the stage while making funny faces at Sammy and Eric.

"And that's how Chuck Berry does it," Frank heard Skeezer say.

Sammy slapped the tops of his thighs and laughed hard. "That's great, man! Who else can you do?"

Skeezer looked at Sammy slyly from under his pale blond eyebrows. "I do a wicked Buddy Death imitation," he said modestly.

"Do it, Skeezer," Sammy insisted. "Come on, man. We could all use a good laugh."

Skeezer smiled and shook his head. "No, I better not. What if His Highness sees me? We could all be in the soup then."

"Oh, go ahead, Skeezer," Eric prodded.

"Okay, okay," Skeezer said, taking off his bass and handing it to Joe. He took a moment to compose himself, then threw out his chest and began strutting around the stage pretending to sing into a microphone.

"I am the greatest rock star of all time!" Skeezer howled in a hilariously accurate parody of Buddy's voice.

Frank smiled and heard the other band members and roadies laughing. Frank had seen Buddy perform only in music videos, but he had to admit Skeezer had Buddy's mannerisms down perfectly.

Skeezer strutted from one side of the stage to the other until the roadies were howling with laughter. Frank noticed Sammy lying on his back, laughing so hard his legs were kicking in the air.

Wearing a near-perfect copy of the sneer Buddy wore on the cover of his first album, Skeezer strode over to Buddy's mike stand and grabbed it. As soon as he touched the mike stand his eyes got wide and his body went rigid. Frank immediately knew something was wrong. Skeezer began shaking as if he were having a fit. Frank heard sizzling sounds and smelled a sharp tang of ozone.

Frank heard the laughter end abruptly as everyone realized that Skeezer was being electrocuted!

Chapter
7

IN A FLASH Frank scooped up a wooden broom and flicked the long end of the broom handle, knocking the mike stand away from Skeezer.

As soon as Frank broke contact between Skeezer's hands and the mike stand Skeezer collapsed on the stage and lay there twitching. Frank threw down the broom handle and bent over Skeezer, ready to administer CPR if Skeezer needed it.

Everyone crowded up onstage, roadies and rockers alike, and they all surged forward to see if Skeezer was all right.

Joe flicked a glance over at Schacht and saw the promoter mopping his face with his handkerchief and talking to himself.

"Not Skeezer," Schacht muttered. "As if I didn't have enough disasters on my hands already."

Schacht suddenly turned to Tex and shouted, "Where's Jake? Where's Bobby? Is somebody calling an ambulance?"

Realizing that nobody else had had the presence of mind to do so, Joe ran toward a pay phone he remembered seeing near the mouth of tunnel A. He dialed 911 and requested an ambulance.

When Joe returned he saw, to his relief, that Skeezer was sitting up, supported by Frank.

Joe pushed through the people standing around Frank and Skeezer. "How is he, Frank?"

Frank looked up, his face serious, and replied, "He's had a bad jolt and has some burns on his hands, but I think he'll be all right."

Sammy knelt down and patted his friend on the shoulder.

"You hear that, Skeez? The man says you'll be okay."

Skeezer nodded. "Yeah, great," he whispered in a dry voice.

Kong suddenly appeared at the top of the stage-left ladder and slid down it. He ran to Skeezer's side with a wild-eyed expression. "Is he all right? I just heard."

"I called an ambulance. It ought to be here soon," Joe told him.

"Sit still until it comes," Frank instructed Skeezer. "Sammy, would you stay with him until the ambulance arrives?"

"Sure, man," Sammy said with a nod.

"Let's check out that mike stand, Joe," Frank said.

"I'll kill the power," Kong volunteered, and he ran over to a bank of amplifiers and began flipping switches.

When Kong had finished, Frank used a voltmeter one of the sound men handed him to be sure the mike was dead. Then he picked up the mike stand, and he and Joe began taking it apart.

At that moment Jake appeared from the wings.

Joe, checking over Frank's shoulder, saw that a thin copper wire had been taped to the inside of the mike stand rod, and it was spliced into the main power cable.

"This thing was deliberately wired to electrocute whoever touched the stand," Frank observed.

"And since it was Buddy's mike stand, it's obviously another attempt on Buddy. It was just chance that Skeezer touched it first," Joe said.

Jake had come over and was looking down

at the mike stand in Frank's hands. "I'm glad Skeezer'll be okay," he muttered.

A rising wail in the distance drew Joe's attention away from the mike stand, and he saw an ambulance emerge from access tunnel A and pull up to the stage. White-suited medics got out and put Skeezer onto a stretcher.

As the ambulance drove off Buddy appeared in the doorway of his motor home. "What's going on now?" he shouted. "Don't you realize I need to rest?"

Kong separated himself from the group of roadies around the stage. "You jerk! Skeezer could have died because of you! He grabbed your mike stand and almost got electrocuted!"

"What?" Buddy was stunned. "It was Blade! I know it! That nut won't stop until he gets me! That's it! I'm not performing here! It's too dangerous!"

"Hold on, Buddy," Schacht shouted, running after the rocker, who was rapidly retreating into his motor home. Joe watched as Buddy slipped through the door before Schacht could catch him. Schacht pounded on the door for several moments before Buddy finally let him in.

Joe heard the sounds of a heated argument from inside the motor home, though as before it was impossible to make out who was saying what to whom.

"Well, there goes the ballgame," Joe said

in disgust. "I think Blade may have scared Buddy out of performing in Bayport."

"Yeah, you may be right, Joe," Frank agreed regretfully. "If Buddy just had the guts to hang on, I'm sure Blade would give us another shot at him. I do feel like we're getting closer to catching him even if we don't have any evidence to nail him."

"Hey, look over by tunnel C. Here comes Bobby Mellor waving something," Joe said suddenly.

"He looks pretty excited," Frank observed.

"Where's Syd?" Mellor asked breathlessly.

"He just went into Buddy's motor home, and I have a feeling he'll be there awhile," Joe told him.

"What happened?" Mellor asked with a look of dread on his face.

"Someone rigged Buddy's mike stand and got Skeezer instead," Frank said.

Mellor paled under his deep tan. "Oh, no! Is Skeezer okay?"

"We think so," Frank answered. "He was sitting up when the ambulance came. Didn't you hear the siren?"

"No," Mellor replied. "I've got a temporary office back in the dressing rooms. I can't hear much from in there. But while I was working I heard a thump on my door and thought somebody was knocking. When I opened the door I found this," Mellor said, holding out a note on white paper and another military dagger identical to the first one.

"Was there anyone around when you opened the door?" asked Frank.

Mellor shook his head. "No. By the time I got to the door all I heard was someone a long way off, running. I ran out into the hall and looked, but I couldn't see anybody."

Joe unfolded the slip of white paper. Like the previous notes from Blade, this one was printed in block capital letters in pencil. Joe studied it intently.

> This is a final warning. If Buddy Death performs here, he dies. Nothing and no one will stand in my way.
>
> Blade

"I guess he was pretty sure that mike stand stunt would scare Buddy off if it didn't kill him," Joe commented.

"If Syd manages to get Buddy onstage I'm sure Blade'll try again," Frank commented grimly.

"Hey, can I have that back?" Mellor asked. "I want to show it to Syd."

Joe gave Frank a questioning glance, and Frank nodded, so Joe handed it over. Mellor slipped the note and the dagger into his pocket.

"Maybe you shouldn't let Buddy see that

new note and the dagger," Frank told him. "He's ready to quit now."

"We'll see about that," Mellor told them with a determined gleam in his eye. "Me and Syd have too much riding on this concert to let him quit now."

With that Mellor left, striding quickly toward Buddy's motor home.

After Mellor was out of earshot Joe turned to his brother and said, "I don't like it. Mellor finding that note strikes me as just a little too convenient."

Frank looked skeptical. "You still think Mellor is Blade, huh, Joe?"

"Yes, I do," answered Joe.

"But why, Joe? It's not logical. What would Mellor have to gain? Think of all the money that's been sunk into this tour," Frank insisted.

"But it's Schacht's money that's financing the tour. Mellor doesn't have as much to lose, and maybe he has something to gain," Joe said thoughtfully.

"Like what?" Frank shot back.

"Like maybe Mellor insured Buddy's life for more than he'd make on the tour," Joe suggested.

"Not bad, little brother, and if we can find something like that in Mellor's office, it might be the motive we've been missing."

"Then there's no time like right now for searching his office. He'll probably be in with Buddy and Schacht for a while."

"Okay, you do that," Frank told him, "but make it quick. It could get sticky if Mellor catches you going through his files."

"Don't worry, Frank," Joe replied with a smile. "Let's meet back here in half an hour and compare notes."

"Okay," Frank agreed. "While you're doing that I'll look around to see if I can find any more booby traps."

Joe left the stage and headed for the dressing rooms. He made a right at the corridor junction and went along a curving passage set into the outer wall of the arena that contained the arena offices and dressing rooms. He passed a dozen tan-colored doors until he came to one that had a hand-lettered sign with the name B. Mellor taped to it.

Joe tried the knob to confirm that it was locked. Checking left and right first, he fished his plastic-coated driver's license from his wallet, and after a few tense moments of fiddling with the lock he heard it click open.

He slipped inside and closed the door behind him before flicking on the lights. The first thing he noticed was that Mellor's office was a mess. There were stacks of business papers and newspaper clippings about Buddy Death piled everywhere. Mellor's small desk was stacked with manila file folders and rock magazines. A wide ceramic ashtray in the center of the desk was overflowing with cigarette butts and ashes, and there were half-empty coffee cups sitting on almost every flat surface.

Against one wall was a dart board to which Mellor had pinned a glossy photo of Buddy. There were four darts in the board, all centered around Buddy's head, and the photo had dozens of punctures in it.

"Nice," Joe said to himself, shaking his head.

Joe quickly began going through the manila folders but soon found out that they contained nothing of interest, just contracts with the arena and various companies that had rented equipment to the band. Joe spent ten tense minutes sifting through the pile of folders before giving up on them. He moved on to a cardboard carton in the corner.

He was reaching for the top drawer when he heard footsteps in the corridor. Joe held his breath and noiselessly slid the drawer open.

The first thing he saw was a file marked "Buddy's insurance." He opened the folder and scanned the form for the name of the beneficiary. It was Bobby Mellor.

THE HARDY BOYS CASEFILES

The footsteps stopped by the door just then, and Joe froze.

Then he heard the jingling of keys being taken from a pocket. Then came the *thunk* of a key being inserted into the lock, and finally the sound of the door handle being slowly turned.

Chapter

8

FRANK ANGRILY POUNDED his fist on the edge of a packing crate. He felt as if he and Joe were getting nowhere and time was running out. He hadn't found any more booby-trapped mike stands, but he knew that sooner or later one of Blade's assassination attempts would succeed.

Frank's mind kept going back to the photos of Blade on the catwalks, their main clue so far. Mentally he turned the images over and over again, wondering if they contained something that he was overlooking.

"No use stewing about it," Frank muttered. He trotted over to the pay phone near the mouth of tunnel A and punched in Callie's number. Remembering that Callie was coming over to the arena that morning to interview Mellor and Schacht, Frank asked her to bring the photos and negatives so he could make better enlargements.

Frank felt slightly better after doing that, but he was so caught up in his thoughts that he almost failed to notice Bobby Mellor leaving Buddy's motor home. By the time Frank was aware of it Mellor was already almost at the entrance of access tunnel C, the one closest to his office.

Oh, no, Frank thought. Joe's still in Mellor's office! He leapt off the stage and raced for Mellor, hoping to stall him long enough for Joe to get out of his office.

Mellor was already so far ahead of him that Frank feared he'd never catch up. He poured on the speed until he skidded to a halt at the junction where tunnel C intersected with the corridor that curved inside the outer wall of the arena. Frank wondered which direction would be quicker, took a guess, and ran to his right.

To his relief, he spotted Mellor a short distance up ahead in the curving passage. Mellor had his hand on the knob of his office door and was just removing his key.

"Mr. Mellor, wait!" Frank shouted.

Startled, Mellor turned to look in the direction of Frank's shout. "What is it, kid? I'm real busy right now."

"Give me a minute to catch my breath," Frank panted, leaning against the wall. His mind raced as he tried to come up with some plausible excuse for stopping Mellor.

"Come on! Come on!" Mellor said impatiently. "What's so important that you nearly busted a gut to catch me, huh?"

Figuring he'd taken his ruse as far as he could, Frank pulled away from the wall where he'd been leaning and told Mellor, "Mr. Schacht sent me to, to, uh, ask you if you had a duplicate set of keys to Buddy's motor home."

Mellor's eyes narrowed suspiciously as he answered, "Sure. But why does Syd want them?"

"Just in case Buddy locks himself in again. Mr. Schacht wants to be able to get right in to talk to him so he doesn't have to waste any time," Frank replied, thinking quickly.

"So he needs my keys to make duplicates, huh?" Mellor said thoughtfully. He detached a set of keys from his ring and held them out to Frank. "Here you go, kid."

Frank made no move to take them but simply shook his head. "Mr. Schacht said he wanted you to bring them to him. I think he said he wanted to talk to you about something."

Mellor threw up his hands in frustration, saying, "When am I going to get my work done?"

Mellor reached for the knob to his office door, and Frank's heart skipped a beat.

It began beating again when he saw Mellor reinsert his key and lock the door before turning in the direction of tunnel C.

"I'd better get back to work, too," Frank said for Mellor's benefit before going a short distance in the opposite direction. He waited until he was sure Mellor had gone, then tiptoed back to the office.

"Joe! It's Frank! Get out of there!" he whispered.

The door popped open, and Frank saw one of Joe's blue eyes shining through the crack. Joe pulled it open wide enough to slip through and carefully locked it behind him.

"That was nice work, Frank," Joe said with a smile. "I thought for sure Mellor was going to catch me when I heard his key in that lock."

"Save the compliments. Let's just get out of here in case Mellor decides to come back. Find anything interesting in there?" Frank asked as he began walking toward tunnel A.

"My hunch about one thing was right," Joe told him. "I found a life insurance policy on Buddy, with Bobby Mellor listed as the beneficiary!"

Frank shrugged. "That doesn't really prove anything. It's probably a normal business precaution. What else did you turn up?"

70

"I found a photo of Buddy that Mellor was using for a dart board," Joe offered.

"That's no proof, either. We already know Buddy and Mellor don't get along. Did you see anything, anything at all that would link Mellor to Blade?"

"Just those two things and what I already told you about," Joe replied, sounding disappointed.

"Well, we'll need a lot more than that to prove he's Blade," Frank said as they emerged into the bowl of the arena from tunnel A.

"Hey, you Hardys!" someone shouted from the edge of the apron that jutted out from the front of the stage. Frank turned to see Kong hailing them.

"What's up?" Joe called as they walked over to him.

"That pretty blond girl from the Bayport paper came by looking for you guys, but Jake thought it was too dangerous to have her wandering around here. You know, if she was my girlfriend, I'd keep a close eye on her," Kong said with a nasty smile.

"What do you mean by that?" Frank snapped.

Kong shrugged, grinning casually with hostility glittering in his eyes. "I think a girl that pretty needs a real man to take care of her, not some know-it-all schoolboy," he said tauntingly in a low voice.

Frank felt anger surge through him, but he tried to keep it from showing. He knew that Kong was testing him and that the situation could turn violent if he showed any weakness.

"Well, excuse me, Kong," he replied, letting a cold edge of sarcasm creep into his voice. "You must have me confused with someone who cares about your opinion."

With that, Frank turned away, followed by Joe, and started to walk off. Abruptly he stopped and turned to ask Kong, "Where did Jake tell her to wait?"

Kong glared at him for a long moment before sullenly answering, "She's over by the lunch tables."

"Boy, for a second there I thought you and Kong were going to go at it," Joe said as they mounted the stage-right stairs.

"For a second, so did I," Frank admitted.

"What's Callie doing here today, anyway?" Joe asked, changing the subject.

"Since she was coming here to interview Schacht and Mellor, I asked her to bring those photos I took. I thought I'd take another stab at enlarging that design to see if it can tell us anything about Blade."

Joe looked skeptical as they walked across the stage to the lunch table where Callie was waiting.

"Still sounds like a dead end, Frank."

"It's a long shot, but those photos are the

best clue we have to Blade's identity," Frank replied.

"Hi, guys!" Callie said cheerily as soon as she saw them. "Here are your photos, Frank." She handed him the large manila envelope containing the photos and enlargements. Frank opened the envelope and briefly glanced at its contents.

"I'm curious about something," Callie said. "I thought you had decided these pictures were no help."

"I'm going to make another batch of prints on finer-grained paper. I feel that there's something important in them that I'm just missing," Frank said.

"Hey, fellows, we're behind schedule on the new sound tower," Jake interrupted, poking his head around the backdrop at the rear of the stage. "I need all hands right now," he said breathlessly.

"Gee, Jake, I was going to ask if I could have a couple of hours off," Frank responded.

"You've got to be kidding. You'll have to leave, Ms. Shaw. Sorry, but there's going to be a lot of steel flying through the air, and it might get dangerous."

"Okay," Callie replied. "I guess I can interview Mr. Schacht and Bobby Mellor by phone."

"That might be best," Jake agreed. "It's going to get crazy here this afternoon."

73

She turned to Frank and said, "Call me when you get off tonight, okay?"

"I will," Frank promised. Then, remembering the envelope in his hand, he said, "Since I won't have time to look at these, I want them in a safe place. Would you please put them in the safe in the van?" He reached into his pocket for his keys.

"Okay," Callie agreed, smiling.

Kong suddenly poked his head around the backdrop. "Come on, lover boy. There's hard work to do, and I'm sure you don't want to miss any of it."

Frank glared at Kong, then turned back to Callie. "See you later."

" 'Bye, Callie," Joe shouted over his shoulder. He stopped when he saw Kong run over to Callie. Wordlessly, Joe grabbed Frank's arm and pointed at Kong and Callie.

Frank watched Kong walk up to her wearing an expression that he guessed was Kong's attempt at an ingratiating smile.

"Hi," Kong said. "What you got in the envelope, sweet thing?"

"Photos," Callie snapped, adding in an icy tone, "and I'm not your sweet thing, so watch it, buster, or I'll tell your boss you've been manhandling a reporter."

"Hey, I was just trying to be friendly," Kong said before turning on his heel and stalking off.

A moment later Frank saw Syd Schacht come out of access tunnel B. Callie noticed him, too, and she went right over to him and began talking excitedly. Frank couldn't hear what she was saying, but he guessed from her gestures that she was complaining about Kong.

Suddenly he felt a tug on his shirt and heard Joe whisper, "Come on, Frank. Whether we like it or not we have to work, or we'll blow our cover. Callie can take care of herself."

The two boys walked around to the front of the stage and joined the work gang passing steel to roadies at the base of the tower. They passed along the scaffolding and watched as the gleaming structure was built higher and higher. The boys shared a look. The tower would stay up.

Something was nagging at Frank. Kong was nowhere to be seen, and Frank couldn't help feeling uneasy as he thought of Callie's run-in with the big roadie. Frank abruptly stopped pulling steel from the pile and slapped himself in the forehead.

"What's the matter, Frank?" Joe asked.

"I just remembered. I didn't see the negatives in that envelope. I've got to make sure Callie left them for me, or we're not going to have any new enlargements. Joe, can you cover for me for a few minutes? I'll be right back."

"Sure." Joe shrugged. "After all, it's only rock 'n' roll."

"Thanks," Frank yelled as he ran off to catch Callie.

As soon as he set foot inside the tunnel Frank knew something was wrong. All the lights were out.

"Callie?" Frank yelled. "You in there?"

There was no answer, and a dreadful chill snaked down Frank's spine. He ran down the center of the tunnel as fast as he dared in the pitch darkness, furiously wishing for a flashlight or cat's eyes.

Frank had counted off about fifty paces when he heard the sounds of a struggle off to his right.

"Callie?" he yelled as loud as he could.

He heard a slap, a man's harsh whisper, and then, to his horror, Callie's scream—a scream that was abruptly cut off.

Frank strained to hear in the darkness and ran for the spot where he'd heard the scuffle. Some muffled grunts that sounded like Callie trying to scream with a hand over her mouth came next.

Furious, Frank ran faster, his arms outstretched, hoping to snag Callie's attacker. He heard the man whirl around at the sound of his approach.

"Frank, be careful!" she shouted.

Then suddenly Frank felt a karate chop

strike him at the base of his neck. The blow drove him to his knees, but he managed to grab his assailant's ankles and trip him.

Frank could dimly make out his enemy's dark form as the guy fell with a dull thud. Frank hoped he'd stunned him, but the attacker was up again in an instant and charging Frank with a flurry of karate blows.

Frank spun away and launched a counterattack, aiming kicks and punches where he thought his enemy's head and torso were. The attacker absorbed all the punishment Frank dished out.

They sparred in the darkness for several more tense moments before Frank was driven back by a furious rain of body blows. As he retreated his left heel caught on something and he tumbled backward.

He rolled when he hit and bounced back up again quickly, but his attacker met him with a kick to the head that knocked him flat to the floor.

"Frank! He's got the pictures!" he heard Callie scream before he lost consciousness.

Chapter

9

I**T WAS DIFFICULT** to hear much of anything over the clank of steel pipes and the orders being shouted, but Joe was sure he'd just heard someone shout, "Help!" He paused and cocked his head to listen, then he knew he'd heard the scream.

Joe threw down the support rod he'd just picked up, startling the other roadies in the crew.

"Hey—what gives, Joe?" asked Tex.

Joe didn't waste his breath answering. He saved it for running flat out across the arena floor toward tunnel A. As he entered the dark tunnel he heard the same female voice scream for help. It was Callie.

"Hang on, Callie! It's Joe. I'm coming!" he shouted.

"Over here, Joe! Hurry! Frank's hurt!" Callie shouted.

Guided by the sound of Callie's voice, Joe quickly found her. He struck a light from a book of matches he had in his pocket and saw Callie kneeling against a wall.

"What happened?" asked Joe.

"The lights went out when I was halfway down the tunnel," she replied. "Then someone attacked me. He got away with the photos and knocked Frank out cold."

The match burned down to Joe's fingers, making him yelp. He lit another one and handed the matches to Callie.

"Light another one so I can find Frank," he instructed.

Callie held the match until Joe found his unconscious brother. He lifted him over his shoulder in a fireman's carry. By the time they reached the tunnel's entrance Frank was starting to come around.

"Did you get the license number of that truck?" Frank muttered.

Joe laughed and knew Frank was all right.

"Frank, are you okay?" Callie asked anxiously.

"He's all right, Callie," Joe answered her, "or he wouldn't be making bad jokes."

Joe set Frank down in a sitting position and leaned him against the inner wall of the arena.

"Frank, did you see who it was?" Joe asked.

Frank rubbed his temples and shook his head.

"Callie, do you know who it was?" Joe asked her.

Callie bit her lip and shook her head.

"I know what you're thinking, Joe," Frank said, "but don't even bother looking for our attacker. I'm sure whoever it was is long gone."

As soon as Frank finished speaking Joe heard a shuffling sound in the dark tunnel.

"I'm not so sure about that, Frank," Joe whispered before he went over to the tunnel entrance. He stood for a few seconds, listening, staring into the darkness. The shuffling grew louder.

Suddenly Jake Williams staggered into view holding one hand to the left side of his head. Jake lurched against a wall, and Joe hurried over to hold him up.

"Jake, what happened?" asked Joe.

"I can't say," Jake mumbled, holding his hand to his left temple and wincing. "I was putting together the compressed-air cannon when the lights went out. While I was looking for the door somebody came up from behind and conked me."

"Someone attacked Frank, too," Joe said

grimly. "Whoever it was, he could still be in the arena."

Jake looked up at Joe for the first time.

"Why don't you wait here until you feel better, Jake?" Joe suggested.

Jake shook his head. "No, I'll be okay. I've been hit worse than this before."

With those words he strode off toward the road crew. As he walked past, Joe noticed an ugly purple bruise starting to form across his temple.

"What really burns me up is that he got the pictures," Frank said after Joe rejoined him. "Now I'll never know what the enlargements might have shown."

"Not necessarily, Frank," Callie quietly told him. "The negatives weren't with the photos. They're still in my purse."

Joe smiled as he watched a broad grin spread across his brother's face. "Callie, you're great!" Frank and Joe said almost together.

Roadies kept stopping by to ask what had happened to Jake. Kong was the last to arrive, sporting a bad bruise on his left cheek.

Joe sauntered over to Kong. "That's a nasty bruise, Kong. What happened?" he asked casually.

Kong glared at him. "Mind your own business, punk," he growled.

"No need to get hostile, Kong," Joe said

81

easily. "I was just asking. It's not like you to have anything to hide, right?"

Kong whirled on Joe, wearing a wrathful expression. "I—" he began, then swallowed what he was going to say. "Yo, Jake, what happened to you, man?" he asked instead.

"Never mind," Jake replied. "Go see if you can get the lights back on in tunnel A, then check around the main power cables to see what went wrong."

Wordlessly Kong nodded and left.

"Hey, Jake, do you know where Buddy is?" Joe called.

Jake smiled grimly over his shoulder. "Tex told me that when he heard what happened to me he ran back to his motor home and locked himself in. Schacht and one of Hubbard's people are with him."

"What about the other guys in the band?"

"Schacht told them to stay in their dressing rooms. Bobby Mellor's with them, so they ought to be safe."

Callie shuddered. "I just wonder if anybody's safe with this Blade character creeping around attacking people."

"Callie, we don't know for certain it was Blade who attacked us," Frank pointed out.

Casting an uneasy glance at Jake and the other roadies who stood almost within earshot, Joe bent down and suggested, "If we're

going to analyze this case, we should go somewhere a little more private.''

They got up and moved to the center of the
arena floor, at least fifty yards from anyone.
Joe said, "Frank, so far this investigation is
getting us nowhere. I think we need more
background on Buddy.''

"Hey, guys, don't forget I'm on this case,
too," Callie put in. "Why don't you let me
do some of the legwork while you're stuck
here?''

"Okay, Callie. See what else you can find
on Buddy. Meanwhile I'll make another batch
of photos and hope I can get a clearer look at
that design. The rap on the head I took is a
perfect excuse to take a couple of hours off,''
Frank said. "I'll just tell Jake I'm going to the
doctor.''

"What about me?" Joe asked.

"Somebody's got to stay here and maintain
our cover, Joe. If all three of us are gone, it
might tip Blade off that we're not what we
seem to be.''

Joe would have preferred developing photos
to slinging steel and lugging road cases, but
he had to admit that Frank was right. "I'll
check around to see if I can dig up anything
else," Joe said.

"See you," Frank called, leaving with
Callie.

The guys were having a break, so Joe began

to search the perimeter of the arena. As he walked around the outside of the domed space he kept thinking about the bruises he'd seen on Jake and Kong. Frank had said that some of his blows had connected with Blade, and Kong and Jake both had bruises on the left sides of their faces. Frank was right-handed and usually led with his right when they were sparring, Joe remembered. If he hit somebody with a solid right hand, he'd have a bruise on the left side of his face.

Jake had offered a seemingly plausible explanation for his bruise. Kong had offered none at all. Could Kong be Blade?

Joe kicked at an empty paper cup on the ground. He felt angry and helpless. Blade was out there somewhere, he thought, and he and Frank could only guess who he was or where he might strike next.

He and Frank had only suspects, no hard evidence. Buddy's concert was set for the following night. Joe was certain that if they didn't catch Blade before then, he'd strike at Buddy during the show—maybe endangering thousands of innocent fans.

Joe was occupied with those gloomy thoughts when a flash of movement around the corner of a Dumpster caught his eye. He immediately sought cover, then began to ease up to the Dumpster and slide around to its corner. He paused for a moment, gathering himself, then charged around the corner.

"Hold it right there!" Joe shouted to the leather-jacketed back bending over near a door in the outer wall of the arena. The person spun around, wearing a look of utter astonishment. It was David Pauling, the fan who'd been in the arena the night the spotlight had nearly crushed Buddy.

Joe's gaze dropped from Pauling's startled face to his hand. Light glinted off an open switchblade as David came at him.

Chapter

10

"HEY, W-WAIT—" Joe stammered as he took in the gleaming knife blade and David Pauling's wild-eyed expression. There was no time for more than a quick glance. Pauling was only an arm's length away, holding the blade at waist height and close to his side so Joe couldn't knock it away.

As Pauling rushed him Joe pivoted on his left foot and sidestepped the knife. Expecting another attack, he wheeled around to face Pauling again. But to his surprise, Pauling had kept on running toward a gate that led to the parking lot. Joe followed and spotted a beat-up red racing motorcycle through the chain link fence that surrounded the lot, and he guessed it was Pauling's.

"You can't get away that easy," Joe muttered as he took off after Pauling.

Pauling poured on the speed and passed through the gap in the chain link fence into the wide parking lot. Joe caught a glimpse of Pauling's pale face as the teen shot a glance over his shoulder.

Joe ran even faster, trying to close the gap before Pauling got to his motorcycle. The fan zigzagged as he ran, and Joe did gain on him. But just as he stuck out a hand to grab Pauling's shoulder Joe's foot hit an oily patch on the pavement. Both feet slid out from under him, and he slammed into the ground.

"Oooff!" he cried as the air rushed from his lungs.

As he tried to pick himself up he heard a motorcycle engine roar to life. He got to his feet just in time to see Pauling take off across the parking lot and through the lot's wide main gate.

"Nuts!" Joe muttered disgustedly as he watched Pauling disappear down the road. Totally discouraged, Joe limped back to the arena, rubbing the hip he had landed on.

After Frank walked Callie to her car he got into his van and drove to Speedy Photo.

When Frank appeared at the front counter of the photo shop Duke Wampler's long jaw dropped in surprise.

"What are you doing back here?" Duke asked, brushing his long brown hair out of his sleepy-looking eyes.

"I need to make another set of blowups, Duke," Frank said seriously. "It's important that I do it quickly."

"Jeez, Frank, my boss would skin me alive if he knew I was letting you use his enlargers and stuff," Duke said gloomily.

"Okay, okay, I get the message," Frank replied. "Now I owe you a favor. I'll help you study for the final exam in calculus. Fair enough?"

"I guess," Duke replied, a little less gloomy. "All I want is a B in the class so my dad will stay off my back. Help me get a B and we're square."

"No problem," Frank answered.

He and Duke shook on their deal, then Frank asked, "Where do you keep the really fine-grained developing paper, Duke? I've got an idea."

Within a few minutes Frank had put the negative showing Blade's shirt design in the enlarger and was slowly turning the focus knob, trying for the clearest image possible.

He raised the head of the enlarger by turning a hand crank on its side, then turned the focus knob a fraction of an inch before he was satisfied.

Acting on a sudden inspiration, Frank overexposed the image slightly, hoping to bring out some of the detail in the design that had been lost in shadow. Then he made six more prints of the enlargement, varying the exposure times so that he would have the greatest possible range of dark to light values in the photos.

He finished his enlargements and slipped the first photo into the shallow tray of developing bath.

As the first image emerged from the blank paper Frank felt a thrill of satisfaction. He'd been right about a finer-grained paper bringing out greater detail. Without waiting for the photo to dry he took it into the next room, where he could examine it under bright light with a magnifying glass.

The details of the design were clearly visible. Frank saw an intricate flowing piece of artwork that seemed oddly familiar, though he wasn't quite sure if it was a T-shirt or something else entirely.

Frank went back into the darkroom and pulled the other prints out of the developer tank. He had five new 8 x 10 prints showing large, clear images of the design.

He was at the front counter scrutinizing them under Duke's magnifying glass when the phone rang. Duke took the call, then handed the phone to Frank. "Here. It's for you."

"Hi, it's Joe." His voice sounded faint on

the other end of the line. "They need you at the arena."

"What's up?"

"Buddy was too jumpy to play, so Schacht canceled this afternoon's rehearsal. He wants us to drive the band back to their hotel so they can rest up before the press conference tonight."

"I'll be right there," Frank assured him. "I think I've finally found a decent clue in my photo."

"Great!" Joe replied. "See you soon."

After thanking Duke for the use of the lab Frank gathered up his photos and raced back to the arena.

When Frank parked the van he saw Buddy's motor home and a black stretch limousine parked near an exit. Joe lounged against the side of the motor home while Schacht and Bobby Mellor stood tensely beside the limousine, checking their watches and talking into Mellor's walkie-talkie. Frank locked the van and trotted over to join them.

"About time you got here!" Mellor snapped at him.

"I came from the doctor's office as soon as I got Joe's message," Frank replied.

"How's your head, Frank?" asked Schacht.

"We can talk about it later, Mr. Schacht," Frank replied.

"Yeah, later is a good time to talk about it," Mellor said impatiently as Joe joined the group. "I'd like to get our star to his hotel before he has a nervous breakdown."

"I'm ready whenever you are," Frank said to Mellor, a note of irritation creeping into his voice. "What do you want us to do, Mr. Schacht?"

"I want you to drive the limo, Frank," Schacht told him. "I fired the driver. Buddy's inside with Sammy and Eric. I'll ride with them. Joe will follow in Buddy's motor home with Bobby. I figured having you two drive the vehicles would be safest. I know neither of you is Blade."

"Syd, can we get this circus rolling, please?" asked Mellor.

"Take it easy, Bobby," Schacht said firmly. "Getting bent out of shape won't help anybody."

"Which hotel, Mr. Schacht?" Joe asked.

"They're staying at the Branford Towers," Mellor cut in.

"We'll get everybody there safely. Don't worry," Frank said. He opened the door of the limousine. As Schacht climbed inside Frank saw that Joe was already behind the wheel of the motor home, with Mellor sitting next to him in the passenger seat. Joe gave him a thumbs-up sign to show that he was ready to go. Frank slid behind the wheel of the limo.

The car's engine started up with a powerful roar, and Frank threw it into gear. It took him a few moments to get used to the handling of the long car, but it was easy once he caught on.

Frank had never driven a stretch limousine before and marveled at all the features on the dashboard, from the phone to rows of switches that controlled the windows, sun roof, and door locks. Frank experimentally flicked a switch, and the glass panel separating him from the passenger cabin slid down noiselessly.

"Hey, how's it going, dude?" came Sammy's cheerful voice from the backseat.

"Hey, what's going on?" Schacht asked.

"I was just checking out the dashboard," Frank replied a little sheepishly.

"Well, concentrate on your driving and give us some privacy," Buddy said in a haughty voice.

"Yes, sir!" Frank retorted, flicking the switch for the panel. What a creep, Frank thought. That jerk never lets up.

Frank drove on in silence, concentrating on the extra-long vehicle. He got on the highway encircling Bayport and headed toward the exit for the center of town. He turned off at the downtown exit ramp and hit the brake.

As he turned onto the off ramp the brake pedal sank all the way to the floor with no slackening of the limo's speed. "Uh-oh!" Frank said out loud. He stomped on the brake pedal again. No effect.

"Slow down, Frank!" Schacht's voice crackled over the intercom.

"Uh, that might be a problem, Mr. Schacht! The brakes don't work!"

"What!" came a chorus of panicky voices over the intercom.

Frank felt a flash of fear, then remembered the emergency brake. He pulled it back, but the handle came off in his hand. Frank looked at it in horror for a split second before tossing it aside.

"Do something, you moron!" Buddy shouted over the intercom.

Frank kept a tight grip on the wheel. The big car sped down the off ramp, heading straight into oncoming traffic!

Chapter

11

"WHOA!" Frank didn't hear himself shout as the limousine careened out of control, speeding straight at a delivery truck. His heart in his throat, Frank spun the wheel hard to the right. The tires screeched as the big car veered back into its own lane, hit the guard rail, and bounced away.

Grimacing with the effort, Frank leaned on the wheel, forcing the fender against the guard rail in a screaming shower of sparks and tortured metal. Seventy-five yards down the road the car finally slowed to a jerky stop.

Watching from the driver's seat of the motor home, Joe felt relief flood through him.

"Way to go, Frank! Way to go!" Joe exulted.

"I saw it, but I don't believe it!" Mellor said with wonder.

Joe guided the big black-and-white motor home around the other car and parked it on the shoulder of the road. Before Joe had completely stopped Mellor was on the car phone calling for taxis to pick up the band.

As Joe climbed down from the motor home he saw Frank emerge from the limousine and disappear under the front of the car. Joe hurried to join his brother.

"Frank, are you okay?"

"Just scared out of three years' growth," came the muffled reply from under the hood.

Joe knelt down by Frank's legs so he could talk to him more easily over the roar of the passing traffic. Some passenger cars with teenagers in them, attracted by the sight of Buddy's motor home, slowed to a crawl, and the kids shouted and honked their horns.

"Heeey, Buddy! We love you, dude! Buddy rules!" the teenagers shouted.

Joe glanced over at them and shook his head.

"Do you think those kids would love Buddy if they knew the guy?" he wondered aloud.

Frank didn't reply. All Joe heard was a thoughtful "hmmm" coming from his brother. It was followed by a triumphant, "Aha! I knew it!"

A moment later Frank crawled out from

under the car with a smudge of grease on his cheek, rubbing his hands together to clean them off.

"What did you find?" Joe inquired.

"Someone fixed the brakes for us," Frank replied, wiping the grease from his face with a handkerchief. "They punched a tiny hole in the brake line so that I'd have normal brakes for a mile or two. Then as I lost brake fluid in traffic—*whammo,* major accident. I wonder who had access to this car."

"I got there only a few minutes before you did," Joe answered. "We'll have to ask Schacht."

The Hardys went over to the side window of the limo and knocked. The tinted window lowered several inches. They could see Syd Schacht's face through the gap. It was drawn and pale.

"What's up now, boys?" Schacht asked.

"Can we talk to you privately?" Joe asked.

Schacht nodded and climbed out. He came around to the front of the limo and knelt down by the front wheels. Joe and Frank knelt down and joined him.

"Mr. Schacht, was this limo left unattended at any time before we left?" Frank asked.

Schacht considered his question for a moment. "No. Either Bobby or I was beside it or in it at all times until the band arrived."

"Let's check with Mellor," Joe suggested, heading for the motor home.

When Joe pulled open the driver's-side door Mellor, who was talking on the car phone, looked over, annoyed.

"What is it?" he snapped.

"Mr. Mellor, did you leave the limo alone before the band arrived?" Joe inquired.

Mellor held the phone to his chest while he answered. "Well, yeah. A few minutes after Syd left Kong came out and told me I had a call on one of the pay phones in tunnel A."

"Who called you?" Frank asked.

"I don't know. By the time I got there the line was dead," Mellor answered.

"Thanks for the info, Mr. Mellor," Joe told him before closing the door.

"That few minutes when the limo was unattended had to be when the brakes were tampered with," Frank speculated.

"Unless Mellor was lying about the phone call and he monkeyed with the brakes himself," Joe countered.

"Then again, it could have been Kong," Frank guessed.

Joe shrugged. "Maybe, but maybe somebody else put him up to getting Mellor away."

Joe's speculations were cut off by the arrival of a pair of sedans bearing the Bayport

Taxi Company logo, followed by a lumbering tow truck.

While Frank oversaw the limo getting hooked onto the back of the tow truck Joe checked the motor home's brakes to make sure that they hadn't been tampered with.

Buddy and the other band members piled into one taxi. "I'll ride in the motor home with Joe," Frank volunteered as Bobby Mellor climbed into the second taxi with Schacht.

The drive to the Branford Towers was uneventful, for which Joe was thankful. But when he pulled up in front of the hotel Joe noticed a large crowd of Buddy Death fans wearing BDB T-shirts and holding up a large homemade banner that read: Buddy—We Love You!

Joe drove to the underground parking lot, and the crowd of teenagers surged around the vehicle.

He gazed out over the sea of bodies wearing T-shirts that bore Buddy's face or the band's logo, then looked over and noticed Frank's concerned expression.

"Maybe we should have parked this thing on the next block, Joe," Frank said quietly.

"They'll leave us alone when they realize neither of us is Buddy," Joe said.

"Let's hope so," Frank muttered.

Joe grinned. "Relax. The worst thing that'll

happen is a bunch of girls will tear your shirt off. How bad can that be?''

The fans had surrounded the motor home while Joe parked it and were pounding on the sides, chanting, "We want Buddy!" Frank and Joe were mobbed as soon as they opened the doors.

"Hold on a minute! Buddy's not here! We're just on the crew!" Frank shouted to the fans who pressed in, tugging on his clothes.

After a few minutes the Hardys finally made it into the elevator. When they arrived at the top floor of the hotel, where Schacht had reserved an eight-room suite for Buddy and the band, Frank and Joe found a pair of huge, muscular men wearing dark warm-up suits flanking the door to the suite. One had short blond hair. The other had dark hair and a neatly trimmed beard. Both wore no-nonsense expressions.

"Hi," Joe said. "We're Frank and Joe Hardy. We're here to see Mr. Schacht."

The dark-haired man checked a small notebook, then nodded to his companion, saying, "It's okay, Matt. They're on the list."

The other man grunted and opened the door for the Hardys, slamming it as soon as they were inside.

"Wow. Not bad." Joe whistled as the brothers surveyed the wide, expensively carpeted corridor with closed doors leading off at regular intervals.

"Plenty of privacy," Frank remarked. "This suite must take up at least a quarter of the floor." Down the corridor to their right the brothers heard loud talking and the clink of ice in glasses. They followed the sound to a large sunken living room at the end of the corridor. It was filled with comfortable-looking leather couches, glass-and-chrome coffee tables, and a black baby grand piano. Schacht was sprawled on one couch drinking a cup of coffee, and Bobby Mellor was hunched up on the edge of another couch, staring tensely at the phone on the table in front of him.

"Hi, Mr. Schacht," Joe announced from the top of the steps leading down into the living room.

Schacht looked up in surprise. "What kept you boys?"

"We ran into a mob of Buddy's fans in the garage and had to wade through them," Frank replied. "Say, who are the two gorillas outside?"

"Buddy's bodyguards."

Suddenly Joe heard the sound of a door opening. He flicked a quick look down the corridor to his right and saw Buddy come out of his room, followed by Sammy and Eric.

"Yo, dudes! What's happening?" Sammy

called cheerily. Behind Sammy, Eric wore a worried expression.

Buddy sauntered past the Hardys without a word and stepped down into the living room. He went right to the phone.

"Did you tell room service that I don't eat meat?" Buddy asked.

"Buddy, sweetheart, don't worry. Uncle Syd takes care of everything," Schacht told him in a soothing voice.

Buddy tossed his tangled black mop of hair, put the phone to his ear, and began ordering.

"And I want fresh hummus. And send up some bottles of mineral water," he said, finishing his order.

"I'll be in my room resting up for the press conference," Buddy told them. "All this excitement has got my nerves ragged. I want to look good tonight."

As Buddy was leaving Sammy went down into the room to ask Schacht, "Hey, Mr. Money—any word on Skeezer?"

Schacht's answer was interrupted by the phone ringing. Mellor snatched it up before the first ring ended.

"Hello?" he spat out.

Then suddenly Joe saw the tense expression leave Mellor's face. He smiled broadly.

"That was Skeezer. They're letting him out of the hospital. He'll be okay for tomorrow night's show."

"All right!" Sammy shouted.

With a flourish he produced a pair of drumsticks from the back pocket of his frayed jeans and beat a rapid drum roll down the corridor walls to Buddy's door.

"Hey, Buddy!" he shouted. "Skeezer's okay!"

"Great, Sammy," Buddy said impatiently. "Leave me alone."

Sammy made a face at the door, then looked back down the corridor with a grin.

"I'm feeling restless. Hey, you Hardys! Eric! Let's party! My buddy Skeezer's coming home!"

Joe followed Eric into Sammy's room, with Frank trailing him. Although the band had been in Bayport for only two days, Joe saw that Sammy had already turned his room into a shambles. A lamp was overturned, and there were clothes, drums, and empty food containers strewn everywhere. Sammy swept a pile of clothes off the bed and offered it to his guests with a low bow.

"Uh-oh," Eric said with a slow grin. "Sammy's on a roll. Bear with him, guys. He always gets like this before a show."

For the next ten minutes Sammy entertained all three of them with a stream of jokes, funny stories, and snatches of songs. Joe relaxed and began enjoying himself for the first time in two days. If this was stage fright, it wasn't so bad, he told himself. Sammy should perform more often.

"So then Bowie said to me—" Sammy stopped in midsentence when he heard a knock at the front door of the suite. Joe saw a devilish gleam appear in his eyes. Then he leapt up and ran out of the room.

"What's up?" asked Joe with a grin.

"With Sammy, your guess is as good as mine," Eric replied.

Sammy reappeared a moment later carrying a covered tray of food.

"Here's Buddy's food. Let's play a joke on him," Sammy said, chortling.

"I don't think that's a good idea, Sammy," Frank told him. "Buddy's edgy enough right now."

"No, no, it's cool," Sammy insisted. "Buddy could use a good joke. It'll loosen him up for the press conference."

"What are you going to do?" Joe asked.

"Nothing too rotten," Sammy chuckled. "I'll just eat his lunch myself and send Mr. Health Food a treat from my room."

Sammy scanned the room until he spotted a tray shoved under the nightstand, where the maid must have missed it.

"Perfect!" Sammy dived for the tray. He came up with a day-old cheeseburger and a pile of limp, greasy fries.

"Come on, Sammy," Frank insisted. "I really don't think Buddy will laugh at this."

"Sure he will," Sammy replied. "It's in excellent taste!"

Sammy wolfed down Buddy's hummus, pita bread, tabbouleh, and steamed vegetables, but no one laughed.

"No kidding, he'll love this," the rocker insisted as he started out the door with the room service tray containing the stale burger and fries. He never made it to the door. Joe heard a choking sound, and the next thing he knew, Sammy had dropped the tray.

"What happened?" Joe got up to help. Sammy clutched his throat, making gagging noises. His freckled face turned pale. He was having trouble breathing. He coughed again and fell forward into Joe's arms.

"Frank," Joe cried. "Buddy's food was poisoned!"

Chapter

12

FRANK WAS AT JOE'S SIDE almost before he caught the choking musician.

"Set him down easy, Joe. I'll call an ambulance," Frank instructed.

Frank dashed over to the phone. He told the dispatcher that there had been a poisoning and requested an ambulance.

"What happened?" Eric was bending over Sammy, terrified.

"Buddy's lunch must have been poisoned," Joe guessed. "Go tell Schacht and Mellor. Let them know an ambulance is on the way."

"Check," Eric simply said, and then vanished through the door.

Frank knew that Sammy shouldn't be moved until proper medical care arrived, so he only rolled the unconscious rocker onto his side to keep a close watch on his breathing.

Schacht and Mellor appeared in the doorway. Schacht mopped his bald head with his handkerchief while Mellor stared at Sammy with a horrified expression and wrung his hands.

"Eric told us," Schacht said. "How is he, Frank?"

"He's alive. That's all I know," Frank said without looking up.

The paramedics arrived soon after, and they put Sammy on a gurney and wheeled him down the hall.

As they passed Buddy's door he stuck his head out and peevishly asked, "What's all the racket? I'm trying to re—"

Buddy's words faltered when he saw Sammy being wheeled past.

"W-what happened to Sammy?" he asked in a soft voice.

"He got poisoned eating your lunch," Eric told him crossly.

Buddy turned a shade paler than usual before he slammed his door and locked it.

"Syd!" he screamed through the door. "Get in here."

As the medics pushed Sammy through the door Frank realized that if Blade was indeed responsible for the poisoning, he might have left some clues in the hotel kitchen. "Joe!" he called. "Let's check the kitchen."

Frank and Joe rode to the ground floor with Sammy and the medics. As the elevator doors slid open the Hardys took off through the lobby toward the kitchen. They burst through a pair of swinging doors, startling a chef, who dropped a mixing bowl full of dough.

"What are you kids doing in here?" he demanded angrily.

"One of your guests was just poisoned. Where is the room service food prepared?" Frank asked sharply.

The chef's mouth dropped open, and he simply pointed to a cook's prep station in the corner of the kitchen, where a male and female chef were bustling around half a dozen room service carts.

"But I don't think *they'd* do it. They've been with the hotel for years and their credentials are perfect," the chef said.

Frank started to stride over to the station, but Joe grabbed his arm to stop him.

"Look over at the dishwashing station, Frank," Joe told him, pointing to a bored-looking teenager loading a big industrial dishwasher with racks of dirty plates.

"I don't see—" Frank began, then he stopped as soon as he recognized the dishwasher. "It's David Pauling!" he whispered.

"Maybe he poisoned Buddy's food," Joe suggested.

"There's only one sure way to find out," Frank replied.

Frank and Joe quietly slipped up behind Pauling, who was concentrating on his work.

"David Pauling—we want to talk to you," Joe told him firmly.

Pauling spun around, wide-eyed, and tried to bolt past them. Joe caught him easily and pushed him back against the dishwashing machine.

"You're not going anywhere until you answer a few questions, David," Joe told him.

"I didn't do anything! Honest!" Pauling said in panic.

"Take it easy," Frank assured him, coming a step closer. "We just want to talk to you."

"What's going on here, eh?" a voice asked behind them.

Frank looked for the speaker and saw the first chef glaring at him.

"Somebody from the Buddy Death Band got poisoned a few minutes ago," Frank explained. "We've seen David at the arena twice, both times after accidents. We think he might have something to do with the poisoning."

The chef snorted contemptuously. "That's ridiculous. David is no murderer!"

"How long have you been here today?" Joe demanded.

"He came on at two," the chef told them before Pauling had a chance to answer. "Here, I'll show you," he said, leading the Hardys over to a time clock and a rack of cards.

He pulled out the one bearing the name David Pauling and shoved it under Frank's nose. Frank saw that David had clocked in at 2:03 P.M.

Frank then asked the chef, "Is there some record of when the room service orders go out?"

The chef's head bobbed up and down. With a curt wave he led the Hardys over to a wire spindle at the room service station and pawed through the stack of orders before extracting one and handing it to Frank. Frank checked it out and saw that the order had come in at 1:22 and had gone out at 1:47, almost fifteen minutes before David Pauling had clocked in.

"Are you sure David clocked in at two?" Frank asked the chef.

"Positive," the man replied. "I remember, because I scolded him for being three minutes late."

"Did anyone else see him come in then?" Joe asked.

The chef turned to the male and female prep cooks, who'd stopped working and were staring at them with interest. "What about it, Carol? Ralph?"

"It was just after two. I remember because you were standing under the big clock over the kitchen entrance while you chewed David out."

The chef glanced back at the Hardys with a satisfied expression. "There. Three witnesses. Is that enough?"

"I guess this puts David in the clear about the poisoning," Joe agreed. "But I still want to know why he lied to Captain Hubbard about being unemployed."

"Well?" Frank asked.

Pauling fidgeted and stared down at his feet before answering. "I didn't want to tell anybody where I worked 'cause I just got this job, and I was afraid that if I got in trouble I'd get fired."

"Why did you try to knife me at the arena earlier?" Joe asked, fixing David with a hard stare.

"I—I—" David stammered. "I didn't want to hurt you, man. You just surprised me, and I wanted to get away."

"You were warned not to come back to the arena. What were you doing there?" Frank asked.

"I thought maybe if I sneaked inside I could talk to Buddy and let him know that I'd never hurt him. That's all. I just wanted to talk to my man Buddy. Honest!" he added, his eyes wide.

"Why did you have a knife in your hand?" Joe persisted.

"To jimmy the door lock so I could sneak in without the arena cops grabbing me."

Frank realized that questioning Pauling was fruitless. He turned back to the trio of cooks.

"Did anybody else notice anything out of the ordinary around the time Buddy's order went out?" Frank asked, scanning their faces.

The female cook, a petite, dark-haired woman, spoke first. "I remember thinking we had a new waiter—one I didn't recognize. Come to think of it, he was the one who took the order up to Buddy Death's suite."

"What did he look like?" Joe jumped in excitedly.

She shrugged. "I only noticed him out of the corner of my eye. All I remember was that he was a big guy in a waiter's jacket."

"Where's the service elevator?" Frank asked.

"Through there." The chef pointed toward some battered steel swinging doors in the far corner of the room.

"Let's check it out," Frank suggested.

The brothers went through the doors. Facing them was the gray service elevator. To their right was a pair of swinging doors like the ones they'd just opened.

Frank turned and called over his shoulder, "Where do those other doors lead?"

"To a service corridor that leads to the rear of the lobby," the chef answered.

Joe opened the doors and peered into the corridor.

"Frank, I found something!" he shouted.

Frank followed him into the corridor. He found Joe bending over an industrial ice machine set in a niche in the wall.

As Frank watched, Joe pulled something out of the narrow space between the side of the ice machine and the wall.

"Look at this." Joe held up a wrinkled red waiter's jacket and black pants. "Blade could have changed out of this waiter's outfit on his way to the lobby after delivering the poisoned food."

"If you're right," Frank pointed out, "then Buddy's bodyguards should be able to give us a decent description of the guy."

As they pushed through some swinging doors into the lobby Joe said, "I don't care if there was a poisoning, I'm starved. Before we quiz the bodyguards, how about getting a couple of burgers?"

"As long as they're not from room service," Frank agreed.

As the Hardys crossed the Branford's wide lobby to the coffee shop Joe suddenly grabbed Frank's arm and pointed to the front entrance.

Syd Schacht was standing just inside the door, scanning the lobby. He quickly spotted the Hardys and crossed to join them.

"Blade is back," Schacht said grimly. "A couple of minutes after you left we found a note outside the suite."

"Another threat against Buddy?" Frank asked.

"No. This time he threatened to get you and your brother if you don't lay off. I'll show it to you when you come up."

"We'll be right there," Frank informed him. "Your bodyguards may be able to give a description of Blade. They probably took the tray of food from him."

When Schacht had gone the brothers eyed each other. "Let's hit the coffee shop," Frank said.

As they stepped inside the restaurant Frank spotted a familiar couple in the farthest booth.

"Say, Joe, isn't that—" Frank began.

"Jake and Clare Williams?" Joe said, completing Frank's sentence. "It sure is."

"Let's see if we can get close enough to hear what they're talking about," Frank said quietly.

"Lead on," Joe responded.

Jake's attention was totally occupied with his sister. It was easy for Frank and Joe to sneak across the crowded coffee shop and slip into a booth behind them.

"So what are you going to do about those poems, Clare? They're yours!" Jake was saying.

"Just drop it, Jake, okay?" she said wearily. "I'm tired of fighting about it."

"Well, if you're not here about the poems, you're here to see him, aren't you?"

"I—" Clare began defensively.

"I knew it!" Jake said tightly. "Stay away from Buddy, Clare. That's an order. I won't have you chasing after him, living in rat traps like that Star-Lite Motel. Once the tour starts it could be dangerous just to be around that creep. Sammy just got poisoned, and who knows who'll be next?"

"But I—" the pretty girl began.

Jake's voice rose hysterically. "You hear me, Clare? You stay away!"

"YOU'RE MY BROTHER, not my boss!" Clare flared angrily. "I'll go where I please and see who I want!"

"I'm telling you for your own good!" Jake shouted louder.

Joe noticed Jake's tool bag on the floor beside him. Sticking out of the unzipped top was a bright orange lineman's phone, the type telephone repairpeople carry to tap into phone lines. Joe wondered why Jake would be carrying that around, but his train of thought was interrupted when Clare suddenly sprang from her seat. "I don't have to take this, Jake! I'm going back to my motel!"

"Good!" Jake shouted, following her out. "You stay there until Buddy leaves town!"

When he was sure Jake had gone Joe spoke to Frank. "What do you make of that?" he asked.

"What Jake said about it being dangerous to be around Buddy?" Frank replied.

"It sounded like he knows more than he's saying."

"Yeah," Frank agreed. "Something else bothered me, too. How did Jake know about Sammy so fast?"

"We'd better check whether someone told him," Joe said. He looked at his watch. "Let's get our food and head upstairs."

When Frank and Joe got back to the band's suite they found a pair of Bayport police officers quizzing Schacht and the two body-guards. To Joe's relief, one of the officers was Con Riley, a friend of the Hardys. Joe knew Con to be fair and hoped he would give them the elbow room they'd need to help solve the case.

"I don't really see how I can keep a lid on this, Mr. Schacht," he overheard Con saying. "Attempted murder is serious business."

"All I'm asking for is a little cooperation to keep these incidents quiet until after Buddy's concert," Schacht pleaded.

Con Riley didn't appear to be persuaded. "Well . . ." he hedged.

Joe saw an opportunity to jump into the conversation, and he took it. "Con, Frank and I are working on tracking Blade down."

"In fact, these two bodyguards may have seen Blade," Frank quickly added. "Did they give you a description of the room service waiter?"

"I can answer that, kid," the blond bodyguard replied in a gravelly voice. "The waiter was a big guy, over six feet tall, with dark hair and a bushy beard."

"Could be almost anyone with a wig and fake beard," Con noted.

I can think of at least two people it could be, Joe thought to himself. He could tell from Frank's expression that the same thought had occurred to his brother.

"I agree it's not enough of a description to pin the poisoning on anybody, but we've narrowed our list down to only a few suspects. All we need is a little more time to unmask Blade."

"And would you mind telling me who the suspects are?" Con asked sarcastically.

Frank appeared to be uncomfortable. "Right now our evidence is too thin for us to make any accusations. That's why I asked for more time before we name names."

"Well, you boys have a pretty good track record. Mr. Schacht has confidence in you. I'll tell you what. I won't interfere with you yet on this case. But I'm assigning extra officers to the arena. At the first sign of danger to the public I'll stop the show. In the meantime, we'll keep a lid on everything."

"Great! That's great, Officer Riley. Thanks a lot," Syd Schacht said. Then he turned to the bodyguards. "Everything said here is confidential, fellows. Nobody's to know the Hardys are working for me."

Wordlessly the big men nodded.

"Thanks, Con. You won't be sorry," Joe said.

Con gave Joe and Frank a skeptical look as he and the other officer left the room. I hope not, he seemed to be thinking.

As soon as the two police officers had left Schacht turned to the Hardys. "Okay, you wouldn't tell the cops who your suspects are, but I have to know—is it someone on my staff?"

"There are several possibilities," Joe answered, "but it's probably better that we don't tell you who they are right now."

"Why not? I'm trustworthy!"

"That's not what's in doubt, Mr. Schacht," Frank cut in. "If we tell you who our prime suspects are, you might accidentally tip the real Blade off. We want to sneak up on him so nobody else gets hurt."

"Well, as long as you can keep things quiet, I'll let you run this investigation your own way," Schacht told them.

"You can help a lot by making sure Buddy's bodyguards stick to him like glue, just in case Blade gets past us," Joe said seriously.

"Don't worry, I'll keep Buddy under wraps," Schacht said. "Now, you guys better get back to the arena. I want to make sure there are no surprises at tonight's press conference."

To Joe's annoyance, he and Frank had to share a taxi with Bobby Mellor on the ride back to the arena, making it impossible for the Hardys to discuss the case.

Joe's frustration doubled when he and Frank were separated as soon as they arrived at the arena. Jake sent Frank to work with the sound crew in the tech booth suspended over the center of the arena.

Joe was assigned to the crew in charge of the smoke machines. He waited in the wings for the climax of the special effects display, at which time he was supposed to drop a twenty-pound block of dry ice into the smoke machine's tank of water. Carbon dioxide fog would be pumped through a tube to create a thick white wall of "smoke."

Joe spotted Callie sitting onstage in a metal folding chair with about twenty other print and television reporters. She would be covering the press conference for the paper.

Syd Schacht had arranged for the media people to sit in the center of the stage so they could get a clear view of the spectacular light show that would accompany Buddy's performance the following night.

To Joe's relief, the press conference went smoothly. Joe had to admit that Buddy, Skeezer, and Eric handled themselves well. Buddy in particular took to the limelight like a pro. He appeared charming, funny, and humble as he answered questions and posed for pictures.

If I didn't know better, I wouldn't believe it was the same guy who's been behaving like a jerk for the last two days, Joe thought.

The press conference climaxed with the special effects preview, the moment that had Joe worried as the most likely for Blade to strike.

From beside his smoke machine Joe kept a close eye on Buddy. He knew Frank was high up in the tech booth, scanning the catwalks with binoculars. The brothers kept in contact with walkie-talkies that Schacht had given them. Con Riley had sent a dozen officers to guard the arena.

Joe hoped that the increased security might scare Blade off, but then he recalled Blade's notes. Blade was determined to stop Buddy— no matter what the cost.

After the final laser display Schacht and Bobby Mellor ushered the press out of the arena. Callie waved to Frank and Joe as they joined the other roadies in cleaning up the stage and making sure all the lights and other equipment were ready for the concert.

It was well after two A.M. when Jake finally told Joe he could go home. He'd have to report for work at six P.M. the next day, though. Joe was so tired he could scarcely keep his eyes open. When he spotted his brother slowly coming down the stage-left ladder, Joe knew Frank was just as tired.

Joe saw the arena lights go out as he and Frank wearily trudged down tunnel A to the parking lot and through the knots of teenagers waiting for the show the next night.

"Boy, I thought I couldn't wait to talk about the case with you, Frank, but now all I want to do is fall into bed."

"I can't even think straight," Frank agreed. "Maybe we should wait and discuss it with Callie over breakfast."

Joe was still dressing when Callie arrived at the Hardy home the next day at two o'clock. He pulled on a clean T-shirt and greeted her from the top of the stairs. "Morning, Callie. Thanks for joining us for breakfast."

"Good *afternoon*, Joe. I'm not just joining you, I'm the chef, Mr. Hardy," Callie replied smartly. "I figured I'd better give you two at least one decent meal while your mom and aunt are out of town. I'm making western omelets, whole wheat toast, and juice. How's that sound?''

"Great, especially since I don't have to cook it," Joe replied with a smile.

"Oh, did you hear? Sammy's going to be okay. They got his stomach pumped soon enough."

Joe smiled again. That was a relief.

While Callie dished up the steaming omelets filled with chunks of ham, green pepper, and onion, Frank and Joe filled her in on everything they'd learned so far.

"Have you eliminated David Pauling and Bobby Mellor as suspects?" Callie inquired.

"Well, Mellor does hate Buddy, but he's got a lot riding on the success of this concert, so it doesn't make sense that Mellor would threaten his own interests. Besides, Mellor was with Schacht when Buddy's food arrived. Unless he was working with an accomplice, he couldn't have poisoned Buddy's food," Frank pointed out.

Callie thought for a minute. "Well, you said David Pauling worked in the hotel kitchen. Could he be Blade's accomplice?"

"Pauling came on his shift after the bogus waiter picked up Buddy's food, so that eliminates him," Joe said, shoveling in the last bites of his omelet.

"Then what about the two times Pauling

showed up at the arena, Joe? He did attack you with a knife!" Callie's voice rose excitedly.

Joe smiled slightly. "It was a pretty lame knife attack, Callie. He was just trying to get away. My guess is that Pauling is just a victim of lousy timing. He's always in the wrong place at the wrong time."

"Then if neither of them is Blade, Jake and Kong are the only reasonable suspects, right?" Callie ventured.

"That makes sense, Callie. Those two are the only ones who would match the size of the fake waiter," Joe put in quickly.

"The tactics and booby traps Blade has used so far indicate some kind of military training, which both Jake and Kong have had," Frank observed.

"Yeah, but didn't you learn that Kong was a SEAL?" Callie asked. "I'd say that meant he knew more about booby traps and ambushes than Jake."

Frank considered that while sipping his orange juice, then finally said, "True, but Jake specialized in demolition. That tells me he probably knows something about booby traps, too."

"All I know is that Kong gives me the creeps," Callie said with a small shudder. "My gut feeling is that he's probably Blade."

"Well, so far everything we have is just circumstantial. We can't go around making accusations against that tattooed ape without solid proof,'' Joe reminded her.

Suddenly Joe snapped his fingers. "Tattoos! Hey, Frank—where did you leave those photos of Blade?''

"They're in my room. Why? Did you get an inspiration?''

Joe shrugged. "More of a hunch, really. But I think I can prove who Blade is.''

Joe ran to Frank's room, where he grabbed the photo blowups and a magnifying glass. Joe then hurried downstairs to his father's office, tossed the envelope onto the desk, and began scanning the bookshelves for the specific title he needed.

He spied it on a bottom shelf and pulled out the thick volume covered in a glossy dust jacket. After he found the page he was looking for he pulled the photos from the envelope.

With growing excitement Joe compared the glossy color photo in the book to the design in Frank's photo.

"That's it!" he said triumphantly.

He snatched up the photo and ran back to the kitchen. "Frank, Callie, I've got it!''

"What've you got, Joe?'' Frank asked.

Waving the photo at them, Joe said excitedly, "The proof that Kong is Blade!''

Chapter

14

FRANK FELT A THRILL of excitement, but his natural caution asserted itself immediately.

"Let's see the proof," Frank said calmly.

"It's here in this picture you took, Frank," Joe replied excitedly. "It was here all along. We were just interpreting it wrong."

Frank examined the enlarged design in the photo again but saw nothing new. "Okay, Joe," Frank said carefully. "What about this T-shirt design makes you think it's Kong in the photo?"

"That's the whole thing, Frank—it's not a T-shirt design! It's a tattoo!"

Frank's jaw dropped in disbelief. "Of course! Kong is covered with tattoos! If he's got one that matches this one, that's our proof!"

"Great work, Joe!" Callie told him excitedly. "What made you think of tattoos?"

"Well," Joe answered, "something about that design struck me as familiar. I remembered a book on tattooing that our dad used to break a case a few years back, and something clicked. I compared the tattoo in the photo to one of the Japanese Yakuza-style tattoos, and they were very similar."

Frank rubbed his chin for a moment, thinking hard. "Kong could have gotten that tattoo when he was stationed in Japan."

Joe nodded, a look of intense satisfaction on his face. "Since Kong was in the SEALs, that might explain the commando tactics Blade used to try to kill Buddy. This is all starting to fall into place, Frank."

"I'm beginning to think so, too, but we can't have Kong arrested just on guesswork."

"Then let's talk to someone who knows Kong and who'd know if he has that particular tattoo at his waist," Joe answered. "Like Clare."

"In the coffee shop Jake mentioned that she was staying at the Star-Lite Motel. Let's head over there now. You gather all the photos and any equipment we'll need. I'll get the van warmed up," Frank said decisively.

"What can I do to help?" Callie asked.

"Well, I don't know if you should—" Joe began, but Callie cut him off.

126

She stood nose to nose with Joe, her fists on her hips. "Joe Hardy, don't give me any of this you-can't-come-because-it's-too-danger-ous-for-a-girl stuff. Besides, I can get you in to see Clare without arousing her suspicions. I'll just tell her I want to interview her for my article on Buddy."

"Clare's not exactly wild about discussing Buddy, Callie," Joe insisted.

"She may not talk to you, Joe, but she will respond to the power of the press. Almost everybody wants some kind of recognition. I'll tell Clare the article's about her. I'll flatter her silly if I have to. Whatever it takes!" She shook her finger in Joe's face.

Frank kept out of the discussion. He knew from long experience that Joe's arguments would be futile.

"Give it up, Joe. Admit you're beaten."

Joe smiled and tried to look like a gracious loser, but Frank could tell he was annoyed.

With Joe behind the wheel the three located the Star-Lite Motel in a run-down neighbor-hood near the arena.

Frank was surprised when he saw how shabby the two-story motel was. It badly needed new siding, and there was garbage scat-tered all over the parking lot.

"No wonder Jake didn't want his sister stay-ing here," Frank said.

127

"Really," Joe agreed. "This place is an eyesore."

They parked the van near the front office and went inside. "Where can we find Clare Williams?" Frank asked the unshaven desk clerk.

"Room Twenty-three. Other side of the motel," the clerk replied with a toothless grin.

They drove around to Clare's door and piled out. Before locking the door Frank grabbed his camera and the envelope full of photo enlargements. Callie was in the lead, so she rapped sharply on the door of Room Twenty-three.

They waited for what seemed a very long time before they heard someone coming up to the door. It popped open a crack, and Frank could see Clare's face in the dim light just beyond the door chain.

"Who's there?" she asked.

"It's Callie Shaw, Miss Williams," Callie explained quickly. "I'm a reporter for the Bayport *Examiner*. Can I talk to you for a few minutes?"

"What about?" Clare asked, opening the door a little wider.

"Your influence on Buddy Death's music," Callie answered.

Clare started to slam the door, saying, "No thanks. I'm through talking about that bum!"

Callie stuck her foot in the door and pressed

forward. "Wait, Clare. I've heard about your
playing and singing from Joe. I want to talk
about the material you've written."

"It's nothing," Clare said, exasperated because Callie kept moving into her room.
"Besides," she said wearily, "I'm not really
a musician. I'm more of a poet."

As Joe and Frank slipped in behind Callie,
Clare gave them a quick once-over.

"Hey, what is this? Look, I'm really not up
to having my room invaded by the press right
now," she said, running her fingers through
her hair. "What are those guys doing here,
anyway?"

"They're helping me with my story," Callie
said. "I'm sorry if we're intruding, but it's
more important than you might realize."

"You might even save Buddy's life," Frank
added.

"You think I care what happens to that
louse?" Clare said defiantly.

"I think you care a lot," Callie replied
softly, "or you wouldn't be following him all
over the country on the chance that you'll get
to spend five minutes with him."

Clare buried her face in her hands.

"You're right," she said tearfully. "He—
he hurt me, but I still care about him. Kong
told me about this whole Blade business, and
I'm scared for Buddy!"

Callie put her arm around Clare's shoulders.

"Take it easy, Clare. Look, I know a way you can help Buddy right now."

Clare looked up at Callie with red-rimmed eyes. "How?"

Frank stepped over to Clare and handed her the enlargements he'd made. "I took these photos of Blade in the catwalks just after the spotlight missed Buddy. Look at the closeups of the tattoo around Blade's waist and tell us if you can identify it," Frank instructed.

Frank noticed that Clare paled visibly as soon as she glanced at the clearest enlargement of the design.

"Oh, no," she muttered.

"What's wrong?" Joe jumped in.

Clare stared at the trio surrounding her and pointed to the photo in her hand. "Kong has a tattoo like this." Her expression grew more serious, and she added in a quiet voice, "And so does Jake. They got them together in Tokyo."

Callie gently took the photos from Clare's hand and led her to the edge of the bed.

"Clare, you may just have saved Buddy's life," Callie told her. "I'll explain all of this to you soon, but I can't right now. Stay here. Don't call anybody or go out. I'll call you after Buddy's show, okay?"

Clare nodded, stunned.

"I knew it!" Joe said triumphantly as soon

as they were outside Clare's room. "Kong is Blade!"

"Don't jump to any conclusions," Frank warned. "Jake has the same tattoo. We can't go around making rash accusations without better proof!"

"Well, we can at least warn Schacht about our suspicions," Joe said forcefully.

"All right," Frank said. "That's reasonable."

Frank made the call, but when he got through to Schacht's office in the arena he was informed that Mr. Schacht was with Buddy and could not be reached until shortly before the concert. Frank left a message for Schacht to contact the Hardys as soon as possible.

He turned to Joe and Callie with a grim expression. "Schacht's not available. He's got Buddy under wraps."

Frank flicked a glance at his watch. "Let's get to the arena before Buddy and make one last search for Blade."

"If we can surprise Kong, maybe we can 'persuade' him to show us his tattoos," Joe said with a hard expression gleaming in his eyes.

"Let's roll," Frank said impatiently. "Time's wasting, and we're not that much closer to catching Blade."

The trio walked around the corner of the

motel to where Joe had parked the van, and Frank and Callie climbed in.

"Hey, the hood's unlatched!" Joe shouted. "Somebody's been tinkering with our van!"

"Leaving it parked in this neighborhood, it wouldn't surprise me if somebody swiped our battery," Frank said angrily.

Joe stepped quickly over to the van and raised the hood.

Immediately he ran to the door and waved Frank and Callie out of the van.

"What's wrong, Joe?" Frank asked.

"There's a bomb wired to the engine! Both of you get out of the van! *Now!*"

Chapter

15

JOE RAN BACK to look at the compact bundle of plastic explosive wired to the van's battery again. It was a simple, deadly apparatus: Yellow wires that ended in alligator clips were attached to the battery terminals and the starter. It was all designed to explode when the driver started the engine.

Joe's blood ran cold as he thought about what would have happened if he hadn't noticed that the hood was unlatched. They would have been blown to bits.

"Get around the corner and call the cops!" Joe yelled as they took off past him to the corner.

Joe then turned his attention back to the bomb. He traced the two yellow ignition wires to a place under the packet of plastic explosive that was taped to the rear wall of the engine compartment, only a few inches from the cab. Joe gingerly examined the wires, knowing he had to be sure there was no additional time fuse.

Joe slowly reached over to the two alligator clips attached to the battery and unclamped them, letting out a sigh of relief when nothing happened.

Suddenly Frank stuck his head around the corner of the motel. "Bomb squad's on their way. Do you need any help?" Frank called.

"No!" Joe yelled back. "I'm trying to disarm the bomb. Stay back! Get everyone out of the motel!"

"You're crazy," Frank shouted. "Leave it for the pros, Joe!"

"I can't. There's too much stuff here. I think there's a time fuse that'll detonate it automatically if we wait too long," Joe said. He waited until Frank had pulled his head back around the corner, then Joe carefully peeled up the tape from the outer edge and lifted up the packet of explosive to expose the underside.

Joe felt a little chill down his spine as he realized that his hunch had been right. There was a small digital clock and a D battery wired to a blasting cap with a thin wire.

Joe's eyes flicked down to the timer, which

read :05. It changed to :04 as he pulled out his Swiss army knife and flipped open the scissors. The little clock read :03 as Joe put the scissor blades to the ignition wire. It changed to :02 as Joe snipped the wire.

To Joe's horror, the clock kept ticking. But when it hit :00 without the bomb exploding, Joe knew the circuit had been broken. The clock had continued ticking because it was wired directly into the battery.

He carefully lifted the inert bomb off the engine wall and set it on the asphalt beside the van.

"Frank! Callie! All clear!" Joe shouted with relief.

First Frank, then Callie cautiously emerged from around the corner of the motel wall.

"It's okay. I disarmed it," Joe told them with a smile.

"Thanks, Joe," Frank said, punching him lightly on the shoulder. "That took guts!"

Just then Joe saw two Bayport police cruisers and a big van marked Bomb Disposal Unit pull into the Star-Lite parking lot. All three police vehicles braked to a stop just before the corner of the motel.

"What's the story?" Con Riley barked at the Hardys as soon as he jumped out of his police car.

"There was a bomb in our van, Con. I disarmed it," Joe explained.

"You *what?*" Con shouted as the entire bomb squad and three uniformed cops crowded around excitedly.

"I had to," Joe said quickly. "The bomb was wired to a backup fuse and a timer so it would go off automatically unless it was disarmed."

"Let's check this out," the sergeant in charge of the bomb squad ordered. He walked cautiously to the corner, followed by two men from the squad carrying blankets that dampened explosives. They were pulling a little cart that supported a spherical bomb-proof containment chamber.

While the bomb squad investigated for the next hour and a half Joe and Frank were forced to explain to an irate Con Riley what had happened.

"So you see, Con, we thought Blade planted this bomb to stop us from returning to the arena tonight, where he obviously plans another attempt on Buddy Death." Joe spoke rapidly, hoping Con would buy his story.

"I don't know," Con said doubtfully. "I should bring you down to the station house to make a statement."

"But, Con, if you keep us here, that might give Blade enough time to kill Buddy!" Frank said loudly.

"You've got to let us get to the arena!" Joe added.

136

"You boys are not the law. This is very serious business, and I don't know why I'm letting you stay on the case, but I will. Remember, you're only helpers—not the law. I'm calling for backup. If that nut's inside, we'll find him," Riley asserted.

At that moment the bomb squad came by, pulling their cart.

"It's safe," the sergeant announced.

"The kid did a good job of disarming this baby," one of his men commented.

Joe and Frank thanked the sergeant, then, along with Callie, they piled into their van.

With Frank behind the wheel they drove to the arena, following the screeching siren of Con's police car.

As a uniformed cop waved them in through an emergency entrance Joe noticed that the huge parking lots surrounding the arena were already filled. The excited talking and shouts of the arena crowd mixed with snatches of recorded warm-up music blasting over the sound system.

Con and a squad of cops led the way into tunnel A, with Frank, Joe, and Callie following.

The entrance to the tunnel was jammed shoulder to shoulder with teenagers, many wearing Buddy Death Band T-shirts and black leather pants. The atmosphere was electric. Joe heard crazy laughter and shouting all around him. As he pushed through a close-packed group of teens he couldn't help noticing one long-haired fan playing air guitar in sync with the rock music that pounded through the mammoth sound system at an almost earsplitting level. The would-be musician was totally oblivious to the squad of Bayport cops that was pushing toward the bowl of the arena.

Tex, who stood near the entrance of tunnel A, tossed a walkie-talkie to both Frank and Joe as soon as he saw them. Tex looked sweaty and totally frazzled.

"Where've you guys been? It's six-thirty. Jake's fit to be tied!" Tex said anxiously.

"I can't worry about that!" Frank shouted. "Where can we find Schacht?"

"I don't know where anybody is!" Tex raised his voice to be heard over the racket. "I haven't been able to raise Kong or Jake on their walkie-talkies for a while. I can't get Bobby Mellor, either! I'm swamped, boys!"

"If you see Schacht, tell him we have to talk!" Joe shouted.

Tex nodded, then turned and pushed his way through the crowd of fans to the stage, which was guarded by a ring of muscular bouncers dressed in black Buddy Death security T-shirts and jeans.

"If Blade is out in the open, maybe we can bag him quietly before the show starts," Joe shouted to Frank.

"Somehow I don't think Blade is the type to come quietly," Frank shouted back, smiling grimly.

For the next hour or so Frank and Joe checked out the arena floor. They came up empty.

They flashed their crew badges to gain admittance to the backstage area next. Buddy's motor home had been driven directly behind the stage. The two bodyguards stood on either side of the motor home's door, their eyes moving constantly to scan the area for any sign of danger.

A small trailer had been set up next to it as a temporary office, and a steady stream of roadies, cops, and arena security guards flowed in and out of it.

"Unless I miss my guess," Joe observed, "that is where we'll find Syd Schacht."

Joe led the way into the cramped trailer, where they found Schacht seated behind a makeshift desk talking on a telephone and mopping his brow. As soon as he caught sight of the Hardys he abruptly hung up on whomever he'd been talking to.

"Am I glad to see you guys," Schacht said with relief. "What's up?"

"There's no time to explain now," Joe said breathlessly, "but we need to know where Jake and Kong are."

"Jake's working with the special effects

gear in the catwalks," Schacht replied. "As for Kong, the big goon disappeared. Where do you think Blade will strike?" he asked anxiously.

"If he follows his past pattern, it's likely he'll strike from above," Frank replied.

"I agree," Joe said. "Backstage is crawling with cops and guards. It'd be much easier for him to get at Buddy from above, so that's where we'll be standing watch."

"While you guys do that I think I'll join the press corps. I still have a story to get out," Callie told Frank. "And don't forget my exclusive, Mr. Schacht," she called over her shoulder as she headed off toward the crowd of press people. Joe saw her pull out her press pass and clip it onto her blouse.

"If we bag Blade, she'll probably get a Pulitzer prize," Frank joked.

"Come on, Frank," Joe said, hurrying out the trailer door toward the backstage ladders that went up to the catwalks.

He noticed Buddy coming out of the trailer and joining the rest of his band. He was relieved to see Sammy up and around, though he did look almost as pale as Buddy was naturally. Skeezer stood behind Sammy, leaning against an equipment case.

Eric seemed to be extremely worried as he waited near Sammy and Skeezer, his blue electric guitar strapped across his chest.

By the time Joe and Frank reached the ladders to climb up to the catwalks the audience had been let in and was chanting for Buddy. Recorded intro music continued to blare out, but as the boys climbed into the flies it ceased. Spotlights blasted pinwheels of multicolored light in all directions for twenty minutes. Then finally, at showtime, the smoke machines kicked in, creating a thick wall of smoke through which Buddy and the other band members would suddenly appear. There was no opening band for the group. Joe thought Buddy would be jealous of the competition.

As Joe groped his way along the catwalk with the crazy light from the spotlights strobing below him, red laser beams suddenly began hissing all around.

Involuntarily, Joe ducked and then flattened himself to the deck of the swaying catwalk. Finally he realized that the laser beams were part of the show and not an attack launched by Blade. He sneaked a look behind him and saw that Frank had done the same thing, so he didn't feel so foolish.

"Nervous?" Joe quipped.

"Very funny," Frank said sourly. "I noticed you went down first, though."

"Better safe than sorry," Joe said as he got back to his feet.

"If Blade is going to strike, he probably won't try anything until Buddy hits the stage,"

Frank yelled over the roar of the crowd as Eric and Skeezer appeared onstage. Sammy came on moments later, timing his entrance so that he began his drum roll just as the smoke was clearing across the stage.

"I agree," Joe shouted back. "But where do we start looking?"

A bright spotlight suddenly slashed across a small special effects platform directly over the stage. Joe and Frank both scanned it automatically for signs of danger. Joe started in surprise when he spotted a dark form hunched over a compressed-air cannon normally used to fire confetti over the crowd.

"Frank, do you see him?" he shouted over the electric guitars and thrumming drums.

"It's Blade! He's doing something to the cannon. We've got to stop him!" Frank shouted.

Joe saw the dark figure putting handfuls of something glittery into the barrel of the cannon. He swiveled it around and pointed it down directly at the stage. The electric guitars rose to a raucous wail, and then Buddy leapt into the spotlight to stand center stage at the edge of the apron.

"He's right in the cannon's sights!" Joe shouted.

Chapter
16

FRANK RAN as fast as he dared on the swaying catwalk. The special effects platform where Blade stood was still thirty feet away.

Up ahead he saw Joe snatch something from an open toolbox one of the roadies had left sitting on top of a speaker cabinet suspended next to the catwalk. A moment later Joe stopped moving abruptly, and Frank was just able to avoid running into his back.

Joe braced his feet in a pitcher's stance and hurled a silver crescent wrench at Blade with all his might. Frank thought Joe's aim was bad, because the wrench missed Blade and slammed into the back of the cannon, knocking it down and swinging the barrel up. He hadn't been aiming for Blade after all. With a grunt muffled by his black mask Blade swiveled the cannon around to face the Hardys. Then he thumbed the cannon's electric trigger.

Boom!

The cannon fired a second after the Hardys hit the deck again. As Frank hugged the catwalk he heard small missiles whizzing overhead.

After a moment Frank risked a peek and saw that the black canvas covering over the catwalks was studded with winged metal darts. Frank shuddered when he thought of what the little darts would have done to him. Or to Buddy. But before Blade had a chance to reload Frank was up and charging toward the platform.

Since he and Joe were running at full speed toward the only ladder that led to the small effects platform, Frank figured they had to have Blade cornered. He realized how wrong he was a moment later when Blade whipped a stubby pistol from his belt and fired it—not at the Hardys, as Frank had expected, but at a crossbeam over the stage. The pistol fired with a loud report, shooting out a small grappling hook attached to a light nylon line.

As Joe and Frank hurried along the catwalk above the special effects platform Blade wrapped the line around his right wrist and swung to a section of catwalk over the opposite side of the stage.

"He won't get away!" Frank insisted, putting his walkie-talkie up to his mouth. "The cops can surround the stage right now!"

"Con Riley, over. This is Frank Hardy! Blade is here! He's on the east side catwalk—" Frank paused while he listened to Con's instructions. "All right," Frank agreed. "Your men will surround the stage, and we'll drive him down to you."

Frank turned back to Joe. "Where's Blade now?"

"Still over the stage, on the catwalk," Joe said, pointing. "What's the plan?" he asked.

"Con's giving us one chance before he sends his boys up here. He doesn't want the crowd to panic," Frank replied.

"What if Blade doubles back on us?"

"Then it's up to us to stop him," Frank replied with a grim set to his jaw. "You go ahead, Joe. Keep Blade busy."

"And where will you be?" Joe asked.

"I'm going back to prepare a few surprises for Blade."

Moving fast, Frank found the roadie's toolbox on the speaker and pulled out the pliers and other things he knew he'd need, then returned to the spot where the side catwalk intersected with the catwalk that bisected the dome.

He stretched a four-foot length of piano wire at ankle height between the two upright supports just before the intersection, then he strung another piece chest-high.

Before leaving, Frank sprayed some slippery lubricant on the deck of the catwalk about two feet in front of the wires. He hoped his booby trap would catch Blade off guard.

Frank quickly booby-trapped the catwalk on the opposite side of the arena as well, then sprayed the lubricant on the deck behind him and hurried along the catwalk to meet Joe.

To his horror, Frank saw Joe grappling with Blade on the catwalk that ran over the width of the backstage area.

"Hey!" he yelled.

Frank raced along the catwalk toward them, his running causing it to rock perilously.

Joe and Blade were locked in a battle of strength. Blade had Joe's left wrist, and Joe held on to Blade's right wrist for dear life, trying to keep Blade's stubby pistol pointed away from him.

Joe and Blade were dancing in a tight circle as Blade slid his foot behind Joe's ankle with snakelike speed. Joe went over backward, and Blade pulled his gun hand free.

Frank felt a cold ball of fear in his stomach as Blade lowered his pistol to point it right at Joe's head. Frank ran headlong down the catwalk, heedless of the danger, screaming, *"No-o-o-o!"*

Blade glanced up, and his pistol wavered between the two brothers, which gave Frank time to pull the pliers from his back pocket and throw them at Blade.

The pliers struck Blade's wrist, knocking the stubby gun from his grip, sending it tumbling over the edge of the catwalk.

At the same moment Joe grabbed Blade's left ankle and pulled it out from under him. Frank watched as Joe pounced on Blade like a tiger, pinning him to the deck.

Blade quickly pushed Joe off with a tremendous heave just as Frank arrived. Joe stumbled backward into Frank, who teetered on the edge of the catwalk, desperately trying to regain his balance.

Frank snagged a guy wire with one hand. A split second later Joe grabbed his other hand and pulled him to the center of the catwalk.

The boys looked around for Blade and saw him sprinting down the catwalk.

"He's getting away again!" Joe yelled.

"He won't get far," Frank assured him as he took off after Blade.

Far ahead of him Frank watched as Blade suddenly ran into an invisible barrier, then slid over the edge of the catwalk.

Blade managed to snag the edge of the catwalk as he fell.

"Take it easy," Frank cautioned as he edged over to Blade's gloved fingers.

"Stay back or I'll let go!" Blade threatened.

"I wouldn't do that," Frank said tensely, edging closer to his hands.

"I won't be taken alive," Blade shouted.

"Oh, yes, you will, *Jake!*" Frank shouted, and dived over his booby trap to make a grab for Jake's hands. The surprise of being recognized kept Jake from reacting for a second. In that last possible instant Frank caught his hand.

"Help me pull him up, Joe," Frank urged through gritted teeth.

A few hours later, after the concert was over, Frank, Joe, and Callie were sitting in Schacht's office trailer with Schacht, Con Riley, and Captain Hubbard.

The flood of relief Frank had felt after capturing Blade had left him about an hour earlier, and he just felt tired. He glanced at his watch, wondering when Con would let them go. He and Joe had explained almost every aspect of Blade's crimes.

"I still don't see how you knew Jake Williams was Blade, Frank," Con Riley was saying.

"Well, he wasn't our only suspect, but when I saw him fighting with Joe on the cat-

148

walk I realized Jake had to be Blade because Kong would be too tall."

"Whatever happened to Kong, anyway?" Joe inquired.

Captain Hubbard chuckled, "I found the big galoot bound and gagged in a storage closet. He'd found Williams while he was getting into his Blade outfit, so Williams decked him, then tied him up."

"Did you get a motive for his attempts on Buddy?" Callie asked.

"Maybe I can explain that," Clare said quietly. "Jake did it for me. He—he's not really bad, he just thought he had to stick up for his little sister."

"But why try to kill Buddy?" Joe asked her.

"Because Buddy stole my poems. You see, I had a notebook full of poems that I'd been writing ever since I was a little girl. I showed it to Buddy when we were dating, and he really liked them. Then, after he dumped me, I went to look for my notebook, and it was gone. I found out later that Buddy had stolen it."

"Do you know that for a fact?" Frank inquired.

Clare nodded sadly. "The first time I heard Buddy's album I already knew all the lyrics because they were from my poems. But because Buddy had stolen my book there was no way I could prove it.

"Jake felt totally frustrated about the way Buddy had gotten away with hurting me and stealing my poems. I guess he wanted revenge and knew only one way to get it."

Clare's voice fell off, and she stared down at her lap. An awkward silence fell over the group for a moment until Con Riley broke in.

"Well, we're almost finished if you'll just bear with me, people," he said, opening his notebook to a fresh page. "I'm still fuzzy on how Blade—er, Williams—performed his acts of sabotage."

Frank sighed. "It was easy. Jake was the special effects supervisor. He had access to all the equipment. All he had to do was walk a little way down the catwalk, loosen four bolts, and *bang*—down comes the light. It was easy for him to rig the mike stand to electrocute someone."

"Yeah, and he used Kong to decoy Mellor away from the limo just long enough so he could sabotage the brakes," Joe put in. "The guy is definitely a mechanical wizard. In a lot of ways his special effects work was great training for this. Real life—real murder—is a lot simpler than faking it."

"But how did he know when Buddy's lunch was coming up so he could poison it?" Con asked.

"What I suspect is that Jake hid somewhere in the hotel, eavesdropping on Buddy's room phone with that lineman's handset I saw," Frank explained. "When Buddy ordered the food Jake disguised himself as a waiter, slipped into the kitchen, and did his dirty work."

"Okay, I'll buy that," Con said. "But why do you think he tried to blow you two up?"

"Panic. He knew he was running out of time to kill Buddy, and Frank and I had spoiled his plans several times. He got careless, too. That bomb might have killed his sister as well as us, but at that point Jake wasn't thinking too clearly.

"One of the things that made me suspicious of Bobby Mellor initially was that life insurance policy he had on Buddy," Joe said thoughtfully.

Schacht dismissed that with a wave of his hand. "Insuring your star's life is a standard practice in this business. There's nothing mysterious about it."

Frank grinned at Joe. "Didn't I tell you that before?"

Joe was annoyed. "Well, I wouldn't have been so suspicious of Mellor if the guy had a normal past. His past ended after five years. That's pretty strange."

Schacht chuckled. "You boys are pretty thorough," he said admiringly. "Bobby's past only goes back five years because Mellor's not his real name. He ditched his old identity after a partner of his ran out on him and left him with a lot of bad debts and his reputation in tatters. He's been rebuilding and repairing ever since.''

"Well, that explains a lot," Joe said, satisfied.

"Say, what would you say to joining my outfit permanently? I could use a couple of bright boys like you."

Frank and Joe exchanged grins, then looked at Schacht and shook their heads.

"No thanks, Mr. Schacht," Frank said with a smile. "I think we'll stick to being detectives. Being a roadie is too much like work!"

CHOKE HOLD

Chapter

1

"GIVE UP, FRANK! You're beaten!" Joe Hardy said, his blue eyes flashing as he tightened his hold on his older brother.

"Never!" Frank replied through gritted teeth. He strained against Joe's viselike hammerlock.

Joe thought he and Frank were about evenly matched in terms of strength, but Frank was slightly quicker.

Frank's speed wouldn't help him this time, though. Joe bore down on his older brother, forcing his shoulders closer to the mat. Frank tried to kick out with his legs, but he couldn't dislodge Joe.

"Don't let him pin you, Frank," a cheerful voice called from outside the ropes of the wrestling ring. "Come on! You can do it!"

1

"Hey!" Joe called to the man coaching Frank. "Whose side are you on, Sammy?"

Sammy Rand, better known to his fans as the Kung Fu King, was a compact, heavily muscled man whose straight black hair hung down to his shoulders. He was dressed in a gold-colored muscle T-shirt, black sweatpants, black kneepads, and wrestling boots.

His almond-shaped brown eyes sparkled as he shrugged his broad shoulders and smiled. "Fair's fair, Joe. Since you're on the Bayport High wrestling team, I know you're a better wrestler than Frank."

"Sammy, if you've got any suggestions to avoid getting pinned, I could use one right about now!" Frank panted.

"It won't do you any good, anyway, Frank. You're licked!" Joe said as he shoved Frank's shoulders down to the mat. "One, two, th—" Joe didn't finish his count.

With catlike quickness Frank kicked out and got to his feet. He faced Joe in a combat crouch, knees bent, hands ready.

"Brace your feet wider, Frank!" Sammy called. "And next time Joe gets you down, take a deep breath and really expand your chest. Flex your shoulders in and out quickly to keep him from getting a good grip on you."

Joe circled his opponent, trying to size up the situation. Although Frank was an inch taller, Joe thought that his extra weight would be an advantage.

Joe feinted left with his head. Frank moved to counter this, but Joe stepped inside, sweeping Frank's left foot out from under him. At the same time he grabbed Frank and shoved him backward.

Frank fell to the mat with a bone-jarring thud. But before Joe could pin him, Frank inflated his chest and flexed his shoulders and wriggled free of Joe's grasp. Then Frank grabbed one of Joe's arms and twisted it behind his back and shoved him into the mat.

"Time!" Sammy called. "You guys are looking good," he commented as the brothers walked toward him. "And with a little more work, Frank, I think you could take Joe. You've always been quick. After all, you were one of my best karate students back home in Bayport."

"Thanks, Sammy," Frank said as he stepped through the ropes and drank from the jug of ice water Sammy held out. Joe was right behind his brother, taking the water jug and draining it in two gulps.

"After you guys catch your breath, how about spotting for me while I do my free-weight workout?" Sammy suggested.

"Sure, Sammy," Frank agreed, pushing his dark hair off his face.

"And maybe then you'll explain why you

wanted us to come out here to Allentown, Pennsylvania, posing as wrestlers," Joe said.

"I've got my reasons," Sammy replied, walking to a weight bench and sitting on it. "Joe, is anybody close enough to overhear us?"

Joe scanned the cavernous interior of the International Wrestling Association training center. He noticed a pair of wrestlers rehearsing their moves in each of the three wrestling rings that were located in the center of the room. And at the far end of the gym several wrestlers were on the mats, stretching and practicing falls.

As he checked out the area, Joe wondered what Sammy was worried about. Joe and Frank had known Sammy since he had been Frank's karate instructor in Bayport. Joe thought about how in a few short years Sammy had gone from being an obscure martial arts teacher to one of the most successful wrestlers in the country.

Joe turned back to Sammy and sat down on a mat next to his brother. "Coast is clear. No one's close enough to overhear us. Now, what gives, Sammy? Why all the precautions?"

"I'm more than a little curious now myself," Frank added. "You said you needed us to investigate a problem for you." Sammy was well aware of the Hardys' reputation as detectives, which was why Frank assumed he had called them.

"I'm in trouble, guys," Sammy said quietly. "You remember that bout I had with Major Disaster about three months ago?"

"The one where he creamed you with a chair?" Joe responded. "I saw that. I can't believe Disaster got away with it!"

"Yeah, well, the chair was supposed to be a breakaway, made of balsa wood, so he could hit me with it without hurting me, but somehow a real one got substituted. When he hit me, I went down for real. That little mishap resulted in four cracked ribs. I was out of commission until a couple of weeks ago."

"Do you think Disaster switched the chairs?" asked Frank.

"I didn't at first," Sammy answered. "The Major and I had choreographed our moves ahead of time like pro wrestlers do for every bout. So I thought he'd made an honest mistake and grabbed the wrong chair. Disaster's no mental giant, you know."

"What changed your mind?" asked Joe.

"I started to suspect Disaster a couple of weeks ago, when I got into the ring for the first time after my 'accident' for a little training session."

"What happened?" Joe prompted.

"I took a break and went for a drink of water, but as I raised my bottle up, it smelled

5

funny. When I checked it, I found out it was filled with ammonia. Somebody had to have put it in there deliberately.

"So I started to think," Sammy continued, "that since Disaster didn't permanently knock me out of commission with the chair, he might be trying to get me again."

"Did you do anything about it?" asked Frank.

"Sure," Sammy replied. "I went to Stanley Warfield, the International Wrestling Association president, and told him about both incidents. But he said they were just accidents and refused to do anything. That was when I decided to call you guys."

Sammy sighed. "Like I don't have enough other problems now. Daniel East, who runs the TV network that broadcasts all the bouts put on by the National Association of American Wrestlers, the IWA's main competition, has been after me for weeks to switch to the NAAW.

"When I finally gave him a definite no last week, he got really mad. Warfield told me East tried to sell his operation to him after I turned him down. Warfield refused his offer and got the same kind of reaction I did from East.

"Anyhow," Sammy continued, "that's the least of my problems right now. I need you guys to help me nail whoever is responsible for these 'accidents.' "

"Glad to help, Sammy," Joe assured him.

The worried expression on Sammy's face left as he broke into a wide grin. "Great! I knew I could count on you guys. I've already started telling the other wrestlers that you two are trying to break into the biz and are acting as my assistants."

"Sounds good," Frank commented. "That should give us freedom to check around without arousing any suspicion."

Suddenly a hoarse bellow cut the air inside the training center. "Kung Fu, you better drag your sorry tail into that workout room and get in shape! You're going to need it to avoid total humiliation on Saturday!"

Startled, Joe turned in the direction of the voice and saw Major Disaster, the IWA's number-two wrestler and resident bad guy. He was standing near the entrance of an adjoining workout room. Disaster was a big burly man whose brown hair was shaved in a military crew cut. Joe guessed that his battered nose had been broken more than once. Disaster was clad in baggy camouflage pants, a khaki T-shirt, and brown wrestling boots. The lights overhead gleamed off his mirrored sunglasses.

The next person Joe noticed was a petite, blue-eyed, blond woman standing at Disaster's side. She was dressed in a tight royal blue jumpsuit, with a long blue feather boa.

"Who—" Frank began, but Sammy cut him off.

"That's Major Disaster," Sammy said out of the corner of his mouth.

"Who's his blond sidekick?" Frank wanted to know.

"She's Marvelous Missy Mayflower, Disaster's manager," Joe replied as Sammy stood up and turned to face Disaster.

"Disaster, you windbag—if that's the best you can do, you'd be better off letting Missy get in the ring with me Saturday. I'll tie you up in knots, you brass-plated phony!"

"Why wait for Saturday, creep?" Disaster shouted, taking a step toward Sammy. "We can settle it right here! Right now!"

"Come on, Major—save it for the paying customers," Missy said, grabbing Disaster's arm and trying to drag him toward an exit.

"I'm ready any time, you wimp! I'll stuff that championship belt down your throat!" Disaster shouted over his shoulder as Missy did manage to pull him away.

As soon as the door swung shut behind Disaster and Missy, Sammy turned to the Hardys. "That guy's had it in for me ever since I won the IWA championship two years ago. I really don't trust him or Missy."

"Then checking out Disaster and Missy is

a good place to start our investigation," Frank observed. "What's the Major's real name?"

"Fred J. Stone," Sammy replied.

"Gee, Missy looks pretty trustworthy to me," Joe interrupted with a devilish grin.

Before Frank could reply, he noticed Slim Sorkin, Sammy's trainer, approaching. Although Slim stood about an inch taller than Frank's six-one, Frank guessed that Slim weighed about fifty pounds less than he did. Slim's big brown eyes seemed to pop out of his gaunt face, and his dark hair fell straight and flat against his head.

"Sammy!" Slim shouted. "Get into the workout room. You've got to get into shape for your next two bouts."

"What are you working on next, Sammy?" asked Joe.

"Upper arms," Sammy replied. "I think I'll do some rope climbing in the V position. That way I can work on my arms and my abdominals at the same time."

"Want us to time you?" Frank asked.

Smiling, Sammy shook his head. "Not the first time," he replied. "I've felt really out of shape since my ribs got hurt. I'll probably be slow as molasses."

"I'll get you into shape, Sammy. Never fear," Slim said seriously. "Come on." Sammy and the Hardys followed him to the workout room.

Sammy grabbed the thick rope dangling from the ceiling of the workout room and stuck his legs out in front of him at a forty-five-degree angle. Joe was amazed at how easily Sammy pulled himself up the rope. And he was fast!

"If that's being out of shape, I'd hate to see Sammy when he's in shape," Joe commented to his brother.

Frank glanced at the second display on his digital wristwatch. "Ten seconds to the top," he observed. "Not bad for someone who just came off the disabled list."

Joe glanced at the top of the rope, to watch Sammy. Just below the hook that attached the rope to a support beam, the rope was unraveling!

"Sammy—the rope's going!" Joe shouted.

Frank raised his eyes, and for a moment his heart stopped. Strands of rope were popping one after another. In another second Sammy would plunge to the floor!

Chapter

2

FOR A SECOND Frank thought Sammy was doomed, but the wrestler's lightning reflexes saved him. His hands shot up and wrapped around the beam the hook was screwed into.

Frank heard Sammy grunt with pain as he grabbed the beam. Frank guessed the sudden jarring had sent a shock of pain through Sammy's healing ribs.

"Help me, guys—I can't hold on long!" yelled Sammy.

"We'll figure out something!" shouted Joe.

Frank scanned the room for a ladder to climb to reach Sammy. Nothing. Frank watched as Joe rushed over to a tall pile of wrestling mats stacked in one corner. Slim followed Joe to the mats.

"If we stack these mats up high enough,

Sammy will have something to break his fall!" Joe shouted, grabbing two mats and dragging them to a spot directly under Sammy.

"I don't know about this," Slim said doubtfully as he grabbed the opposite ends of the mats Joe was dragging. "It's a long shot."

"It's the only shot we've got." Joe turned and ran back to the pile of mats.

"I'm slipping!" Sammy shouted desperately. "Hurry, guys. Hurry!"

Realizing that they would never get enough mats piled up in time, Slim ran to the doorway of the workout room and cupped his hands around his mouth. "We need everybody's help! Hurry! Sammy's in trouble!"

Joe was throwing another mat onto the pile when a dozen wrestlers and trainers came pouring into the room. In moments the pile of mats was two feet high.

"There's a big stack of mats under you, Sammy. Let go and just go limp when you fall!" Frank instructed.

"Here goes nothing!" Sammy shouted. He released his grip on the beam. Sammy fell backward with his arms and legs spread wide and landed in the center of the pile with a muffled thump.

Frank, Slim, and Joe rushed to Sammy's side. Sammy had the wind knocked out of him, but otherwise he seemed unhurt.

"How're your ribs?" Slim asked as he helped Sammy to sit up.

"Okay. They're okay," Sammy gasped. He sat on the edge of the stack of mats to catch his breath. The other wrestlers and trainers tried to crowd around Sammy, but Joe kept them back.

"All right, everybody, back off. Give Sammy room to breathe," ordered Joe.

"Thanks for your help, folks," Frank announced. "The rope broke, but Sammy's okay." Slowly the crowd began to disperse.

"I'll tell the maintenance boys about this rope," Slim volunteered. "I'll be back in a little while."

"That was close," Sammy said to the Hardys after Slim left. "If it hadn't been for you guys, I would've been splattered all over the floor."

"I'm just glad we were here," Frank said, shooting a quick look up at the frayed stump of rope hanging from the beam. "I think this is another of those 'accidents' you were telling us about."

"Major Disaster and Missy Mayflower were the last ones in this room," Joe said. "Do you think they could have cut the rope?"

Sammy shrugged. "Disaster hates me, but I don't know if he hates me enough to kill me."

"Maybe Disaster wants to be the IWA

champion more than you know. Maybe enough to try to kill you," Joe suggested.

"I've wrestled against him many times, but I don't really know the guy. He's a very private person," replied Sammy.

"I'll do a background check on him," Frank said, whipping out a small notebook.

"What about Missy? Any reason other than Disaster for her to want to hurt you?" asked Joe.

"Well," Sammy said slowly. "If you remember some wrestling history, Joe, the name Mike Mayflower should sound familiar."

"Mike Mayflower," Joe said excitedly. "Sure, Mike Mayflower, one of the first wrestling superstars! You mean Missy's—"

"His daughter," Sammy finished. "And Missy might be out to get me because of her brother, Mitch."

"Why? What happened with Mitch?" asked Frank.

"Two years ago, Miracle Mitch Mayflower was the IWA champ. I took away his title belt in our first match. During the match Mitch tore some ligaments in his knee and had to retire from wrestling."

"And you think Missy blames you for ruining his career?" asked Joe.

"I'm sure of it," Sammy said quietly. "Before that match, Missy was friendly to

14

me. Ever since Mitch got hurt, she won't give me the time of day.''

"Well—" Frank began, but his sentence was cut off by a loud commotion coming from the next room.

With Sammy in the lead, the Hardys went out into the huge, brightly lit gym of the IWA training center.

In one corner of the room, near the main entrance, Frank spotted a television camera crew clustered around a muscular black giant decked out in a snakeskin jacket, pants, and cowboy boots. Standing next to the giant was a smaller, older man.

"Oh, no! Warfield's going to go through with that challenge promo. I thought I convinced him to drop it," Sammy said angrily.

"Who's the big guy?" asked Frank.

"That's my buddy Ethan Berry. He's known in the ring as the Constrictor. He's one of my chief rivals, and the IWA's most popular 'bad guy.' We're actually best friends, but the fans don't know that.''

"What do you mean by 'bad guy'?" Frank asked.

"In professional wrestling you're either a good guy or a bad guy," Sammy explained. "We choreograph most of the moves ahead of time so that sometimes the good guy wins and sometimes the bad guy wins.''

15

"You mean wrestling matches are fixed?" Frank asked in surprise.

"It's all show biz! Now I have to go over and listen to the Constrictor bad-mouth me. Then I've got to sound off at him. It's to publicize our bout for a week from Saturday."

"And who's the older guy standing next to Constrictor?" asked Joe.

"That's Stanley Warfield, the IWA president—the guy who's making me go through this," answered Sammy.

Joe studied Warfield and thought that he had probably been a good athlete when he was younger. But he'd let his body get out of shape now. Warfield was almost completely bald, except for a neatly trimmed fringe of dark hair around his shiny dome. The hairiest parts of his head were his thick mustache and bushy eyebrows.

Joe's thoughts were interrupted as the Constrictor grabbed a microphone and began to speak.

"I'm here to challenge the IWA's so-called champion, the Kung Fu King, to wrestle me for the undisputed IWA championship! He doesn't deserve to be called champion! I'm calling you yellow, Kung Fu! I'm saying you're afraid to face the awesome might of the Constrictor!"

Frank saw Sammy take a deep breath and

angrily stalk across the gym toward the Constrictor.

"Constrictor, I'll wrestle you anywhere, any time. You're nothing but an overrated loudmouth!"

The camera crew quickly wheeled around and trained their camera on Sammy.

Sammy stalked up to within a foot of the Constrictor and yelled, "You hear me, punk? I'll throw you out of any ring you're stupid enough to enter with me!"

"You think I'm afraid of a wimp like you?" The Constrictor lunged at Sammy.

Stanley Warfield stepped between the two wrestlers to prevent any punches from being thrown.

Frank observed that a large crowd had gathered. Wrestlers had stopped their practices to witness the confrontation. Trainers in warm-up clothes and managers in rumpled suits moved forward to watch the shouting match between Sammy and the Constrictor.

Frank also noticed that Missy Mayflower and Major Disaster had come back and joined the crowd. Disaster's expression was unreadable behind his mirrored sunglasses, but Missy looked as if she was enjoying the show.

Suddenly Frank felt Joe jab him in the ribs with his elbow. Joe gestured with his head toward a different part of the crowd.

"Take a look over there, Frank. Check out

17

the short guy standing next to the big dude in black with the sunglasses.''

"Who are they?'' asked Frank.

"The short one's Daniel East, president of East Broadcasting Corporation. The big one is the Living Weapon, the NAAW's top wrestler.''

"But what are they doing—'' Frank started to ask, then stopped as he saw Disaster leave the training center.

"Disaster's splitting. I want to tail him to see where he's going. It might be a lead,'' said Frank.

"Good idea,'' Joe agreed. "I'll stay here and keep an eye on Missy and East.''

Frank gave Joe a knowing look. "I had a feeling you were going to say that. Let Sammy know that I'm borrowing his car, okay? I'll leave the van for you.''

Joe nodded and walked over to where Sammy and the Constrictor were hurling insults at each other. Stanley Warfield stood watching, his arms folded, and seemed to be pleased with something.

Frank ducked out a side exit of the training center and ran around to the parking lot. He hoped he'd be able to catch up with Disaster.

Just as Frank reached the parking lot, he spotted Disaster climbing into a black sports car. Frank hopped into Sammy's red convertible and felt under the dash for the spare key hidden there. He quickly started the car and took off after Disaster.

Disaster drove fast, weaving expertly in and out of traffic. Frank kept on his tail for about twenty minutes. They passed through the center of Allentown and then into an area across from a railroad track where the streets and buildings looked run-down. As he drove, Frank noticed nothing but dilapidated office buildings and stores, many of which were boarded up with For Rent signs nailed to their doorframes.

After driving a few blocks in this neighborhood, Disaster made a left turn and pulled into a parking lot. Frank noted that the parking lot was next to the tallest building on the block. I wonder where he's going? Frank thought.

He drove slowly past the parking lot, watching as Disaster got out of his car and walked through a back entrance of an office building.

Frank parked his car around the corner and made his way back to the building through broken bottles and other trash.

As he neared the rear entrance of the building, Frank heard what sounded like a conversation coming from behind the window next to the doorway. Frank stole up to the grimy window and tried to peer inside. The window was too filthy even after Frank wiped some of the dirt off with a piece of newspaper. The window was as filthy on the inside as the outside.

As Frank crept up to the next window, he heard the distinctive sound of glass being crunched somewhere behind him.

He started to turn his head, but an iron grip on his neck held him in place. He couldn't shake it free. Then he felt his body being slammed into the brick wall with amazing force!

Chapter

3

AS JOE WALKED up to the edge of the small crowd surrounding Sammy and the Constrictor, he noticed that Daniel East and the Living Weapon had been joined by two other men. Joe recognized the guys as the Roman brothers.

Like the Constrictor, the Roman brothers were bad guys. The two men were almost identical, except that one of them stood two inches taller than his brother. The shorter one had a scar on the left side of his chin. Both men had dark wavy hair cut in the style that reminded Joe of ancient Roman sculptures. I get the feeling I'll be seeing more of those guys, Joe said to himself.

Joe then turned back to watch Sammy's confrontation with the Constrictor.

"Get out of my way, Warfield. Let me tear his head off!" the Constrictor shouted.

"Easy, big guy," Warfield said, his fleshy face gleeful. "You'll get your chance. Just wait till you meet in the ring."

"That's right, Kung Fu, wait till we meet in the ring. But I'll tell you right now, you don't stand a chance against me, you little nothing!"

"That's just like you. Your mouth against my muscle. Do you think I take a third-rater like you seriously, Constrictor?"

"Third-rater! Why you—" The Constrictor lunged at Sammy over Warfield's shoulder.

"Go ahead, Constrictor, knock his block off!" Joe heard a female voice shout. "I'd like to see that, in the ring or out of it!"

Joe swiveled around to see Missy urging on the Constrictor. Her pretty face was now twisted in hate. Her hostility toward Sammy was very obvious.

"Kung Fu, I'm going to lay such a hurting on you that you're going to have to retire—in a wheelchair!" the Constrictor shouted.

"Yeah? We'll see about that, pinhead," Sammy retorted. "In the meantime, I can stay in the company of a loser only so long, so I'm going back to my dressing room. I'd advise you to leave now before I throw you out."

"You and what army, punk?" the Constrictor snarled back.

Sammy ignored the last of the snakeskin-clad wrestler's threats. Turning, he sauntered across the gym toward his dressing room.

Joe saw Warfield give the cut signal to the camera crew, and they turned off their lights and camera. The fun was over, and the crowd began to break up.

As he turned to follow Sammy into his dressing room, Joe heard Warfield call, "That's a wrap!"

Joe looked around for Daniel East and the Living Weapon, but they had disappeared.

"Hey, Sammy, wait up!" Joe called after him.

Sammy stopped long enough for Joe to catch up. When he reached the big wrestler's side, he noticed that Sammy was seething.

"What's wrong, Sammy?" asked Joe.

"I'm still mad at Warfield for making me go through with this challenge promotion with the Constrictor," Sammy replied, barely controlling his anger. "You'd think he'd give me a break after today with the rope snapping and all. But not him! He'll do anything for a buck and publicity."

Sammy threw open the door to his dressing room and angrily kicked over a folding chair just inside. Joe followed him and watched Sammy pace back and forth in front of a large mirror lined with light bulbs.

Joe slowly took in the dressing room. The

wall to the right of the door was lined with three tall metal lockers containing Sammy's wrestling costumes and workout clothes. A TV, VCR, and small cabinet filled with videotapes sat in the far corner of the room beneath a poster from Sammy's campaign against steroids. Joe recalled how Sammy had toured the country lecturing on the dangers of steroids.

"I've got enough to deal with, with somebody trying to wreck my career and maybe kill me! I don't think it's fair to make me go through with those stupid promos. Warfield doesn't even believe I'm in danger!"

"Take it easy, Sammy! Frank and I are going to help," Joe reminded him.

Sammy drew a long breath and collapsed into a padded leather swivel chair. "Yeah, you're right, Joe, I've got to calm down. Sorry I lost my temper," Sammy said quietly.

"Forget it. Anybody would get a little freaked out after what happened with the rope," Joe said sympathetically.

Joe picked up the chair Sammy had kicked over and sat down in it a few feet from him. Spotting a pad of paper and a pencil on the counter, Joe picked them up and began making notes.

"The important thing now is to figure out who our main suspects are. Once we have a list of suspects, we'll investigate to find out

who has the strongest motive for knocking
you out of the business," Joe told Sammy.

"You should probably start with Missy Mayflower and Major Disaster. I don't think Major
hates me enough to kill me, but he doesn't
exactly like me, either. And I think Missy
could be capable of just about anything—
maybe even murder," Sammy said.

"It's hard to think that someone as young as
Missy could be a killer," Joe said dubiously.

"Don't let that sweet face of hers fool you,
Joe. Missy may be only nineteen years old,
but she's one tough customer. Here, let me
show you what I mean."

Sammy walked over to the VCR and
searched through a stack of tapes. After a few
seconds he pulled one out. "This is a tape
of the match where I got hurt. Watch," he
instructed as he popped the tape into the
VCR.

Joe watched as Sammy fast-forwarded the
tape and stopped it. Then he ran the tape at
normal speed, and Joe watched as Missy
handed a wooden folding chair to Major Disaster. Disaster grabbed it, then charged forward,
slamming Sammy in the side with it. Joe
winced as he watched Sammy crumple to the
mat, his face contorted with pain.

"Ow, that hurts just to look at it," Joe
commented.

"That move was all worked out before the

match,'' Sammy explained. "It was supposed to be a breakaway chair.''

"So you think Missy probably substituted the real chair before the match?'' Joe asked, quickly scribbling notes.

"Someone did. I sure wouldn't put it past her. She blames me for what happened to her brother. And I think she'd stop at nothing to make sure that I have to quit wrestling like he did.''

Sammy had picked up the remote control device and was automatically rewinding the tape when Joe said, "Run the tape back to the point just before Missy hands the chair to Major.

"Sammy—freeze that frame!'' Joe shouted excitedly. He stood up so fast his own chair toppled backward. "Look there!'' he said, pointing to the upper portion of the screen. Joe and Sammy watched as a pair of hands moved a folding chair into position just before Missy grabbed it.

Joe hit the Rewind button on the VCR and ran the tape back a few more frames.

"What are you doing?'' Sammy asked.

"Trying to see if I can get a look at the person who moved that chair,'' Joe replied, staring intently at the screen.

Joe ran the sequence through several times before finally admitting defeat. "It's no use, Sammy,'' Joe said glumly. "The lighting's not good enough, and there are too many people in the foreground to make a positive ID. About all I can tell from this tape is that whoever moved the chair is probably a man because of the size of the hands."

"Well, I know more than I knew before," Sammy offered. "I watched that tape four or five times and never noticed someone move that chair."

Joe frowned, tapping the notebook with his pencil. "You told me Mitch Mayflower hurt his knee where you took away his title. Can you tell me anything more about what happened then?"

"Well, let's see," Sammy said as he sank back into the swivel chair. "I'd been in the IWA for less than a year, and when Mitch Mayflower said he'd take me on, it seemed like my big break. Mitch was the champion, and I was the new kid on the block."

"Did Mitch have bad knees already?" Joe inquired.

"Yes, he did," said Sammy. "That was pretty common knowledge. Frankly, he shouldn't have been wrestling with such bad knees. Mitch was taking chances."

"And you think Missy believes you deliberately went after his knees to cripple him," said Joe.

Sammy nodded. "Definitely. See, before that match I was on friendly terms with both

Mitch and Missy. Since then, she bad-mouths me to the wrestling press every chance she gets. And she manages only bad-guy wrestlers, with the hope that one of them will take the title away from me. So far, she hasn't had any luck."

"How did Mitch feel about you?" Joe inquired.

"When I went to see him in the hospital after the match, he told me not to blame myself," Sammy replied. "Mitch is a good guy. I don't think he holds a grudge."

Joe scribbled down a note, then asked Sammy, "Is there any other wrestler who might want to take you out, Sammy?"

Sammy shrugged. "It's possible. Maybe some guy's been using steroids and feels threatened by the campaign I began last year to keep steroids out of the IWA.

"Ever since Duke Dixon had a heart attack from using steroids last Christmas, I've been trying to convince Warfield to institute mandatory testing of all IWA wrestlers. He keeps saying he agrees with me one hundred percent, but he's still dragging his feet about mandatory testing. Maybe he's afraid he'll lose too many wrestlers."

"That's a possibility," Joe observed. "Who do you think uses them?"

"Major Disaster for one. I don't have any proof, but he bulked up awfully fast."

28

"Okay," Joe replied. "What about Tomahawk Smith?"

"I don't know," Sammy answered. "He's new to the IWA, and I don't know him well enough to say."

"How about your pal the Constrictor?"

"No way!" Sammy laughed. "Ethan would never use that garbage. He's too much of a health nut!"

"What about the Roman brothers?" Joe asked.

"It's possible. They're pretty pumped up, and I never see either of them do really serious weight lifting."

Joe put down his pencil. "Well, since Frank's tailing Disaster, I think I'll keep an eye on Missy. It's not much, but it's a start."

"Good," Sammy agreed. "I'll feel better if I know what she's up to."

"I hope she hasn't left." Joe went to the door and stuck his head out. Missy was standing with Warfield, the Constrictor, and a couple of guys from the camera crew, talking with them in a friendly, easy way.

Turning his head, Joe told Sammy, "I'm in luck! She's still here."

Joe watched then as Missy shook hands with Warfield and the Constrictor. Then she walked through the training center's main entrance.

"There she goes, Sammy. I'm going after her," Joe said in a low voice.

"Good hunting, pal," Sammy said as Joe slipped through the door.

Moving as quietly as possible, Joe trotted across the huge room after Missy. He paused at the entrance to make sure she wasn't in the lobby, but all he saw was a busload of tourists gawking at the photos of the IWA wrestlers on the wall. Joe moved forward to peer through the wide plate-glass windows at the front of the lobby and found Missy getting into a powder blue sedan.

When Joe stepped outside, Missy was already pulling out. Joe ran to his and Frank's black van and took off fast. He had to keep her in sight.

Missy turned right onto Tilghman Boulevard, the main thoroughfare that ran through Allentown. She traveled west on Tilghman, and Joe guessed she was heading for Bethlehem, the town right next to Allentown. Missy drove for about half an hour, seemingly unaware that she was being followed. Just before reaching Lehigh University, Missy made a quick left onto Fourth Street.

He followed her down Fourth until she turned into the front gates of a white two-story mansion. Joe looked up at the row of Greek columns in front of the house. Wow, this is some place, Joe thought to himself. His

30

eyes traveled along the low stone wall surrounding the property and read the name Mayflower on a wrought-iron sign affixed to the wall.

Missy pulled her car in through the gates and parked in the circular driveway. She hopped out and hurried up the front steps.

Joe pulled up to the entrance and parked just in front of a gatekeeper's cottage. He still had a clear view of the front of the Mayflower mansion, including the driveway.

"Now at least I know where she lives," Joe said quietly to himself.

He watched the house, but absolutely nothing happened during the hour that the late-afternoon sun slowly dropped in the sky. Joe yawned as he began his second hour of surveillance.

He began to realize how tired he was from his workout with Frank and wished he could catch a quick nap. Before long his eyelids got heavy, and he drifted off to sleep.

It seemed as if his eyes had closed only for an instant when he felt a sharp jab on his shoulder.

Joe jerked awake to find himself looking down the two holes at the end of a double-barreled shotgun.

Chapter

4

FRANK'S ASSAILANT let him drop, and he fell flat on the ground. What's going on? Frank thought frantically to himself as he scrambled to his feet. He found himself face-to-face with Major Disaster.

"I saw you working out with the Kung Fu King at the gym today. Who are you, kid?"

"My name's Frank." Disaster grabbed Frank by the front of his shirt and lifted him until the two of them were nose to nose.

"Hey, take it easy! I'm a wrestler, too!" Frank cried out.

"What are you doing snooping around here?" asked Disaster.

"I'm one of your biggest fans, Major. I was working out with Sammy because he offered to show me the ropes. But I'd rather be a bad-guy wrestler like you. I've been wanting to meet you, so I followed you."

I hope he buys my story, Frank thought to himself.

"So can you put me down, please?" Frank pleaded, pretending to be more scared than he actually was.

Disaster held Frank out at arm's length for a moment, intently studying his face. Finally he let go of Frank.

"Thanks, Major," Frank said, brushing the dirt from his pants.

"I don't know if you're telling the truth or not, but you seem like too much of a kid to worry about."

"Hey, I'm a lot tougher than I look," Frank said defiantly. "I really thought if I could learn from you, I could make it as a pro wrestler. Can I at least talk to you?"

"No!" Disaster snarled. "Get out of here and don't follow me anymore! I might not be so gentle the next time I see you hanging around."

Frank turned away and walked around the corner of the building. He ducked into the doorway of a vacant storefront and gave Disaster a few minutes to go back inside. Then he made his way toward the parking lot. Frank saw that Disaster's car was still the only one in the lot.

Moving cautiously, Frank went around to the front of the office building, opened the double doors, and slipped inside.

He scanned the dimly lit lobby and saw that it was as shabby and dirty as the surrounding neighborhood.

"Must be the janitor's year off," Frank said as he took in the filthy floor, the graffiti on the walls, the dusty windows, and the overflowing ashtray beside the elevator doors.

Attached to the wall, just above the ashtray, Frank noticed the directory for the building, faintly illuminated by a twenty-five-watt bulb. Frank cast a quick glance around to see if anyone was approaching, but the building was as silent as a graveyard.

Frank hurried over to the directory and ran his finger down it. He saw that the tenants on the first floor were an accountant, a beauty salon, and a Jacob Walsh, M.D. He shot a quick glance down the hall and spotted the door to Dr. Walsh's office. The office was set along the outer wall of the ground floor, and Frank guessed that he had been outside one of Walsh's windows when he'd overheard the muffled shouting.

So the rear doorway Disaster had used probably opened right into Walsh's office, Frank thought. But why would he sneak in the back way? Unless he had a reason for not wanting to be seen.

Hearing voices raised down the hall, Frank turned and quickly left. He didn't want another run-in with the big wrestler. I'd better ask Sammy if he's ever heard of this Dr. Walsh, Frank decided. Maybe he knows of some connection between him and Major Disaster.

Once outside the building, Frank made a beeline to Sammy's car. He put the top down and sped off, grateful for the cool evening air that flowed over him.

Frank drove directly to Sammy's house. He aimed the automatic garage door opener at the small attached building and pulled the vintage sports car inside.

The door leading into the house from the garage was open, but Frank knocked before entering. Sammy called out a big hello from the kitchen counter, where he was eating a huge ham and cheese sandwich.

"How are you doing?" Sammy asked around a mouthful of sandwich. "Help yourself to some eats."

"Thanks. I will," Frank replied, moving to a cutting board on the kitchen counter piled high with sliced cheese and cold cuts. "Any word from Joe?"

"Nope," Sammy said, shaking his head. "Last I heard he was tailing Missy Mayflower."

"Leave it to Joe to follow the women!" said Frank, spreading mustard on a slice of rye bread.

"Did you learn anything?" Sammy wanted to know.

35

"Possibly. Have you ever heard of a Dr. Jacob Walsh?"

"I sure have, and none of what I've heard is good. He's got a bad reputation," Sammy answered, putting his sandwich down. "I'm pretty sure he supplies steroids to some guys in the IWA."

"Do you think Major Disaster uses them?" Frank asked as he piled ham and cheese on the bread.

"As I told Joe, it's possible," Sammy replied. "Disaster got an impressive physique in a big hurry. It's probably one of the reasons Missy Mayflower was able to make him into a star so fast."

"Speaking of Disaster, I ran into him outside of Walsh's office. Actually, he grabbed me while I was trying to look through one of Walsh's windows," Frank continued. He put his sandwich together for one big bite.

"Did he rough you up?" asked Sammy, concerned.

Frank shook his head as he chewed. "Not much. He recognized me from the gym, and I told him I was a big fan of his. I probably inflated his ego—if that's possible."

"Walsh and Disaster together . . . something stinks here," Sammy said. "I announced the other day that I'm going to make a public statement against steroid use before my match against Major Disaster on Saturday."

36

"So, you think maybe Walsh might be using Disaster to try to shut you up?" Frank speculated. "Maybe Walsh convinced Disaster that it was in his best interests to keep you quiet.

"Are there any other wrestlers besides Disaster who you think might use steroids?" he added.

"A few," Sammy replied. "But nobody knows how many because Stan Warfield keeps stalling about testing all the wrestlers in the IWA.

"If it could be proved that Disaster or any other wrestler was using steroids, he'd be kicked out of the IWA. Just like in any other professional sport, it's against IWA rules to use steroids."

Frank took another big bite of his sandwich as he quickly ran over what he'd learned about the case so far. He knew he had to find out what Joe had uncovered before he could decide what to do next.

"Well, if Disaster thinks you're trying to get him kicked out of the IWA, that could give him a strong motive to knock you out of wrestling. Say, Sammy, can I borrow your car again? I want to go buy a six-pack of soda," Frank added as he stood peering into the refrigerator.

"Sure," Sammy said with a wave of his hand. "I forgot I was out of soda."

"Stay on your toes until I get back, Sammy," Frank said after he finished his sandwich. "There's no telling when the next attack on you will come."

"Don't worry. I've got the best alarm system money can buy. Besides, Ethan's coming over to watch videos tonight and keep an eye on me."

As Frank walked into the garage, he passed through an electric eye that triggered the outer garage door. The door was rising as Frank slid into the sleek red sports car and fastened his seat belt.

Enjoying the soft comfort of the car's leather interior, Frank revved the powerful engine, threw it into reverse, and backed out into the street.

Suddenly the lights of a car parked nearby flicked on, and its engine roared to life.

Frank was still backing up when he realized that the car was accelerating and heading straight toward him.

Hey! Frank thought. Is that guy blind? He's going to broadside me!

Frank tried to push the gearshift into first, but the clutch stuck. Frantically he pushed on the stick, trying to put the car into a forward gear.

The mysterious sedan raced closer, and still the shift wouldn't move. Frank glanced out at the oncoming car. The light from its headlights moved forward and quickly filled the side window. Unable to see, Frank tensed for the crash that he knew was coming.

Chapter

5

"MIND TELLING ME what you're doing trailing my sister, kid?" the guy at the other end of the shotgun asked Joe.

"I wasn't—" Joe started to say, but the big man holding the double-barreled twelve-gauge cut him off. Hey, this guy is Miracle Mitch Mayflower, Joe thought to himself.

"Don't try to deny it. Missy saw you following her," Mitch said, pulling open the door on the driver's side of the van. "Come on." He motioned with the shotgun barrel. "You're coming into the house. I have to decide whether or not to call the cops."

"There's no need to do that," Joe said, flashing an embarrassed smile. "It's easy to explain."

"Explain inside," Mitch replied, and he backed off a few steps.

Joe stepped out of the van, conscious of the shotgun that was still leveled at his chest.

Joe walked slowly up the driveway, Mitch Mayflower at his side. From the corner of his eye Joe glanced at his captor. He noticed the man's pronounced limp, undoubtedly the result of his wrestling injury. Joe caught a dangerous gleam in Mitch's eyes when their gazes met briefly. This guy knows how to handle himself in any rough situation, Joe thought.

"Hey," Joe said, "aren't you Miracle Mitch Mayflower?"

The big man's hard expression broke, and his blue eyes widened in surprise. "Yeah! Are you a wrestling fan?"

"I'm not only a fan, I'm a wrestler, too," Joe replied.

"Oh, yeah?" Mitch said. "Well, then we ought to have a lot to talk about," he said good-naturedly, opening the front door of the house and backing inside. Although Mitch was acting sort of friendly, Joe noticed that the ex-wrestler still kept the shotgun trained on him.

Joe stepped through the doorway and found himself in a foyer with pearl gray walls, a black marble floor, and an ornate crystal chandelier overhead. Joe was very impressed.

"Over here." Mitch gestured toward a door just off the hall.

40

Joe pushed the door open to see Missy Mayflower lounging on a huge black leather sofa.
Her icy stare cut right through Joe and almost
made him shudder.

Mitch motioned for Joe to sit down on a
chair across from the couch. Then Mitch
tapped Missy so she would scoot over to give
him room to sit down. He sat next to his sister, laying the big gun across his knees.

"First things first," Mitch said. "What's
your name?"

"Joe Hardy, Mr. Mayflower."

"Okay, Joe, why were you following
Missy?" Mitch asked bluntly.

"I—" Joe pretended to stumble over his
words. He lowered his head and tried to look
embarrassed as he answered. "Well, it's like
I started to tell you, Mr. Mayflower, that I
want to be a professional wrestler. While I
was working out at the IWA gym today, I saw
Missy, and . . ." Joe's voice trailed off.

"So, you've got a crush on my little sister,
huh?" Mitch chuckled.

Joe dropped his head. "Uh, yeah, Mr. Mayflower, I guess I do. I followed Missy to find
out where she lived. I was sitting in my van,
trying to get up enough nerve to come up to
the front door to ask her out. I guess I fell
asleep. I had a pretty tough workout at the
gym today."

Joe raised his eyes to Missy and Mitch to

see if they were buying his story, and he was relieved to see that Missy looked a bit flattered. When he checked out Mitch, he saw the big man flick the safety catch on the shotgun, which he set on the glass and marble table before him. The big man's handsome face was creased with a broad grin.

"What do you think, Missy?" Mitch asked. "Should we introduce him to the old man?"

"No! I saw him at the gym today hanging around with that creep Sammy Rand. Any friend of—"

"Stop it, Missy! It wasn't Sammy's fault that I got hurt. You've got to stop blaming him for that," Mitch said sternly.

"I'm sorry, Mitch," Missy said, and lowered her head. After a moment she glanced up at Joe. "Do you know who our dad is, Mr. Hardy?"

"Sure. He's Mike 'the Maestro' Mayflower, the man who succeeded Gorgeous George as the superstar of wrestling," Joe said, grateful that he'd remembered the article he'd just read in a wrestling magazine.

"Okay, Mitch, perhaps Daddy should meet this guy," Missy said, her expression softening.

Before he knew it, Joe was being ushered into a room on the other side of the hall. It was filled with souvenirs and trophies from Mike Mayflower's professional wrestling career. Mike himself was sitting in a huge armchair reading the newspaper. On a television set in the corner, columns of stock-market quotations scrolled down the screen.

The first thing Joe noticed was the amazing resemblance between father and son. Mike was an older version of Mitch, with white hair and a few more wrinkles. Next Joe noticed the way the old man's chest and arm muscles bulged under what was obviously an expensive yellow cashmere sweater.

"What have we here, a visitor?" the older Mayflower asked in a gravelly voice.

"A would-be wrestler with eyes for Missy," answered Mitch.

"Is that a fact?" Mike rose to shake hands. "What's your name, son?"

"I'm Joe Hardy, Mr. Mayflower. It's a real honor to make your acquaintance."

"Can the mister, Joe. Call me Mike," the older wrestler said in a friendly voice.

"Thanks, Mike," Joe replied. "Meeting you and your son in the same day is a real treat. I've got videotapes of some of your matches from the fifties and sixties, against Gorgeous George, Man Mountain Dean, and the Swedish Angel."

"No kidding." Mike's eyes twinkled with pleasure. "I'm amazed any of those matches survived. Not that many of them were filmed, you know."

43

"The tapes I have were copied from old kinescopes, made before they had videotape," Joe explained, glad he had seen his friend Chet Morton's old wrestling videotapes.

"Boy, it's been years since I've seen some of that stuff. You'll have to tell me where you got those tapes," Mike said enthusiastically as he motioned for Joe to sit down. Joe saw Missy and Mitch seat themselves in chairs on either side of their father. Joe sat down on a chair across from them.

Joe glanced over at Missy. Although she appeared to be relaxed, she still looked suspicious.

Joe turned his attention back to Mike Mayflower. "If you'd like, Mike, I'd be happy to send you the video company's address."

"You would?" Mike's eyebrows shot up as he grinned. "That'd be great. Then I could show Mitch how I creamed Man Mountain Dean in fifty-two. Now, that was a great match.

"Hey, I know what," Mike suggested. "Let's have Joe to dinner tonight." The old man leaned forward and slapped Joe on the knee. "How about it, Joe? Have you eaten yet?"

"No," Joe replied, delighted not only at the prospect of digging deeper into the case, but also at getting to know Missy better.

"Missy, would you tell Clarice that we have one more for dinner?"

After a dinner of roast beef, baked potatoes, and double-chocolate cake for dessert, Mike Mayflower pushed away from the dinner table, patting his stomach in satisfaction. Then he looked over at Joe and said, "Come on. I'll take you on the five-cent tour of my little shack.

"Want to help me show Joe around the house, kids?" Mike asked.

"I'd like to. Dad, but I've got a date later," Mitch explained.

"Okay, have fun," Mike said with a smile. "How about you, Missy?"

"No, thanks, Dad. I have to make some phone calls about the Major's next match."

"Suit yourself," Mike replied. Then he turned to Joe and said, "Well, Joe, I guess it's just you and me."

Joe decided that this would be a good time to try to learn as much as he could about Missy and Disaster from Mike. But he knew he had to be careful not to get Mike suspicious.

Mike led Joe through the long dining room, past a wall of stained-glass windows, and into the next room. Every inch of wall space was covered with framed swords, pistols, knives, flintlocks, crossbows, and other weapons so obscure Joe didn't immediately recognize them.

"Wow," Joe said, impressed. "This is quite a collection."

"It's taken me twenty years to put it together," Mike said modestly. "It's one of the best private collections on the East Coast."

"I read that Major Disaster is a real military buff. I bet he's fascinated by all this stuff," Joe ventured.

The cheery expression left Mike's face at Joe's mention of Major Disaster. "The Major's never seen it. I won't have him in my house."

"Why is that? Your daughter *is* his manager."

"I don't like the guy. I'm sorry Missy ever got mixed up with a jailbird like him," Mike growled.

"A jailbird! What'd he do?"

"He used to be a leg breaker for a loan shark. He got into wrestling after he got out of prison."

"Exactly why is Missy managing Disaster?" Joe asked.

"She's determined to manage any wrestler who can take away Sammy Rand's title. Missy hates Sammy so much she doesn't care how she does it," Mike told him, an edge of anger creeping into his voice.

"Mitch doesn't blame Sammy for what happened to him," Joe pointed out. "Why does Missy?"

"I don't know, kid," Mike said with a bewildered expression. "It's an obsession with her."

Sensing it was time to change the subject, Joe asked Mike another question. "Say, Mike, were steroids a problem when you were wrestling?"

"Huh?" The old wrestler gave Joe a strange look. "Steroids? Nope. Wrestlers didn't use that stuff in my day. Why do you ask?"

"Sammy Rand thinks steroids are a major problem with the IWA. He's even trying to get Stanley Warfield to make testing for steroids mandatory."

"Yeah? Good for Sammy," Mike said approvingly. "I keep trying to convince Missy that Sammy's okay, but she just won't listen."

"How does Missy feel about steroids?" Joe inquired.

"She's against them," Mike replied firmly. "I know she felt pretty bad about that kid in the IWA who died from using steroids last month."

"Do you think Major Disaster uses steroids?"

"I don't know. But I'll tell you one thing—if he is using them and Missy finds out about it, she'll drop him like a hot potato."

Filing that bit of information away for future reference, Joe decided he'd better make his exit. He was eager to tell Frank about his eventful evening.

"I think it's time I go. Please say good night to Missy and Mitch for me," Joe said politely.

"Will do. Good night, Joe, I'm sure you can find your way out."

With those words Mike turned and walked down the hallway toward a wide staircase that led upstairs.

Boy, the Mayflowers are some family, Joe said to himself as he walked toward the front door. He passed a small side table beneath a gold-edged mirror and noticed Missy's purse, which had been carelessly tossed on top of the table. Its clasp was open. Casting a quick glance behind him, Joe stuck his hand into the purse and immediately touched something cold and hard wrapped loosely in a silk scarf. Puzzled, Joe withdrew the heavy object and whipped the scarf off it.

It was a bowie knife. As Joe scrutinized its sharp, wedge-shaped blade, he realized it was the perfect tool for sawing through a thick rope.

Chapter
6

WHAT'S GOING ON? Frank thought to himself as the sedan raced closer and closer. At the last possible instant before impact, Frank slammed his foot down on the gas pedal and spun the wheel hard, to the right. The car zoomed backward and swung out in a wide arc. The sedan zipped past.

Frank breathed a sigh of relief. He strained to check out the sedan, but it was moving too fast for him to identify. Besides, whoever was driving the car had put out the rear license plate light.

The first thing Frank wondered was if Disaster had trailed him from Walsh's office. Then, since he was driving Sammy's car, he wondered if the attack had been meant for Sammy. Who-

49

ever's responsible for those attacks on Sammy might have been behind that wheel, Frank thought to himself.

Frank was afraid to drive Sammy's car after it wouldn't go into gear. He managed to get it back to neutral and pushed it back into Sammy's garage.

"I thought you were going to the store," Sammy commented when Frank came in.

"I changed my mind. Your car wouldn't shift, and then somebody decided to play chicken with me as I was pulling out."

"What?" Sammy's eyes widened in surprise.

"Someone tried to broadside your car. They split before I could get a plate number or a make on the car."

"Man, what a day," Sammy said, shaking his head. "All these incidents are starting to get to me. I think I'll cancel with Ethan and just go to bed. Tell Joe I said good night."

"Okay, Sammy. Why don't you double-check the alarm system before you turn in. I'm going to do some background checks on the computer while I wait for Joe."

Frank sat down at the small desk in Sammy's guest bedroom, where he had set up his computer, modem, and fax machine. He quickly gained access to the national law enforcement data network his father, Fenton Hardy, used in his work as a private investigator.

First Frank keyed in Major Disaster's real

name, Fred J. Stone. Frank had a strong suspicion that Disaster had a criminal record—he was right, of course. Quickly scanning the screen, Frank noted multiple arrests for assault and illegal possession of firearms, and one for attempted murder! Bingo, Frank said to himself.

Next Frank requested a copy of Disaster's "rap sheet" to be faxed to him. Frank did have to admit to himself that a criminal record alone was no proof that Disaster was behind the mysterious attacks on Sammy.

Frank finished reviewing the rap sheet and next keyed in Missy Mayflower's name. Frank found no information on her in the national law enforcement data bank, so he tried the Allentown police computers next. Besides a few parking tickets, he saw that Missy had only been cited twice, both times for making harassing phone calls to Sammy Rand. A quick check of the dates showed that this had occurred immediately after the match with Mitch. In both cases the charges had been dropped. Frank called up a copy of Missy's record on the fax anyway.

Next Frank decided to check out some of the other wrestlers. He started with Tomahawk Smith, but Smith had no criminal record. Frank was about to check out another one when Joe walked in.

"Hi, Joe. How'd it go?"

"Well," Joe began as he seated himself across from Frank at the small table. "It started with Mitch Mayflower getting the drop on me with a twelve-gauge shotgun."

"What! How did that happen?"

Joe looked abashed. "I fell asleep while I was watching Missy's house."

Frank let out a sigh. "Whew! You were lucky you didn't get your head blown off."

"I talked my way out of it by pretending to be a novice wrestler with a crush on Missy. Mitch even took me in to meet his dad, Mike 'the Maestro' Mayflower."

"Hey, wasn't he an old-time wrestling star?" asked Frank.

"Yep," Joe replied. "So, anyway, after I had dinner with the Mayflowers, I talked with Mike and got some info on Missy and Major Disaster. Then on my way out I saw that Missy had left her purse lying on a table by the door, so I checked through it for any clues. Inside, I found a very sharp bowie knife that would have been perfect for slicing through a thick climbing rope."

"I found something else that doesn't look good for Missy," Frank announced, quickly filling Joe in on what he had learned about Missy's harassment of Sammy. "And it gets worse. Fred Stone, also known as Major Disaster, has a rap sheet as long as my arm."

"That coincides with what I learned from Mike Mayflower," Joe told his brother.

"I think Major Disaster and Missy might be trying to shut Sammy up permanently so he won't speak out against steroids," Frank said. "I ran into Disaster outside the offices of a Dr. Walsh, who Sammy thinks has been supplying steroids to some of the wrestlers."

"If Sammy's antisteroid campaign *is* the motivation for the attacks, then maybe we can cross Missy off our list of suspects. Mike told me that Missy is totally against the use of steroids," Joe pointed out.

"Well, maybe Disaster's working alone," Frank suggested. "Anyway, while you were gone, a car almost broadsided me while I was driving Sammy's car.

"I'm not sure if that means I was followed by Disaster, or if it was because I was driving Sammy's car, but either way we all have to be very careful.

"There's not much more we can do until morning," Frank told his brother, stifling a yawn. "Let's hit the sack so we can get an early start tomorrow."

The next morning, after a quick breakfast, the Hardys and Sammy set out for the garage and then the IWA training center. Frank rode with Sammy in his car, and Joe followed them to Sammy's mechanic's garage in case the car broke down on the way. After dropping off the car, they all piled into the van and drove to the IWA center.

When they entered the main gym of the center, Frank saw that there were already at least thirty wrestlers and trainers beginning their workouts. Among the group Sammy pointed out the Constrictor, Tomahawk Smith, Baron Von Krupp, and Major Disaster to him. Missy was nowhere to be seen.

In the center of the room and just beyond the three main practice rings, Frank noticed a pair of almost identical wrestlers working out on a mat. Several mats were laid out on the floor near them.

"Let's limber up over by those guys, Joe," Frank suggested.

"You guys go ahead," said Sammy. "I have to check in with Slim."

"Sure," Joe said, following Frank into the locker room. The Hardys set down their gym bags and changed into wrestling tights, knee pads, boots, and protective headgear.

"Ready to try a few falls, Frank?" Joe challenged as they walked over to the mats. "I bet I can pin you today without Sammy coaching you."

"I wouldn't be so sure of myself if I were you," Frank retorted.

"If you guys are looking for a match, how about trying something really challenging?"

Joe heard a slightly sarcastic voice from behind him.

He turned around to see the two nearly identical wrestlers standing at the edge of his mat.

"Both you guys look like you could use a serious workout," said the taller of the two men.

"We're tough enough to take on you two refugees from a Hercules picture," Joe snapped.

"Who are these guys, anyway?" Frank asked Joe.

But before Joe could reply, the shorter brother rolled his blue eyes disbelievingly and snapped, "We're the Romans, the hottest tag team in wrestling. My name's Victor, short for Victory, punk!"

"Yeah, and I'm Jimmy," his brother added. "Who are you guys?"

Joe turned to his brother with a look of disgust on his face. Then he turned back and focused on the opposition. "We're Frank and Joe Hardy. How do you want to do this?"

"In a tag-team match, of course," Victor answered with a sneer. "I'm sure you rookies can use the practice."

"That remains to be seen," Frank retorted.

"I'm going to enjoy teaching you two a lesson," Jimmy Roman said as he smacked a huge fist into the palm of his other hand.

"Follow us, rookies," Victor Roman said,

leading the Hardys to the ring in the center of the room.

When they were all assembled in the ring, Frank noticed that the other wrestlers and trainers had stopped their workouts and were clustered along the ropes that surrounded the ring.

"Now, you two know the rules of a tag-team match?" Jimmy Roman asked with a sneer.

"Sure," Joe replied. "Only one wrestler from each team in the ring at a time. The man in the ring can make a substitution only by touching his partner's hand. The untagged man has five seconds to get out of the ring."

"Very good," Victor Roman said sarcastically. "Little Joey has obviously done his homework."

"Easy, Joe," Frank warned as he passed him on the way out of the ring. "Don't let him rile you. It's just a trick to make you careless."

As soon as Jimmy left the ring, Frank saw Victor and Joe square off against each other.

"Now's the time to pull out your best moves," Victor taunted as they circled each other.

"Ha!" Joe retorted. "You think I'd waste my best moves on you?"

"That's the spirit, kid. Don't let the Romans buffalo you," the Constrictor shouted encouragingly.

"Tear his head off, Victor!" Major Disaster yelled. "If Kung Fu taught him to wrestle, it ought to be easy!"

Suddenly Victor charged forward and tried to grab Joe's head. Joe ducked under Victor's arms, pivoted, and shot his arms under Victor's in a double hammerlock.

Victor went down on one knee and whipped his upper body back and then forward, and Joe was tossed off.

Victor launched himself into the air, landing on Joe with a full body slam.

"Oooohh!" Joe grunted, his face contorted with pain. Using a quick kick, Joe threw Victor off. The Constrictor and a few other wrestlers cheered Joe's escape, while Disaster led Tomahawk Smith and the rest of the bad-guy wrestlers in booing Joe and cheering Victor. Victor rolled to his feet, dived into the ropes, and rebounded back into Joe.

Frank saw his brother sidestep Victor, catching him with a clothesline move across the throat. Victor dropped, and Joe hurled himself on top of the larger man.

"One, two—" Frank counted off, but his count was interrupted by the sight of Jimmy Roman hurling himself over the top rope and into the ring.

Jimmy hurled his entire weight onto Joe's

back, knocking Joe off Victor and onto the mat.

"Hey, you can't do that!" Frank shouted, and he, too, leapt into the ring.

Victor Roman met his charge with a knee to Frank's midsection, and Frank went down.

Then, while Frank gasped for breath on the mat, he saw the Romans grab Joe and hurl him into the ropes. Then Jimmy slammed Joe on the side of the head with a blow from his forearm.

Joe went down hard, and the Romans tossed him into the ropes again, twining the flexible ropes around his arms.

Frank desperately tried to get up, but Victor slammed him back down to the mat with a two-fisted ax-handle punch.

Before Frank could make any countering moves, he felt Victor pick him up around the waist and hold him upside down.

Hanging with his head down, he saw Jimmy Roman climb up to the top of the corner post. From Frank's position it looked as if Jimmy was getting ready to fly through the air. In a flash of realization that sent chills through his body, Frank knew he was being set up for a spiked pile driver, an illegal move that could break his neck!

Chapter

7

JOE TRIED TO FREE HIMSELF from the ropes, but they held fast. In a minute Jimmy Roman would deliver the spiked pile driver move against Frank's feet that would drive his head into the mat and snap his neck!

Joe stopped straining against the ropes for a moment and tried rotating his arms to loosen the ropes. He worked fast, knowing that his brother's life was at stake.

"Hey, you guys are going too far!" shouted the Constrictor. Joe's hopes rose as he realized Sammy's friend was coming to Frank's aid.

Suddenly Major Disaster planted himself in the Constrictor's path. "Not so fast, pal. I think we ought to let them finish their match,"

Disaster said, placing a beefy hand on the Constrictor's chest.

"Get out of my way, Major!" the Constrictor said, slapping Disaster's hand away. "The Romans will kill that kid!"

"Let them!" Disaster snarled, grabbing Constrictor's arm and twisting it behind his back.

"You're way out of line, Major!" Tomahawk Smith shouted as he ran over to the two struggling wrestlers. Joe saw that the Romans had been momentarily distracted by the confrontation outside the ring.

Finally Joe pulled free from the ropes and charged Jimmy Roman.

"Yaaaaaa!" Joe shouted as he plowed into Jimmy, the force of his attack throwing Jimmy off the post and out of the ring.

Victor Roman dropped Frank on his head and rushed to his brother's aid. Luckily, Frank wasn't hurt. He sprang up a second after he hit, then launched himself at Victor, who was just stepping through the ropes.

"If you're so fond of tying people in the ropes, let's see how you like it!" Frank shouted, twining the top and middle ropes around Victor's left arm.

While Frank was occupied with Victor, Joe had gotten out of the ring and was grappling with Jimmy Roman. Joe rolled between Jimmy's wide-spread legs, snagged Jimmy's ankle, and whipped it backward. The hulking wrestler tumbled forward on his face.

Joe instantly leapt on Jimmy, wrapping his arms and legs around Jimmy's spread-eagled arms, with the back of one arm pressing mercilessly against the back of Jimmy's neck.

"What's going on out here?" Sammy shouted angrily from across the gym.

Joe looked over to see Sammy standing outside his dressing room dressed in black sweatpants and a black tank top.

"It's just a friendly little practice bout," Victor Roman grunted from where he strained to free himself.

"Well, it doesn't look friendly to me!" Sammy said angrily as he stalked over to the ring.

"You got that right, Sammy!" the Constrictor said from where he was being held back from Disaster by a couple of trainers. "The Romans were warming up to do a spiked pile driver on your buddy here."

"Oh, yeah?" Sammy said. "If I ever see you Romans try that move again, I'll make double sure you're both kicked out of the IWA! You got me?"

"Yeah, we heard you," Jimmy said sullenly.

"Kung Fu, you wimp! Let them fight! They had a good bout going till you butted in!" Joe heard Major Disaster shout. "Why don't you stop being such a Goody Two-Shoes and mind your own business?''

"Why don't you butt out instead, Disaster? As long as I'm champ, I have an obligation to all the wrestlers in the IWA to make sure nobody gets hurt. I don't want anyone using the spiked pile driver even in a practice bout!" Sammy said, sauntering over to Disaster, his fists lightly clenched.

"In a pig's eye!" Disaster spat out. "You're so high and mighty. You think you can boss everybody in the IWA around, don't you?''

Disaster shoved Sammy in the chest with both hands. Instantly the two men were at each other. Tomahawk Smith and the Constrictor jumped in and tried to keep the two wrestlers apart while the Romans stood back, laughing at the confrontation.

"All right! Take it easy!" Joe shouted, making a grab at Disaster.

Frank pushed between Sammy and Disaster while Tomahawk and Constrictor held them back. "Come on, Sammy, be smart. Don't let him antagonize you," Frank said in a calm voice. "Remember what you always told us about mastering your anger."

"Don't listen to these punks, Sammy! Let's get it on! Right here!" Disaster shouted.

"We won't solve anything here," Sammy admitted. "But I'll see you in the ring Saturday, Disaster, and we'll see who comes out on top then."

"It'll be me!" Disaster sneered. "Better polish up the IWA trophy belt, Sammy. I like it nice and shiny."

Disaster turned and straight-armed Frank out of the way as he sauntered back toward the locker room.

"Come on, guys. Let's practice at the other end of the gym until the air clears. It stinks in here," said Sammy.

Sammy led the Hardys and the Constrictor to workout mats spread out at the far end of the gym.

While Frank and Joe watched, Sammy and the Constrictor practiced their moves. "Guys like Disaster and the Romans make me wonder what I'm doing in this business," Sammy said, disgusted.

"Take those punks the Romans," the Constrictor said as he rose from the mat. "They come off like they're so tough, but the truth is, they're losers."

"Really?" Joe remarked.

"Yeah," the Constrictor went on. "They couldn't make it in the NAAW, so now they're giving the IWA a shot. You see, Victor's got a glass jaw. One tap and he's out like a light."

"I guess that explains why he has to prove he's so tough " Frank observed.

"Uh, Sammy," Joe started. "When you have a free minute, Frank and I would like to talk with you."

"Don't worry," Sammy said, shooting a look at the Constrictor. "Ethan knows that you guys are here to investigate the little accidents I've been having."

"Well, in that case," Joe announced, "I forgot to tell you I found out something very interesting last night during my visit to the Mayflower mansion. As I was leaving, I found a bowie knife in Missy's purse."

"A bowie knife, huh? That could have cut through the climbing rope," Sammy said with a troubled expression.

"Like butter," Joe elaborated. "I know Frank told you about following Disaster to Dr. Walsh's office. It's starting to look like Disaster and Missy are double-teaming you. Disaster's trying to keep you from making that antisteroid speech before your match with him in two days, and Missy's out to get you because she blames you for Mitch's injury."

"Let them try," Sammy said grimly. "Nothing will stop me. I'm going to make that speech no matter what!"

"That's the spirit!" Joe cheered. "If Missy and Disaster are after you, we'll triple-team them—you, me, and Frank!"

"Hey, don't forget me," the Constrictor added.

"How could anyone forget you, Ethan." Sammy grinned, his expression lightening. "In the meantime, there's just one obstacle between me and my Saturday match with Disaster—a six-foot-six newcomer named Tomahawk Smith.

"I've got to be in top shape to wrestle him, because I've seen this kid wrestle and he's good. He's fast and he's got tremendous upper body strength."

"Then let's get to work," the Constrictor said, taking a wrestling stance in the middle of the mat.

After a grueling wrestling workout with the Constrictor, followed by squats, bench presses, and curls with free weights, Sammy said his morning workout was finished.

"Listen, guys. I'm going to hit the sauna for a while. I want to be sure I'm not over my weight limit for my bout."

"Sammy, if I ate like you do, I'd be worried about my weight, too," Joe shot back.

Pretending to get angry, Sammy threw a towel at Joe on his way out of the weight room. "Thanks a lot, Joe," Sammy said sarcastically.

"I'm not up for a sauna, but how about a shower, Joe?" Frank suggested after Sammy was gone. "I feel pretty grimy."

As they crossed the training center's main

room, Joe automatically kept an eye out for Major Disaster and the Romans. Although the huge room was full of wrestlers and trainers, there was no sign of Disaster or the Romans.

Joe followed Frank into the locker room, where they removed their headgear and began unlacing their wrestling boots.

As he was loosening his second boot, Frank heard the locker room door creak open and an angry voice drifted in.

"Man, if there hadn't been so many people around, I'd have kicked Sammy's teeth in for talking to us like that!"

"Keep your voice down, Vic! No point in getting so worked up right now," Joe heard Jimmy Roman reply. "He'll get his. And after Sammy's been dealt with, we'll settle accounts with those two punks. I think the blond one loosened one of my teeth."

"I can't wait to see that creep Sammy get what he deserves," Victor said nastily.

"His time will come, but in the meantime, keep your trap shut, Vic. Your big mouth could blow everything."

Putting a finger to his lips to indicate that they should be silent, Frank led Joe toward the locker room door.

Once they were out in the gym, Joe put his head close to Frank's and whispered, "Do you want to tell Sammy what they just said?"

"Absolutely!" Frank whispered back as he

turned and trotted off toward the steam room. Joe followed him into the hallway that led to the examination rooms, the doctor's office, the hydrotherapy room, and the steam room.

The steam room was deserted when they entered. Joe looked around for the sauna doors, and his heart skipped a beat when he saw them. Looped around the double door handles was a thick steel chain and a padlock.

"Sammy's been locked in!" Joe shouted, tearing over to the door. A moment fumbling with the chain showed him that it couldn't be broken without tools.

Both Joe and Frank tugged on the double doors and succeeded in opening them a crack.

They immediately had to retreat from the intense heat that poured through the crack. Frank checked the thermometer beside the door.

"Joe, it's a hundred and fifty degrees in there! We've got to get Sammy out before he's roasted alive!"

Joe peered through the glass window. "It may already be too late!" he cried as he spotted Sammy's flushed, sweaty form lying face-down on the floor of the sauna.

Chapter

8

JOE POUNDED HIS FIST on the door to the
steam room.

"This'll let some of the heat out. Stand
back—we're in for a real hot blast." Frank
smashed the sauna windows with a metal
bucket he found on the floor. Frank and Joe
stepped back as intense heat poured out.

Frank checked the thermometer and saw
that the mercury was slowly rising. It almost
read one hundred and sixty degrees now!

"The thermostat controls must be inside the
sauna," Frank observed.

"We've got to get inside fast then!" Joe
shouted. He yanked on the doors again.

"Get help! Go find anybody to get these
doors open," Frank said, still studying the

chained doors. He heard the door slam shut behind him as Joe left the room.

Suddenly Frank's expression brightened. "I've got it! I'll pry the pins out of the hinges!"

Frank ran his eyes over the room looking for anything he could use to pry up the hinges. Sammy's gym bag, which sat on a redwood bench beside the sauna doors, caught his attention. He dumped the contents on the bench and quickly pawed through Sammy's soap, toothbrush, razor, and shaving cream.

"Aha!" Frank shouted triumphantly, holding up a metal comb and a hairbrush.

"It isn't much, but I think it'll work!" Frank said, and squatted next to the bottom hinge of the left door. He carefully slipped the teeth of the comb into the narrow space between the top of the pivot pin and the barrel of the hinge. He wiggled the teeth up and down, drawing the pivot pin up until he had enough room to jam one end of the comb under the rim of the pin. Using the metal comb like a wedge, Frank hammered the other end with the back of the hairbrush until he'd knocked the pin out of the top of the barrel.

Frank popped the pin out of the top hinge, too, and then tried to pull the door open, but it was too heavy.

Frustrated, he slammed his fist into the double doors. Luckily, at that moment, the doors to the sauna room swung open, and Joe charged through with the Constrictor and Tomahawk Smith close behind. They pulled on the door until there was a space large enough for Frank to squeeze into the sauna.

"I'll get some cold water and towels!" Joe ran to the shower on the far side of the room.

"I'll get the doctor," Tomahawk Smith said over his shoulder on his way out the door.

"I'll go get Sammy!" Frank shouted as he let a blast of burning hot air escape before he squirmed through the narrow entrance. "Wait here, Ethan, and I'll hand Sammy out to you."

Frank didn't bother turning down the temperature control. He just raced inside the sauna, grabbed Sammy, and dragged him toward the door. Frank strained hard, sweat pouring off him as he pulled Sammy's body to the door. The Constrictor reached in and yanked Sammy through the opening.

"It's like an inferno in there!" Frank said, wiping the sweat out of his eyes. The Constrictor laid the unconscious Sammy on the cool tile floor.

Constrictor and Frank could do nothing until Joe got there except try to remember their basic first aid. Joe arrived with cold wet towels very quickly, and Frank laid them across Sammy's forehead, around his neck, and across his chest.

Then, while Joe went into the sauna to turn off the heat, Frank knelt next to Sammy and bathed his head and limbs with the cold water Joe had brought in a bucket.

In minutes Tomahawk Smith burst into the room, followed by a young black man in a suit who was carrying a medical bag. "I'm Dr. Towner," the man with the bag announced as he knelt beside Sammy. "What happened?"

"He was locked in the sauna with the heat turned up all the way. We don't know for how long," replied Frank.

"I'll need some ice," the doctor said to Tomahawk over his shoulder. "There's a machine down the hall."

The young doctor lifted one of Sammy's eyelids and peered into his eye. "I'll think he'll be okay," the doctor announced. "You did the right thing by cooling him down. Another few minutes and he could've suffered brain damage."

Moments later Tomahawk returned with a bucket filled with ice.

Frank watched as the doctor made compresses with the ice and wet towels and packed them tightly around Sammy's neck and the back of his head. Frank realized that Sammy was in good hands and turned his attention to the sauna.

"I can't shut it off, Frank," Joe said as he

emerged from the sauna red-faced and dripping wet.

"I'll get one of the maintenance guys to trip the circuit breaker for the sauna," the Constrictor volunteered.

"How's Sammy?" Frank asked Dr. Towner.

"His temperature's down, and he's starting to breathe normally. I think he'll be okay," Dr. Towner answered cautiously.

A moment later the Constrictor stuck his head through the sauna room doors and gave the Hardys a thumbs-up sign. "Sauna's off, guys."

"Great, thanks, Ethan," Frank told him.

"Let's see what's wrong with it, Frank," Joe suggested eagerly.

"Hold on," Frank replied. "Let's wait for it to cool down."

Frank waited a few more minutes before he led Joe into the still hot, but now bearable, sauna.

Frank immediately went over to the control panel to check for what temperature Sammy had set on the thermostat. He was surprised to see it set at only ninety degrees. When Frank touched the control knob, it felt wobbly.

"I think the thermostat's been tampered with."

"Can you get the cover panel off?" Joe asked, crowding closer behind his brother.

"I can try." Frank dug his fingernails under the edge of the cover. It pulled right out.

When Frank studied the thermostat mechanism, he saw that it had indeed been tampered with. Someone had jammed the thermostat in the maximum On position. Then the metal post that the control knob was attached to had been broken off.

"Looks like it was ripped out of the wall, then just shoved back in the hole," Frank observed, handing the panel to Joe.

"It's been tampered with, all right," Joe said, looking into the space containing the thermostat mechanism. "The control's been jammed all the way on!"

"Whoever did this had to know Sammy was heading for the sauna," Frank pointed out.

"Disaster and the Romans were in the training center before Sammy went into the sauna. It could have been one of them," Joe speculated.

"They're strong suspects, but we don't have any hard evidence to prove they're involved. We still have lots of investigating to do before we find out who's trying to kill Sammy," said Frank.

"Hey, speaking of Sammy," Joe said, "let's see how he is."

When they emerged from the sauna, they were relieved to see Sammy sitting up, supported by Dr. Towner. Tomahawk Smith had left, but the Constrictor was still standing near the door, watching Sammy with a relieved smile on his face.

"How are you doing, Sammy?" asked Joe.

Sammy smiled weakly. "I'm alive, thanks to you guys."

"If you're feeling better, I'd like to take you to a hospital to be examined," the doctor told Sammy.

"I'm fine, Doc, really," Sammy assured him.

"I don't agree, Sammy. You could have died in there. You're weak and dehydrated," the doctor said.

"You'd better listen to the man, Sammy," the Constrictor mumbled.

"But, Ethan," Sammy interrupted, "you know I've got two important bouts in the next two days. Plus, I have to work on my speech against steroid use. I can't afford to go to the hospital right now."

The young doctor shrugged and closed his medical bag. "All right," he said, sounding resigned. "It's your funeral. But I won't be held responsible for a patient who ignores my advice."

"Don't worry about Sammy, Dr. Towner," Joe put in. "Frank and I will take care of him."

"Make sure he gets plenty of rest and

drinks a lot of water," the doctor instructed before leaving.

"I see you're in good hands, so I guess I'll go finish my workout," the Constrictor said He started to follow the doctor out.

"Oh," Sammy said quietly, "Slim's at the dry cleaner's picking up my costumes. When he gets back, let him know what happened."

"Will do, buddy," the Constrictor said over his shoulder as the door closed.

"Sammy, if you won't go to a hospital, at least let us drive you home," Frank suggested.

"Okay. I just hate hospitals—they give me the creeps," Sammy replied. "But I do feel pretty shaky. It probably would be a good idea to get some rest at home."

Frank dropped Joe off at the garage to pick up Sammy's car on the way to Sammy's house.

"Are you sure you feel good enough to wrestle Tomahawk Smith tomorrow, Sammy?" Frank asked, concerned.

"I have to, Frank. Don't you see, if I have enemies because I'm against steroids, they'll think they've stopped me if I don't wrestle Tomahawk Smith tomorrow or if I don't make my speech before the bout with Disaster on Saturday. I can't allow anyone to stop me!" Sammy declared.

"We're with you Sammy," Frank said.

"Joe and I will do everything we can to protect you and find out who's behind all these 'accidents.' "

They drove in silence the rest of the way to Sammy's house.

"Sammy, do you mind if I raid your refrigerator?" Joe asked as soon as he got back to Sammy's.

"Go ahead," Sammy said. "Get some stuff out for all of us. I'm feeling a little hungry myself."

Frank smiled to himself. That sounded more like the Sammy he knew.

"Sammy, do you remember who was around the sauna before you went in?" Joe asked as he popped a frozen pizza into the microwave.

Sammy scratched his head thoughtfully. "Yeah, I bumped into Major Disaster and Missy in the hall outside."

"Where was Missy? I didn't see her in the gym today," said Joe.

Sammy shrugged. "I think she was meeting with Warfield or something. Anyway, I had words with both of them, and Disaster promised to stomp my tail during Saturday's bout. I told him to give it his best shot, and then I went into the sauna."

"Was anyone else arou—" Frank began.

"Yeah," Sammy replied quickly. "I ran into Victor Roman coming out of the room.

He was in such a hurry he almost knocked me down.''

At the mention of Victor Roman's name, Frank and Joe exchanged looks.

"Did he seem jumpy?" Joe asked.

"Uh-huh," Sammy answered. "But I just thought he was uncomfortable about bumping into me." Suddenly Sammy snapped his fingers as if remembering something. "Excuse me a minute, guys. I'd better check my phone messages before I forget."

Frank followed Sammy out of the kitchen and into the living room. He was relieved to see that Sammy's mood had begun to lighten a bit.

Sammy began to relax as he listened to a few messages from friends, along with a reminder from his agent about a television interview he was scheduled to do after the bout with Major Disaster. Sammy froze, though, as the next message began to play.

The gravelly voice on the tape was unfamiliar to Frank, but the menacing message was all too familiar. "Sammy Rand, you'd better not deliver that antisteroid speech you're planning. If you do, you'll wish you'd never been born!"

77

Chapter

9

THE ANSWERING MACHINE clicked off just as Joe entered with the pizza. He immediately noticed the worried look on Sammy's face.

"What happened?" Joe asked.

"There's a threat against me on my answering machine," Sammy told him.

"Who has your number?" Joe asked, setting down the tray of food.

"Even though my number's unlisted, my agent's got it, and Slim, and Sue, my girlfriend. She's in Europe right now. They have it at IWA headquarters, too," Sammy replied.

"Almost anybody in the IWA would have access to it, then," said Frank.

"Let's play back the message and see if we can get a clue as to who it is," suggested Joe.

78

"Good idea," Frank agreed. He turned to Sammy.

"Do you have a noise reduction system built into your stereo system?" asked Frank.

"Sure do," Sammy replied.

"Good, I want to play with the sound levels on the tape to see if there are any clues in the background noises." Frank popped the incoming-message cassette out of the answering machine.

Then he walked over to the stereo system and slipped the tape into the cassette deck. After it played out, Frank rewound the tape and adjusted the levels on the graphic equalizer.

The message played through several times, with Frank making various adjustments. But no one could pick up anything from the background noises.

"I'm stumped," Joe admitted. "There's nothing on that tape that gives us any idea where that call was made from."

"You're right," Frank said in a discouraged tone. "Do you recognize the voice?"

Sammy shook his head. "My guess is that whoever made the call was disguising his voice."

"With all these threats, Sammy, I think you should try to get Warfield to take them seriously. Make him listen to you!" said Joe.

"Joe's right," Frank agreed. "And if Warfield won't help, then maybe you have to go to the police."

Sammy sat down on the couch and thought for a few moments, pursing his lips. When he looked up at the Hardys, he spoke simply and with great resolve. "I'm still going to make that speech Saturday night, no matter what threats are made."

Frank exchanged a quick look with his brother and slowly shook his head. He knew that Sammy was determined to make his speech, and he also knew Sammy's attacker was just as determined that he wouldn't make it. Frank and Joe had to work quickly to find out who was behind all the attacks on Sammy. The next one might just succeed.

"Sammy, you stay here where you're safe and rest up," Joe said, breaking the silence. "Call Slim or Ethan and get him to come over and keep an eye on you. Frank and I are going over to the IWA office to talk to Warfield about what's been happening. We'll see if we can get the IWA to back you."

Fifteen minutes later Joe and Frank were trying to talk their way into Warfield's office. From the look on the face of Warfield's sour, middle-aged secretary, it was going to be an uphill battle, Joe judged.

"Ma'am, we've got to see Mr. Warfield.

I've already told you it's urgent!'' Frank was saying.

"And I've already told you that you can't get in to see Mr. Warfield without an appointment. He's a very busy man," she replied with a glare.

Just then Warfield's door flew open.

"Mrs. Briggs, I need—"

"Mr. Warfield, we need to speak with you! It's an emergency!" Joe jumped in.

Warfield looked at the Hardys as if noticing them for the first time. "I've seen you two around the gym. Who are you kids?" he asked.

"We're Frank and Joe Hardy," Frank explained. "We're, uh, protégés of Sammy Rand, and we're very concerned about the recent attempts on his life."

"You mean all the accidents Sammy's been staging?" Warfield asked sarcastically.

"This isn't a joking matter, Mr. Warfield," Joe said. "Sammy's life is at stake."

"Okay," he said with resignation, "why don't you step into my office and tell me about it.

"Hold my calls for a few minutes, Mrs. Briggs," Warfield told his secretary as he stepped aside to let Frank and Joe enter before him.

The Hardys sat down on two chairs that faced Warfield's big wooden desk. Frank checked out the office, its walls covered with wrestling posters and framed pictures of various wrestlers.

Warfield sat down behind his desk. "Is this about the thing with the chair and the ammonia in the water bottle?"

"It's more than that now, Mr. Warfield," Joe cut in. "Since then there have been several more attempts on Sammy's life, as you well know. What about the climbing rope that got cut?"

"Or about the attempt to roast Sammy in the sauna?" Frank added.

"Of course I heard about the rope, but he could have cut that himself. My maintenance chief told me about the sauna, but I figured it was just a publicity stunt."

"A publicity stunt!" Joe shouted. "Sammy could have died in that sauna!"

"And if that's true, Mr. Warfield," Frank asked sarcastically, "do you mind telling me how Sammy chained the sauna doors from the outside?"

"Now, w-wait a minute, boys," Warfield sputtered. "I don't know how well you know Sammy, but he's a complete publicity hound. Publicity is the main reason for his antisteroid kick. He's trying to milk it for personal publicity because steroids are in the news now. Next month it'll be something else."

"Haven't you listened to a word we've

said?'' Joe asked. Despite his frustration at Warfield's stubbornness, he tried to keep the anger from creeping into his voice. "Just a little while ago somebody left a message on Sammy's answering machine that threatened him if he went ahead with his speech.''

Warfield dismissed that with a wave of his hand. "So what? Wrestlers are always looking for ways to drum up publicity. A threat on a wrestler is always good for a few lines in the evening paper or a mention on the TV news. The fans eat this stuff up, boys.''

"Does this mean you're not going to do anything about the attempts on Sammy's life?'' Frank demanded.

"I don't believe that Sammy's in serious danger,'' Warfield said smugly. "If you can give me some real proof that his life is being threatened, then I'll have the IWA investigate. Until then, don't waste my time. I've really got better things to do, like promoting wrestling through legitimate channels.''

With that, Warfield stood up and showed the Hardys out. Frank and Joe reluctantly left his office.

"That was a waste of time,'' Joe said, feeling angry at the way Warfield had dismissed them.

"I can't understand it,'' Frank commented. "It's almost as if Warfield wanted something to happen to Sammy.''

"I'll say. He sure didn't seem too concerned about the welfare of the man who's the IWA's biggest drawing card," Frank said as they walked down the hall toward the lobby.

"He seemed to believe that everything that's happened to Sammy is just for publicity," Joe pointed out. He stopped walking as a sudden thought struck him.

"Okay, Joe, I know that look. What are you thinking?"

Joe paused for a moment before answering.

"It just hit me—Warfield seems so unconcerned about Sammy's safety, yet he's very concerned about publicity. Could it be possible that Warfield's behind these assaults on Sammy? Maybe he's doing it to hype interest in Sammy's next matches."

"If that's true, then there might be some people in the IWA who have similar stories about Warfield," Frank pointed out. "Let's go back to Sammy's place and check out that idea with him."

Joe agreed, knowing now that they would get little help from Warfield or the IWA in protecting Sammy.

The next morning was bright and hot, and Joe and Frank rose early. Over a quick breakfast of pancakes and eggs, the duo discussed the next stage of the investigation. Sammy had been asleep when they got back the day before, and they hadn't wanted to disturb him.

"What do you think about the possibility of Warfield being behind your accidents? He seems pretty bent on the publicity angle. Do you think he could be doing this to you to drum up publicity for the IWA?" asked Frank.

"I never thought of Warfield as a suspect," Sammy said, "but what you're saying does make sense. I guess we should keep our eyes on him."

"That's a good idea, Sammy. I also think Frank and I should go back to Walsh's office to see if we can establish a solid connection between him and Disaster," Joe suggested. "After that message on your phone machine, I feel Walsh and Disaster could be up to something."

"You may be right, Joe," Sammy agreed. "Put those two sleazebags together, and they're capable of anything. Go, check them out with my blessings."

"We'll catch up with you later at the training center," said Frank.

"Okay. Good luck, guys. And be careful."

An hour later Frank directed Joe to turn into the parking lot next to Walsh's office.

"Are you sure this is the right place?" Joe asked skeptically, studying the building and the surrounding neighborhood with obvious distaste.

"Yep. Here's the plan," Frank said as they climbed out of the van. "We'll say we're novice wrestlers who want to see Walsh. Then, if we can get in to see him—"

"We'll try to get some proof that he's supplying steroids," Joe finished excitedly.

"You got it," Frank agreed as they entered the run-down office building. "If we can get Walsh for supplying steroids, then maybe we can tie him to Disaster and the attacks on Sammy."

They passed through the building's dingy lobby and down the narrow hallway that led to Walsh's office. Joe opened the door to Dr. Walsh's office and stepped through the doorway into a small reception room.

Joe noticed a small receptionist's window in the corner and went over to it, with Frank following.

"Hi! We're here to see Dr. Walsh," Joe said brightly to the young nurse with bleached-blond hair.

She gazed back at Joe suspiciously. "Do you have an appointment?" she asked coldly.

"Uh, no, we don't," Joe replied. "But we're from the IWA, and, uh, some of the other wrestlers said that Walsh is the man to see."

"What, precisely, is wrong?" the nurse

asked. Joe noticed that she seemed to perk up at the mention of the IWA.

"We're feeling kind of run-down, miss," Frank interjected. "We thought maybe Dr. Walsh could give us some kind of tonic or vitamins to pick us up."

The young nurse looked doubtful. "Well, he doesn't usually see new patients without an appointment—"

"But we're wrestlers," Joe insisted. "I thought Dr. Walsh specialized in wrestlers."

The nurse looked a little uncertain. "I guess it'll be okay. Why don't you go into the examining room and wait for the doctor."

The nurse led Frank and Joe down a dingy hallway to the examining room.

"Well, what do you think?" Frank asked as soon as they were alone. "Should we do a little snooping?"

"I'm right behind you," replied Joe.

Frank walked across the black- and white-tiled floor to a set of cabinets.

Just as Frank suspected, they were locked. "This won't stop me," Frank said as he pulled a lock pick from his wallet.

Frank pulled the first cabinet open, and he and Joe began to examine the boxes of prescription medicines and various medical implements.

"Find any steroids?" asked Frank.

Joe glanced over at the garbage can and got an idea. "I'll check in here, Frank." Joe lifted the lid and carefully began to go through its contents. After a moment he spotted a small white box labeled Anabolic Steroids and grabbed it.

"Frank, I've got it," he said excitedly.

Suddenly Joe froze as he heard a man's voice loudly demanding to see Walsh immediately. He shoved the steroid box into his pocket.

"I'm sorry, Mr. Stone, Dr. Walsh isn't in right now, but if you could have a seat . . ." Joe heard the young nurse say in a flustered voice.

"And I think you're lying, little lady! I think that sleazy pill pusher's hiding in his office, 'cause I heard you talking to someone as I came in."

Joe heard footsteps rapidly approaching their door. He quickly scanned the small room for another way out, but there was only one door into the room.

Joe and Frank turned to the door just as it flew open. There stood Major Disaster, his huge form filling the doorway. When his gaze fell on Frank, his ugly face turned red with rage.

"I told you I'd take care of you if I saw you here again," Disaster said as he stepped toward Frank, wearing a deadly expression.

Chapter
10

"THIS IS THE SECOND TIME I've caught you here, kid!" Disaster snarled at Frank. "Didn't I tell you not to come back?" Disaster took a step closer to Frank.

"Hey, wait a minute! I can explain, Major!" Frank replied quickly.

"Yeah, what's your story this time?" Disaster took a step closer to Frank.

"You see, Major, I wasn't exactly truthful when you found me outside the office before." Frank tried to look sincere. He shot a look at Joe to make sure he'd play along. Joe met his eye and gave a slight nod.

"Yeah, I thought you were giving me the runaround," Disaster growled.

"The fact is, I wasn't feeling too well, and I thought Dr. Walsh could—"

The rest of Frank's words were drowned out by the arrival of Dr. Walsh.

"What's the meaning of this ruckus in my office?" Walsh shouted as he barged into the small examining room.

Frank took Walsh's appearance in at a glance. Walsh was a pot-bellied, round-shouldered man with thinning blond hair and a wispy blond mustache on his upper lip. He wore black-rimmed glasses with thick lenses. Behind his thick lenses, his pale blue eyes were small and beady. Frank disliked him immediately.

"It's easy to explain, Doctor," Joe said quickly. "My brother and I were waiting here to see you, when this guy came in and accosted us."

"You're not patients of mine," Walsh snapped. He peered at them suspiciously through his thick glasses. "What are you doing here?"

"Uh, well, the fact is, Doctor," Frank said, pretending to fumble with his words as he improvised his story, "Joe and I came to you on the advice of the Roman brothers."

"You see, we're wrestlers, Doc," Joe interjected. "The Romans said if we wanted to get bulked up quick, you were the man to see."

Frank saw Walsh's small eyes narrow even further. "I don't know what you're talking about. If you want to see me, you call me and make an appointment."

Frank acted disappointed. "Gee, Dr. Walsh, we were sort of hoping we could see you today before we went back to our training."

"You heard the man, make an appointment," Disaster growled in a low voice. "Now get out!"

Not wanting to anger Disaster any more, Frank and Joe left the examining room.

As they made an appointment with Walsh's nurse, Frank heard Disaster shouting angrily, "I'm a two-time loser, Doc. If they catch me doing what you've asked me to do, I might get into deep, deep trouble!" Walsh's reply was inaudible. The Hardys exchanged looks, and then left the office.

"Should we tell Sammy what we found at Walsh's office?" Joe asked when they reached the lobby.

"I want to do a little more snooping first," Frank said in a low voice. "Come on." He led Joe out of the building and cautiously went around to the rear of the building, where he spied a rusting Dumpster.

"Keep an eye out for Walsh and Disaster." Frank climbed up and leaned into the Dumpster, where he began sorting through its contents.

"Anything interesting?" Joe asked when Frank came up for air.

"I want more than just one steroid box as evidence. If we can find a bunch, we have a much better case against Walsh."

Frank leaned into the next Dumpster and began digging through it rapidly. After a few moments he emerged with a small cardboard box full of empty steroid ampules. "Bingo! I hit the jackpot!" Frank said excitedly. "Look!" He pointed to Walsh's name and office address on the box, which also bore the return address of the manufacturer.

"That's great!" Joe replied. "I don't see how a legitimate doctor could be giving out steroids in this quantity."

Frank turned back to the Dumpster. "I want to see if I can find out who else Walsh is giving steroids to. Maybe I can find some old prescription forms or something."

He spent several minutes digging through the rest of the garbage before coming up with some dog-eared sheets of typing paper covered with names.

"What have you got now, Frank?" Joe asked.

"I think it's a list of Walsh's patients," Frank said after examining it.

"Look here," Frank said, indicating a note from Walsh scrawled in the margin that read: "Sue, please update the names and addresses of all current patients. J.W."

"Great work, Frank. Let's cross-check this

list of patients against a list of IWA wrestlers and see how many of them are seeing Walsh."

"My thinking exactly," Frank agreed. He looked up and down the alley. "If the coast is clear, let's get back to the van and go see Sammy."

As they drove to the training center, Joe turned to Frank and asked, "We know now that Walsh and Disaster are connected, but where do you think Missy fits in?"

"She's his manager, Joe. If Disaster's trying to kill Sammy, then Missy's probably involved, too."

"I sure hope not," Joe said bleakly.

When the Hardys returned to the IWA gym, they found a worried Sammy and Slim in the weight room.

"More trouble," Sammy greeted them.

"What happened now?" Joe asked.

"Sammy found a threatening note under the door of his dressing room when he came in this morning," Slim said glumly.

"Where is it?" Frank asked quickly.

"In my gym bag," replied Sammy.

Joe stepped over to Sammy's gym bag to retrieve the note. The note was hastily scribbled in pencil on coarse white paper.

It read: "Sammy Rand, if you make your speech on Saturday, you won't live to regret it. Don't make the speech! You have been warned!''

There was no signature, but a tiny grinning skull had been pasted to the bottom of the note.

"Do you think there's any point in showing this note to Warfield?'' Joe asked.

Sammy rolled his eyes. "You've talked to the man—what do you think? Every time I've mentioned anything to him about the threats, he just tells me I'm making them up for the publicity.''

"Maybe if we can show Warfield that a sizable number of IWA wrestlers are using Walsh's steroids, he'll get involved,'' Frank observed. "In the meantime, we can send out the note to have the handwriting analyzed.''

"I want you guys to stick close to me,'' Sammy told them. "I have a feeling that they're going to try something at tonight's bout.''

They went back to Sammy's dressing room, and Joe and Sammy cross-checked the list of Walsh's patients against a list of IWA wrestlers. Frank got on the phone to his father and arranged to have the handwriting in the note analyzed by an expert.

When he got off the phone, Frank found Joe and Sammy still poring over the list of Walsh's patients. They both looked deadly serious.

"We found at least six IWA wrestlers besides Disaster on Walsh's patient list," Joe told him.

"There's the Roman brothers, Baron Von Krupp, the Chain Gang tag team, and Pit Bull Parker," Sammy said.

"That's some roster," Frank commented. "Do you want to go to Warfield with this information?"

Sammy glanced at his watch. "It'll have to wait, Frank. I've got to rest for the match tonight. I'm still worn-out from yesterday."

That evening, as the trio drove up to the big covered arena, Frank noticed that the parking lot was filling up fast. Hordes of people were streaming through the main door of the arena, and the atmosphere was electric. People were milling about, obviously eager to see their favorite wrestlers in action.

Frank read the huge banner that hung over the entrance to the arena: IWA Wrestling Tonight! Sammy the "Kung Fu King" Rand vs. Tomahawk Smith. Major Disaster vs. Curious Cat. Tag-Team Action: The Romans vs. The Chain Gang.

Joe drove the van around to the entrance for wrestlers, and they all piled out.

Sammy went straight to the dressing room set aside for the good guys and quickly changed. Frank and Joe waited outside in the hallway. Frank scanned the bustling passageway for any signs of danger, but he didn't sense any threat to Sammy among the wrestlers, managers, trainers, and reporters who streamed past.

Sammy emerged fifteen minutes later, clad in his wrestling costume. His gold lamé karate jacket gleamed under the fluorescent lights in the hallway. Sammy was smiling broadly, but Frank could tell that the big wrestler was nervous. A reporter, notebook in hand, came over to Sammy, but Slim waved him off. "See him after the match, huh, George?"

Joe noticed how worried Sammy was, too. "Don't worry about a thing, Sammy. Anybody who tries to get at you tonight will have to come through us first."

"Thanks, Joe. I'm glad you guys are around tonight."

The bout preceding Sammy's still had a few minutes remaining. Frank and Joe got the satisfaction of seeing Major Disaster being dropped to the floor in a full body slam. A few seconds later the Major was pinned. The Major got up and shook his fist at his opponent, vowing vengeance the next time they met.

"You're up, kid," Slim told Sammy.

"Let's do it," Sammy replied, and began walking down the aisle toward the ring.

The crowd roared as Sammy entered the arena. Frank saw that almost every person in the packed arena was standing and cheering as Sammy walked up the aisle.

A group of elderly women in outfits like Sammy's leaned over the barriers along the aisle to touch Sammy and wish him luck. Smiling, Sammy went over to the group, kissed some of them, and then continued on his way to the ring followed by Slim.

Smiling and waving with both hands, Sammy walked up to the ring, then climbed through the ropes that the referee held open for him. As he stepped into the center of the ring, the tuxedoed announcer grabbed a microphone suspended just over his head. His deep voice boomed over the arena's loudspeakers: "And now we proudly present the Heavyweight Champion of the IWA, Sammy the 'Kung Fu King' Rand!"

At this announcement the cheering from the crowd became even louder and more frenzied. Chants of "Sam-my! Sam-my!" rang out and echoed back and forth under the big domed roof.

The announcer next called out Tomahawk Smith's name as Sammy's challenger, and the tall wrestler stalked toward the ring from the bad guys' dressing room on the opposite side of the arena.

Frank saw that Smith's elaborate costume included fringed buckskin pants and a quill vest. Tomahawk gave a shrill cry and shook his tomahawk at the fans who were jeering him.

Glancing past Tomahawk, Frank suddenly noticed two oddly familiar faces in the crowd. He realized they were Daniel East and the Living Weapon. Frank wondered what they were doing there, then decided they must be checking out the competition.

Frank's attention was suddenly distracted from East and the Weapon by an ominous creaking sound. He looked around to find its source, and realized it was coming from above.

The creaking grew louder and louder. Frank looked up. The sound was coming from the huge, two-sided scoreboard that hung across the ring—it was hanging by only one corner!

Oblivious to the danger, Sammy was standing directly beneath the scoreboard, smiling and waving to his fans. In the next few seconds Sammy could be crushed!

Chapter

11

"SAMMY, WATCH OUT! The scoreboard's about to fall!" Frank ran to the edge of the ring.

The sound of screeching metal cut through the noise in the crowded arena. The audience's cheers had turned into screams. Joe looked up and saw the scoreboard swaying now by its single corner.

Joe immediately sprang into action. He, too, charged toward the ring. Joe knew that Sammy, the announcer, and the referee were in grave danger. They obviously didn't understand why everyone was screaming at them. The warnings must have sounded like just more noise.

In the next instant Frank slipped through

the ropes and physically knocked Sammy aside. They tumbled through the ropes.

Meanwhile, Joe had grabbed the referee and announcer and hauled them out of the ring.

A mere second after everyone was safe, the scoreboard tore loose. Frank cringed as the board slammed into the center of the ring, caving in a spot right where Sammy had been standing.

Joe stared at the scoreboard, which was sticking out of the canvas floor of the ring at a crazy angle. Then he glanced over at Sammy, who was sitting on the floor of the arena, cradling his right arm.

"Sammy, are you hurt?" asked Joe.

"No, not bad," Sammy replied, "but when Frank knocked me out of the way, I landed on my elbow. I think it's sprained."

The short, mustached referee appeared at the side of the ring. "Sammy, are you okay?"

Grimacing, Sammy shook his head. "Not really. It's my elbow. I can't wrestle tonight."

"The match is canceled anyway," the referee replied. "Nobody can wrestle in this mess," he said, gesturing toward the ring.

While Slim hovered anxiously in the background, Joe and Frank helped Sammy up and led him down the aisle. Joe noticed Stanley Warfield standing in front of the crowd.

"Still think Sammy's pulling publicity stunts, Mr. Warfield?"

"Nope," Warfield replied grimly, then he fell into step behind Sammy, Slim, and the Hardys.

Despite the pain he was in, Sammy managed to wave to the fans as he trudged up to the locker room door. The fans responded with loud cheering and applause.

Even before the Hardys got Sammy back to his dressing room, gray-uniformed maintenance men had begun to clear away the scoreboard.

Back in Sammy's dressing room Warfield took the Hardys aside while Dr. Towner and Slim examined Sammy's sprained elbow.

"Look, fellows," Warfield said, "I'm sorry I didn't believe you before about the attempts on Sammy. I'll do anything I can to help you catch the people responsible for these attacks."

"Thanks, Mr. Warfield," Frank said. "We'll let you know what you can do."

After Warfield left, Joe turned to Frank and shot him a questioning look. "Think we can trust him, Frank?" Joe asked in a low voice.

"Maybe, maybe not," Frank replied with a shrug. "We'll have to see how cooperative he is about protecting Sammy. In the meantime, let's check out the cables that held the scoreboard before the police get here."

"Sammy, can we leave you for a few minutes?" asked Joe.

"Sure, guys. I'll be okay. It's just a sprain—it

could have been a lot worse," Sammy said, taking a deep breath.

Frank and Joe left Sammy's dressing room and walked down the hall to a service elevator that went to the upper levels of the arena.

"These attacks on Sammy are getting more and more dangerous. A couple of seconds more and it would have been goodbye, Sammy," Frank said as the elevator doors slid shut.

Joe nodded. "Let's hope we can find some kind of a clue this time. So far we're just shooting in the dark."

They stepped out of the elevator, and Joe saw that a small maintenance catwalk had been lowered from the arena ceiling. Two electricians were working on a circuit breaker box on the other side of the dome. Joe and Frank walked around the curving gallery that hugged the arena wall just below the ceiling until they came to the end of the catwalk.

It swayed slightly when Joe took his first step on it, but it seemed sturdy enough. Joe and Frank moved cautiously out to the scoreboard's support cables, which were dangling from the center of the ceiling.

Joe grabbed the cable nearest him and examined the end. He saw that it had been partially sawed through—probably with a hacksaw.

"Frank, this one's been cut!" he said excitedly.

"So's this one!" Frank replied, examining the other cable. "Looks like it was sawed partway through, then gravity did the rest."

"Yeah, that's what I think," Joe echoed. "And whoever did this must be getting pretty desperate to stop Sammy. If that scoreboard had fallen slightly askew, it could have landed in the audience."

Frank stared down at the arena below. The disappointed fans were filing out through the exits. "That could have been a catastrophe. Who knows how many people would have been hurt.

"But what we have to keep in mind," Frank continued, "is that the scoreboard didn't land in the audience. Whoever did this knew exactly what he or she was doing. And that was to try to kill Sammy!"

The Hardys finished their examination of the cables and went back along the catwalk to the gallery just as the police flooded into the building. On the way back to the elevator Joe spotted something small and metallic gleaming on the floor.

"Hey, what's this?" he asked, bending over to pick it up. Holding it up to the light, he saw that it was a platinum lapel pin embossed with the logo of the East Broadcasting Corporation.

"What do you make of this, Frank?" Joe asked as he handed the pin to his brother.

Frank studied the pin. "EBC. Hmmm. Hey, I saw a pin just like this on East's lapel two days ago. We might be stuck with a new mystery here. These attacks on Sammy may not have anything to do with his antisteroid campaign."

"I don't follow you. Who else could be behind the attacks?"

"Daniel East, president of EBC," Frank said. "Remember what Sammy told us about East trying to get him to switch to the wrestling conference he broadcasts the meets for and the threats he made?"

"Oh, yeah!" Joe said, his face lighting up. "I got so involved in the steroid angle, I forgot that. Maybe these attacks are East's way of getting revenge on Sammy. Chet Morton told me that up until Sammy came along, the NAAW was bigger than the IWA."

"Maybe East is crazy enough or desperate enough to think that eliminating Sammy would put his wrestling conference back on top," Frank speculated.

"Let's go back to Sammy's place and show this pin to him," Frank said, heading for the elevator. "It's too late to visit the EBC now, but we can go there first thing in the morning."

"We should use our cover as young wrestlers to get in the door at the EBC," Joe suggested the next morning as they drove along the highway toward the EBC's headquarters.

Frank parked the van in front of a tall, black-glass office building. The sign on the lawn outside read East Broadcasting Corporation.

Inside the lobby of the building Frank scanned the directory. After a minute he determined that they should head to the fourth floor.

As soon as they stepped off the elevator, they were greeted by a pretty young receptionist who was sitting behind a sliding glass window.

"Hi, can I help you gentlemen?" she asked brightly.

"I sure hope so," Joe said, flashing his most charming smile. "We're wrestlers, and we'd like to speak with your wrestling programmer about signing on with the EBC."

"Wrestlers, huh?" The pretty receptionist smiled. "Who are you? Maybe I've heard of you."

"We're pretty new at the game," Frank answered, smiling. "I'm Frank Hardy, and this is my brother Joe. We call ourselves the, er, American Flyers."

"You'll want to speak to Miss Greta Yothers. I'll buzz her office and see if she's free." The receptionist spoke quietly into her phone, then told the Hardys, "She'll see you now.

Her office is the third one down on the right.''

"So far so good," Joe whispered as they walked toward Miss Yothers's office. The EBC offices hadn't been maintained very well for the past several years, Joe noted to himself. The walls needed painting and the carpeting was worn. Overhead, several fluorescent tubes had burned out and hadn't been replaced.

At Greta Yothers's office they knocked on the door. "Come on in," Joe heard a female voice call. The woman who asked them in was plump and in her late forties, with frosted blond hair and square-framed glasses.

"Hi, Miss Yothers, we're the American Flyers," Joe said, extending his hand to her.

"What can I do for you?" Greta Yothers replied, shaking hands with both of them.

"We were hoping the EBC would sign us on for their wrestling show," Frank quickly told her.

Miss Yothers's expression was very doubtful. "Well, business is a little slow right now, so we're sticking with proven commodities like the Living Weapon, Smash Bradley, and Firehouse Taylor."

"But wait till you get a load of our act," Joe insisted. He walked away from Frank a few steps, then faced him, holding his hands together in a stirrup at waist level. "Let's show her, Frank," Joe prompted. "Alley oop!"

Frank stepped back a pace, then ran forward, putting his left foot in Joe's joined hands. Joe smoothly tossed Frank up in the air, and he did a tight flip just below the ceiling.

But when he landed, Frank's foot slammed into a small coffee table, tipping it up and catapulting a heavy onyx ashtray through the air. It narrowly missed Miss Yothers's head, but it did crash through the window behind her.

"All right! I've seen enough! Get out of here!" she shouted angrily, pointing toward her door.

Miss Yothers furiously punched a button on her intercom. "Security!" she shouted into it. "Come to my office immediately!"

In seconds a broad-chested guard filled her doorway.

"Okay, let's go," the man said in a hard voice.

As Joe stepped out into the hall, he looked past the hulking security guard to the office at the end of the hall. A sign next to it identified it as Daniel East's office. The door was open and he could see East sitting behind his desk. East raised his eyes, and when he saw the Hardys he did a double take, and then he looked surprised.

It was obvious to Joe that East recognized

them. But why does he look so guilty? Joe wondered.

In the next instant the other two people in the room turned, too, and Joe saw they were the Roman brothers. They, too, were obviously shocked to see the Hardys.

"Let's go! Let's go!" the security guard shouted, pushing them down the hall.

As soon as the elevator door slid closed, Joe turned to his brother.

"Frank, did you notice East's expression?"

"Yes," Frank answered tightly. "He sure looked guilty."

"What do you think the Romans were doing there?" Joe asked. "I thought they had left East's wrestling conference to join the IWA."

"Maybe that's what we're supposed to think. Maybe the Romans are still working with East—undercover," Frank speculated.

"If the Romans are working for East, maybe they're the ones who've been trying to kill Sammy," Frank said as they stepped outside.

Passing a service alley next to the EBC building, Frank was suddenly grabbed and dragged into an alley. When Joe turned, he saw his brother struggling with a man in a ski mask.

But before Joe could even make a move to come to Frank's aid, a fist connected with his jaw. As Joe staggered around, he heard a gunshot echo deafeningly in the alley!

Chapter

12

THE BULLET MISSED Frank's ear by an inch.
After it whizzed by, he shot out with his foot
and knocked the gun out of the masked man's
hand. He was on it in a second and kicked it
behind a row of garbage cans.

The gunman didn't give up. He ran and
butted his head into Frank's stomach, driving
Frank back against the brick wall.

"Yow!" Frank cried, shaking his head to
clear it. He countered with a karate chop to
the gunman's neck.

"Oof!" the man grunted, but he quickly
recovered to deliver a sharp punch to Frank's
midsection again.

Frank momentarily lost his breath and doubled over in pain. The assailant moved in for
the kill, and Frank waited for the perfect

moment to raise an elbow and catch the masked man in his windpipe. The gunman dropped to the ground and lay there like a sack of potatoes.

"Well, that's one down," said Frank.

Frank checked Joe to see if he needed any help. Joe was struggling against another masked assailant, who had him immobilized in a headlock. Just as Frank stepped forward to come to his brother's aid, Joe stomped down hard on his opponent's instep and followed up with a quick karate chop to his side.

Howling with pain, the man released his grip on Joe, who immediately spun away. Then Joe's attacker turned to face Joe again.

Frank started off to help Joe, but was knocked off his feet by the recovered gunman. Frank smashed against the wall with his shoulder and soon felt himself sliding to the ground.

I guess he really wasn't out, Frank thought, reaching back to rub his shoulder in pain.

Seeing Frank on the ground, the gunman raised his foot to kick Frank in the face. But Frank shot out his hand and grabbed the guy's ankle. In an instant Frank pulled the thug's foot out from under him, and the man crashed to the ground, hitting his head.

"This time it doesn't look like you'll get up so quickly!" Frank said to his downed opponent.

Meanwhile, Joe's opponent looked over and

saw his partner on the ground. He left Joe and ran up to him. With strength and speed Joe hadn't thought possible, the thug scooped up his partner and sprinted down the alley toward the next street with his accomplice over his shoulder.

As Frank was getting up, Joe walked over and gave him a hand.

"Can you walk, Frank?" asked Joe.

Frank slowly brushed himself off. "Yeah, I'm okay," he said.

"Then let's go after them!" Joe insisted.

Joe ran down the alley at full speed after their attackers, with Frank following close on his heels.

Joe reached the mouth of the alley and checked in both directions down the next street. When Frank saw Joe punch the wall in frustration, he knew they had lost the two men.

Frank trotted up behind his brother. "No sign of them?"

"Nope. We lost them," replied Joe.

"Before we go back to the van and take care of our war wounds, let's find that gun," suggested Frank.

"Since those thugs got away, it might be the only clue we've got," replied Joe.

Remembering where he had kicked the gun, Frank led Joe back to the row of garbage cans. The Hardys began pulling them away from the alley wall until Joe spotted the gun on the ground.

"Got it!" Joe shouted as he scooped up the snub-nosed revolver.

"Has the serial number been filed off?" Frank asked.

"Nope," Joe replied, holding the gun out for Frank to examine.

"Great! This might be our first real break in this case," Frank said enthusiastically.

"Unless it's stolen," Joe pointed out. "Still, let's give it a try and call Dad with the serial number. Maybe he can track down the owner."

The cuts and bruises from their fight momentarily forgotten, the Hardys took off for their van.

"Are you sure, Dad?" Frank asked eagerly. "Great! Thanks a million. Yeah, we'll tell you all about it when we come home."

"Sounds like good news," Joe ventured.

"It is. Dad traced the serial number for us. It's registered to Daniel East, *and* it was never reported stolen."

"Well, now we have two pretty solid clues that connect East to this case," Joe said. "First we find an EBC lapel pin lying near the cut cables at the arena. Now we find out that the gun those two thugs tried to permanently silence us with belongs to him.

112

"I wouldn't be surprised if those two thugs we just fought were the Romans. They would have had time to get down here," Joe continued.

"Well, since those guys did get away, we don't know for sure, unfortunately," Frank pointed out. "Though their style of fighting did remind me of the Romans."

Frank was silent for a moment.

"Joe, do you remember when East showed up at the IWA gym with the Living Weapon?"

"Sure. Why?"

"We also saw the Weapon at the arena last night before the scoreboard fell. Since the Romans were wrestling, they couldn't have gotten to the scoreboard without attracting attention, so maybe the Weapon was the one who sabotaged the cables," Frank speculated.

"That makes sense," Joe agreed. "The Weapon's strong and fast enough to shinny up those cables and saw them partway through, then come back down and join East before the scoreboard falls."

"Our evidence definitely is pointing at East as the source of the attacks on Sammy," Frank concluded.

Joe nodded. "I agree. Now we need to know East's motive."

"Let's do a financial check on his company. It might be interesting to see how he's doing."

* * *

An hour later Frank was at his computer in Sammy's house, tapping into the network that supplied financial information on American companies for potential investors.

"Well, what kind of shape are East's holdings in?" Joe asked impatiently. "You know I can't read this stock market gibberish."

Frank smiled at his brother. "Wait a second and I'll call up an investor's newsletter that specializes in media companies. It ought to have a rundown on the performance of all of East's holdings for the last year or so."

Frank's fingers flew across the keyboard, and in moments dense columns of type scrolled down the screen. Both Hardys read in silence for several minutes, mentally digesting a large amount of information.

At length Joe broke the silence. "Frank, if I understand this correctly, both the EBC and the NAAW are on the verge of filing for bankruptcy. They're both heavily in debt.

"Remember how Sammy told us that East wanted to sell out to Warfield, and Warfield turned him down? I bet East plans on killing two birds with one stone. He gets revenge on Sammy for turning down an NAAW contract, and he eliminates him so he won't be overshadowing the NAAW wrestlers!"

Chapter

13

LATER THAT DAY, with Sammy working out at the IWA gym and Frank out, Joe thought Sammy's house was too quiet. But as he paced up and down Sammy's living room, he had to admit he was glad to have a little time to himself to sort out the flood of information they had unearthed in the last few days.

Just then the doorbell rang. Joe was surprised to find Stanley Warfield waiting on the front step.

"Mr. Warfield, what are you doing here?" Joe asked.

"I wanted to talk to you and your brother in private about these threats to Sammy."

"I'm glad you finally do believe the threats are real." Joe led Warfield into the living room.

Warfield shrugged. "I'm sorry I was so skeptical, but I've seen wrestlers pull every kind of stunt imaginable just to get publicity. One year Baron Von Krupp staged his own kidnapping to get on the front page of the papers. The FBI was called in, and it was a real mess."

Looking a little sheepish, Warfield added, "To be honest, this steroid campaign of Sammy's has been getting so much press, I felt as if he were stealing my thunder. Maybe that's why I was reluctant to take the threats seriously. Until that scoreboard fell," Warfield added, "I was sure Sammy was behind all this stuff.

"Sammy's pulled some wild publicity stunts, like the time he parachuted to a bout at the L.A. Coliseum, but I've never known him to do anything to endanger anyone's life."

"Well, the important thing is that you now believe someone's trying to kill Sammy," said Joe.

"That I do," Warfield agreed. "After thinking all night about the scoreboard incident, I'm convinced that someone is out to get him."

"Then we can really depend on your cooperation in clearing this up?" asked Joe.

Warfield nodded. "Absolutely. I'll do whatever I can to protect Sammy."

"Good. So far we've come up with a few suspects within the IWA—Major Disaster, Missy Mayflower, and the Romans," Joe replied.

"Disaster?" Warfield said in surprise. "I know there's no love lost between him and Sammy, but I never thought Fred would try to kill him."

"We've learned the Major's been arrested for attempted murder and has a prison record," Joe pointed out. "Did you know Disaster goes to a doctor who may be supplying him with steroids?"

"If the Major's using steroids, he'll be out. That's a pretty serious charge to make with no proof," Warfield said solemnly.

"We've got proof." Joe walked over to retrieve the steroid packages and Walsh's list of patients from the carton of evidence they'd collected so far. Also in the carton were the cassette, the damaged thermostat, the pistol, and the printouts of the information on East's companies, as well as Disaster's rap sheet and Missy's police record. Joe considered showing Warfield the other evidence, but a nagging doubt about Warfield's true motives made him cautious.

"This looks serious," Warfield agreed after examining the patient list and steroid box. "I want to get back to the office and contact the IWA board of directors about this. I'm sure they'll want to take some disciplinary action against Disaster. And while I'm at it, I'm going to contact the American Medical Association about this Dr. Walsh.''

Warfield shook hands with Joe, then let himself out.

Half an hour later Frank returned with a handwriting analysis of the threatening note. He was also carrying a pizza.

"What's the verdict on that note?" Joe asked, hungrily digging into the pie.

"The analysts compared it with Disaster's signature on the rap sheet I sent them, and they say the handwritings are a match."

"Well, this complicates things," Joe pointed out. "Do you think Disaster's working with East?"

"No, I don't. I think East is behind the murder attempts on Sammy, with the Romans and maybe the Living Weapon helping him.

"We only have concrete proof linking Disaster to the threats against Sammy, not the murder attempts. It's possible he's just working with Walsh to make Sammy lay off steroid users."

"So maybe your theory about Sammy being under attack from two groups at once is correct," Joe speculated. "Maybe the threats and murder attempts are unrelated."

"But we can't cross Missy off our list of

suspects just yet," Frank added. "Don't forget about the chair incident or the big knife you found in her purse. Sammy also saw her and Disaster near the sauna before he got roasted."

"I can't shake the feeling that those things are just circumstantial. I'm sure Missy is innocent," Joe said.

"Well, if you're that sure, then there's only one thing to do," Frank said. "Confront Missy directly with our evidence and get her story."

"I'm for that," Joe replied, wolfing down another slice of pizza. "It's pretty late now. Let's turn in and go see her tomorrow."

The next morning Sammy left early to tape a public service announcement against steroid use. He left a note for the Hardys saying that he'd meet them later at the gym. After a quick breakfast Frank and Joe headed over to the Mayflower mansion.

Joe steered the van through the wrought-iron gates and up the driveway, stopping near the front door.

The Hardys walked up the mansion's front steps, and Joe rang the ornate bell beside the front door. After a moment the front door was swung open by Missy.

"Hi, Joe," she said in a friendly voice. "What are you doing here?"

"I need to talk to you, Missy," he said seriously. "It's about all the accidents that have been happening to Sammy Rand."

"I don't care what happens to Sammy. He ruined my brother's career."

"Please, Missy," Joe said. "This is really important."

Missy stepped aside and ushered the Hardys inside. Joe briefly introduced Frank as Missy led them into the library.

"We can talk in here. Dad and Mitch are out back doing some skeet shooting," Missy explained.

Joe met her gaze and felt distinctly uncomfortable. "Well, I guess there's no nice way to ask this, but here goes. Have you had anything to do with any of Sammy's 'accidents'?"

"What? You mean that time with the chair?" Missy asked.

"That's one of the incidents," Frank put in. "Do you have an explanation for that?"

"Sure," Missy responded. "I didn't know the chair I gave the Major wasn't a breakaway. Victor Roman handed it to me."

"Oh, really?" said Joe.

"I had no idea Sammy was going to get hurt so badly. I felt awful about it, though I never said anything to Sammy because of the bad blood between us."

"Okay, that makes sense," Frank agreed. "But what about the knife Joe saw in your purse the night someone sawed through the climbing rope Sammy was using?"

Missy glared at Joe. "I wasn't aware that rifling through a lady's purse is among your habits. That's pretty sleazy."

"Ordinarily I don't. But I felt my friend's life was in danger," Joe explained.

Ignoring Joe, she stared at Frank.

"I can explain what the knife was doing in my purse. It's a birthday present for my dad for his weapons collection."

"But you and Disaster were in that room before the rope was cut," Frank pointed out.

"We weren't the last ones. The Romans were in there after us. Look, I'll take a lie detector test and swear that neither of us touched that rope," Missy stated. "We only ducked into that room for a few minutes to talk about business."

"There's something else about Disaster that needs to be addressed," Frank told her seriously. "Do you know he's been seeing a doctor who gives steroids to wrestlers?"

"Steroids?" Missy said in surprise. "I don't know anything about that."

"I talked to Stanley Warfield today, and he's checking into it," Joe said.

"We first suspected that you and Disaster might be involved in a vendetta against Sammy. Disaster because of his antisteroid campaign, and you because you hate him for hurting Mitch," Joe explained.

"If Warfield wants to clean up steroid use in the IWA, then I'm all for it, even if Sammy's spearheading the campaign," Missy said decisively.

"But what about the Major?" asked Joe.

"If he's violating IWA rules, then I won't help him," Missy replied. "Rules are rules. Let me know if there's anything I can do to help you protect Sammy. I don't know if I'll ever forgive him for hurting Mitch, but I'd like to make up for the chair incident."

"Thanks, Missy," Joe replied with a broad grin. "We'll tell Sammy you said that."

Frank stood up and went over to Missy. He shook hands with her. "And speaking of Sammy, Joe and I had better get over to the gym and check in with him."

Frank went over to the library doorway and turned to look at Joe, who was lingering over his goodbye to Missy. "Are you coming, Joe, or are you going to stay for dinner again?" asked Frank.

Half an hour later Frank and Joe found Sammy dripping with sweat as he practiced kicks and punches before a mirror. Joe noticed the bandage and tape around Sammy's elbow and saw that he was moving carefully, favoring his injured elbow.

"Hi, Sammy," Joe called as they walked over to him. "How's the elbow?"

Sammy stopped practicing and looked over at them. "It's a little sore, but I'm ready for tonight's bout with Disaster. Have you learned anything?"

"Plenty," Frank replied. "Like for instance, Daniel East is going broke."

"No kidding," Sammy replied. "I knew the IWA was clobbering him in the ratings, but I didn't think he was that bad off."

"He didn't used to be," Frank told him. "But I did a little digging into his finances and learned that the decline of EBC and the NAAW coincided with your stardom and the rise of the IWA."

"Do you think East blames me for his problems?" Sammy asked. "Is he after me because I wouldn't join the NAAW?"

"It's starting to look that way," Joe answered. "We also think the Romans might still be working for East. We saw them at the EBC offices yesterday."

"And right after we left there, we got jumped by two guys who definitely knew how to wrestle," Frank added.

Sammy looked thoughtful as he wiped the sweat from his face. "Come to think of it, I heard the Romans' trainer complaining that they'd missed a training session yesterday."

"That's one more piece of circumstantial

evidence against the Romans,'' Joe commented.

Sammy turned away from the mirror. ''Guys, I want to hear everything you've dug up so far, but I have to keep working out to keep my elbow from getting stiff. How about working out with me while we talk?''

''Sounds good, Sammy. We'll just go and get changed.'' Joe and Frank headed for the equipment room.

Joe stepped through the door of the equipment room to look for Slim or one of the other trainers.

The door to the back office in the equipment room was open, so Joe led his brother toward it.

They made their way down a narrow aisle between two racks of training gear toward the office. But as they neared the door, Joe felt himself being grabbed from the side by strong hands.

He struggled unsuccessfully against the unseen enemy and felt a wet cloth being pressed over his mouth and nose. The last thing he was aware of as he lost consciousness was the sickly sweet odor of chloroform filling his nostrils.

Chapter

14

FRANK RETURNED to consciousness with a splitting headache. He tried to open his eyes but soon realized that he had been blindfolded and gagged. He also tried to move his hands, but they had been securely tied behind his back. He took a deep breath and started to adjust to his surroundings.

Frank felt something warm resting against his back and knew it must be Joe. He heard muffled noises that sounded as if Joe was trying to speak with a gag in his mouth. He could feel Joe struggling and knew he was tied up, also.

Both of them were rocking back and forth where they lay, and Frank guessed that they were shut up in the back of a moving vehicle.

After what seemed like forever, the vehicle lurched to a stop, and Frank heard doors slamming. A moment later he heard another set of doors open and could sense light streaming in on him.

Frank's heart was racing and sweat was pouring down his face. What do these people want from us? he thought. In the next instant he was picked up and roughly slung over someone's shoulder. I'd better relax, he told himself, so they'll think I'm still unconscious. Frank was carried a short distance before he was dropped on the floor of a dark room. A moment later he heard a heavy thud that he assumed was Joe being dropped beside him on the floor. Then he heard a door shut and a bolt thrown.

Frank knew he had to come up with a quick plan to free himself and Joe. He rolled from side to side until he was lying facedown on the floor. He scraped the lower part of his face along the wooden floorboards until he felt the tape come loose on his mouth.

He lay in that position for a moment, breathing hard, his face sore from the scrapes.

"We've got to get out of here, Joe," Frank whispered. "Can you move your hands?"

"Uh-huh," he heard Joe grunt.

"Good," Frank answered. "I'll roll over to you and try to put my hands next to yours.

See if you can loosen the ropes around my hands.''

Joe grunted affirmatively again.

Frank rolled onto his side again and bumped toward the sound of Joe's voice. After a moment his back nudged against Joe's. He felt Joe struggling to get up on his side and groped blindly for Joe's hands.

To Frank's great relief, he soon felt one of Joe's hand in his own and pulled it toward his back. Frank lay on his side for what seemed like an eternity while Joe fumbled with the ropes tied around his brother's wrists. Just as Frank began to feel his arm going numb, he felt a knot loosen. He strained against his bonds and felt his left hand slip free.

"Way to go, Joe!" Frank whispered triumphantly.

Pushing himself over on his chest with his free hand, Frank got off his sore right arm and flexed it to start the circulation. Then he quickly pulled the ropes from his wrist and whipped off his blindfold.

He strained his eyes, trying to get a look at the room they were in. In the dim light that filtered under the door of the windowless room, Frank could see they were in an empty storeroom.

Next he turned his attention to untying Joe. His fingers felt clumsy after being immobilized, but he did free Joe's hands in a few minutes.

As soon as his hands were free, Joe pulled the gag off his mouth and tore off his blindfold.

"How do you feel?" Frank asked as he stood up and stretched his stiff muscles.

"Like garbage," Joe replied, massaging his arms. "That chloroform gave me a massive headache."

"Me, too," Frank admitted. "But at least neither of us is seriously hurt."

"Not yet, but what happens when our play-mates decide to come back and finish us off?"

"I hope we'll be out of here before that happens," replied Frank. "Speaking of which, let's find a way out of here, pronto."

Joe stood up and, after stretching his arms, began examining the door and walls.

"I heard a bolt being thrown after they dropped us in here," Joe observed. "And the hinges are on the outside of the door, so we probably can't get out that way."

Frank walked over to the wall, and ran his fingers over it, looking for any kind of open-ing, but the walls were bare. Then suddenly his hands hit a grille set high up in the wall opposite the doorway.

"Hey, Joe, here's something!" Frank whis-pered excitedly. "It's an air-conditioning grille. And it feels wide enough to crawl through."

"Great!" Joe whispered. "But how are we going to get it off the wall?"

Frank felt around in his pockets for a moment. All he found was some loose change.

"It feels like a dime would fit into the slots in the screwheads. Do you have a dime?"

"I think so," Joe answered, and handed Frank a dime.

Wasting no time, Frank and Joe began removing the screws that held the corners of the grille in place. It was hard work and Frank's wrist ached by the time he felt the last screw come loose.

"Quietly now," he cautioned Joe as they pulled the grille from the wall.

They set the grille on the floor as silently as possible, then Frank put his hands on the edge of the air-conditioning duct and chinned himself up into it. It was a tight fit, but Frank was able to crawl forward at a moderate pace. He heard Joe clambering up behind him.

"Where to now, Frank?" he heard Joe whisper behind him.

"Wherever this takes us. I don't think we have much choice," Frank said.

"Lead on," Joe replied in a hoarse whisper.

Frank crawled forward about thirty feet and came to a junction of two ducts. He thought he heard the faint sound of voices to his right, so he crawled in that direction. He'd like to be able to identify his kidnappers for the police. He continued on for another fifty feet. The sound of the voices grew louder and louder.

He finally came to a grille with light streaming through. As he approached it, he could hear talking and the sounds of people moving around below. He crawled over to the grille and peered through it.

Below him Frank could see a table with an automatic shotgun and boxes of ammunition resting on it. Frank also saw several wrestling boots, a spool of thread, and some small bottles that looked as if they contained medicine of some kind.

He crawled up a little farther and was able to see more of the room. He froze when he saw Victor Roman standing by the table. Frank peered around the room and also made out Jimmy Roman and the Living Weapon.

Frank couldn't see him, but suddenly he heard Daniel East's nasal voice saying, "So, what do you think of our little booby trap, Victor?"

"Cute." Victor smirked, picking up one of the wrestling boots from the table. "But are you sure it'll work on Sammy?"

"Since he's wrestling Major Disaster tonight, it's a cinch. I've seen Disaster wrestle maybe forty times. He always uses the flying dropkick move. Always!" Frank identified that speaker as the Living Weapon.

Frank saw Victor turn the boot upside down and press his thumb into the heel. A sharp silver needle popped from the heel.

"Hey, Victor, be careful with that thing, or you'll get a dose of that heart attack drug," Frank heard Jimmy Roman caution his brother.

"I'm being careful," Victor shot back. "Stop being such a worrywart, Jimmy."

"You really should be cautious how you handle that thing," East told him. "A few drops of heart stimulant can induce a massive heart attack."

"But what if they do an autopsy on Sammy?" Victor asked. "Won't they find the drug in his body?"

"No," East replied, chuckling nastily. "That's the beauty of this stuff. It breaks down very quickly in the bloodstream. It's practically untraceable unless you know what to look for. And when Sammy dies, it'll just look like he had a heart attack.

"The boot with the poisoned needle is already in Disaster's locker at the arena. So, very shortly after he steps into the ring, it's goodbye to the Kung Fu King."

Frank felt a surge of anger when he realized the fate East and his cronies had in store for Sammy. Frank silently beckoned to Joe to follow him.

They kept crawling until they came to another branch in the ductwork. Frank crawled to his left until he came to another grille that looked out on a wide empty room. He rolled over on his back and braced his feet against the grille. Frank shoved hard and felt the grille loosen. He gave it a hard kick with both feet and felt the bottom of the grille pop out from the wall as the screws went flying. He quickly wormed his way back to the opening and crawled through, hoping East and the others hadn't heard the noise.

After dropping to the floor, Frank stood up and helped Joe crawl out of the opening. Then when Joe was out, Frank turned around to see where he was.

Frank saw that they stood against one wall of a large, mostly empty warehouse that contained only a blue sedan, a big black Lincoln Continental, and a white paneled van.

Against the far wall of the warehouse Frank noticed several glassed-in offices. He could make out East and the Romans in one of them.

There was a row of fifty-gallon drums near the wall, and Frank ducked behind them, with Joe quickly following his example. Frank peered over the top of the row of drums and saw East open a small leather shoulder bag and brandish a compact Ingram Mac-10 machine gun.

He grabbed Joe's shoulder and pointed at

it. Joe nodded, indicating that he had seen it, too.

Joe leaned over to Frank's ear and whispered, "This is getting out of hand, Frank. Let's call the cops on these dirtbags right now."

"We've seen and heard enough to put them all away," Frank agreed. "But in order to call the cops, we have to get out of here!"

Frank scanned the inside of the warehouse for an exit. Finally his eyes fell on a pay phone at the far end of the building.

"Joe, I don't see an exit, but there's a phone down there! I'm going to try to sneak down and phone the police," whispered Frank.

"Okay, but stay low and out of sight," Joe warned him.

Frank crouched and ran toward the phone, using whatever cover would shield him from East and the others.

Frank's heart was pounding when he reached the phone. He punched in 911 and heard a guttural voice announce, "Bethlehem P.D. How may I help you?"

"I've got an emergency, officer. My name's Frank Hardy. I've been kidnapped, and my kidnappers are planning to murder someone later tonight. If you send some squad cars over right now, you can bag the whole gang."

"Where are you, Mr. Hardy?" the voice asked.

Frank felt a sudden flash of panic. "I don't know! I was blindfolded when I was brought here."

Frank looked at the pay phone and got an inspiration. "Wait a minute. If I tell you the number where I'm calling from, can you find this place? It's a big warehouse somewhere in Bethlehem."

Static crackled over the line as the anonymous cop pondered Frank's request.

To his relief, the cop answered, "Yeah, that's no problem. What's the number, Mr. Hardy?"

Reading it off the front of the phone, Frank told the cop, "The number's 555-9997. Hurry, please!"

"We're on our wa—" the cop began, then the line fell silent.

"Hello? Hello?" Frank whispered, frantically tapping the switch hook.

"It's too late for that, kid," an angry voice rasped from somewhere to Frank's left. He whirled around and saw the Living Weapon standing there with a bundle of severed phone wires in one hand and a gleaming military combat knife in the other.

The Weapon dropped the wires and moved toward Frank, the long knife pointed at his heart.

Chapter

15

FROM HIS HIDING PLACE behind a row of rusting fifty-gallon drums, Joe watched the Living Weapon advance on Frank with a drawn knife.

Joe frantically searched around for some weapon he could use to stop the hulking wrestler before he reached Frank. Raising his eyes, he spied a block and tackle dangling by a rusty chain from an overhead beam.

Joe jumped up on a packing crate below the block and tackle, then leapt high and grabbed it. The block and tackle swayed when Joe put his weight on it. Joe added to his momentum by pumping his legs back and forth. He swung backward into the wall, grabbed a metal bracket jutting from the side of the wall, and hung there for a split second.

135

Joe let go of the bracket and swung forward, straight toward the Living Weapon, who was backing Frank into the wall.

"Yaaaaa!" Joe screamed as he swung down on the Weapon. The wrestler turned around just as Joe's feet connected with his chest, sending him tumbling backward.

The Weapon landed heavily, and his knife went flying off behind a pile of rusty compressors.

"Frank—run for the exit! Straight ahead!" Joe shouted as he landed on all fours.

Frank wasted no time following his brother's advice. He sprinted for the huge double doors, with Joe only a few steps behind him.

But although the Weapon was down, he wasn't out. Behind them, Joe heard the Weapon shout, "Dan! Victor! Jimmy! The kids are getting away! Stop them!"

Joe risked a glance over at the office where East and the Romans were. He saw all three of them appear in the doorway with weapons. Jimmy Roman leveled a pistol at them, but East grabbed his arm and pulled it up.

"No shooting!" East snarled. "Do you want to bring the cops down on us?"

Jimmy jammed the pistol into the waistband of his pants and charged after the Hardys. Joe noticed that Victor was not slow to follow his younger brother.

Joe saw Frank reach the big double doors.

He grabbed a door handle and threw his shoulder into it, shoving it slowly back along its track. Joe was there several seconds later, throwing his weight into helping to move the heavy door.

As soon as they pushed the doors open wide enough to squeeze through, the Romans arrived.

Jimmy grabbed Joe by the shoulder and spun him around. He threw a savage roundhouse punch, which Joe successfully ducked. Out of the corner of one eye, Joe saw Victor leap on Frank, knocking him to the ground.

Jimmy threw a hard left at Joe's face, which Joe knocked away with a forearm block. Joe countered with a straight punch to Jimmy's midsection, which caught him off guard and sent him reeling backward.

Joe kept up a barrage of punches, driving Jimmy back more. The dark-haired wrestler's heels caught in a deep groove in the pavement, and he fell flat on his back.

Suddenly Joe heard an approaching police siren cut the air. "All right! Just in time!" he exulted.

His exultation was short-lived, however, for he saw East and the Living Weapon run to some windows at the front of the building. East carried the Ingram Mac-10 Joe had seen earlier. The Weapon carried a folding stock automatic shotgun.

137

The two gunmen smashed out the windows and peered over the sill, holding their guns at the ready.

Joe looked around for Frank and saw that Victor Roman had gotten the upper hand. Victor had Frank down on the ground and was twisting his arm behind his back.

Joe got up to go to Frank's aid, but the Living Weapon suddenly noticed the movement and snapped off a shot at Joe. The shower of shotgun pellets missed by inches as Joe dived for the pavement. He looked over at the Weapon, but he and East were concentrating on the police and could spare no more attention for the Hardys.

Joe glanced over at Frank, who was struggling to escape the arm bar Victor had him in. Joe saw Frank blindly grope for a piece of scrap metal that was lying on the floor.

With a desperate heave, Frank swung his arm and smashed the metal piece down on Victor's foot. Howling with pain, Victor released his grip on Frank's arm and danced around holding his injured foot.

"Frank—his glass jaw!" Joe shouted.

Joe saw Frank walk over to Victor and deliver a solid right to the jaw. Victor fell to the warehouse floor.

Joe heard more police cars arrive. He looked over toward East and the Weapon, and saw them let off a few rounds at the police.

The police returned fire, and Joe ducked for cover behind the white panel van. Frank joined him a moment later, panting from exertion. "There's not much we can do now without risking a bullet!" Joe shouted over the din of sirens and gunshots.

"I agree," Frank shouted back. "Let's let the cops handle this!"

The gunfire within the warehouse suddenly ceased, causing Joe and Frank to trade questioning looks. Joe crawled around the rear of the van to see what East and the Weapon were doing.

"More cops!" East shouted in frustration.

"There's too many to fight!" the Weapon called back. "Let's blow this joint before we're surrounded!"

East looked uneasily out the window, then jumped back as the cops fired at him. He stepped back against the wall beside the window and dropped the spent magazine from his machine gun.

"You start up the Lincoln!" he commanded. "I'll lay down covering fire to keep them off our backs!"

The Weapon nodded, then sprinted over to the big black Lincoln Continental. He dived behind the wheel, and a moment later its powerful engine roared to life.

East fired two long bursts from his powerful gun, then ran frantically for the Lincoln. Even before he had closed the door, the Living Weapon had thrown the car into gear and was roaring toward the rear door of the warehouse.

"Those maniacs! They're going to smash through the door!" Joe shouted in amazement.

"I think that's exactly what they have in mind," Frank agreed a moment before the big car hurtled through the outer wall of the warehouse in a shower of splinters and glass.

The cops kept shooting at the window where East had stood.

"Somebody better stop the shooting," Frank suggested.

"You go," Joe told him. "I'll make sure the Romans don't get away before the cops come in."

Frank gingerly edged over to a window and waved a white handkerchief at the police. Meanwhile, Joe took down a canvas fire hose and tied up the Romans.

A moment later a pair of cops carrying pump shotguns came through the door, their weapons at the ready.

"Don't shoot, officers! We're the ones who called you!" Frank shouted, holding his hands up.

"Where're the creeps with the heavy artillery?" a tall cop with a booming voice asked.

"They went thataway!" Joe told him, pointing at the gaping hole in the rear door of the warehouse.

"They were driving a black Lincoln Continental hardtop."

"Did you get the license number?" the tall cop asked.

Joe shook his head. "Sorry, there was too much going on."

"I did, officer," Frank said calmly as he joined Joe. "It was GRA one-nineteen."

"Thanks kid," the tall cop replied. "Dudley, you call that in while I check this place out," he told his partner.

The shorter officer nodded his head once and trotted off.

"You two kids stay here!" the tall cop ordered. Then he walked over to the glassed-in offices on the opposite side of the warehouse.

Joe suddenly grabbed Frank's arm to look at his watch. "Frank, look at the time!"

Frank's watch read 8:05. With a feeling of dread, Joe realized that Sammy's fatal bout with Major Disaster had already begun.

"We've got to get out of here!" Joe said urgently.

"Joe, the cops aren't going to let us go before questioning us," Frank reminded him.

"Then we'll have to make a break for it," said Joe. "Out the back the way East went."

Keeping an eye on the cop checking the offices, Joe led Frank to the van.

"You get the van started, Frank," Joe ordered. "I'll stay outside to distract them if

I have to. Leave the side door open, and I'll jump in at the last minute.''

"What if there are no keys in the van?" Frank asked.

"Then hotwire it. Just do it! Sammy's life may depend on it.''

Giving his younger brother an I-hope-you-know-what-you're-doing look, Frank sneaked over to the van and climbed in. He cranked the engine on and spun the van backward and in a circle so it faced the rear opening. He hit the gas, and the van shot forward. As it passed Joe, he leapt in through the side door.

"Hey—" Frank heard the tall cop shout from the far end of the warehouse.

As the van roared out of the warehouse, Frank checked the rearview mirror and saw the tall officer draw and raise his pistol. Then he heard him shout, "Stop. Stop or I'll shoot!"

Chapter

16

FRANK'S HEART was in his throat as the van screeched up to the arena. Even though he had made great time, Frank knew Sammy's match was already under way. He glanced at his watch. It now read 8:19.

Sammy could already be dead from the effects of the heart drug on the needle concealed in Disaster's boot.

Frank felt as if he were moving through molasses as he and Joe pushed through the boisterous crowds of wrestling fans clogging all the entrances to the main ring.

Joe's expression was worried when he turned to Frank. "I don't think we're going to make it in time!" he shouted over the screaming of the crowd.

"Keep pushing!" Frank shouted back. "Sammy's life may be riding on what we do next!"

Frank and Joe pushed and squirmed through hordes of wrestling fans, all wearing T-shirts bearing the names and faces of their favorite grapplers, or in some cases even dressing like their favorites. Finally they made it to the interior of the arena. Frank stood on tiptoe to peer over the heads of the crowd and saw that Sammy was still alive. He and Major Disaster were circling each other, each looking for an opening to strike.

"Sammy's still alive, Joe!" Frank shouted excitedly.

"Then let's keep him that way!" Joe yelled, pushing through a group of Major Disaster fans dressed in Disaster's trademark khaki muscle T-shirt, crisscrossed with bandoliers of machine-gun cartridges.

"Hey, watch where you're going!" a fat Disaster fan with a camouflage headband snarled at Joe.

"Sorry, but it's an emergency!" Frank called over his shoulder as he followed in Joe's wake through the rowdy crowd.

"Hey—come back here!" the fat man shouted at Joe's and Frank's backs as they pushed their way to the edge of the ring.

Major Disaster climbed up on the ropes and was preparing to spring in a flying drop kick. But just before he could make his move, Joe charged up behind him and locked both arms around Disaster's waist.

Across the ring Sammy's jaw dropped in surprise. "Joe, what—" he sputtered.

"Sammy, get out of the ring!" Joe cut him off. "Get out before Disaster kills you!"

Missy Mayflower, dressed in a low-cut royal blue evening gown and matching feather boa, rose from where she was sitting at ringside with Stan Warfield.

"No! Joe, get out of the ring!" Missy screamed.

"We can explai—" Frank started to say, but Missy was charging Joe, brandishing one of her royal blue high-heel shoes like a weapon.

Frank intercepted her, lifting her up by her waist.

"Put me down!" Missy shrieked, kicking and flailing around. She struggled so hard that Frank almost dropped her.

All around the arena, Frank heard loud booing and shouts of "Unfair!" erupt from Major Disaster's fans.

Frank shouted at the top of his voice to make himself heard over Missy's shrieking and the crowd's noise. "Sammy—get out of the ring! Listen to Joe! You're in danger!"

Sammy looked very confused and backed away from Disaster. This move prompted Disaster's fans to boo even louder and shout

"Chicken!" and "Coward!" at Sammy. Some of them even hurled popcorn bags and soda cups at the bewildered champion. Sammy's fans rallied to his defense, and a number of fistfights erupted between fans of the two wrestlers.

Sammy stepped through the ropes and walked toward Frank.

"Sammy, you yellowbelly—come back here and fight!" Disaster snarled, struggling to break Joe's grasp.

When Sammy left the ring, Disaster growled at Joe, "Kid, when I get loose I'll murder you and your brother, too!"

"I don't suppose it would help if I explained why we're doing this," Joe said through gritted teeth.

Suddenly Disaster drove both elbows back into Joe's arms, which stunned Joe and caused him to loosen his grip. It was all Disaster needed. He grabbed Joe's hands and pulled them apart, then jumped away from the ropes. Disaster was moving so quickly, Joe didn't have time to react. Disaster grabbed Joe's arms and yanked him over the top rope, hurling him to the far side of the ring. Ecstatic cheering erupted from Disaster's fans when he did this. "Kill him, Major!" a female voice shouted. And a rhythmic chant of "Drop kick! Drop kick!" started up.

Joe tried to roll when he landed, but it hurt

him. Shaking his head to clear it, Joe tried to rise. Disaster pounced on him, knocking Joe to the mat with an ax-handle blow to his back.

Next, Disaster picked Joe up to raise him overhead for a full body slam. But before he dropped Joe, Disaster turned to Frank and snarled, "You're next, punk!"

Shoving Missy into the startled Sammy's arms, Frank said, "Hang on to this wildcat, Sammy!"

Before Sammy had a chance to object, he was hanging on to Missy, trying to keep her from smacking him on the head with her shoe.

In the next instant Frank launched himself into the air, slamming into Disaster's midsection with a body block. A chorus of boos rained down from Disaster's fans.

Disaster fell like a collapsing house of cards, with Joe on top of him. Frank put all his weight on Disaster's legs, holding them to the mat.

Major Disaster growled and thrashed, but he was unable to dislodge the Hardys.

To Frank's surprise, he saw the perplexed-looking referee get down on the mat next to them and make a count of three.

When the Hardys didn't immediately release Major Disaster, the referee indicated that they should get up, saying, "The match is over. You two won."

Frank got off Disaster's legs while Joe

untwined his arms and legs from Disaster's arms. They stood up together, and the referee grabbed Joe's left hand and Frank's right hand and held them up in the air.

"I hereby declare—" He paused and whispered to them from the corner of his mouth, "Quick, what are your names?"

"Frank and Joe Hardy," Frank whispered back.

"I hereby declare Frank and Joe Hardy the winners of this bout," the ref said with a smile. Disaster's fans booed and hurled trash at the Hardys. "Hey, what can I do, folks?" the ref said. "They pinned him!"

"I demand a new match!" Major Disaster shouted angrily. "This wasn't supposed to be a tag-team bout, or I would've brought a partner!"

"Take it easy, Major," Sammy told him as he put Missy down and stepped through the ropes into the ring. "I'm sure the Hardys have a good reason for what they did."

"Garbage!" Missy shot back. "I bet you put them up to it, Sammy!"

"Yeah," Disaster growled. "You can't beat me fairly, so you use kids!"

"Sorry we had to horn in on your bout, Major," Frank told him, turning away from the referee. "But we had to stop you before you killed Sammy with your flying drop kick.

You were being set up as the fall guy in a plan to murder Sammy."

"What?" Disaster said in surprise.

"What's going on here?" Stanley Warfield suddenly shouted from the edge of the ring. "I thought you guys were investigating the threats against Sammy, not trying to break into wrestling."

"I demand to know what's going on," Missy Mayflower shouted from beside Warfield.

"This is going to take a lot of explaining," said Frank.

"Yeah, but first we need to talk to the Major in private," Joe put in.

"If you're going to interrogate him, then I demand to be there!" Missy insisted.

Joe and Frank exchanged looks, then nodded.

"Okay," Frank agreed. "That's reasonable."

A few moments later Missy ushered the Hardys into Major Disaster's dressing room, where the Major waited for them wearing a sullen expression.

"What's this about?" Missy asked as soon as Frank and Joe closed the door behind them.

"We have proof that the Major was the one threatening Sammy with notes and phone calls," Joe told her.

"What proof?" Disaster snarled.

"A note in your handwriting, for one thing,"

Frank explained, adding, "And a taped phone threat that could be matched with your voice print even though you tried to disguise your voice."

"Look, if you cooperate, it'll make things easier," said Joe.

Disaster glared defiantly at the Hardys for a moment, then dropped his eyes. "Okay, I guess you're right. What do you want to know?"

"Why were you threatening Sammy?" Frank asked.

"Dr. Walsh was blackmailing me. He threatened to tell Warfield and the wrestling press that I used steroids unless I shut Sammy up. Walsh was afraid Sammy's antisteroid campaign would ruin his business of supplying steroids to wrestlers."

"What about the attacks on Sammy?" Joe asked. "The cut rope, the chair, the ammonia in the water bottle?"

"Not to mention the falling scoreboard and Sammy's getting locked in the sauna," Frank added.

Disaster's eyes widened. "I didn't have anything to do with that stuff, I swear!"

"Tell them the truth, Fred," Missy ordered.

"I *am* telling the truth, Missy! I swear on my mother's grave!" Disaster pleaded.

Missy looked over at the Hardys. "Can you

leave us alone, guys? I need to talk to Fred in private."

"Sure, Missy," Joe replied. "Come on, Frank."

"We'll be in Sammy's dressing room," Frank told her, then turned to Disaster and said, "Major, we'll need your wrestling boots before we go."

Disaster took them off and handed them to Frank without a word.

Frank and Joe joined Sammy and Warfield in Sammy's dressing room, where Frank set the boots on Sammy's makeup counter.

"Those are the Major's boots. Do you mind telling me what this is about?" Warfield asked sternly.

"Major Disaster was being set up by Daniel East to kill Sammy in the ring tonight," Frank explained.

"What do his boots have to do with that?" Warfield asked testily.

"I'll show you," Frank explained, picking up the right boot and pressing a spot near the center of the heel. Joe couldn't help noticing Warfield's look of surprise and Sammy's shocked expression when a needle popped out of the boot.

"That needle is coated with a drug that would have induced a heart attack," Frank told Warfield and Sammy. "East, the Romans, and the Living Weapon kidnapped us from the

IWA gym. But we escaped and overheard East explaining his plan to the Romans.''

Sammy clutched his throat and turned white.

"Your success with the IWA was driving East Broadcasting and the NAAW out of business," Frank told him.

"That's what all those attempts on your life were about, Sammy," Joe continued. "Our guess is that East thought that eliminating you would improve his own fortunes. He had the Romans and the Living Weapon helping him. Since you ran into Victor Roman coming out of the sauna, I'm sure he and his brother were the ones who rigged the thermostat and locked you in."

"And who were those two goons who jumped you in the alley?" Sammy asked.

"The Romans," Joe answered. "It had to be them because of their fighting style and because they saw us at EBC when we went there."

"But who did all that other stuff to me?" Sammy asked.

"We're sure it was the Romans and, in some cases, the Living Weapon, acting under East's orders," Frank told him. "Missy said that Victor Roman handed her the chair that Disaster hit you with. She also saw the Romans coming out of the workout room just before we discovered the rope was cut. So they had to be the ones who did it. One of the Romans put the ammonia in your water bottle, since neither East nor the Weapon was seen in the gym that day."

"The Living Weapon had to be the one who cut the scoreboard cables," Joe put in. "But East had to have helped him because of the lapel pin we found."

"So who was threatening to stop me from making my speech?" Sammy asked.

"I can answer that," Frank cut in. "Disaster. He wasn't trying to kill you, but he sure was behind those threats."

"Do you have proof of that?" Warfield asked.

"Solid proof," Frank replied. "The handwriting in the last note threatening Sammy matches Disaster's handwriting exactly."

"Well, if Disaster wasn't working with East, what was he after?" Sammy wanted to know.

"Dr. Walsh was blackmailing him to stop your antisteroid speech. Walsh threatened to expose Disaster's own steroid use and get him thrown out of the IWA."

There was a knock on the door, and Missy appeared in the doorway.

"Mr. Warfield, I've talked with the Major, and he's prepared to testify that Dr. Jacob Walsh gave him steroids illegally. He also offered to point out the other steroid users in the IWA."

"Well, if Major Disaster's willing to cooperate, maybe he'll be allowed back in the game eventually. He'll have to be banned for a while, though," Warfield said.

Suddenly the phone in Sammy's dressing room rang. Sammy answered it, then handed it to Warfield, telling him, "It's for you, Stan."

Warfield grabbed the phone and said, "This is Warfield. Yeah? Uh-huh, uh-huh. Well, that's certainly good news."

He hung up the phone, telling Sammy and the Hardys, "That was a friend of mine in the Allentown P.D. The Bethlehem cops captured East and the Living Weapon about fifteen minutes ago. The Weapon's making a full confession in exchange for leniency. They have Daniel East and the Romans cold."

"All right!" Joe said. He turned to Frank and slapped him a high five. Frank slapped back.

"Looks like everything's pretty well wrapped up," Joe said, grinning broadly.

"I want to apologize to you, Joe," Missy said sweetly. "You guys did the right thing."

"Now that we've solved this mystery, how about going out with me tonight?" Joe asked, turning on the charm.

Missy reached over and squeezed his arm briefly. "Joe, I'd love to, but since the Major's going to be out of action for a while, I need a new wrestler to manage. I'm going to try to talk Tomahawk Smith into letting me manage him.''

Frank couldn't help smiling at the crestfallen expression on Joe's face after Missy left. He went over to his younger brother and clapped him on the back. "Don't take it so hard, Joe. Maybe you can still get her if you come up with a good enough costume.''

"Yeah!" Joe said, his eyes lighting up. "Got any ideas?"

"Well," Frank said, carefully moving out of his brother's reach. "How about something, say, in powder blue? It always was your best color!"

UNCIVIL WAR

Chapter

1

"PROFESSOR DONNELL! Can I have your autograph?"

Joe Hardy's step faltered as he walked beside Professor Andrew Donnell as he made his way toward the baggage claim area of the Memphis airport. Joe turned to watch a skinny, gawky college-age student in thick glasses and a Tennessee State University sweatshirt run toward them, a small bag dangling from his hand. The student's voice sounded shaky, and he called to the professor with the wild-eyed expression of a fan spotting a movie star.

"Do you know that guy?" Joe asked the professor, eyeing the pale-faced boy rushing up to them. Frank, Joe's older brother, turned, too, to take in the intruder.

"No, don't believe I do," Professor Donnell boomed. He stopped to squint at the boy through his wire-rimmed bifocals.

Joe guessed that the professor didn't mind the public attention. With his shock of thick white hair, pale blue eyes, rumpled tweed sports coat and wrinkled slacks, he appeared as if he had dressed that morning for the role of Famous Professor.

"Well, he sure wants to meet you," Joe remarked. He covered his mouth and tried to stifle a yawn.

Joe and Frank had just flown down to Memphis from their hometown of Bayport to take part in a reenactment of an American Civil War battle for which Professor Donnell was acting as consultant. The professor, who taught in a large New York City university, was an acquaintance of their father, the internationally known detective Fenton Hardy. Fenton had run into the professor at a party, heard about the Memphis reenactment, and suggested it would be a perfect extra-credit history project for his two sons. The brothers' teachers thought it was a great idea, too.

Joe was glad when Donnell agreed to let Frank and him accompany him to Memphis. What better way to study history than to play war for a couple of days? Joe thought.

Now that they were in Memphis, though, Joe only wanted to go to bed. It had been a long flight, there hadn't been enough to eat on the plane, and now some beady-eyed fan was slowing them down.

"You *are* Professor Andrew Donnell, aren't you?" the boy exclaimed abruptly, stopping just in front of them. He spoke with a thick southern drawl, and his voice was deeper than Joe would expect from someone so scrawny.

"Right you are, my boy," Donnell said, smiling at the young man like a lion contemplating his prey. "Forgive me, but have I met you before?"

"Oh, no, sir!" The young man blushed to the roots of his pale hair. He fumbled in his bag and pulled out a hardcover book with the title *Gettysburg Revisited* across its cover. "But I've read just about everything you ever wrote. I heard you were coming into Memphis this afternoon"—the young man stuck the book out toward the pleased professor—"and I was hoping you'd autograph this."

"Certainly, my boy!" the big, brash professor roared, taking the book. "To whom shall I inscribe it?"

"To—to Dennis, sir. Dennis Kincaid."

Joe glanced quizzically at Frank, whose dark eyebrows were raised. He seemed to be surprised. Obviously, he hadn't expected a history professor—no matter how well-known—to be chased down by a fan at an airport.

"Do you always hang out here, hoping your

heroes will wander by?" Joe asked, only half kidding.

"Yes—I mean, no," said Dennis, blushing as he accepted the signed book back from the professor. "I live in Nashville, see. I'm a freshman at State—a history major. I'm going to perform in the reenactment of the Battle of Shiloh here tomorrow. My parents gave me the chance to do it as my birthday present. I'm even staying at Magnolia House."

"The Battle of Shiloh?" Frank said, grinning. "That's what Joe and I are here for."

"What about me?" protested Donnell with good humor. "I'm the star consultant for it, or so I understand." He turned back to Dennis, unwilling to let his admirer go. "Tell me, boy. How'd you recognize me in this crowded place?"

"Th-that's easy, sir," Dennis stammered. He turned the book over, revealing a photograph of the professor on the jacket. "See? It looks just like you."

"I should hope not!" Donnell laughed, obviously flattered. "That picture was taken twenty years ago!"

"And what about you?" Dennis demanded of the brothers. "Why did you come to participate?"

"Extra credit. We need it because we missed a lot of school this year," Frank explained.

"You're being too modest, Frank," said the professor. "Tell the boy why you missed school."

He went on without waiting. "They're famous detectives and were off solving cases."

"Who cares?" said Joe cheerfully, obviously uncomfortable with the praise. "The important thing is that participating in this battle earns us credit for history class. Writing a report about it takes care of English. Figuring the hit-miss ratio for each day aces math. And arguing over who should have won takes care of debate class. Plus, we get a free vacation!"

"This is hardly a vacation for me," the professor snapped. "I happen to be at work on a biography of General Pierre G. T. Beauregard, the leader of the Confederate troops at the battle. I assure you, this battle was no laughing matter."

Joe's grin froze on his face. He shot a puzzled look at his brother but kept his mouth shut.

Dennis seemed to be almost pleased at Joe's reprimand. He cleared his throat and spoke. "Don't you think, sir, that a case could be made that the Battle of Shiloh was General Beauregard's greatest victory? Just because the Yankees claimed to have won doesn't mean—"

"The 'Yankees,' as you call them, didn't *claim* to have won," roared the professor. "They beat that coward Beauregard fair and square, and that's what I intend to prove—once and for all."

Dennis stared, thunderstruck, as the professor wheeled around and took off again to claim his baggage. "Sorry," he whispered to the professor's back.

5

"Don't worry about it," Joe muttered, heading past the mortified student to catch up with the professor. "My dad warned us that he talks like that all the time."

Still, Joe thought as he hurried after Donnell, that didn't make the professor's rude behavior acceptable.

"Donnell!" A voice called to them from the crowd gathered in the baggage claim area.

"Merriweather!" the professor boomed. Joe spotted a heavyset, nervous-looking young man with slicked-back hair and a closely trimmed beard hurrying toward them. The man's eyes were dark and narrow—ratlike, in Joe's opinion.

"Where's my luggage, man?" Donnell demanded. "We were held up back there. I thought you would have had the bags off the carousel by now."

"They aren't even off the plane, Professor," Merriweather reported, flustered. His dark eyes flicked from the professor to the boys. "Hi. You must be the Hardys. Merriweather's my name. I'm Professor Donnell's graduate assistant. He asked me to accompany him on this trip."

"Not for long, if you don't get our bags," the professor snapped. With that, he stormed off toward a nearby lounge, leaving Joe and Frank with the flustered assistant.

"Does he always treat you like that?" Joe asked.

"What difference does it make?" Merriweather's preoccupied tone surprised Joe. "You have to make allowances for great men."

Frank's eyebrows shot up. "You think Donnell's a great man?"

Merriweather's reverent tone convinced Joe that he had no doubts. "Among Civil War historians, Donnell's the most highly respected, influential thinker of all. He can be as rude as he feels like being."

Joe started to laugh at Merriweather's solemnity but thought better of it. Luckily, the bags had started to arrive, and Merriweather hurried off to retrieve the professor's bags as fast as his chubby legs could carry him.

Behind him, Frank shook his head and Joe chuckled. "I don't get it," Joe said goodnaturedly. "So a guy writes a bunch of books on the Civil War. What's so great about that? It's not like he had to invent the story or anything."

"There are plenty of questions about the Civil War, and about this battle in particular," Frank, who was the more studious of the brothers, informed him. "I don't really understand what all the fuss is, either, but maybe we'll find out more tomorrow."

"Yeah," Joe said, rubbing his hands together and grinning. "Rifles, boots, sharp-looking uniforms. I can't wait."

"Just make sure you learn something in the process," Frank chided cheerfully. Then he added, "Look at Merriweather. He's got a whole cart filled with Donnell's stuff. What do you think the professor has in all those boxes?"

"Papers and books," Joe answered. "I asked him when he checked it in New York. He spends a lot of time down here researching and working on his book. He even has an office here."

Joe spotted his and Frank's two garment bags on the luggage carousel. The two boys walked over and swung them off and then plopped them on top of Merriweather's overflowing cart. "Where to now?" Joe asked the assistant.

"We need to catch the shuttle bus to the car rental office," Merriweather replied. He flagged down a porter and instructed him to load everything onto the bus. "Let's go to the lounge to pick up the professor. By the time we get back to the bus, all the bags should be loaded."

"Joe says Donnell has an office in Memphis," Frank said as they entered the lounge. "Where is it?"

"On Tyler Pardee's estate." The assistant peered around the crowded room for his boss. "Pardee's a great guy. He owns the old plantation house outside of town that we're all staying in. He's converted it to a very profitable hotel. He keeps a room on the second floor reserved exclusively for his buddy the professor."

Merriweather spotted Donnell and made his way toward him, explaining to Frank over his shoulder as he moved. "Pardee hosts the reen-actment every year."

"Indeed he does," boomed the professor, slap-ping his assistant on the back. "Wonderful man, Pardee! And incredibly rich! Owns all the land around the Shiloh battlefield. What he didn't use for his hotel he turned into an amusement park— a park with a historic theme, though, so I approve."

"Let's not keep him waiting." Merriweather led them toward the airport exit. "I promised Pardee you'd be there in time for dinner. He eats at six."

"Ah, southerners," Donnell crooned. "Charm-ing, how they eat before sundown."

"Charming," Joe whispered mischievously to his brother as they strolled outside toward the bus, "how Professor Donnell loves food. I don't know about you, but I'm starving."

"Ah, there we are!" The professor spotted the shuttle bus across the lane and down forty feet. The porter was loading the last of his boxes. He started diagonally across the blacktop, ignoring the pedestrian crosswalk. Frank, Joe, and Merri-weather followed in his wake.

As he stepped onto the road, Joe became aware of an engine revving. It sounded unusu-ally loud.

"What's that?" he muttered, turning to look to his right. A large blue pickup truck with a Confederate flag covering its front license plate hovered at the end of the lane. The top half of its windshield was tinted dark blue, preventing Joe from seeing into the cab. But the way the engine was being revved made the hairs on the back of his neck stand up in alarm.

"Joe?" he heard Frank say. Too late. The truck was already moving toward Donnell and Merriweather at an alarmingly fast speed.

"Watch out!" Joe leapt toward the professor as Frank charged for Merriweather. The truck careened closer.

It was headed straight for them—and it wasn't slowing down!

"WHAT ON EARTH—" Merriweather started to protest as Frank knocked him flat to the ground, out of the path of the speeding truck.

Professor Donnell cried out as Joe smashed into him with the full force of his running-back physique. The two of them rolled safely in front of the shuttle bus just as the truck's muddy tires passed inches from them.

"What? I'll b-be—" the professor sputtered as he tried to pull himself to his feet. Joe reached over to help him up.

The porter who had loaded their luggage, the driver of the shuttle bus, and a few other passersby had gathered to stare at the four intended victims. Frank and Merriweather, brushing their pants, joined Joe and the professor.

11

"Did you see the driver?" Frank asked his brother under his breath.

"No. You?"

Frank shook his head in frustration.

"Are you folks okay?" the shuttle bus driver asked.

"Of course we're all right!" the professor snapped, slapping at the dust on his jacket. "These boys are having trouble controlling their high spirits, that's all. Let's go."

"Wait a minute." Frank stared at the professor, dumbfounded. "My brother just saved your life!"

"Saved my life?" The professor sniffed haughtily. "Ridiculous. My life wasn't in danger."

"But the truck!" Frank turned to Merriweather, but the assistant just stared at the ground and shifted his weight from one foot to the other. The watching crowd backed away slightly, as if they were in the presence of crazy people, and murmured among themselves.

"That truck would've run right over you if Joe hadn't pushed you out of the way!"

"Nonsense." The professor brushed past the brothers and climbed onto the bus.

Furious, Frank thought about pursuing the professor but realized it would be useless to argue with him.

Shaking his head, Frank joined Joe. Merriweather, still stunned, followed behind.

"Who would have tried to run us down?" Frank asked Joe as they approached the bus.

"I was wondering the same thing," Joe admitted. "The only person we've even talked to here was that Dennis Kincaid."

"Why would he want to run us over?"

Joe shrugged his shoulders and grinned ruefully. "We embarrassed him, maybe?"

Frank laughed. "Maybe it was just an accident," he said finally. But he knew that neither he nor Joe believed that.

By five-fifteen the foursome was driving in a rented car through the rolling green hills of the Memphis countryside, each lost in his own thoughts.

Finally Frank could stand the tense silence no longer. He leaned forward from the backseat and asked the professor in a polite voice, "Sir, could you tell us about the Battle of Shiloh."

The professor's face instantly brightened. "Certainly, Frank. It began, on this land we're riding through, back on April sixth, 1862. It was the largest, most devastating battle to that date in the Civil War—some twenty thousand men killed in two days of fighting—and it killed any hope on either side that the war would be over quickly."

"Why did Dennis say the South might have won the battle?" Joe's mind was still on the college student.

The professor's face twitched in annoyance. "Actually," he explained, "the South *was* victorious the first day. But the second day, April seventh, General Grant counterattacked with fresh reinforcements and won. Unfortunately for the rebels, the battle enabled the Union forces to advance north and capture Memphis, thus effectively controlling the state of Tennessee. History places the victory squarely in the Union camp."

"And General Beauregard led the Confederate forces?" Frank asked.

"Brilliant soldier," the professor said, nodding. "But he made some major errors at Shiloh."

"Like what?"

The professor blinked. "First, he should have attacked on the evening of the first day of battle when he had the Union on the ropes. But instead he chose to rest for the night."

"What else?"

"The next day," Donnell continued, "when he might have made a tougher stand against the North, he chose to retreat." He readjusted his jacket. "Many people blame old Beauregard for the South's defeat that day. I count myself among them."

"Where'd the fighting take place, exactly?" Joe asked eagerly.

"Right out there." The professor nodded out the window. "That's the Tennessee River. To the west is the Shiloh National Military Park.

And here to the east are Mr. Pardee's mansion and Rebel Park, which is nearly twice the size of the national park, I'm told."

"Wow." Joe craned his neck to see past his brother's shoulder. "Not bad."

Frank spotted a large, ornate wrought iron gate with the words *Magnolia House* expertly woven into its design where it arched over the paved private drive. The gate swung open automatically as Merriweather guided the car off the main road and onto the estate.

"This is an amusement park?" Joe gazed around at the well-tended lawns, magnolia trees, and the pine forest that lined the property.

"Of course not," Merriweather scoffed. "These are the grounds of the plantation house. Rebel Park is on the right, past those trees. The annual reenactment takes place just beyond that."

Joe whistled. "Sounds like a lot of land."

"Certainly is." The professor smiled.

"Wow. Look." Frank nudged his brother in the ribs, then pointed at the enormous, white-columned mansion that swung into view as the car rounded the last curve in the long drive. It was a classic, three-story plantation house with a veranda that wrapped around the two lower stories and enormous windows looking out onto the manicured lawns. "Some hotel, huh?"

As Merriweather shut the engine off, a uniformed valet approached the car. "Welcome, Dr. Donnell," he said. "Mr. Pardee is waiting

15

for you in the library. We'll take care of your bags."

Frank and Joe followed the professor and his assistant into the house. Frank was even more impressed with the inside of the mansion than the outside. The ceiling of the foyer soared thirty feet above the marble floor. Richly varnished wood paneling made the huge space seem warm and cozy.

In the middle of the lobby the marble floor gave way to a marble staircase that rose majestically to the second floor. "Come on," Frank said, eager to explore the rest of the house. He led the way up the stairs behind the professor and Merriweather.

As they reached the top of the stairs they could already hear the professor loudly greeting his host in one of the rooms at the end of the hall. Frank and Joe entered behind him and found themselves inside a large library with a huge fireplace and floor-to-ceiling bookcases.

"Good to see you again, Andrew," a man was saying to the professor, shaking his hand. "Welcome back to Magnolia House."

Frank, watching their slender, middle-aged host, smiled to himself. Pardee was a friendly-looking man, with well-trimmed brown hair that had turned white at the temples and intelligent, pale green eyes.

"You must be Joe and Frank Hardy," Pardee added, reaching out to shake their hands. "The professor's told me about you two, not to mention that dad of yours. I'm pleased to make the acquaintance of two such clever detectives.''

"We're on a sort of learning vacation here,'' Frank said, smiling at him.

"We hope so, at least,'' his brother added in a low voice.

"Good,'' replied Pardee. "Because it so happens that you have to attend a dinner party for all the folks participating in tomorrow's battle down at the amusement park. Better two teenagers at a party than a couple of ace detectives, don't you agree? But first''—he winked conspiratorially at Frank and Joe—"I've got a surprise for Andrew.''

Frank watched as Pardee walked toward the fireplace. On the wall above it hung an impressive array of knives, sabers, and bayonets, which Frank logically guessed dated to the Civil War. Pardee took a saber from the wall and handed it to his friend. "Look at this,'' he said to the professor.

Frank watched as Donnell turned the saber over in his hands, inspecting the shiny blade and ornately carved handle with growing disbelief. "It can't be,'' he said at last to Pardee. "When you told me about this, I didn't really believe you had come up with it.''

Pardee beamed. "Well, sir, I did. This here's the genuine article.''

"What is it?'' Frank asked.

17

The professor slowly continued to shake his head. "Tyler claims this is the saber that General Beauregard carried into the Battle of Shiloh."

"I do more than claim," Pardee retorted. "Look here."

He pointed to the base of the blade. Both Frank and the professor peered closer. Frank made out the name *P. G. T. Beauregard* engraved in tiny letters.

"Had it authenticated at Tennessee University a week ago," Pardee said. "One of my men found it when we were excavating for all those new rides we're putting in at the park."

The professor shook his head, gazing at the valuable saber. "Better to be lucky than rich," he said.

"To tell you the truth," said Pardee, grinning widely, "it's better to be both."

He took the saber from the professor and replaced it on the wall. "Now we'd better get down to that party."

Though separated from Magnolia House by the tall wrought iron fence, Rebel Park was only about a hundred yards from the mansion. As Frank and Joe accompanied the others along the brick walk to the park's entrance, they could hear a band playing in the distance, as well as the sounds of talk and laughter.

"How long has your family had Magnolia House?" Frank asked as they approached a gate to the park.

18

Pardee grinned. "Depends on who you talk to, I reckon," he said. "My people first settled this particular land back in the late 1700s. Been adding bits and pieces ever since. The professor here doubts my claim, but after all, possession *is* nine-tenths of the law."

The professor cleared his throat, seemingly annoyed, and Pardee laughed. Frank wondered what the hotel owner meant, but there was no time to ask. They had reached the entrance to the park. On the other side of the gate stood an enormous red-and-yellow tent that Pardee said housed the band, dinner, and most of the guests. Frank grinned at Joe's eager expression. Joe had obviously forgotten how tired he was and was now ready to party.

"Ah, gentlemen!" Pardee called out to several men standing just outside the entrance to the tent. He led his guests toward them, saying expansively to the professor, "About time I introduced you to a few of our more fascinating locals.

"Andrew Donnell, meet Martin Crowley," Pardee said, gripping the arms of both men. "Andrew, Martin's read every one of your books. He's our recorder of deeds in Memphis, so I guess he has a taste for history."

"I know Martin quite well already," the professor replied, beaming at the round-shouldered, pasty-faced man in the three-piece suit. "We've had a number of conversations regarding my

19

THE HARDY BOYS CASEFILES

new book. In fact, I'm considering acknowledging you in it, Martin."

"Really, Andrew?" the man said tentatively. "I didn't realize I'd been so helpful."

Frank noticed annoyance flash across Pardee's face, but he quickly recovered and turned toward the other two men.

"Okay, then, let me introduce Wayne Robinson of Macon, Georgia, and our own Wesley Hart," he said to the professor. "Two more loyal readers."

Donnell smiled and bowed slightly to the two men.

Frank studied them. Robinson was a short, paunchy man with a bulbous nose and squinty blue eyes. Hart, younger and more muscular, had the hooded eyes of a hungry hawk.

"Gentlemen," Donnell said, "it's always a pleasure to meet fans. The name Wayne Robinson rings a bell."

Before Robinson could answer, Hart said to the professor, "Just because a man reads your book doesn't mean he believes what you write."

The professor's smile faded. "Indeed," he said, straightening up. He seemed to brace himself for an argument.

But before Hart could continue, they were interrupted by Joe, who muttered, "Wow!" in a too-loud voice.

They all turned to watch Joe smiling at a slender girl in a simple summery blouse and skirt

20

who was heading toward the group. Her long red hair was lifted off her shoulders in the slight breeze. Frank couldn't help but notice how attractive she was. Uh-oh, he thought. Joe's just found his own fascinating local.

"Daddy, I just called for more soda water," the girl said to Tyler Pardee in a soft, southern-accented voice. Then she noticed the Hardys. Her face, which was splashed with freckles, broke into a wide grin.

"You're the Hardys, aren't you?" she asked, putting her hand out. "I'm Jennifer Pardee. Daddy's told me all about you."

Frank waited for his brother to take Jennifer's hand, but the girl had Joe forgetting what to do. Frank grinned and shook the girl's hand instead. "I'm Frank," he said to Jennifer. "This dumbfounded blond, blue-eyed loon here is Joe."

"Pleased to meet you, Frank and Joe," Jennifer drawled. "Welcome to my amusement park. If y'all want free tickets to the rides later, just let me know."

"*Your* amusement park?" Joe managed to say, his voice cracking just a little.

Pardee and the other men chuckled. "You heard right," Pardee said, putting an arm around his daughter's shoulders. "Jennifer's been working here since she was thirteen. When she turned eighteen last month, I handed the reins over to her."

"Not the whole thing," Jennifer protested,

blushing. "I run the ideas department. Party schemes, new concessions, promotions and stuff. Daddy still handles the money end."

"Not for long, though," Pardee said proudly. He turned toward Jennifer. "Why don't you show the boys around, honey?"

"Sure!" Jennifer smiled at Frank and Joe.

To Joe's relief, Jennifer asked them if they'd rather eat first. While they loaded their plates at the buffet, she described the park's rides, games, horse rentals, and Civil War–related shows.

"How do you manage to run all this and go to school, too?" Joe wanted to know as they chose a table and sat down to eat.

She smiled. "I'm used to it, I guess. Other girls wait on tables or take piano lessons after school. I call the repairman for the merry-go-round. Of course, this weekend I'll be especially busy. The battle reenactment always attracts lots of folks to Rebel Park."

Frank was about to ask her another question when a commotion near the entrance to the tent distracted him. Frank recognized the voice of Professor Donnell.

"Get your hands off me, man!" he shouted. His voice was loud enough to cut through the party conversation. The band members, who had stopped for a short break, all turned to stare at the two men from their place on the stage.

"You don't tell me what to do!" Wesley Hart shouted back at the professor. Frank wondered where Pardee and Robinson were as he saw the younger man push the professor in the chest. The professor staggered backward, causing several onlookers to scream.

"Stop that or I'll call the police!" the professor shouted wildly. Frank stood, ready to run to help the professor. But he was too far away to stop Hart from attacking again.

As Frank, Joe, and Jennifer watched, Hart pushed the professor once more. As the older man fell backward onto the ground, Hart stood over him, shouting, "I'll kill you, Donnell! I swear I will!"

Chapter
3

INSTANTLY JOE AND FRANK sprang into action. They pushed through the crowd to where the professor sat stunned on the ground and pulled the red-faced attacker away from him.

Frank, holding one of Hart's arms, demanded, "What's this all about?"

"None of your business." Hart glared at the professor, whom Joe was helping back to his feet for the second time that day.

"It was nothing, dear boy," Donnell said, glaring at Hart. "A mere misunderstanding."

"Misunderstanding?" Hart shouted. "I understand perfectly! You're filling your book with a pack of lies about General Beauregard. You ought to be shot!"

"Hey, watch it." Joe held up his hands. "It's

a free country, right? He can write what he wants."

"He can't tell lies and get away with it," said Hart. With that, he turned and stomped off.

Joe looked around. Now that the argument was over, the other guests had gone back to their celebrating again. The band struck up a good dance tune, and everyone ignored the professor and the two brothers.

"What's going on here?" Joe asked Frank after Pardee rushed up and took the professor to a table, where they were now sitting.

Frank shook his head. "I know one thing. This is no get-together of the Andrew Donnell Fan Club. Hart may not be the professor's only problem," he added quietly. "Look, there's that Dennis Kincaid—over there, talking to Mr. Hart. Kincaid seems to be as angry as Hart is."

"Thank goodness you boys were here." Joe jumped at the sound of Jennifer's soft voice in his ear. He turned to find her standing behind him. "That Wesley Hart has always had a terrible temper," she confessed. "People like him give the South a bad name."

"And what about people like you?" Joe said with a smile, everything else instantly vanishing from his mind.

Jennifer took his arm and began to lead him out of the tent. "Southerners like me take good care of their guests at parties. And I'm going to give you a tour of Rebel Park."

She turned back to Frank. "Would you like to come along?" she asked, smiling welcomingly.

Frank grinned. Whether he wanted to or not, Joe would kill him if he ruined his get-together. "No, thanks," he said. "I'll hang out here and eat a bit more, then I'll turn in early. It's been kind of a long day."

The next morning Frank awoke to a dark room and a shrieking alarm clock. Sitting straight up in bed, he slammed the clock with one hand.

Across the room he saw Joe lying half on and half off his bed, oblivious to the noise. Joe was still dressed in the clothes he had worn the day before. Frank shook his head, remembering how he had awakened around midnight when Joe had come tiptoeing in.

"Get up, little brother." Frank tossed a pillow at Joe. "Don't say I didn't warn you."

"Mmmph." Joe shoved the pillow off his face and sat up, blinking sleepily. "Tell 'em to have the war without me, okay?"

Frank laughed as he got out of bed and started dressing. "No way. The troops meet in the dining room in twenty minutes."

Joe yawned and stretched, then slowly climbed out of bed and went to the closet, where his dark blue Union uniform was hanging. "How come I'm North and you're South?" he asked.

Frank was studying himself in the mirror. Confederate gray was a good color for him, he decided. "I'm not sure how they divided up the sides. You know what they said about the Civil War, though, don't you? Brother against brother?"

"Yeah." Joe grinned. "Let's fight."

Leading the way down to the dining room, Joe was surprised to see more than four hundred men crammed into the huge room, and dressed in authentic-looking Civil War uniforms, the colors equally divided between gray and blue. He spotted the professor wearing the uniform of a Southern general, with Merriweather beside him, dressed in Union blues.

"Good morning, boys," roared the professor when he saw Joe and Frank standing in the doorway. "I trust you slept well."

"We did." Frank glanced at Joe, who was stifling a yawn. "Did you sleep well?"

"Sure." Joe led the way to the professor's table. "But then, I always sleep well. Clear conscience. Clean living. Works every time."

"How about you, Robert?" Frank asked Merriweather amiably as he and his brother sat down at the table.

Merriweather didn't answer right away. Frank decided the assistant was either still half asleep or lost in thought.

"Oh—er, fine," Merriweather said at last. "Fine, I guess."

"Well, I feel much better," Joe said as a wait-

27

ress served him and Frank heaping plates of scrambled eggs, grits, bacon, fried potatoes, and biscuits. "Nice to know that no matter which side you're on, you still get fed right before the battle."

The others were too busy eating to answer. In fact, they downed their meals in near silence. As they were finishing their breakfast, Tyler Pardee appeared at the front of the room.

Joe glanced up from his breakfast long enough to notice that Pardee wore the uniform of a Union general. I guess I'll have to address him as sir for the next couple of days, he told himself.

Pardee's speech interrupted his thoughts. "Good morning, men," the slender man was saying, smiling broadly at his guests. "I hope you're enjoying your breakfast at Magnolia House. We do our best to please you folks going into battle. In any case, rest assured it's better than the food those first soldiers—on both sides—had to eat that morning at Shiloh."

The crowd murmured its agreement. Joe glanced around at the attentive faces—more alert now than they had been before they were served.

"The reenactment is set to begin at dawn," Pardee continued. He checked his pocket watch. "That's in about an hour. We'll leave here in ten minutes. Those of you in Union uniforms will follow me. Confederate soldiers are under

28

Professor Andrew Donnell's supervision. Stand up, Professor.''

The professor rose and nodded to the men, then sat down again.

"There's a room just off the foyer where you'll pick up your rifles and blank ammunition," Pardee said. "Sheriff Bradley Walker and I will be monitoring the ammunition, to be on the safe side. If you run out of cartridges during the day, there's a supply tent on the battlefield not far from Shiloh Church where you can get more. That tent is being supervised by Wesley Hart."

Wesley Hart seemed to be almost cheerful as he stood up across the room from Joe and Frank.

"Okay," Pardee concluded. "Now, finish your breakfast and we'll see you outside the hotel."

Shortly before dawn Joe found himself with more than two hundred other blue-uniformed actors in tents at the site of the Shiloh battlefield. Through the open flaps of the tent, Joe could see Tyler Pardee surveying the scene from atop an enormous white horse. A crowd of spectators shivered in the chilly morning air.

Joe also spotted Robert Merriweather wandering back and forth in the predawn light as though searching for something or someone. Joe wondered if he should ask the assistant whether he could help him when a voice interrupted his thoughts.

"Hey, remember me?"

At the sound Joe turned quickly and stepped outside into the gray morning. The voice belonged to Dennis Kincaid.

"Sure," Joe said, controlling the urge to cross-examine the student about pickup trucks and his real feelings about Professor Donnell. "What are you doing in a Yankee uniform?"

Kincaid's smile faded, and he looked down, flustered. "Well, er, they didn't really give me a choice. How about you?"

"Ditto." Joe was becoming restless. "What happens now?"

The college student scanned the field for a moment. "Well," he said at last. "When the sun comes up, I reckon the South will rise again."

Meanwhile Frank and the rest of the Confederate troops were lining up just behind the top of a bluff near the Union camp, preparing to attack. Frank hunched down in the cold air, watching his breath form clouds that floated lazily away.

"Nervous?" said the soldier beside him.

Frank nodded.

"This your first battle?"

"Yeah," Frank answered.

"Don't worry. These blanks just give a little sting. Can't hurt nobody unless you shoot 'em at point-blank range."

Frank was about to say that that was just what he'd been telling himself, when he realized he'd seen his neighbor before. "Hey, you're Wayne Robinson, aren't you? We met last night."

Robinson grinned and was about to answer, but just then the ball of the sun broke over the horizon and Frank watched as Professor Donnell, riding a chestnut mare, gave the signal to charge. Instantly Frank joined his fellow soldiers and hurtled downhill, shouting, toward the Union camp.

To Frank's gratification, the Union soldiers were caught completely by surprise. But it didn't take them long to regroup as the first wave of Confederate foot soldiers descended on them. Within minutes, resounding cannon blasts were exploding among the rebel troops.

"Take shelter!" Frank heard someone yell. He dove behind a large rock and waited, while others hid behind trees and in ruts in the ground. The cannon fire ceased, and Frank and his fellow soldiers ran out from their hiding places to attack.

Frank wasn't prepared for the noise of battle. The two armies faced each other across less than fifty feet of dust and filled the air with the explosions of four hundred rifles at once.

At first Frank thought he would never get through the day. He wondered if there was some way he could quit the reenactment early. He also wondered how the real soldiers had

31

managed to drag themselves through battle after battle for the many years of the war.

After thirty minutes Pardee signaled the Northerners to pull back. Frank and the other Confederate soldiers also withdrew to the steep banks of the Tennessee River. Frank hoped that would be the end of the fighting for a while, but instead the professor ordered his troops to attack.

Not my lucky day, Frank thought gloomily as he prepared his rifle for the onslaught.

The fighting by the river was even worse than before. Dust filled the air. Cannonballs splashed into the river and drenched the soldiers who clung to the riverbank. The weary fighters grew increasingly clumsy as they aimed their heavy rifles at one another.

At some point Frank saw Professor Donnell himself struggling at the bottom of the riverbank nearby. "Fantastic, eh, boy?" he shouted to Frank. "This is where General Johnston was killed the first day of fighting and Beauregard became the sole commander. Beauregard might have changed history if he had fought on instead of pulling back!"

Before Frank could answer, the shooting started again. The professor turned away and struggled up the riverbank, waving his rifle and shouting at his men.

Frank watched him, startled. Something was wrong. There was the same stench of gunpowder, the same clouds of smoke that he had been smelling and seeing all day. Frank rubbed his eyes. Something was different, but what?

Then he realized that a tree beside Donnell was suddenly sporting a hole. He could see splinters spraying out of it.

"Wait!" he shouted after Donnell.

But Frank could see that Donnell had no intention of stopping the battle now.

"Professor! Wait! Stop the—"

Frank never finished his sentence. He stopped in his tracks atop the riverbank. All around him he could hear the high whine of bullets. He could see dust flying as the shells hit the ground around him.

Suddenly he felt something hit him, and he put a hand to the back of his head.

He'd been shot!

Chapter

4

"OH, MAN, are you okay?"

Frank, facedown in the mud of the riverbank, was dimly aware of someone running over to help him. Hands flipped him over roughly. Then he was staring into a pair of terrified brown eyes. He had never seen this Confederate soldier before.

"Oh, gee, I got one of my own men," the soldier moaned. Frank grinned, astonished at how seriously the stranger was taking this.

"But it was only a blank, right?" the soldier said, trying to convince himself. "You must have been pretty close to me, but you'll be okay, right? It's not even bleeding."

"Naw, it's just a bruise." Frank shifted his gaze and saw another soldier in gray standing over them. His rifle rested over one shoulder,

34

and he looked more like an insurance salesman than a soldier, Frank thought.

"You just startled the kid, that's all," the man added to calm their frightened colleague.

Frank started to laugh. "That's the great thing about reenactments," he said. "The bullets aren't real."

Suddenly he remembered. The bullets! They *were* real! He sat bolt upright. Something had to be done!

"Professor!" he yelled, struggling to get to his feet while the two soldiers struggled to hold him back so he could rest. "Professor Donnell!"

"What's he saying?" asked the soldier who had hit him with the blank. "Ain't Donnell Union?"

"No, he's one of us," said the insurance salesman. He pointed to a rise about twenty feet away. "There he is, right there."

Frank spun in that direction and spotted the professor astride his chestnut mare. His back was to Frank, and he obviously hadn't heard him over the noise of the gunfire.

"Professor!" Frank broke free of the soldiers and ran toward the gray-suited general. "Listen to me!"

Miraculously, Donnell heard him. He turned in his saddle and fixed Frank with an angry glare.

"What?" he shouted impatiently, cupping a hand to his ear.

Frank started to answer, but his foot caught on a tree root and he stumbled slightly, catching himself on his hands before he hit the ground face first. When he raised his eyes, it was too late.

Frank watched as a bullet caught the professor in the chest, sending him spinning off the back of the horse. The chestnut mare reared and whinnied and took off at a gallop.

"Get the horse!" Frank shouted back over his shoulder at his fellow soldiers and stumbled forward to the wounded professor. At the first sight of the bleeding wound, both sides had stopped fighting. Frank's words to get the horse rung out in an eerie silence. An instant later a hundred men ran forward to help the professor.

It was too late. Frank searched for any sign of life. There was none. In the distance he could hear the sound of an ambulance siren. He just stared at the dead professor, stunned into silence, until the paramedics arrived to take the body away.

"Frank!" Frank became aware of Joe beside him as ranks of soldiers moved past them to watch Donnell's body being loaded into the back of the ambulance.

"It's okay, Joe," Frank managed to say. "I mean, I'm fine. It's the professor."

"We all saw. What happened?"

"That's what we want to know, son."

Frank looked up to see a pale, grim-faced

Tyler Pardee approaching them with an equally grim-faced companion also in Union blue.

"Frank, this is Sheriff Walker," Pardee said, his tone all business. "He has some questions for you."

"Okay, son," the sheriff said. "Just tell me what happened."

Eager to cooperate, Frank related the events of the last few minutes. He mentioned the flurry of real bullets and the blank in the back of his head.

"Hmm. Anything else?" the sheriff asked, scribbling notes in a pad he had pulled from the pocket of his uniform.

"Nothing I can think of." Frank rubbed the back of his head, which was still sore. "Before I could stop him, he was dead."

"Any idea where the shots came from?"

Frank shook his head. "I'm just not sure."

The sheriff looked around the site and shook his head. "Okay, son," he said, slapping Frank on the shoulder. "Thanks for your help. Stick around the hotel for the next couple of days, okay? I might need to question you further. I'll be over there or here most of the day to continue the investigation."

By early that evening news of Donnell's death had spread through town. Magnolia House was swarming with reporters and curiosity seekers, not to mention most of the four hundred soldiers. Joe and Frank had showered and changed into civilian clothes. Now they were standing at the top of the marble stairs, watching the pandemonium in the foyer below.

"I still can't believe Donnell's dead," Joe said, shaking his head.

"I know what you mean," Frank said. "The scene keeps flashing in my mind. If only I hadn't tripped, Donnell might still be—"

"You can't be so hard on yourself," Joe said, cutting off his brother's sentence.

"I know," Frank said thoughtfully. "While I was showering I was thinking that we didn't tell the sheriff about the pickup truck or that fight Donnell had with Wesley Hart."

Joe's eyebrows shot up. "That's right," he said. "He'd probably want to know about those incidents. I think we should head for the library and have a little talk with the sheriff."

"A pickup truck?" Sheriff Walker's skepticism showed on his face, even in the dim light from the fire in the fireplace. It was too hot for a fire, Frank reflected, shifting uncomfortably in the heat. But Sheriff Walker obviously was enjoying the luxury of his temporary surroundings. April or not, he was going to use the fireplace.

"Yes, sir. A blue truck with a Confederate flag on the front license plate," Frank replied. He watched the sheriff shift his weight in the big leather chair behind the library desk. "We

38

couldn't identify the driver. But if my brother, Joe, hadn't knocked the professor out of the way, that truck would have mowed him down."

"Hmm." The sheriff frowned down at his notes. "Anything else, then?"

Joe stepped forward to tell the sheriff about the fight that had taken place at the party the evening before. The sheriff had been there, and he was soon nodding impatiently, indicating that he had witnessed it, too. Several others had mentioned the argument to him also.

"Wesley Hart's a hothead," he said, putting his pen down and leaning back in the chair.

"Enough of a hothead to carry out his threat?" asked Joe.

The sheriff shook his head, frowning, but failed to meet Joe's insistent gaze. "I guess I'll have to check it out," he said at last. "I sure don't have much else to go on."

The boys sat in uncomfortable silence for a moment. Then the sheriff stood, reaching out to shake their hands. "Thanks for your help," he said. "I'll let you know if I have any more questions."

"Uh, Sheriff," Joe stammered, shaking the man's hand. "We were wondering, Frank and I. . . ."

"Wondering what?"

Frank stood up, facing the older man. "Would you mind if we hung around while you questioned the others?" he asked. "We feel kind of responsible for what happened. I mean, we didn't know it was going to happen or anything, but—"

"We're pretty good at investigations," Joe put in. "It seems that if we couldn't prevent Dr. Donnell's death, at least we can help catch the killer."

The sheriff hesitated, eyeing the boys. Finally he cleared his throat. "Don't go blaming yourselves," he said. "Doesn't seem like there was much you boys could have done. And who knows, maybe it was just an accident after all."

"You don't really believe that, do you?" Joe protested.

The sheriff sighed. "At the moment I don't believe anything," he said.

Two hours later Frank had to ask himself if he and Joe weren't useless in the investigation. All day they'd listened to witnesses tell the same stories of seeing Donnell hit during the battle and of hearing the argument at the party the night before. And as far as Frank could tell, no one had offered a single clue as to who the killer might be. No one had seen Hart anywhere near the professor. In fact, no one had seen Hart all that day.

Frank glanced at Joe, who appeared to be half asleep on a loveseat. Frank knew his brother felt as bad as he did about the professor. But he also knew how hungry he must be by now. Maybe the two of them should take a break, he thought.

Go downstairs for dinner. Maybe the food would recharge their mental batteries and they'd come up with a new idea.

"Wesley Hart," the sheriff said. Frank's head jerked up. Hart had just been let into the room and was crossing the carpet to shake the sheriff's hand. He still wore his Confederate uniform and looked pale and muddy—and scared, Frank realized. He must have understood how bad his threats from the night before made him look.

"What're they doing here?" he asked, nodding toward Frank and Joe.

"Helping with the investigation," the sheriff said smoothly. "Now, sit down, Wesley, and tell me what you were doing during the battle. No one can recall even seeing you there."

"I was in the ammo tent." Hart scowled at the boys, then sat down grudgingly in a leather-upholstered chair. "Handing out blanks, stocking cannons. I got a dozen people who can back me up."

"Can you give me a list of names?" the sheriff asked.

"You heard me," Hart said belligerently. "Give me paper and a pencil and I'll write 'em down."

Frank stood up abruptly. "Thanks for letting us stay, Sheriff," he said to Walker. "I think Joe and I will go downstairs and have a look around."

The sheriff glanced up at him. "Suit yourselves," he said curtly.

41

As he left the overheated library, Frank heard Joe hurrying to catch up with him.

"What's up, Frank?"

"Nothing," Frank muttered, walking slowly down the hall. "Hart wasn't going to spill anything, that's all. That is, if he had anything to spill. I figured we could spend our time more wisely by checking out the other men who were in the field."

"Good idea." Joe licked his lips, and Frank grinned, knowing he was dreaming of food again.

"You go down the back stairs," Frank said. "They lead directly to the dining room and kitchen. I'll take the front stairs and talk to the guys in the foyer."

"Yes, sir!" Joe saluted, then turned and jogged down the hall toward the back stairs. He was hungry and in a hurry. As he raced down the dark, narrow staircase, Joe heard something behind him. It sounded like the door at the top of the staircase slowly opening and closing.

He turned, but saw nothing—it was too dark. He also heard nothing more. Must have been my stomach growling, Joe thought to himself.

But as he continued down the wooden stairs, a leg suddenly swung down from behind him and kicked him on the back of the neck. Joe had no time to react as he flipped forward and fell into the long darkness.

Chapter

5

JOE WAS FLYING, out of control. He screamed once and grabbed for the banister, but got nothing but a fistful of air.

Throwing his arm wide, he reached again and got a piece of it this time. He slowed his fall enough to save himself from landing head-first on the stone floor in the hall at the bottom of the stairs. He heard the door at the top of the stairs open and close as someone called out, "Joe!"

A door banged open in the back hall right beside Joe. Frank was standing in the doorway, the light from the dining room behind him. "You okay?" he asked.

"I'll live," Joe said, leaning against the wall. Frank checked his head for cuts and bruises.

"What happened?"

"All I know is, someone or something drop-kicked me halfway down the stairs."

"Maybe we'd better stick together after all," Frank muttered, leading the way into the dining room.

"I'm for that," said Joe, massaging a sore spot on his shoulder. "Where do we start?"

Frank hesitated in the doorway. "How about Dennis Kincaid?" he said. "He said he was staying here at the hotel, remember. I have a couple of questions to ask him."

"No food first?" Joe asked as they moved through the large room, which smelled of roast beef, fried chicken, and hush puppies.

"Tell you what, Joe. Ask Dennis some nice sharp questions and dinner's on me."

Dennis Kincaid answered the door of Room 311 on the second knock. Joe noticed that he didn't seem at all surprised to see the Hardys.

"I wondered when you guys would get around to looking me up," he said as he led them into his room and motioned them to sit on the small sofa.

"What made you think we'd want to see you?" Joe asked.

Kincaid sat on the bed. "Makes sense, doesn't it? I mean, you saw the professor insult me at the airport. You might figure I could have killed him for that."

44

"Is that a confession?" Frank asked.

"Of course not. I'm not a killer."

"Fine," Joe said. "Then what can you tell us about the shooting?"

"Not much." Kincaid leaned back against the headboard of the bed. Joe reflected that he was remarkably calm for someone whose hero had just been murdered and for someone who might easily become a suspect. "As you know, I was on the Northern side, same as you," he said to Joe. "And it was loud. I was having a great time, to tell you the truth. It was my first time at a reenactment. I had never shot a muzzle-loader before. But I was on the edge of the battle when the professor got killed. I didn't see anything. Some people said maybe it was a spectator."

"Somebody would probably have noticed if a spectator had a gun," Frank pointed out.

"One more question," Joe persisted, leaning forward. "Last night, at the party, after Wesley Hart threatened to kill the professor, you and he were talking together."

"So?"

"So, what were you talking about?"

Kincaid blinked. "Nothing," he said. "I mean, I don't remember."

"Don't remember, or won't remember?" asked Frank.

Dennis's eyes darted from one Hardy to the other nervously. "Look, I'm telling you, I didn't do anything wrong."

"Then tell us what you and Hart were talking about." Joe's voice was starting to rise.

Frank reached out to calm his brother. "You aren't in any trouble—yet," he said to Kincaid. "Anything you tell us will be confidential. But a man has been killed, and your help in finding out who did it is vital."

Joe waited, listening to the intense silence in the room, for Kincaid to speak.

When he finally spoke, it was in little more than a whisper. "I don't want to get anybody in trouble."

"Professor Donnell is dead." Joe was almost seething.

"It might make you feel better to tell us," Frank said. "We can help you."

Kincaid said, "After you broke up the fight last night, I was standing alone, minding my own business when Hart came over to me. I guess he saw my Tennessee sweatshirt and figured I'd be sympathetic. He didn't say much, really. We got to talking about General Beauregard. I told him I was going to do a paper on the general. He seemed happy that I was going to write something nice about the man—"

Kincaid stopped talking abruptly. Finally Joe said, "Excuse me, Dennis, but what are you holding back?"

"I don't—I don't think he was serious."

"Who?" Joe demanded. "Hart?"

Kincaid nodded. Joe realized he was very upset.

"What did he tell you?"

Kincaid studied Joe in silence for a moment. There were tears in the corners of his eyes. "He said not to worry about Beauregard's reputation being sullied by that Yankee," he said. "That's what he called Professor Donnell. He said once the battle began, things would be taken care of."

When Frank and Joe ran up to the door of the library on the second floor, they saw that the sheriff was wrapping up the questioning of his last witness. The witness, a solemn middle-aged man in an ill-fitting Confederate uniform, was just nervously edging out the door. Joe stepped back to let the man pass, impatient to tell the sheriff what they'd found.

"I don't know, Joe," the sheriff said after the boys told him everything Kincaid had said. "I know you don't want to hear this, but I don't think all this amounts to much."

"But I was attacked on the stairs!" Joe reminded him.

"Yes, and we'll have to look into that," the sheriff admitted. "But one thing isn't necessarily connected to the other."

"Okay, suppose we agree with you that the attack on Joe isn't related to the professor's death," Frank offered. "That still doesn't explain why you don't think what Wesley Hart said to Kincaid is important."

The sheriff's tired face grew suddenly animated. "Fact is," he said angrily, "I'm the sheriff here, and I don't really have to explain anything to you two."

Joe stepped forward, eager to object, but the sheriff held up a hand to calm him. "I've known Wesley Hart all his life," he said wearily. "He's been a hothead ever since he was a boy, and he'll always be a hothead. He blows off steam, and then it's over. Far as I know, he never hurt a fly."

"There's a first time for everything, Sheriff," said Frank.

The sheriff agreed. "Of course there is. Look, I'll go ahead and talk to Wesley again myself. But don't you boys get your hopes up. And don't go getting involved, either. I'm telling you, Wesley is not our man."

Having said that, the sheriff stood up and announced, "I have not left this room in I don't know how long, and I intend to find myself something to eat. You're welcome to join me if you'd like."

"No thanks, Sheriff," Frank said to Joe's surprise. "But I did just think of something we could do for you. Has anyone checked the ammunition supply room downstairs, where the blanks came from?"

"Sure. My deputies went over it this afternoon and found nothing," answered the sheriff.

"Oh." Frank hesitated. "Well, you think we could have a peek at it?"

The sheriff hesitated. Joe could tell he didn't want to involve the Hardys any more than he had already. On the other hand, Joe knew, there was no real reason to bar them from a room that had already been searched by the police.

"Oh, okay," the sheriff said at last, taking a key out of his pocket. "Here. Tyler Pardee gave me this passkey. Go ahead, if you want to try your luck."

"Thanks," said Frank. "We will."

"Wow," said Joe as he followed his older brother into the dark, windowless ammunition room in the basement. He could tell that the room was fairly large, even before Frank flicked on the light. Once the light was on, Joe saw two rows of eight-foot-high metal shelves running down the center of the room. They were stacked high with boxes of blank cartridges.

"What are we looking for?" Joe asked his brother.

"Your guess is as good as mine," Frank said. "I thought if we found some live ammunition—but I don't know, maybe it'll be a waste of time."

Joe shrugged. "Well, we can try," he said. "I'll start here. You take that side."

Minutes passed as the brothers searched the boxes on the shelves. "Anything?" Joe asked.

"Not so far. Keep looking."

More minutes passed. Joe was about to suggest that they give up when he reached inside one more box of blanks and removed some bullets.

"I don't believe it," he said.

"Believe what?"

As Joe started to walk to Frank, Joe heard the door open behind him, and then the room went black—pitch-black.

Someone had come in and switched off the lights!

Chapter

6

"FRANK! YOU OKAY?"

"Yeah—shh." There was silence.

Frank knew that someone else was in the room. He strained his ears to hear any unusual sound and cautiously took a few steps forward, his hands out in front of him. Nothing. He took a few more steps and felt something brush against his shoulder. Just then an entire row of shelves toppled forward onto him, pinning him to the floor.

"Aaaaah!" he screamed.

"Frank," Joe cried.

The door flew open, and Joe caught a glimpse of a figure silhouetted for an instant against the light. Then it disappeared as the door was pulled closed.

"Frank!" Joe called again.

"I'm okay," Frank assured him, wondering if he was telling the truth. Just then the room was flooded with light. Joe had found the switch.

As Joe was digging his brother out of the rubble of shelves and ammunition, the door opened again and the sheriff appeared in the doorway, a chicken drumstick in one hand. Tyler Pardee stood beside him, and behind them was a small crowd of onlookers obviously drawn by the sudden noise.

Frank got to his feet cautiously, testing himself for broken bones. He grinned sheepishly at the crowd, noticing that Wesley Hart, Robert Merriweather, and Dennis Kincaid were among the onlookers.

"What on earth—" the sheriff said.

"I can explain, sir." Frank hobbled toward the men and, after the crowd had been dispersed, explained to him what had happened.

"Did you get a look at whoever did this?" Tyler Pardee asked when Frank had finished.

"Just a silhouette," Joe said. "I think it was a man." He glanced at his brother. "I have something else to tell you, Sheriff. Before the lights went out, I found this."

He handed a box of ammunition to the sheriff. "Take a look inside."

As the sheriff lifted out the shells, his eyes widened. "Well, I'll be."

"What is it?" Tyler Pardee and Frank asked.

The sheriff held up one of the shells. Unlike the flat-topped blanks, Frank observed that this one carried a hollow-nosed slug. "These are real bullets. This just might explain the shooting. It was an accident—a horrible accident, but not murder. I reckon the professor's family will have a beautiful lawsuit against the ammunition company, but it looks to me like you've wrapped up the investigation. Good work, boys."

Joe was surprised. "Hold on a minute, Sheriff. There are still a few questions that need answering."

"Such as?"

"For starters, who attacked me on the stairs? And who turned out the lights in the ammo room?"

The sheriff was not impressed. "When you've been in law enforcement as long as I have, son, you learn that it's rare when you can tie up every single loose end. I can't say why those other things happened, but I can say how the professor was probably shot. And that's what my report will state. His death was an accident."

"Does that mean we can go ahead with the reenactment tomorrow morning?" Pardee asked, shuffling his feet.

"I don't see why not," the sheriff answered. "I'll assign some men to go through the soldiers' ammunition and the shells in this room to make sure there aren't any more boxes like this one."

The sheriff paused and seemed very pleased.

"Well then, Tyler, that's that. Now I think I'm going to sample some of the Magnolia House's famous pecan pie."

Pardee threw an arm around the sheriff's shoulders. "Sheriff Walker, I'll not only join you, I'll treat."

He turned to the Hardys. "You boys care to come along?"

"No, thanks," Frank said absently before Joe could speak. Joe glanced at his brother, who seemed to be lost in thought.

"Suit yourself," said Pardee, and he and the sheriff left.

"What are you thinking?" Joe asked his brother as they straightened up the shelves.

"I'm thinking that there's more to this case than either Sheriff Walker or Tyler Pardee will admit. And I'm wondering why they both were so quick to say it's been solved."

Joe started to answer, but just then he saw something that turned his concerned expression into a smile. Jennifer Pardee had just breezed into the room. When she saw Joe, she approached him with a big smile on her face.

"Joe Hardy, there you are," she said. "I've been looking all over for you."

"I'm sorry," Joe said simply.

The look on Jennifer's face told him she understood. "It's so horrible about the professor," she said softly. "Daddy and I knew him for such a long time. But I just met Sheriff Walker upstairs, and he told me it was an accident."

"Yes, well—yeah," Joe said awkwardly, not wanting to talk about the case.

His answer left an awkward silence, made worse by the fact that Frank was still lost in thought and hadn't even greeted Jennifer. Then quite suddenly Frank's face lit up and became animated. "Of course," he said. "Why didn't I think of it sooner?"

"Think of what, big brother?" Joe asked.

As an answer, Frank began to hurry toward the stairs to the first floor. "I have to check something out."

"Wait a minute. I'll go with you."

"You're leaving again?" Jennifer cried, sounding a little frustrated.

"Don't bother," Frank said, already on the stairs and taking them two at a time. "Get something to eat. I'll see you in our room later."

"But what—" Joe started to say, but was interrupted by Jennifer taking hold of his arm.

"It's okay. Frank'll take care of it, whatever it is," she said. "Come on, Joe, how about some supper. Then I'll take you over to Rebel Park and show you the rides. There's a real crowd there tonight, and that's when it's most fun."

"But he—" Joe started to tell Jennifer that he couldn't let Frank take on the burden of the case by himself. But Jennifer didn't know there *was* a case, and Joe knew his brother wouldn't want him to tell her. Better not to involve more people than necessary, he decided.

Jennifer tugged on his arm. Joe looked down at her and relaxed. "Okay," he said. "Sure. To tell you the truth, Jennifer, I think I could eat everything in the Magnolia's kitchen."

Frank still had the sheriff's passkey in his pocket, and he meant to use it to get into the professor's room. But when he got there, the door was standing open. Frank peered inside and saw Robert Merriweather sitting glumly on the bed, leafing through a stack of papers.

Frank hadn't seen the professor's room before. Bookcases stacked with volumes and papers lined one wall. On the far wall, in front of a large window, stood an enormous wooden desk piled high with more books and notebooks.

"Am I disturbing you?" Frank asked quietly.

Merriweather took a long time answering. When he did it was with a sad, softspoken no.

The assistant cleared his throat, sat up straighter on the bed, and said, "I mean, not at all. Come in. I was just trying to organize the professor's papers."

"I didn't realize he had so much stuff here," said Frank, entering the room and peering around. A large fireplace made it seem more like a library than a bedroom.

"Amazing, isn't it?" agreed Merriweather. "The professor used this room off and on for about two years. He'd come here approximately every other month for a few days to research the book on Beauregard.''

"Have you found anything at all," Frank said as gently as he could, "that might suggest who'd want to harm the professor?"

Merriweather smiled wanly. "The question is, who *wouldn't* want to harm him. But, no, I haven't come up with any name in particular. Of course I just started looking through his things."

Merriweather picked up the papers he had been reading, then put them down again. "You know, I don't think my heart is in this tonight," he said.

"That makes sense," said Frank.

Merriweather stood up and sighed. "I think I'll call it a day."

He started for the door. "You coming?"

"I was wondering," Frank said, "if you'd mind if I hang around for a few minutes, see what I can come up with?"

Merriweather hesitated. "I don't know—"

"I won't disturb anything. I just figured it couldn't hurt—you know, before I go down to supper."

Merriweather's face seemed to drain of all its color. He waved a hand toward the professor's desk. "Fine," he said, moving through the doorway. "You're a detective, right? Just lock up after you go."

After Merriweather left, Frank ran his eyes

around the room, trying to decide where to begin his search. The stack of papers that Merriweather had left on the bed proved to be of no use in pointing to a killer.

"Maybe the sheriff's right," Frank said out loud. "Maybe it was just a freak accident."

Even though he felt discouraged, Frank was no quitter. He moved to the bookcases to begin a systematic search for any clue to the identity of the person who had decided to do Donnell in.

"And this is my latest ride. The new disco tilt-a-whirl."

Joe stood next to Jennifer, watching the speeding circular ride. Its exterior was painted with southern plantation scenes to help it fit in with the park's theme. But the ear-splitting music, screaming passengers, and teenage disk jockey kept it planted firmly in the present.

"Not bad," Joe shouted over the noise, just as fifty passengers raised their hands off the safety rail and screamed in unison.

Jennifer giggled. "How do you know? You haven't even tried it yet! Come on, this ride's on me."

She pulled him toward the entrance to the ride. Joe held back at first. He was wondering what Frank was up to and wished he'd gone to help him. He was also a little worried about the food he'd eaten less than half an hour earlier. Would he be able to take this ride? Just watching the passengers whirling up and down and around made him feel a little woozy.

"What are you, chicken?" Jennifer teased. Then she saw his uneasy expression. "I'm sorry. You're thinking of the professor again," she said as though she could read his mind. "You know, Daddy told him not to write a book about Beauregard. He said there were too many people down here who'd get angry to hear their hero called a coward."

Joe just stared at her. "I thought you said his death was an accident."

Jennifer's green eyes widened. "I did. I just mean, if he hadn't been killed that way, sooner or later something even worse might have happened to him."

Joe shook his head, trying to make sense of what she said. But Jennifer pulled him toward the tilt-a-whirl.

"Come on," she said. "The ride's about to start again. Let's see what Yankee men are made of!"

Frank wearily tugged at the last drawer of Professor Donnell's desk. *I guess I'll have to give up and accept that the professor's death was an accident after this drawer.*

For nearly two hours Frank had searched every corner of the professor's room, read through every bit of correspondence, turned each book upside down and riffled through its pages for any kind of clue. All he had to show for it was dust up his nose and red eyes from reading.

Most of the papers had been photocopies of court records, old letters, and military orders—nothing that would indicate the identity of the professor's killer. This was the last desk drawer, and Frank was exhausted. He pulled at the drawer again, but it was stuck in its frame. Frank thought about not bothering to unstick it but decided finally to yank one last time.

Now the drawer stood open—and there it was.

Frank picked up the letter, noticing that it was dated just two weeks earlier. Reading, he learned that the professor's great-great-grandfather, a Union soldier, had killed the letter writer's great-great-grandfather, a Confederate soldier at Shiloh. "Maybe, at the reenactment, we can even the score," the letter ended.

Frank peered excitedly at the signature. It read, "Wayne Robinson."

Chapter
7

I DON'T BELIEVE IT! Frank read the letter one more time to make sure he hadn't misinterpreted it. It seemed clear enough—Robinson was threatening to avenge his great-great-grandfather's death at the reenactment.

Frank ran out of the room with the letter. I just hope Robinson hasn't left Memphis, he thought as he raced down the marble stairs in search of the sheriff. The little man, he remembered, lived in Georgia, but surely he'd wait until after the reenactment to go back home.

Frank hurried through the first-floor rooms, searching for the sheriff. At last he found him, still in the dining room, sipping coffee and chatting with Tyler Pardee.

Incredible. Frank shook his head in wonder as he watched the sheriff guffaw at one of Pardee's jokes. He really thinks the professor's death was accidental!

He stuffed the incriminating letter into the pocket of his jeans and approached the sheriff's table.

"Frank!" Tyler Pardee smiled at the detective. "Sit down, relax! Let me get you a piece of pie."

"No, thinks, sir. Uh, Sheriff, I was wondering if I could have a word with you."

"What about, Frank?" The sheriff seemed to have completely forgotten about the professor.

"It's—uh, private."

The sheriff's face flickered with annoyance, but he wiped his mouth with a napkin, balled it up, and set it down as he stood up. "Okay," he finally said. "How about this table over here?"

It wasn't as private as Frank would have liked, but he was in no position to argue. He followed the sheriff to the table, pulled out the letter, and handed it to him before he sat down. "I found this in Professor Donnell's room. I think you should take a look at it."

As the sheriff read the letter, his expression changed.

"Pardee," the sheriff called, looking up from the letter. "What room's Wayne Robinson staying in?"

"How should I know?" Pardee called back with a grin. "Go ask at the front desk. Why do you want to know, anyway?"

Frank stood up, angry that the sheriff had let Pardee in on his discovery. Professionals knew better than to let everyone in on all the information, but the sheriff didn't seem to care who knew about this letter.

Not meeting Frank's eyes, the sheriff stood up and sauntered out of the dining room. "We've got another suspect," he called over his shoulder to Pardee. "Seems Wayne Robinson wrote a threatening letter."

"Robinson?" Pardee laughed. "He's nothin' but a good ol' boy."

Joe staggered off the tilt-a-whirl with Jennifer right beside him.

"How'd you like it?" she asked, her eyes shining with excitement. "That's just about my favorite ride."

"Mmm. Yeah," Joe said, trying to focus his blue eyes. "Especially that part where it went backward real fast and the disk jockey made us let go of the safety bar."

"Want to do it again?" Jennifer asked eagerly.

"Uh, not right now. But thanks."

Joe ran a hand through his blond hair. He wondered where Frank was and what he was up to. He felt guilty, leaving his brother alone while he was out having fun. Well, maybe fun wasn't the exact word for his ride on the tilt-a-whirl.

"Hey, come with me," Jennifer said as she tugged on his arm and led him across a still undeveloped field behind the rides. "I'll show you my favorite part of the park."

She took him nearly a quarter of a mile away from the glittering midway, to a large corral standing in open meadow and filled with horses softly whinnying and nickering in the moonlight.

"See?" Jennifer leaned against the corral, gazing out at the beautiful horses. Joe leaned against the fence beside her, admiring the stallions and graceful mares.

"They're still wild, most of 'em," Jennifer explained, reaching out to pat a curious filly on the nose. "They're my dad's hobby. He breaks them himself. For a guy his age he's a terrific horseman."

Joe nodded, reaching out to pat the filly himself.

"We put on a horse show every day, to show folks what a Southern cavalry unit looked like. Daddy says if we'd had as many men as we had good horses, things might have turned out differently." She shrugged and gave a little laugh. "Anyway, I love coming out here and looking at them in the moonlight."

"Yeah. Me, too," said Joe.

He gave a big yawn, and they both laughed.

"Tired?" asked Jennifer.

"Me? Well—maybe."

Jennifer smiled teasingly. "Just one more ride?"

Joe's face fell. He remembered the way his

stomach had felt when he stepped off the last time.

But he managed to take a deep breath, put an arm around her shoulders, and say, "Sure."

Frank walked with the sheriff toward Wayne Robinson's door at the big hotel. "I appreciate your doing this," Frank offered, trying to make up for the sheriff's obvious reluctance. "Maybe it is a wild-goose chase, but I feel as if we ought to check out every lead."

The sheriff was a good deal less amiable this time, Frank noticed, than he'd been before. "Fine" was all he said. "We'll check it out. Then I'm going home."

Wayne Robinson had apparently gone to bed for the night. It took him a long time to answer the door. When he did, he had on a bathrobe and appeared confused.

"Can we come in?" the sheriff asked.

"Yeah. Sure."

He nodded sleepily to Frank as he, too, stepped into the room. Frank eyed Robinson curiously. Half a foot shorter than Frank, he sure didn't look like a killer. Still, Frank told himself, you never knew.

Without wasting time, the sheriff showed the letter to Robinson and explained why they had come. Robinson sat down in a chair and read the letter, his face growing increasingly red.

"Yeah, I almost forgot about this," he said.

"Happened a few weeks back. I'm a big Civil War buff, see. Read all of Andrew Donnell's books. Why, I was the one who came across this information that his great-great-grandaddy killed mine. I remember, now, finding their names in some old battle records and laughing about it."

He tossed the letter down on a low table and gazed steadily at the sheriff. "This letter was meant as a joke, because I thought the coincidence was funny. I don't like what Donnell was saying about Beauregard any more than the next Southerner, but I had no grudge against him personally. And I don't take the past seriously enough to use it as an excuse to kill a man."

He shook his head. "I guess, under the circumstances, my little joke doesn't look too funny."

The room became silent. As though it had just occurred to him, Robinson added, "I've got people who can testify to where I was when Donnell was gunned down. I was way over on the other side of the field."

The sheriff nodded. Then he turned to Frank. "Satisfied?" he asked sharply.

Frank nodded. "Thank you," he said to Wayne Robinson. "We had to check this out."

"Sure you did." Robinson, weary and sad, accompanied them to the door. "The professor deserves no less."

"The tunnel of love?" Joe stared at the gaudily painted ride at the end of the midway. He was relieved that it wasn't the tilt-a-whirl but uncertain why Jennifer had brought him there.

"Sure. Why not?" Jennifer giggled.

"But, look. The operators are already gone." The midway was practically deserted. "For that matter, where is everybody?" he asked.

"The place is closing, silly." Jennifer playfully slapped his arm. "That's the fun of operating this place, though. I can go on the rides as late as I want. Come on. I know how to run it."

Still skeptical, Joe followed Jennifer to the entrance, where she jumped behind the operator's podium, switched a toggle, and stepped back to watch the lights and music come to life.

"Get in," she ordered, pointing to the first rowboat in a line at the entrance to the dark tunnel. "You row. I ride."

Grinning, Joe obeyed.

Inside, the only sound was that of Joe's oars lapping against the water.

"Don't go so fast," Jennifer teased him. "It's not the Indy five hundred, you know."

Smiling in spite of himself, Joe let up on the oars and tried to relax. After all, he was in a deserted tunnel facing a beautiful red-haired girl. Why couldn't he just relax and enjoy the situation?

"Come here. Sit next to me and stop rowing for a bit," Jennifer suggested, patting the seat beside her.

He started to respond when suddenly, back

from the way they had come, came the clank of a metal door being slammed.

Joe grabbed the oars again.

"What was that?" he yelled, glancing wildly down the dark tunnel.

Jennifer was also trying to locate the source of the noise. "Maybe the operator came back. It's Louie. He's always forgetting something."

"Why would he shut that entrance? That's what it sounded like, didn't it?"

Before Jennifer could answer, they heard a deafening roar from inside the tunnel. Joe spun around to see a pair of bright lights speeding toward them.

"Watch out!" Jennifer screamed. "It's a motorboat! It's going to hit us!"

Chapter

8

"DO SOMETHING!" Jennifer cried.

Joe stared at the headlights coming straight at them. The roar of the outboard motor was deafening.

"Is that where the exit is?" he yelled, pointing at the motorboat.

"Yes! It's behind that boat! There's no time! Joe!" Jennifer screamed.

"Jump!" he yelled, pushing Jennifer out of the boat into four feet of water.

Joe jumped and held Jennifer next to him flat against the tunnel wall. The motorboat plowed straight for the rowboat, sending it flying backward a few feet before splintering it into firewood. Then it roared off back through the tunnel, where the engine was cut off and footsteps could be heard running away.

"Joe?"

Jennifer's voice sounded tentative and scared. "You okay?" Joe asked her.

"Yeah. You?"

Joe pulled her close. "Yeah," he said. "Let's get out of here. Whoever was driving that boat might still be around."

Trembling and shivering in the chilly water, Jennifer led Joe through the tunnel to a service entrance. There they found the motorboat, its outboard motor still warm, bobbing in the gentle wake. Clearly, their attackers had used this boat and then run off.

"Who'd want to hurt us?" she asked. "I don't have any enemies."

Joe gave her a quick hug to console her. "Maybe you hang out with the wrong sort of guys," he commented dryly. "Obviously, somebody doesn't like the way my brother and I have been snooping around. We didn't want to tell you before, but Frank and I still believe the professor was murdered. And obviously, there is a killer, or we wouldn't have been attacked."

"I don't know about that." Jennifer sniffed, and then wiped her eyes. "Let's go back to the hotel," she said. "I've had enough excitement for tonight."

"What happened to you?" Frank sat up in bed, rubbed his eyes, and watched Joe pull off his water-soaked clothes.

70

"A little midnight swim," Joe joked, and then told his brother what had happened.

"Did you report it to the sheriff?"

"We told Jennifer's father, and he called the sheriff," Joe answered. "Mr. Pardee was very upset."

"That's understandable," said Frank.

"Yeah, but—"

"But what?"

"But—well, it seemed like he was madder at me for getting her in this situation than at the attackers. You know what I mean?"

Frank sighed and fell back against the pillows. "Yeah," he admitted. "I do know what you mean—people's priorities seem to be all mixed up. I mean, you don't see anyone weeping over the professor's death, do you? Most people are worried only about whether it's going to mess up the battle tomorrow."

Joe climbed into bed. "So, any news?"

Frank told him about the letter from Robinson. Near the end of the story, though, his words started to blur together and sleep threatened to take over.

"One thing's certain," Frank mumbled as he fell asleep. "Tomorrow we fight on the same side—and we stick as close together as we can."

It was still dark when Joe, in his Union uniform, and Frank, now in a blue uniform of his own, gathered with the troops on the rolling hills of Shiloh.

"What's the plan for this morning?" asked Joe, blowing on his fingers to warm them. It was extremely chilly in that predawn dark.

"We're supposed to attack the Southern camp at dawn," explained Frank, who had read up on the battle. "And whatever happens, we stay as close together as we can."

Joe nodded and yawned.

Frank studied his brother closely. "You don't look too good," he said.

"Two nights without my usual eight hours of beauty sleep," Joe joked. "I'll be okay, though."

Frank started to answer, but he was distracted just then by the appearance of Robert Merriweather astride a large black horse. "Look who's the new commander," Frank said, nodding toward Merriweather.

"That's weird," Joe remarked. "Why him?"

"I guess Pardee didn't want to do it today," Frank murmured. "I don't think Merriweather wanted to, either, but obviously he had no choice."

"Attention!" Merriweather called, trying to appear as commanding as possible in spite of his bulky appearance on the horse. "We'll be moving out soon, and I want you to keep it very quiet." He hesitated, as though trying to remember what he was supposed to say.

"I've chosen a second in command," he

added. "Dennis Kincaid, whom I believe many of you know."

A murmur ran through the troops as Kincaid rode up on another large black horse and saluted the soldiers. He looked very pale and very young, but he gave a perfect salute.

Frank saw the sun appear over the horizon behind the two men. "Get ready, everyone," Merriweather called. "We move out in four minutes."

Checking his gun to make sure it was loaded— and with blanks—Joe said, "I didn't know Merriweather knew Kincaid. He wasn't there yet when we met Kincaid in the airport, was he?"

Frank shook his head. "Just what I was thinking, but they could have met later." He and Joe joined the others in forming a long front line.

As they stood gazing at the Confederate camp, Merriweather rode in front of the troops, raised his right arm, and shouted, "Charge!"

The line, with Frank and Joe among them, moved as one across the fields of Shiloh in the dim light of dawn.

As he marched, Frank went over in his mind what he knew about the battle. The Southern camp was scarcely two hundred feet away, but the historical records claimed that the Confederates did not expect an attack and were caught completely off guard.

This time, though, the Confederates waited in front of their tents only until they heard Merriweather's yell. Then, unwilling to play the part of losers, they sounded their alarm immediately. In seconds Frank and Joe faced a battlefield ablaze with gunfire.

"Watch out!" Frank yelled to his brother as round after round of blanks were exchanged. Despite the noise and confusion, a big smile appeared on his face. As long as nobody got hurt, he realized, playing war could be fun—at least until exhaustion set in.

The Union troops were already using their cannons and had almost surrounded the Confederates, who were led that day by Tyler Pardee. That was why Merriweather was the Union commander, Pardee had obviously wanted to change sides and lead the South. Frank saw Pardee suddenly rear up on his horse and yell for a countercharge.

While Frank watched, the confederates responded with shouts and unintelligible yells. Joe grabbed his arm and pointed toward Merriweather, who was signaling a retreat.

As the Northerners pulled back toward the river, Frank yelled to his brother, "Stay close!"

"I'm with you!" Joe shouted, but with all the noise Frank could barely hear him.

Suddenly the Southerners decided to advance, and charged the retreating Union troops. The blue-uniformed soldiers took off, and Frank and Joe found themselves being pushed and tossed to the side of the battle. Troops rushed past them as they staggered backward into the brush.

"Come on!" Frank called to Joe. "We'll go around this way and avoid the crowds!"

Frank led the way through some thick underbrush. He could hear the battle to their left, but he couldn't see it. Finally he stopped and wiped the sweat from his face.

"Are you sure you know where we're going?" Joe demanded, coming up beside him.

"All I know is, we're somewhere in Tennessee," Frank admitted. The battle sounds were much fainter now. He decided it would be a good idea to take a short rest, then hike back through the clinging brush to rejoin their troops.

But before he could tell Joe his plan, he heard a new and unfamiliar sound.

"What's that?" he said, even as the realization began to dawn on his face.

"Horses!" Joe screamed. "A lot of them! Run!"

There was no time to run. A herd of horses was stampeding directly at the Hardys.

Frantically, Frank high-stepped through the thorn bushes that pulled at his legs and ankles. Behind him, Joe screamed to hurry. The noise of galloping horses thundered closer. There were no trees close enough that were big enough for the boys to climb.

"Too late!" he heard Joe yell.

It was later than Joe thought. Frank took one

last, desperate leap through the bushes, his brother close behind.

"W-what—" Frank stammered. But there wasn't time even to ask the question. The two brothers were falling through space.

They'd run off the edge of a high embankment and were falling toward the roaring Tennessee River!

Chapter

9

"AAARGHH!" the Hardys yelled as they hit the rocky slope, half rolling and half tumbling down toward the swirling waters below.

It was impossible for Joe to control his fall down the steep, gravelly bluff.

He did see his brother splash into the water. An instant later he, too, felt the shock of the cold current as he plunged in.

Joe worked hard to keep his head above the surface, but the current kept pulling him down. He looked for Frank but couldn't see him in the churning waves.

Joe pulled with his powerful arms to bring himself to the surface. But just as he was within inches, a powerful swirling eddy caught at him, forcing him to the bottom and pushing him downstream. Joe fought hard as his lungs quickly ran out of air. Frank, he thought weakly. But his brother wasn't there, no one was, and the weight of Joe's uniform was dragging him down, drowning him.

Suddenly he was tossed out of the churning spiral of water. Joe was free and shot to the surface, where he gasped in lungfuls of cool fresh air.

"Joe!" he heard Frank call out.

Sailing feetfirst, downstream on the current, Joe turned to see Frank near the bank of the river. He was caught up on a branch and was frantically trying to pull himself free. Branches tore at his arms, and his head was being repeatedly dunked beneath the surface of the water.

"Break the branch!" Joe yelled, speeding past.

"What?" Frank heard only the word *branch*, but the logic of the situation finally occurred to him. "Of course," he muttered to himself, attacking the branch. "Why didn't I think of that?"

On the fourth or fifth yank, the branch finally gave way and snapped in two, and Frank went sailing down the river in Joe's path, feetfirst in case of a collision with boulders.

Moments later he was treading water in quiet water downstream. Not fifty feet away, Joe was clinging calmly to a half-submerged log.

"Fancy meeting you here," Joe said with a weak grin.

Frank grinned back. "Let's get out of here."

Slowly, Joe led the way up the riverbank. At last, the brothers fell onto their backs on the grass, letting the morning sun warm them.

"That was close," Joe said after a while.

"Too close," Frank agreed. "Where'd those horses come from, anyway?"

"They could have been the same ones I saw last night, near Rebel Park," Joe mused. "Jennifer showed them to me."

Frank frowned. "You think there's any way this was an accident?"

"Who knows?" With an effort, Joe stood up. "I guess we should get back and find the real answers."

When the brothers rejoined the troops, Joe was surprised to see that the reenactment had been halted for a coffee break. Apparently, Pardee had made a few changes in the original battle plan.

When Robert Merriweather glanced up and spotted the Hardys, his eyes widened in surprise.

"You're—you're—" Merriweather sputtered. He paused and swallowed hard. "Where have you been? We were going to send a search party out for you."

"You're soaking wet," one of the other soldiers said. "What happened?"

Joe kept his eyes on Merriweather. "We were nearly killed by stampeding horses," Joe said. "Didn't any of you see them?"

"Sure we did," snapped Merriweather. "But we didn't know you were in their path. You fell into the river?"

Ignoring his question, Frank said, "How did the horses get out of their corral?"

"How should I know?" answered Merriweather. "You must be hungry. Grab a danish or doughnut and sit."

Joe decided not to argue with that. He walked over to a table loaded with pastries and coffee. Frank hung back to ask Merriweather, "Where's Kincaid?"

"I didn't see him all morning until I caught a glimpse of him going off with everyone else on horseback to round up the horses. That's why the reenactment stopped. Everyone was trying to halt the stampede."

"Except you," Joe pointed out, rejoining them with a plateful of doughnuts.

Merriweather scowled. "I'm not a good rider," he said.

"How about Kincaid?"

"He is an excellent horseman," Merriweather answered.

"There he is now." Joe nodded at a horse galloping toward them. Kincaid dismounted near the Hardys, announcing to the group in his southern accent, "Now, *that* was really something."

"The stampede?" Joe asked.

Kincaid nodded. "Never seen anything like it in my life."

"Is everything under control now?" Merriweather asked.

Joe glanced at the graduate assistant. He sounded awfully nervous.

Kincaid gave Merriweather a significant look, "There's nothing to worry about."

"Where were you when the stampede started?" Frank asked Kincaid.

"With Robert, of course," Kincaid said. "I led the retreat with him."

"But I thought—" Joe started to say. Then he saw Frank signal silence and shut his mouth.

"Joe, can I talk to you for a minute?" Frank asked.

"Sure." Joe followed his brother a short distance away.

"What's going on?" Joe asked Frank as soon as they were out of hearing distance of the other people. "Kincaid's story didn't jibe with Merriweather's."

Frank nodded. "I know. Merriweather denied having seen Kincaid since the battle started, yet they were supposed to have led the retreat together. What really gets me, though, is that I didn't know these guys even knew each other, and they're acting like accomplices."

"I don't know, Frank. Let's forget it and just

get through the rest of the reenactment, okay? After that, we can work full-time on the case."

Frank nodded as Joe heard someone clearing his throat behind him. He spun around.

"Oh. Excuse me." The pasty-faced Martin Crowley jumped back, startled by Joe's sudden movement. "Am I interrupting something?"

"No, Mr. Crowley," Frank said. "What can we do for you?"

Crowley approached the boys again, cautiously. His Union uniform looked awkward on his round-shouldered frame, as though it was a size too big for him. As he approached, he kept glancing over his shoulder at the other soldiers drinking coffee nearby. Joe realized, suddenly, that the little man was very much afraid of something.

"I don't know where to begin exactly," Crowley said in a near-whisper.

"Does it have to do with Professor Donnell?" Joe asked.

"Well, yes and no—" Crowley hesitated. "I guess it's better to just tell you."

"Tell us what?" demanded Frank.

"Well, you see, it's this way. Oh, this is rather embarrassing."

"What?" Joe asked impatiently.

But before Crowley could answer, Dennis Kincaid, back on his horse, rode up to them. Joe couldn't help but notice the look he was directing at Crowley, who trembled visibly. Why is Crowley afraid of Kincaid? Joe wondered.

"Gentlemen, the break is over," Kincaid drawled. "Time to resume battle formation. Move out."

With a last look at Crowley, Kincaid rode away.

"Well," Joe said, turning back to the little man. But Crowley was gone. Joe turned to find him trying to slip away.

"Hey, wait a minute!" Joe started after him, followed by Frank. "What'd you want to tell us?"

"Oh, nothing, nothing!" Crowley called out as he walked quickly away from the brothers. "It was nothing, really. I changed my mind. I'll tell you later."

"When?" Frank called after him, frustrated.

"After the battle. At Magnolia House."

The afternoon's reenactment was as loud and chaotic as the rest of the morning's, Joe decided as he aimed his rifle at the now familiar-looking Confederate soldiers. "I know I already shot that guy," he said out loud to himself as he popped another blank into an enemy soldier's shoulder. The Confederate cried out convincingly and fell to the ground, supposedly wounded, but Joe knew that the minute he turned his back, the soldier would get back on his feet and start shooting.

In any case the enthusiastic crowd of onlookers kept everyone fighting energetically. Whenever Joe "killed" an enemy soldier, he could count on a round of applause, just audible over the noise of gunfire. In fact, he began to really enjoy playing for the audience—braving enemy fire and attempting foolhardy exploits to see how many people he could get to cheer him on.

It came as a nasty surprise, then, when the gunfire abruptly stopped, right in the middle of the battle.

Joe turned to Frank, who'd stuck close to him all afternoon.

"What's going on?" Joe asked.

Frank didn't have time to answer. From the far side of the battlefield, Joe heard a cry.

"He's dead!" the voice was screaming. "He's dead!"

"What?" Joe exchanged a quick glance with Frank, and the two brothers began running toward the source of the uproar. As he drew closer, Joe could see a crowd gathered. Joe pushed his way through the crowd.

In the center of a circle of soldiers, flat on his back, lay Martin Crowley, his eyes closed, his mouth half open, and a widening circle of dark red blood staining the front of his Union blues.

"OH, NO." Frank stared at Crowley's still body. He'd been shot in the chest, just like Professor Donnell.

"I can't believe it happened again," he heard Joe say, while feeling for a pulse in Crowley's limp, white wrist.

Frank heard the moan of a siren in the distance. Too late to help Crowley, Frank knew. The arrival of the paramedics took away all pretense that this was 1862 and that this death was anything but real.

Frank backed away from the scene just as Tyler Pardee rode up. "What happened here?" Pardee demanded.

"Another shooting," Frank explained. "Martin Crowley's been murdered."

"Crowley?" Pardee's expression was stunned. As Frank watched, the hotel owner dismounted and joined the crowd of onlookers.

Better late than never, Frank thought, exchanging a glance with his brother. He listened to the muttering crowd, realizing that there was a feeling of real fear in the air now. He knew that all of Crowley's acquaintances were wondering, How was he killed? Why was it Crowley? And who would be next?

"All right, I admit it," the sheriff was saying to the Hardys as they stood before him in the library at Magnolia House. "I probably should have listened to you boys earlier. Not that I'm entirely convinced about the professor, mind you. But I just don't see how poor old Martin Crowley's death could have been an accident."

Frank watched the sheriff shake his head in bewilderment. You ought to be sorry, he thought angrily. If it wasn't for your stubbornness, Crowley might still be alive. But Frank knew his anger contained plenty of guilt. Hadn't Crowley tried to tell them something earlier? And hadn't it been the Hardys who had let him walk off, unprotected?

"Let's figure out what we should do now," Frank suggested. "Do you think Joe and I should work on finding a connection between the professor and Crowley while you and your men question any witnesses?"

The sheriff leaned back in his leather chair and nodded. "Sure," he said in a low voice. "Sounds okay to me. But meet me back here in, say, three hours, to check in."

Frank stared out the window at the magnolia-strewn lawn and let out a deep, thoughtful sigh.

"It's a tough one, huh?" he heard his brother say sympathetically.

"You can say that again." Frank took a sip of soda from a glass.

"I mean, it's not as if either the professor or Crowley was the most likeable guy in the world," Joe went on.

"That's for sure," agreed Frank.

"But who'd want to kill them? And what I want to know," Joe said, "is why Merriweather acted so nervous today."

"Right," said Frank. "And how come he and Dennis Kincaid are so chummy?"

"Exactly." Joe stood up from his chair in the dining room, where they'd headed to talk after leaving the sheriff. "We've got our work cut out for us, brother."

"Where do you want to start?"

"Let's go back to the professor's room. I know you've searched it already, but maybe a second set of eyes will turn up something new."

This was Joe's first time in the professor's room, and he was suitably impressed. "Wow," he said after walking inside behind Frank, who had unlocked the door with the passkey. "Some roadside inn."

"Yeah. Whatever else you say about the professor, he sure knew how to live," Frank remarked. "Seems kind of weird, though, being in here after he's gone. Where do you want to start looking?"

Joe thought for a moment. "Why don't you check the closet and chest of drawers. I'll go through the desk," he said. "If we can't find a tie between the professor and Crowley maybe something else will turn up to answer some of our questions."

They searched in silence for a few minutes—Joe working his way through the desk drawers while Frank moved from the chest of drawers to the closet. He started searching through the professor's jacket pockets.

Joe glanced over in time to see Frank pull a piece of paper out of one of the pockets.

"Find anything?" he asked.

"Yeah," he said. "A dry cleaner's receipt from Bayport."

Joe turned back to the desk as Frank continued pulling papers out of the professor's raincoat, trousers, and sports coat. "Most of these are notes the professor made to himself," Joe heard him say. "Things about his book. Here's one about travel arrangements."

A moment later Frank remarked, "You know, he was pretty organized. He put the date on every note. Sometimes he even numbered notes consecutively by subject. Pretty amazing."

Joe paused for a long time as he read something interesting he had pulled from the desk.

"Oh, yeah?" he said at last. "Then come look at this."

Joe showed the note he'd found to his brother. "See? A corner's been torn off. Is that where he usually puts the date?"

"Let me see—" Frank read the note.

> Robert,
>   Contact the County Clerk's office at Shiloh to determine who owns the property surrounding the National Park.

Frank looked up, smiling broadly.

"Crowley was the county clerk," he remembered. "Joe, I think you may have found something."

Robert Merriweather was even more nervous now than before, Joe realized as he and Frank interrogated him about the professor's note.

Merriweather sat on the bed in his room, sipping a cup of tea. Joe noticed that Merriweather's hands shook each time he lifted the cup to his lips. With each sip, he spilled some of the tea and nervously replaced the cup on the nightstand. Then, seconds later, he would look at the tea cup and start the whole process over again.

"Robert." Frank's voice sounded amazingly patient. "Why are you so nervous?"

"Why shouldn't I be?" The chubby man looked from one brother to the other. "The professor's been murdered, and now Crowley's dead. I'm terrified."

"You've been nervous ever since we got to Memphis," Joe pointed out.

"I've been under a lot of pressure. Professor Donnell wasn't an easy person to work for."

"All right," Frank said. "Never mind about that now. Just tell us what you can about this note."

Merriweather studied the note Joe handed him. "I never saw it," he finally announced. "He never gave it to me."

"Any idea why it wouldn't have a date on it?" asked Joe. "Or do you think someone tore it off on purpose?"

Joe tried to be patient as Merriweather picked up his teacup, then set it down again. "I haven't the slightest idea," he said at last.

"You don't know who owns the land around the national park?" asked Frank.

"Pardee, I assume. We're on that land." Merriweather laughed weakly.

"Fine," Joe interrupted. "Now tell us this. How long have you known Dennis Kincaid."

Merriweather's eyes widened slightly. "As

long as you, I guess. Just met him two days ago.''

Joe started to protest, but Merriweather's face had suddenly taken on a set, determined look.

''I'm exhausted,'' he said, picking up his teacup and, hands steady, he took a big drink of the hot liquid. ''I don't want to answer any more questions right now.''

''Fine,'' Frank said. He started for the door. Joe hesitated but then changed his mind, remembering how stubborn the assistant could be. Reluctantly he followed his brother out of the room.

''What did all that mean?'' he asked Frank as the two of them strode down the corridor.

''I think it means we're onto something,'' said Frank in a low voice. ''But first I think we should check in with the sheriff. It's nearly time.''

As he spoke, Joe was passing the professor's room, where they'd found the incriminating note earlier. Joe glanced at it, then stopped dead in his tracks.

''I thought you locked the door,'' he said to his brother.

''I did—'' Frank glanced toward the room and he, too, stopped cold.

The door to the professor's room was wide open.

Chapter

11

SILENTLY FRANK MOTIONED for Joe to move to the far side of the doorway.

Once they were in position on either side of the door, Frank raised a hand as a signal to enter. As he brought the hand down he yelled, "Now!"

The Hardys burst into the room to find Dennis Kincaid standing near the desk. When he saw the brothers, he froze.

"Get him!" Frank yelled, leaping for him.

But Joe had already made a flying tackle on Kincaid, crashing with him onto the bed.

Frank relaxed. Very few people could wriggle out of one of Joe's football tackles, particularly not an underweight college kid. But to his surprise, Kincaid refused to stop fighting. He struggled against Joe for several seconds, hitting him hard in the stomach before knocking the breath out of him, and sliding off the bed and onto the floor.

"What's going on?" Kincaid gasped as Frank stepped up to him.

"You tell us!" Joe demanded.

Kincaid said nothing but only fought to control his breathing.

"How did you get in here?" Frank asked.

Kincaid glared at the older Hardy but still said nothing.

"Fine," Frank said, his blood boiling. "You can tell it to the sheriff, then. He's always interested to hear from someone who's into breaking and entering."

"I didn't break in," Kincaid snarled. "The door was open."

"It was—" Joe started to say, but Frank stopped him.

"What were you looking for?" asked Frank.

Kincaid's mouth turned down stubbornly. Suddenly he flared out, "I just wanted a souvenir of the professor!"

"And you were just going to take something?" asked Joe.

"I would've okayed it with Merriweather," Kincaid answered, trying to sound annoyed.

"Did you find anything?" Frank asked in a steely voice.

"No." Kincaid paused. He seemed to be deflated. "No. I didn't find anything."

"Get out of here," Joe growled.

Kincaid struggled to his feet and pushed his pale hair out of his eyes. "I think I will."

After he left the brothers exchanged a quick glance. Frank shrugged. "Let's go find the sheriff," he said, and took out the passkey to lock the door behind them.

"It isn't just the fact that these murders could kill my business—so to speak," Tyler Pardee was shouting as Frank and Joe approached the upstairs library. "But my own daughter's under attack, Sheriff. I'm telling you, Walker, this is not going to look good for you come election time."

"Excuse me?" Frank knocked on the half-open door. "Can we come in?"

Pardee motioned for the Hardys to enter without stopping his tirade. "What have you and your men found so far?" he demanded of the miserable sheriff.

"We know Crowley was shot with the same kind of bullet as Professor Donnell, and from a distance," the sheriff recited in a monotone. He turned to Frank and Joe with dim hope lighting his downcast face. "You boys find anything?"

Frank snapped his head toward Joe, "Let me do the talking." Then he addressed the sheriff.

"Not much, I'm afraid," he said. "But I did have some questions for Mr. Pardee."

"For me?" Tyler Pardee seemed very surprised.

"Only a few, actually," said Frank.

"Shoot."

Frank took the passkey out of his pocket. "I got this from the sheriff. How many more of these are there?"

"Just one other," Pardee said.

"Who has the other one?" Frank asked.

"I do."

"May I see it?" asked Frank.

Frank smiled to himself as Pardee grimaced in exaggerated annoyance. But the middle-aged hotel owner dragged the other passkey out of a trouser pocket and held it up for Frank to see.

"Thanks," Frank said. "Oh, and one other thing. Who owns the property around the national park?"

Pardee's face turned to stone.

"What's this all about?" he demanded.

"Just curious," Frank said mildly. "But I think it might have something to do with the murders."

"Can't imagine why you'd think that. Anyway, all that land's been in my family since before the real Battle of Shiloh."

"The deeds are on file at the courthouse?" Frank persisted.

"Sure," Pardee snapped. "Now you tell me

95

something. What's my land got to do with two men getting shot and my daughter almost getting mowed down by a motorboat?"

"Good question." Frank moved away. "Unfortunately, I don't have an answer yet."

The sheriff's face turned red. "If you boys are onto something you'd better tell me right now," he said. "There's a killer on the loose, and I wouldn't be at all surprised if he went after you two next."

"Don't worry, sir," Frank said, moving toward the door with Joe following. "If we figure something out, you'll be the first to know."

"Now what?" Joe asked as they made their way toward the marble staircase.

"Search me," Frank said gloomily. "I was hoping something would shake loose from Pardee, but all I did was make him mad. I tell you, Joe, right now everyone looks suspicious around here." He glanced at his brother and was surprised to see a thoughtful expression on his face. "How about you?" he asked.

"I was thinking," Joe said slowly as they descended the stairs to the foyer. "Jennifer said something kind of funny last night, before we went on the rides."

"What's that?"

"She said her dad tried to talk the professor out of writing a book on General Beauregard.

96

Now, why would he want to do that? Seems a book could only help his business."

Frank frowned. "Search me. Maybe he figured it would get folks down here too mad."

Joe thought it over. Then he said impulsively, "How about checking out Pardee's horses with me? They should be back in the corral by now. Something about that whole stampede doesn't sit right with me."

Frank was surprised and shrugged. "Sure," he agreed, following Joe to the door. "How can it hurt?"

In the pink light of sunset Joe led Frank through the amusement park to the corral at the far end of the fields. The horses were peacefully grazing, as though they hadn't nearly caused the Hardys' death a few hours before.

"Hmm," Joe said, glancing at a stable and barn with construction equipment lined up against the side of it. "I don't remember seeing all that last night."

"You had eyes only for Jennifer," Frank teased.

Joe grinned. "It was dark," he said, "that's all." Then he nodded toward a spot where the corral had obviously been mended. "It looks like the horses got out through there."

"You got that right," said a voice behind the Hardys.

Frank and Joe were startled by a grizzled old man dressed in dusty cowboy clothes. White hair and a beard stuck out from under his battered hat, and his thin shoulders were hunched up beneath his red western shirt. "Name's Ben," he said. "I run the stable for Mr. Pardee. Can I help you boys?"

"We were wondering how the horses broke out this morning," Joe said.

Ben scratched his chin whiskers. "I figure it was all this new construction. Maybe the digging weakened the fences and somethin' spooked the horses and they bolted."

"Did you see it happen?" asked Frank.

The old cowboy shook his head. "I was in the barn spreadin' hay."

Joe asked, "Did you see a young, skinny, blond guy here around that time?"

"You mean Dennis?"

"You know him?" asked Joe.

"Oh, sure, he's been around a few times."

The Hardys said nothing.

"Can't say if he was here before the stampede," Ben continued. "But I do know he was here before the shooting. I remember 'cause the noise of the battle was still going on. After Crowley got shot, everything went quiet."

The Hardys thought this over while Ben rattled on, oblivious of whether or not they were listening. "Shame about Crowley. I always liked him. Even voted for him, and that could have cost me my job if anyone found out."

"Why's that?" asked Joe.

"You boys don't know much, do you? Crowley wasn't popular around here. Mr. Pardee was campaign manager for his opponent in the last election."

"Who was his opponent?" asked Frank.

"Wayne Robinson," said Ben.

"Wayne Robinson," Frank repeated incredulously. "He lives in Macon, Georgia."

"He does now, but until six months ago he lived right here in Memphis," said Ben. "Listen, I'd love to keep chatting with you boys, but they've got supper waiting for me at the house."

"Of course," said Frank. "Thanks for your help."

"You two take care around here," added Ben, walking away. "Plenty of construction pits to stumble into."

"So Dennis Kincaid was here before," Frank suggested after Ben had gone. "We'll ask him about it when we get back to the hotel. Anything else you want to check out while we're here?"

"The barn?" Joe said. He didn't think there'd be much to see, but all the construction equipment intrigued him. Besides, it was so peaceful away from a hotel full of terrified guests.

The Hardys walked slowly across the meadow to the barn in the evening light. It was painted rust red and had a peaked wooden roof. Tall metal scaffolding hugged the side nearest the boys like a metal shell.

Joe entered the barn first, followed by Frank.

Inside, it was spacious and very dark. Rays of light filtered in through the ill-fitting boards on the roof and landed in pale streaks on the hay-strewn floor.

"Wish we had some light," Joe heard Frank say behind him.

Joe found a switch and threw it, but nothing happened. "Power must be off because of the construction."

"Maybe we should come back in the morning," Frank suggested.

"Yeah, maybe so," said Joe. He heard something—or someone—move behind him in the dark.

"What was that?" he asked.

"What was what?"

Then they both heard a creaking sound.

"It sounds like—" Joe started to say. Then he stopped. No, it couldn't be. He looked up through the darkness toward the front wall, the one with the scaffolding. Was it shifting?

"The wall!" Frank shouted behind him. "It's collapsing!"

Chapter

12

"RUN!" YELLED JOE. He turned and raced toward a side entrance, grabbing Frank by the arm and yanking him outside just in time.

Behind them, an entire section of barn wall collapsed. Enormous clouds of dust blew out all around Frank and Joe.

"That was too close," Frank said, stunned.

Joe slapped dust from his clothes. "You can say that again. And we've had too many close calls since we got here." He and Frank stumbled, still slightly dazed, across to the corral, where the horses were snorting and pawing at the dust nervously, and sat down.

A few moments later Joe looked up to see Tyler Pardee, the sheriff, and Ben running toward them.

"What happened here?" demanded the sheriff.

"You tell us," said Joe."

"You boys okay?" Pardee seemed to be shaken, even in the dim evening light.

"We'll be okay after we clean up a bit," Joe said, still brushing dust and grit out of his hair and off his shirt. "Never dull around here, is it?" he said to Pardee.

"Thank goodness you weren't hurt," the hotel owner replied.

Ben said, "I told 'em to be careful around here. Last thing I said to 'em. Then I was sittin' in the kitchen eating supper and I heard that crash, and I just *knew* it had to be the barn—especially with the rides shut down for the night—"

"Fine, Ben," Mr. Pardee interrupted. "Why don't you round up some men and check out what caused the wall to collapse."

"Yes, sir, Mr. Pardee."

As the Hardys, Pardee, and the sheriff walked back toward Magnolia House, Frank said to the sheriff, "Sir, I was wondering if we could have another private talk with you. It won't take long."

"Doubtful, son," the sheriff said matter-of-factly.

"What do you mean?" asked Joe.

"It means he doesn't need any more private talks," Pardee said with obvious satisfaction. "The case is closed."

"What do you mean, closed?" said Frank.

"It's true," answered the sheriff. "We were looking to tell you fellas when we heard the barn wall collapse. We've arrested Wayne Robinson for the murders of Martin Crowley and Andrew Donnell."

The Hardys stared at him, stunned.

Frank was still going over what had happened the next morning as he and Joe ate breakfast in the dining room.

"It just doesn't add up," he said to his brother, who was digging into a heaping plate of buttermilk pancakes, sausages, and grits. "One minute Pardee's yelling at the sheriff to solve this case pronto, and the next minute he and the sheriff are all buddy-buddy, talking about how Robinson shot both Donnell and Crowley. I don't know. Maybe I'm wrong, but I smell a rat."

"A rat?" Joe turned to see Jennifer Pardee standing behind them, her hands on her hips. "You didn't see one around here, did you? How awful!"

"Not a real one." Joe pulled out a chair for Jennifer.

"Frank was just saying he doesn't think Wayne Robinson's responsible for those killings," Joe explained.

"Why not?"

"First of all," Frank answered, "Robinson has an airtight alibi for the professor's murder.

103

We talked to a crowd of people who were with Robinson on the far side of the field when it happened."

Jennifer said, "But Daddy told me he wrote a threatening letter to the professor, and he did hate Mr. Crowley. I don't think you boys understand southern politics. It can get ugly."

"Ugly enough to lead to murder?" asked Frank.

Jennifer shrugged, turning a little pink.

Joe added, "I honestly don't think he'd do it at all after being suspected of shooting the professor."

Jennifer frowned. "You may be right. What are you going to do now, and how can I help?"

"For starters," said Frank, "while Joe finishes his breakfast, I'll make a quick phone call. Then I want to look at the supply tent on the battlefield where they kept the extra ammo."

"The place Wesley Hart was in charge of," Joe added.

"Right. I haven't ruled him out as a suspect yet," said Frank. He glanced at Jennifer, who was listening attentively. He didn't like discussing the case in front of her, but he sensed that she was really on their side.

"After that, I want to drive to the courthouse to check out some deeds."

"Can I come along?" asked Jennifer.

Frank looked from her to Joe, then back to

her. "We'll need you to show us the way to the courthouse," he said, relenting.

As Joe waited with Jennifer in the foyer of Magnolia House for Frank, he wished that for once he and Frank could have made it through an entire vacation without getting involved in a mystery. Here I am, he thought glumly, with one of the prettiest girls I've ever seen, and all I can think about are dead people. Oh, well. He shrugged. Better luck next time.

Joe's thoughts were interrupted by Frank. "So? What gives?" he asked his brother.

"A lot gives," Frank said with obvious satisfaction. "I just talked to the dean of men at Tennessee State University."

"Dennis Kincaid's school?" Joe interrupted.

"Yes and no," said Frank.

"What does that mean?" asked Jennifer.

"It means that that's where Kincaid says he goes to school, but there's no record that he was ever enrolled there."

Joe shook his head, impressed with his brother's detective work. "What tipped you off?"

"First of all he had a room at the hotel, which seemed very odd. Then Ben, down at the corral. He said he'd seen Dennis around there several times. But Dennis told the professor this was his first time at Magnolia House. Kincaid should have made sure his cover story held water."

"Why would he need a cover story?" asked Jennifer.

"That," said Frank, "is just one of the things I want to ask him. Let's all pay a visit to Dennis Kincaid's room."

This time Jennifer Pardee led the way to the upstairs room. Joe was amused at her determination to help the detectives, and he let her run ahead after he had told her the room number.

But when they knocked at Kincaid's door, there was no answer.

"Not really a surprise," Frank commented.

"What now?" Jennifer asked.

"We could try Merriweather's room," offered Joe. "The two of them seem to be pretty friendly lately."

"Good idea," said Frank.

But to Joe's disappointment, there was no answer at Merriweather's door, either.

"This isn't getting us anywhere," Joe said.

"Right," Frank agreed. "Let's check out the ammo tent as we'd planned, and we'll look for Kincaid later."

Frank was surprised at how calm and beautiful the battlefield appeared in the midmorning spring light. It was hard to believe it was the same place where Frank had watched hundreds of people in uniform firing rifles and cannons.

But sure enough, there in the middle of what

had been designated neutral territory for the reenactment, Frank spotted the ammo tent.

"Hurry up," he called to Joe and Jennifer, who lingered behind him. He started jogging toward the olive green canvas structure. Approaching the entrance, he saw that the tent was about twelve feet tall and perhaps thirty feet on each side.

Frank stepped inside and was once again confronted by shelves stacked with boxes of blank cartridges. He stood in the doorway for a while, trying to decide where to begin his search.

"Here we go again," he said aloud.

"Talking to yourself, big brother?" Joe teased as he and Jennifer entered the tent.

"You caught me."

Jennifer studied the shelves. "Dad should have had someone take this down by now," she commented. "What is it you're looking for?"

"Anything that doesn't look as if it belongs here," Frank replied.

"You'll know it when you see it," Joe explained.

Jennifer was skeptical. "If you say so."

Frank began searching the shelves on the far left of the tent, while Jennifer took the middle and Joe wandered off toward the right. After a few minutes' silence Joe said, "You know, there's an excellent chance we won't find anything."

"I know," Frank admitted, "but let's give it a little time."

It was hot in the tent, and even Frank thought about giving up after another fifteen minutes of fruitless searching. He paused to wipe his face on the tail of his shirt. Then he froze. He heard a very unsettling sound.

"What's that?" he said.

"What?" Jennifer wandered over to him.

"That hissing sound. Like steam leaking from a pipe."

Jennifer looked around. Then she started sniffing. "There's smoke."

Just then one shelf, then another, crashed to the ground behind them. Jennifer screamed as Joe came running toward them as fast as he could.

"Run for it!" he yelled at the top of his lungs. "The tent's on fire! It's going to explode!"

Chapter

13

"IT HASN'T REACHED the ammo yet, though," Frank snapped as the three ran for the entrance, climbing over the shelves Joe had accidentally knocked over.

"Not yet," yelled Joe. "But it could any minute, and when it does it will blow this battlefield off the map."

Frank knew his brother was right. Blanks might not have slugs in them, but they did have gunpowder—and gunpowder explodes.

"Get her out of here," Frank said, pushing Jennifer toward his brother. "I'm going to try to put out the fire."

"What!" Joe was already shoving Jennifer through the entrance. "Forget it, Frank!"

"Nobody can stop this but us," Frank insisted,

looking around wildly for something to fight the fire with. In a corner he spotted a pile of army blankets and charged for them.

"I'll be right back," Joe yelled after him. Frustrated and angry with his brother for taking such a risk, he ran outside and yelled to Jennifer, "Run! We're going to try to put out the fire!"

"You're what?" Jennifer yelled.

"We're going to put it out!" Joe hoped he didn't look as foolish as he felt.

"Don't be stupid!" Joe heard the girl scream as he turned back toward the tent, but it was too late. He saw Frank at the far end of the space, beating at the canvas with a blanket. Instantly, Joe was at his brother's side.

"Fancy meeting you here," Frank joked, pounding at the flames. But the fire continued to grow, and as it did, the smoke grew thicker and blacker. Frank broke down in a fit of coughing.

"Give me those," Joe said brusquely, reaching for some of the blankets. He threw the blankets on the flames, smothering one area after another. But the fire continued to work its way closer to the shelves of ammo.

"Frank," he said. "We've got to get out of here."

Frank was coughing too hard to answer.

"Come on, Frank," Joe said, hustling Frank toward the entrance and up and over the fallen shelves.

He practically pulled his brother to the edge of

the open battlefield, where they caught up with Jennifer.

"Don't stop!" Joe yelled at her. "It'll blow any second!"

Jennifer took Frank's other arm, and the three of them made it to a small knoll a safe distance away.

KABOOOOOOOOM!

The ammo tent erupted in a tremendous explosion that rocked the ground. Tiny bits of debris began to rain down on the trio even as far away as they were. But to Joe's relief, they were safe.

"Looks like we won't be turning up any evidence there," Joe said wryly.

Frank surveyed the remains of the tent. Where he, Joe, and Jennifer had been standing only moments before, there was now a black, smoldering hole in the earth.

Frank studied the field to see if he could spot anyone else, but he wasn't surprised that there was no one in sight. He pointed to a row of trees a couple of hundred feet from the tent. "Whoever set the fire probably ran in there," he said to the others.

"Someone purposely set that fire," Jennifer stated. "But why?"

"We're getting too close to the killer," said Frank, "and he knows it."

Frank spotted a group of workers from Rebel Park running toward them. Among them was old Ben from the corral.

"We heard the explosion," Ben said when he caught up with them on the edge of the blackened field. "We called the fire department. Are you okay, Miss Pardee?"

"We're fine." Jennifer was impatient to be moving. "Ben, would you do us a favor? Would you wait for the sheriff, and when he gets here, tell him that someone purposely set fire to that tent. We don't know who it was. We'd stay but we have to get down to the county courthouse."

"I'll tell the sheriff," Ben said, looking mystified.

"Good," said Jennifer. "Then we're on our way."

The boys started to protest, then shrugged and followed Jennifer to her car.

Fifteen minutes later the Hardys were speeding in Jennifer's red convertible along a Tennessee country road. Jennifer was driving. Joe sat next to her. Frank sat in the back seat, trying to put together the pieces of the case.

"Um, Frank?" Jennifer said, glancing at him in the rearview mirror. "Don't look now, but I think we're being followed."

Frank moved closer to the middle of the back seat and studied the road behind them in Jennifer's rearview mirror. A navy blue pickup truck was perhaps a quarter mile back down the road.

"That could be the truck that nearly ran over

us at the airport," said Joe, who had spotted the truck in the sideview mirror.

"That's what I was thinking," said Frank. "Do you recognize it, Jennifer?"

She raised her eyes to the rearview mirror again, then shook her head no. "There are an awful lot of pickup trucks in Tennessee."

Frank sighed. "Let's just keep an eye on it then," he said, "and see what happens."

A few miles later the blue pickup pulled off the road. The Hardys and Jennifer breathed easier.

When they arrived at the county courthouse, Frank was the first one out of the car. Jennifer and Joe followed him to the office of the recorder of deeds.

"Afternoon, Miss Pardee," said the woman behind the counter. She was a slender blond in her late fifties with what Frank thought might be a permanent scowl on her face.

"Afternoon, Miss Beaumont," Jennifer said. She explained what they were there for, and the woman retrieved a huge, red leather-bound book for them. Frank opened it to see that it contained hundreds of deeds.

"It's unlawful to remove this book from the counter," Miss Beaumont said.

"That's fine." Frank leafed through the pages. Then he said to Miss Beaumont, "All these deeds look new." He pointed to one at random.

"It's dated 1938, but see? No wear and tear at all to the page."

Without looking up from her paperwork, Miss Beaumont snapped, "Fire."

"Fire?" said Joe.

"Recorder's office burned down about six years ago," said Miss Beaumont. Frank noticed that she seemed annoyed at having to share this information.

"And all the deeds were destroyed?" Joe asked.

"Every single one."

Frank came to the page that showed the titles to the land surrounding the national park. The deeds to the property were clearly registered in the name of Tyler Pardee.

"Who was county clerk six years ago?" Joe asked in a friendly voice.

"Martin Crowley," said Miss Beaumont. She peered up at them through her glasses. "Will that be all?"

"Yes, it will," answered Frank. "Thank you."

As they filed out of the courthouse, Jennifer hurried to keep up with Frank. "What does it all mean?" she demanded.

"It means," said Frank, "that you have to show us where Martin Crowley lived."

Martin Crowley's house was about five miles from the courthouse.

"I still don't know why we're here," Jennifer

114

said as she parked her car in front of Crowley's home.

"Because my brother has a hunch," Joe said good-naturedly. "Right, Frank?"

"More than a hunch," Frank said, hopping out of the car and walking up to the front door. He knocked and waited for an answer.

"I'm sure nobody's there," Jennifer told him. "Crowley lived alone."

"Wait here." Joe dashed around the side of the house. Frank waited, scanning the street to see whether anyone was watching. There was no one in sight.

Just then the front door opened. Joe stood there, grinning. "Welcome," he said.

Jennifer laughed and followed Frank inside. But Frank was all business as he ordered, "Spread out."

"What are we looking for?" asked Jennifer.

"Deeds," Frank told her.

Twenty minutes later Frank came out of a spare bedroom, waving a red book over his head. "What did I tell you?" he said triumphantly. "I found it at the top of the closet."

"What does it say?" asked Jennifer.

"Basically what I expected," answered Frank, holding it out for Joe to inspect.

But Joe was listening, his face still. "Uh-oh," he whispered. "We've got visitors."

Frank and Jennifer followed his gaze. Through

a front window, they spotted what they thought was the same blue pickup truck pulling slowly away from the front of the house. Its tinted windows prevented them from seeing who the driver was.

"As soon as it's past the front," Joe murmured, "we make a break for the car."

Just then, as though the driver had sensed he was being watched, the engine roared, and the pickup sped off.

"Go!" shouted Joe.

They ran for the car. This time Joe took the driver's seat, with Jennifer beside him in the passenger seat. Frank jumped over the side of the convertible into the back.

In seconds Joe had maneuvered the car in fast pursuit of the truck.

"Slow down!" Frank cautioned.

"I don't want to lose him," Joe retorted.

"Something's wrong," Frank shot back. "Why is he running from us all of a sudden? He was following us."

"That's what I want to find out," Joe answered, putting more pressure on the gas pedal.

"He disappeared around that turn!" cried Jennifer as they made their way into the countryside now.

Joe started to follow the truck around the turn, and as he pumped the brake pedal twice to slow the car slightly, he felt it go all the way to the floor.

The road not only was turning, it was going downhill now and the little convertible was picking up speed.

"Slow down, Joe!" Frank demanded.

"I can't!" Joe shouted. "The brakes are gone!"

Chapter

14

JENNIFER SCREAMED as the car tore down the hill.

Joe fought to keep the speeding vehicle on the road, but he felt he was losing the fight.

He tried to pull on the emergency brake, but there was too much speed built up. "The brake won't hold!" he shouted.

Joe had to focus all his attention on the road now.

At the bottom of the hill, the road formed a T intersection with another road. Across the intersection and dead ahead was the Tennessee River.

There were no guardrails running along the river, and Joe knew in an instant what would happen.

If he couldn't negotiate a turn—either left or right—they would plunge into the water.

"Get ready to jump if I don't make it!" he shouted.

The car raced forward.

The muscles in Joe's forearms began to ache from the strain of holding on to the steering wheel. I've got to hold on, he told himself grimly, gritting his teeth. All our lives depend on it!

At the bottom of the hill, Joe forced the steering wheel to the left until the car moved to the center of the road.

The car went into the turn with screeching tires. Joe could feel the right side of the car lift for a moment off the pavement.

At that instant, Joe pushed down on the accelerator. The sudden surge forward forced the wheels on the right side to drop back to the ground. To his triumph, he had control of the car again.

They were through the intersection! They had made it!

On the straightaway at the bottom of the hill, the car slowed enough for Joe to downshift, using the gears to bring down the speed. Finally Joe could control the car enough to steer it off the road and into some bushes, where it came to a complete stop.

"You did it, Joe." Frank congratulated him from the back of the car.

"Thanks, Joe," Jennifer said sincerely.

"I wouldn't want to do that every day," Joe admitted, already out of the car and sliding under it. "Frank, someone definitely cut the brake lines."

"It had to be," Frank said. "These perfectly timed accidents are turning into a pattern. The question now is, how do we get back from here."

"We've all got two legs, haven't we?" Jennifer said stoically. "My advice is, we walk."

"How much farther?" Joe groaned two hours later as they continued their stroll through the Tennessee countryside. It was the first really hot and humid day, and Joe could feel sweat trickling down his back and sides. He'd have given anything for a nice cold lemonade.

"About four miles," said Jennifer cheerfully. Unlike the Hardys, she seemed to be cool and comfortable.

"Why aren't there any cars on this road?" Joe asked.

"This is Tennessee, honey," Jennifer teased. "Not New York City."

As they kept walking, Joe glanced over at his brother. Frank had barely spoken during the entire walk. "Why so quiet, Frank?" Joe asked.

"I'm thinking about this book," he said, holding up the red book he had found at Crowley's house. "As soon as we get back, I want to talk to Robert Merriweather about it."

"Merriweather?" Joe was surprised. "Why him?"

"I need some information, and I think he can give it to me," Frank said.

Joe started to question him more, but then thought better of it. He sensed that Frank was reluctant to discuss the book in front of Jennifer.

Sure enough, Frank suggested that he and Joe go up to their room the moment they got back to the hotel.

"You're sure you'll be okay?" Joe said to Jennifer. "Your dad won't be too mad about your car, will he?"

"Why should he be?" said Jennifer bravely. "I wasn't the one who cut the brake lines." Her smile faded. "I'm not looking forward to explaining to him about the ammunition tent, though."

"Don't worry. I'll explain that to him myself," Joe assured her. Then he said goodbye to Jennifer and followed his brother upstairs.

"Okay, Frank," Joe said as soon as the two of them were alone in the room. "You didn't want to talk about the book in front of Jennifer. What's up?"

Frank looked embarrassed. "I didn't know I was so obvious," he said. "Listen, we don't know enough about these people, Joe. We have to be careful."

"So, what did you find?" Joe asked.

"The book contains a duplicate set of deeds," Frank said. "Or actually, not a duplicate, a different set. I'm not sure which book contains the genuine ones. I bet it's these, the ones from Crowley's house, but I won't be able to prove that right away, and we need to act fast."

"What do the deeds show?"

Frank leafed through the big book and said, "They indicate that while Tyler Pardee does own quite a bit of land around here, he doesn't own it all. Much of the property where Rebel Park is now—particularly the new section, where the new rides are going in and the corral is— belongs to several different people."

Frank pointed to a survey plot that showed tracts of land around the national park. Many tracts carried the name T. Pardee, but some others carried the names Hood, Colquist, and Langston.

"Maybe Pardee can explain this," Joe said doubtfully.

"Even if he can," said Frank, "it doesn't change the fact that Crowley was apparently up to something."

"But could that be a motive to kill him?"

"That's what we have to find out."

The Hardys didn't find Sheriff Walker until suppertime, when he approached them in the dining room. Frank saw him coming and silently pulled out a chair for the weary sheriff.

"Sorry I took so long getting to you, boys," the sheriff said, joining them. "It's been a busy day, what with the fire and all. I understand you were looking for me."

Frank smiled politely. He didn't intend to tell the sheriff about the brakes on Jennifer's car. He was sure the sheriff could find a way to dismiss it as just another accident—even though the lines had been cut—and Frank didn't feel he had the patience right then to deal with a reaction like that.

Instead, he filled the sheriff in on the book of deeds they found at Crowley's house and what it showed about who owned the land around the park. He also told him of his discovery that Dennis Kincaid was not a student at Tennessee State as he had claimed.

"Well," the sheriff drawled, "lying about being a student isn't exactly a crime."

"I knew you'd say that, Sheriff, and of course, you're right," Frank argued, "but with two murders on your hands I'd think the fact that somebody is lying about who he is might be of some importance."

The sheriff thought that over for a moment. Then he said, "Sorry, but nothing you've told me makes me disbelieve the fact that Wayne Robinson killed both men."

"Has he admitted to the murders?" Joe asked.

The sheriff smiled. "Not yet. But we expect he'll come around pretty soon."

He stood up. "Unless you boys have something else to tell me, I think I'll head home for some supper myself."

Frank frowned, stifling his anger. "Thank you, Sheriff," he said.

"Stay in touch," the sheriff said, and walked away.

"Yeah, Sheriff," Joe said. "Thanks for nothing," he finished under his breath.

But Frank had already gone on to the next step in his plan. "After supper," he said to Joe, "let's stop by the front desk to see if we can find Dennis Kincaid."

"Fine," Joe mumbled between forkfuls of food. "Just let me get this down first. Walking for miles in the middle of nowhere helps a guy work up an appetite."

After supper Joe accompanied Frank to the front desk, where they learned that Dennis Kincaid had checked out. "Did you get a home address, by any chance?" Frank asked the young clerk.

"I'll check." The clerk thumbed through the registration forms. "Yeah, here it is. The address is in Lowryville. That's about ten miles east of here."

"Great," Frank said, waving his gratitude to the clerk and turning away from the desk. "Now that we know where to find Dennis, let's get upstairs to find Merriweather."

Joe was surprised to see, when Robert Merriweather answered the door of his room, that the assistant was obviously packing. His suitcase was open on the bed and half filled with a package wrapped in brown paper.

"Going somewhere?" he asked Merriweather.

"I'm checking out tomorrow. My flight's in the evening, but I like to get my packing started early. Not that it's really any of your business."

Both Joe and Frank were surprised. "I assumed we were going back together," Frank said. "Why didn't you tell us you'd changed your plans?"

For the first time since they had met him, Merriweather lost his temper. "I don't have to tell you anything," he snapped, red-faced. "Your plans were with the professor. The professor's dead. What I do is none of your business, and vice versa for that matter."

"Look, I just want to ask you a couple of questions," Frank said, trying to edge his way past the door. "Would it be okay to talk to you for just a couple of minutes?"

"What about?"

Frank held up the red book of deeds. Merriweather's face registered shock when he saw it, and his familiar nervousness returned. He stepped back into the room and sat, stunned, on the bed.

Finally he spoke. "What do you want from me?"

"It seems you've seen this book before," Frank said calmly.

"No," said Merriweather, trying to look aloof. "Should I have?"

"You tell us," said Joe.

"Tell you what?"

Frank stepped forward. "Why was the professor interested in who owned the land around the park?"

"I've already told you I don't know."

"Might he have been planning to use the information against Crowley?" Frank persisted.

Merriweather became extremely annoyed now. "Look, I don't mind answering questions when you're asking me something I know about, but since you aren't, I'll have to ask you to leave."

Merriweather stood up and walked toward the door.

Joe hesitated, but Frank reluctantly cooperated. "Thanks, Robert," he said as he passed him on his way out the door. "You've been a big help."

"What a grouch," Joe grumbled as the door closed behind both brothers.

"Don't worry about it." Joe noticed that Frank was surprisingly cheerful. "We won't have to talk to him much anymore. I could stand a little relaxation. How about showing me Rebel Park?"

* * *

126

It was almost closing time when the Hardys entered the gates of the amusement park. Joe noted that there were very few people inside.

"We probably have time for only one ride," Joe said. "You want to try the best one?"

"Sure." Frank smiled. "What's the best ride?"

"Well, if you forget the new tilt-a-whirl, which I suggest you do," Joe said, steering his brother down the midway, "then the best ride is definitely the Rebel Yell roller coaster. Jennifer says it's famous all over Tennessee, and it's the first ride her dad put up on this land."

The boys hurried down the length of the midway to the large roller coaster, which stood a short distance away from the other rides. Joe glanced up at it, noticing how it gleamed in the moonlight. When the ticket taker told them this would be the last ride of the night, Joe was relieved. Despite his love of excitement, he wasn't crazy about amusement park rides.

An instant after Frank and Joe fastened themselves into their seats, the ride began, even though they were the only passengers.

The first curves and loops were tame, but as the inclines became steeper and steeper the roller coaster gathered speed. Joe held on tight, so caught up in the fury of the ride that he didn't even notice the first gunshot.

"What was that?" Frank said, startled.

"What?" shouted Joe over the screeching of the roller coaster.

Just then, a second bullet ricocheted off the metal railing near Joe's head, causing him to duck instantly.

"Company!" he yelled at his brother.

Frank and Joe turned cautiously to look behind them.

Sitting four cars behind them was a masked gunman.

He stared at Joe, lifted his gun, and took careful aim.

Chapter

15

"LOOK OUT!" Joe pushed Frank's head down toward the seat and ducked down himself, just as the gunman fired a third shot and then a fourth.

Aiming a gun on a roller coaster couldn't be easy, Joe assured himself, but when he peered over the top of the car he saw that the gunman had moved down and was now only three cars from the Hardys.

"You okay?" he shouted to Frank over the noise of the ride.

"Yeah. You?"

"So far. Any ideas?"

"There's always prayer."

Joe peeked over the edge again. Now the masked man was only two cars away. The roller coaster swooped into a long, graceful curve and the gunman raised his revolver once again.

Joe wondered who the gunman could be. It was impossible to tell with a red bandanna and sunglasses covering his face. While he was wondering the gunman fired again, missing him by mere inches this time.

Joe ducked lower down into the car.

Joe kept his head down, knowing that the gunman would have a perfectly clear shot if he rose up. Joe hung on to the seat next to Frank, feeling the car lurch into a steep uphill climb.

He heard a cry behind them.

"What's that?" he asked.

"How should I know?" shouted Frank.

Unable to resist a peek, Joe stuck his head back over the edge of the car.

The gunman had fallen backward in his seat! Even better, he'd dropped his gun! He was staring over the edge of the car at the ground, where Joe saw what he guessed was the revolver lying fifty feet below.

"It's our turn now!" cried Joe as he stood up and started climbing back toward the shooter.

"Careful, Joe!" Frank yelled.

The roller coaster was careening madly from one curve to another now, but Joe ignored the wild tosses as he climbed seat by seat toward the gunman, who was running from him as fast as he could.

Joe grabbed the guardrail just in time as the roller coaster zoomed downhill. Just a few more seats now, he told himself. You're doing fine.

But a moment later the roller coaster went into another slow uphill climb. Joe leapt over the last few seats toward the masked man, but his quarry was able to leap down onto the track behind the train and half slide, half climb down the track to safety.

"I can't believe it!" Joe slammed his hand down on the back of the last seat. Wearily he turned to climb back toward Frank, who sat watching from the front.

"Good job," Frank muttered to his brother as the two of them climbed, weak-kneed, off the ride.

They agreed to call the sheriff in the morning. That night they didn't feel up to the man's skepticism.

The next morning the brothers awoke to a horrendous rain storm. Frank rolled over and immediately dialed the sheriff's office but was told the sheriff would have to return his call.

"Bad weather for a day trip," Joe remarked, remembering they had to drive to Lowryville to look for Dennis Kincaid.

"Neither rain nor hail nor dark of night, old buddy," said Frank, climbing out of bed. "Come on, get dressed. I'll meet you downstairs for breakfast."

Frank made a point of checking the brakes on the professor's rental car before they took it on the road.

131

Joe drove, and once they were on their way, with the windshield wipers going and the radio on low, he leaned back against the seat and said, "Okay, partner, you've got a theory. Start talking."

"Not a theory, really. Just a bunch of bits and pieces so far."

"Out with it," Joe insisted.

"Okay," Frank said. "For starters, we know from the sheriff that the same gun, and therefore it could be argued that the same person, killed both the professor and Martin Crowley. That has to rule Crowley out as the professor's killer."

"That makes sense." Joe grinned.

"My first assumption was that the professor was blackmailing Crowley in some way over the different land deeds."

"And now?"

Frank said, "Now I'm not so sure. As soon as we get back from seeing our good friend Kincaid, I want to meet with Tyler Pardee and hear what he has to say about the deeds."

"What else have you got?" asked Joe.

"A bunch of little things. We know Kincaid isn't really a student, but that fact isn't such a big deal. We also know that Crowley wanted to tell us something right before he was shot."

"And we know that Robert Merriweather has been wrought up about something the whole time he's been here," Joe said. "That's it?"

"That's it," Frank admitted. "It may not sound like much, but I think it tells it all."

Frank and Joe discovered that the town of Lowryville consisted of little more than a single row of houses and a gas station. Frank easily learned the location of Kincaid's house by asking the gas station attendant.

He studied the little house through the pouring rain. It would probably look almost as bleak on a sunny day, he decided. The walls were made of unpainted wood and the roof was tin. An old dog crouched on the front porch, trying to keep out of the rain but not having much luck.

"Look." Frank nodded toward a blue pickup truck parked in the gravel driveway. Its right front fender and headlight were smashed. Frank knew they hadn't been broken the day before.

"This must be the place," Joe remarked. "But when did Kincaid smash his truck up? I hope he did it when he almost killed us."

"We'd better be extra careful," Frank cautioned. "Kincaid may be dangerous."

The Hardys dashed through the rain to the house, while the dog barked loudly but made no effort to move.

Frank knocked on the door, and a pretty young woman in a cotton dress answered. She was holding a tiny baby.

"Dennis," the woman called out, not taking her eyes off the dripping boys. "Company."

She silently motioned the Hardys inside. Frank followed her in, peering through the dim light at the cluttered but clean and cozy little living room. Joe entered behind him just as Dennis Kincaid appeared from a back room.

Frank eyed the young man's self-satisfied smile as he greeted the Hardys. He didn't introduce the woman, who disappeared into the back room with the baby.

"So," he said, "the great detectives track me down at last. What tipped you off? The fact that I charged my room at the hotel?" he said sarcastically.

Frank sensed that Joe was having a hard time controlling his anger. "It was you in the truck!" Joe yelled.

Kincaid sat down on a lumpy sofa and grinned. "I registered at the hotel with my real address because I couldn't care less if you found me," he said. "I have nothing to hide and nothing to say. Looks like you boys got wet for nothing."

"Why did you lie about being a student?" Frank asked.

Kincaid glared at him from the sofa. "You think I'm not smart enough to go to college. I have the smarts. I just don't have the bucks."

"Did you try for a scholarship," Joe asked sarcastically.

"Yeah, right," snarled Kincaid, half-rising. "Why don't you just get out of here?"

"Okay." Frank was worried that if they didn't

leave soon, his brother and Kincaid would get in a fight. "We've seen enough."

"But we need to make him talk," Joe protested.

"You and who else?" taunted Kincaid.

"Come on, Joe," Frank insisted, guiding his brother toward the door. "Let's go."

It rained even harder as Frank and Joe drove back to Magnolia House. Joe was still angry, so Frank took a turn at the wheel.

"He nearly killed us with that truck of his," Joe seethed as they neared the hotel.

"But we can't prove that," Frank answered. "There are lots of blue pickups, and we never saw his with that smashed-up fender before." He tried to sound calm and mask his own anger.

"Maybe not," Joe retorted. "But we both know it's true."

The Magnolia House gate swung into sight, opening instantly as Frank turned the car onto the private drive. He wondered why Pardee had bothered putting up this gate if it opened whenever any car approached it.

Jennifer was waiting in the foyer when they returned. "There you are," she said as the boys, still damp, ran in through the big, double front doors. "I thought you might have driven out to look for Kincaid today. Did you find him?"

"The less said about that, the better," Frank remarked. "Jennifer, can you take us to your father?"

Both Jennifer and Joe were surprised. "Sure," Jennifer said. "He's upstairs. Follow me."

Tyler Pardee was sitting at the desk in his third-floor office. Jennifer showed them inside and then left the Hardys alone with her father.

"Come in, come in," he said expansively as the boys entered. "What can I do for you?" He motioned generously for the boys to sit.

"We'll be brief, Mr. Pardee," said Frank. "We've come to ask you a few questions about the deeds to the land around here."

Frank watched Pardee's face carefully, but the man's expression remained blank. "What's on your mind?" Pardee asked pleasantly.

"Well, to put it bluntly," Frank began, "we discovered a duplicate set of books in Crowley's house, and they show that you don't own all the land that the deeds in the courthouse claim you do."

Pardee nodded and smiled. "Those old books. Of course you're confused. You see, Martin was a history buff himself, and he kept those useless deeds as a memento. They're interesting, I suppose, but they carry no legal weight. The ones in the courthouse are the genuine article. Anything else?"

Before Frank or Joe could answer, Pardee's secretary buzzed him and he picked up his phone.

"Yes?" Pardee said. He listened in silence, but Frank saw that he was growing angrier by the moment. "Well, Mr.—" He stopped when he remembered the Hardys. "Remember, my friend," he said into the phone in a whisper, "that my daughter nearly got hurt in that little incident. You went too far, and you can pay to fix your own fender."

Pardee put down the phone and apologized. "Now, where were we?"

"Actually," said Frank, "I think we're all done."

Pardee stood up, obviously relieved. "Well, then, glad I could be of some help."

"Thank you, sir," Joe said, shaking Pardee's hand before he followed his brother out into the hall.

"Tyler Pardee hired Kincaid to stop us?" he questioned Frank the minute they were out of earshot of the office.

"It looks that way," said Frank.

"We have to talk to the sheriff," said Joe. "Let's check to see if he's called us back yet."

Frank was about to agree when they both heard someone shouting. Dreading what might be happening now, they moved quickly to the top of the stairs.

"Fire!" someone was shouting. "Get out! The hotel's on fire!"

Chapter

16

JOE RACED AHEAD of Frank to the foyer, where a crowd was gathering.

"What's going on?" Joe asked a bellhop who was racing by.

"There's a fire in one of the rooms upstairs, and it's spreading fast," the bellboy answered.

"Which room?" Frank demanded.

"Room two forty-five," the bellhop shouted as he ran on.

"That's the professor's room!" cried Frank. "There must be something in it we missed. It's no coincidence that the fire started there."

The Hardys ran quickly up one flight of stairs.

As soon as Joe reached the top of the stairs, he could see smoke billowing out from beneath a set of double doors that closed off the far half of the corridor. "Looks like we may be too late, Frank," he told his brother.

Frank shook his head. "I want to be sure."

He spotted a small fire extinguisher on the wall near the staircase. "Wait here," he said. "If I'm gone longer than two minutes, come after me."

Frank flung open the heavy double doors, and a thick, black cloud of smoke billowed out onto the landing. The smoke burned Joe's eyes and made him cough. He realized after a few moments that he wasn't positive how long Frank had been gone.

He took a few steps back down the stairs to get away from the smoke, which was rolling out from under the doors now. Downstairs, Joe heard the fire trucks arrive. Fire fighters began evacuating anyone left in the hotel.

It's been at least two minutes, Joe told himself. I'm going after him.

Just as Joe reached for the handle of the door, Frank stumbled out, followed by a dense cloud of smoke. His eyes were closed and tears were streaming down his face. He was coughing and could hardly speak.

"Couldn't—I couldn't get through," he gasped. "The smoke was too thick—"

"Take it easy, Frank," Joe said, guiding him down the stairs. "Whatever was in there is destroyed now."

Outside, they joined the other guests and

watched the fire fighters. Joe was glad to let professionals take over.

A couple of hours later the fire was extinguished. All the guests—except those in the professor's wing—were allowed back into their rooms. Joe and Frank ran gratefully to their room.

"I can't believe the whole building didn't burn down," Frank commented. "The smoke in the professor's room was incredible."

"Well, it probably destroyed every single thing in there," Joe pointed out, "but this is a sturdy old house. Built to last."

Frank was reaching for the telephone to try the sheriff again when it rang. Frank answered.

"Hello. A message for Joe Hardy?" The voice was that of one of the hotel clerks. "Miss Pardee has asked to meet him at the hall of mirrors in twenty minutes, please."

"Twenty minutes," Frank repeated, smiling. "Thanks. I'll tell him."

He hung up the phone.

"Tell me what?" Joe asked. "That the fire in the professor's room was the result of arson? That much I already figured."

"Nope. Better than that," Frank said with a smile. "Miss Pardee has requested your presence in twenty minutes at the illustrious hall of mirrors."

140

Joe sat up. "The hall of mirrors? It's raining outside."

Frank shrugged. "I'm only the messenger." Then he grinned. "Chivalry may not be dead, but it's about to get very wet."

"Funny," said Joe. "Very funny."

After Joe had gone to meet Jennifer at Rebel Park, Frank lay down on his bed and thought through the case again. Suddenly he sat up—he knew who committed the murders and why. The memory that triggered the solution was the one of Robert Merriweather packing. It was the package wrapped in brown paper on top of the man's suitcase. The case made sense now—he just needed proof and a look at that package to verify his suspicions. He called the sheriff again.

"I understand he's busy," Frank said in growing frustration to the officer who answered, "but I have to speak to him soon. It's urgent." He paused. "I'll hold, thanks."

Frank hummed to himself as he gazed out the window. Rain continued to pound against the glass.

"Sheriff Walker," came a voice over the phone.

"Sheriff, hi. It's Frank Hardy."

"What can I do for you, son?"

"It's Robert Merriweather. He's at the airport now, and you have to stop him. It's vital—he holds the key to the whole investigation."

There was a spluttering sound coming over the wires. "Now, look here, son," came the sheriff's voice. "I've tried to be patient with you and your brother, but the airport isn't in my jurisdiction." The sheriff was ready to hang up.

"I know that, Sheriff." Frank forced himself to remain calm. "But we're talking about murder here—"

"I've got my murderer," the sheriff snapped. "Wayne Robinson's been formally charged."

"Sheriff, I promise you that Merriweather is carrying evidence that will prove who murdered both Professor Donnell and Martin Crowley," Frank said, crossing his fingers against the slight possibility he was wrong. "Do you have that kind of evidence against Wayne Robinson?"

The sheriff paused and seemed to consider what Frank said. "I'll make a call," the sheriff said finally.

"Can you get him here to Magnolia House along with Kincaid?" Frank asked, knowing he might be pushing his luck. "Also we need Merriweather's luggage," Frank added.

"Well, I hope you're right about all this," the sheriff said resignedly.

"Thanks," Frank said.

Just as Frank hung up the phone, he heard a knock at the door.

It was Jennifer Pardee.

"Well, this is a surprise," said Frank.

"I know." Jennifer smiled. "I'm inviting you both for dinner. My treat."

Frank was confused. "Why aren't you at the hall of mirrors?" he asked.

"In this rain?" said Jennifer. "Are you kidding?"

"But Joe got your message," Frank insisted. He was beginning to get a terrible feeling in his stomach.

"What message?"

"To meet him in the hall of mirrors!" Frank was already moving past her into the corridor. "He's been gone over an hour. How do I get there?"

"Wait for me." Jennifer ran to keep up with him.

"Just tell me how to get there," insisted Frank as the two of them ran down the stairs. "Is it near the roller coaster?"

"Right beside it." Jennifer ran to the front desk and grabbed a raincoat. "But I'm coming, too."

"You call the sheriff's office," Frank ordered, heading for the front doors. "Tell Walker to get some deputies to meet me at the hall as soon as possible. Tell him it's a matter of life and death."

Jennifer tossed the raincoat to Frank.

"Then go to your room and stay there with the door locked. Don't open it for anyone except me, Joe, or the sheriff."

143

"What about—"

Frank was firm. "Me, Joe, or the sheriff. No exceptions. None."

Jennifer wavered. "Okay, I'll do it. But hurry!"

As Frank was running out into the rain, Joe was studying five different versions of himself, all of them wet, angry, and confused.

Joe took a careful step to the left. Now there were only three of him.

He had never liked halls of mirrors, but this day would go down as one of his all-time bad hall-of-mirrors experiences.

He was mad that Jennifer hadn't shown up. Thinking Frank might have gotten the message wrong, he'd taken a quick walk around the park to see if he could spot her, but that had proved fruitless.

In fact, thanks to the rain, there was practically no one in Rebel Park. Everyone else has enough sense to stay in out of the rain, Joe realized gloomily.

Finally, he had returned to the hall of mirrors hoping that Jennifer had just been delayed. At least it's inside, he thought, comforting himself. He felt very wet and alone now, though.

Just then he heard a door open and close. It sounded like the door on the far side of the building.

"Jennifer? Is that you? It's me, Joe. Over here." Joe glanced in front of him and laughed.

144

"I'm not sure where 'here' is, actually, but there are three of me, if that helps."

There was no answer. Joe began to worry. "Who's there?" he demanded.

The distinct click of a revolver being cocked sent chills down his spine. He heard a man's voice say very clearly, "When your brother gets here—and I'm sure he'll come—he'll find you dead. And he'll be next."

As Frank reached the entrance to the hall of mirrors the storm reached its peak. A bolt of lightning flashed through the sky, followed immediately by a huge clap of thunder.

Or was that gunfire?

Frank rushed inside, shouting, "Joe! Are you in here?"

"Frank!"

Frank was relieved to hear Joe's voice. But then his relief faded.

"Be careful!" Joe was shouting. "It's Pardee! He's got a gun!"

FRANK WAS GRATEFUL for his martial arts training as he moved through the dimly lit hall. Martial arts had taught him to be light on his feet—and to control his fear.

In a flash Frank thought he saw Pardee. Instinctively, he stepped back. In the next instant, a shot rang out, and glass crashed all around Frank.

I can't stay in here unarmed, Frank realized. "Joe, stay down," he yelled, and ran back outside to get something, anything, to use as a weapon.

He instantly spotted a stand with stacks of baseballs. He took off and filled his raincoat pockets with as many balls as he could carry.

Back inside the hall of mirrors, Frank announced, "Joe, I'm back. Stay down."

Standing half-hidden in the doorway of the spooky hall, Frank methodically pitched baseballs at the mirrors, smashing them one by one and ducking back after each toss.

"You're not going to stop me with those," warned Pardee.

Over the noise of the storm came the distinct whine of sirens as police cars entered the park. Frank kept silent but threw a ball in the direction of Pardee's voice. Another huge mirror smashed to pieces. Behind where it had been stood Tyler Pardee.

"Give it up, sir," Frank said in a level voice. "It's over. The police are here."

Pardee didn't answer but only raised his gun and aimed at Frank.

Suddenly Joe appeared out of the darkness. As Frank watched, he flew a few feet to tackle Pardee from behind. The gun slipped out of the hotel owner's hand and skidded across the floor.

Frank snatched up the gun. "You can let him up, Joe. I've got him covered."

Just as Joe stepped back from the man, Sheriff Walker pushed past Frank into the shattered hall. "What's going on here?" he demanded as half a dozen deputies followed him inside.

Frank turned Pardee's gun over to Walker with a weary smile. "Sir, that's a story I'd like to tell."

*   *   *

147

After the Hardys had showered and changed into dry clothes, they took off for the library, where everyone was gathered.

Frank knew that the sheriff's colleagues had been able to stop Robert Merriweather at the airport. Merriweather would be waiting in the library, along with Dennis Kincaid.

As the Hardys walked down the corridor, Joe said, "What bothers me most is Jennifer."

"I know." Frank frowned. "This has to be awful for her."

"I wish there was something I could do."

"Not much you can do except be her friend."

Frank was pleased to see a guard posted outside the library. The guard opened the door, and the Hardys stepped inside.

Frank saw Tyler Pardee, Jennifer, Robert Merriweather, and Kincaid seated around the library table in the center of the room. The package wrapped in brown paper lay on top of the table.

Sheriff Walker, who stood in one corner of the room, brightened when the Hardys entered. "Good. Now maybe we can get to the bottom of this," he said.

Joe took a seat next to Jennifer, but to his disappointment she ignored him. Frank remained standing. "I think we can," he told the sheriff. "Is that the package from Robert's suitcase?" He gestured toward the package on the table.

"That's it," the sheriff confirmed.

Frank tore the paper off the manuscript and

148

read what he assumed the title would be. *"Southern Carpetbaggers: A Sad Legacy of the Confederacy."*

He put the manuscript back on the table. "You see," he began, "Crowley knew that not all carpetbaggers came down from the North. He'd been blackmailing Tyler Pardee for years after he'd discovered that the Pardee family didn't really hold fair title to all the land they claimed."

"Is that so, Tyler?" said the sheriff.

Pardee looked at the table. "Talk to my lawyer," he said sullenly.

"My guess is," Frank continued, glancing at his brother for support, "that Crowley's demands weren't so great and Pardee didn't mind paying him off to keep him quiet."

"He tried to get Wayne Robinson elected," Joe put in despite Jennifer's obvious discomfort, "so he could get Robinson to find the real book of deeds and destroy it once and for all. By the way, Sheriff, the real book is hidden in our room upstairs. We pried up a few floorboards."

The sheriff nodded. "Go on."

"After Crowley was reelected, I'm sure his price went up," said Frank. "But otherwise everything was business as usual until the professor and Merriweather started researching the professor's new book."

Frank pulled a note out of his pocket. "Merriweather says he never saw this note, but don't believe him. It asks Merriweather to check into who owns the land around here. See where this corner's been torn off? That's where the professor dated his notes. I think Merriweather tore off the date so he could deny having seen it. Obviously the note was old—from when Donnell was doing his research for *Carpetbaggers.*"

"Why wouldn't he just destroy the note?" asked the sheriff.

"Probably because he was afraid Frank or I had already seen it and might get even more suspicious if it disappeared," Joe offered.

"Once Merriweather found out that Pardee really didn't own the land, he began blackmailing him, too. But Merriweather's most brilliant move," Frank continued, "was in convincing Pardee that it was actually the professor who was blackmailing him."

"Hold on a minute," said the sheriff. "It may be true that Tyler's people took land from their neighbors, but that happened a lot in the South. Families often ran when fighting broke out and just never came back. It's not the biggest crime in the world."

"No, it isn't," Frank agreed. "That's probably why Crowley wasn't able to gouge Pardee for too much. But the professor was a world-famous author, and I don't think the National Park Service would take kindly to a southern carpetbagger running a theme park and a profitable Battle of Shiloh reenactment next to a national historic site. Pardee felt he had to kill him.''

For a moment the room was deadly quiet.

Then Jennifer said to Frank, ''If what you say is true about my dad—and I don't believe it for a minute—explain why he would intentionally try to harm me. Joe and I were attacked in the tunnel of love. And you, Joe, and I nearly died when the brakes on my car were cut.''

Frank gave Jennifer a sympathetic look. ''I'm afraid those two incidents are what started me thinking your father *did* do it.''

''Explain that one,'' said the sheriff.

''Pardee had hired Kincaid to frighten—only frighten—Jennifer and me, knowing that that would divert any possible attention from him,'' Joe said. ''As for the brakes going out, Frank and I overheard Pardee talking to Kincaid about that one. He said he'd gone too far. I don't think he cared if Frank or I got hurt or even killed— we'd be out of his way.''

''So you're saying it was Kincaid who killed the professor and Crowley?'' asked the sheriff.

''No.'' Frank tried to be patient. ''Kincaid only harassed us. He drove that truck at the airport. He knocked Joe down the stairs. He set fire to the ammo tent and knocked the wall out of the barn. He drove the wild horses at Joe and me, and he shot at us on the roller coaster, I'm sure. But only one person could sneak live ammo onto the battlefield: Tyler Pardee.''

"But you found a box of live ammo in the supply room yourself," the sheriff protested.

"Yes, because it was planted there by Pardee to make it look like a random bullet killed the professor."

"And the fire in Donnell's room?" asked the sheriff. "Pardee or Kincaid?"

"Neither," said Joe. "Merriweather did that."

"Why?" asked the sheriff in surprise.

"He wanted to destroy any evidence that might link him to the blackmailing."

The sheriff shook his head. "It makes for an interesting story, boys, but I'm not sure it'll stand up in court."

"You're forgetting ballistics," Frank replied. "I'm certain if you test Pardee's rifle against the bullets that killed the professor and Crowley, you'll find that they match."

"That reminds me, Frank," said Joe. "If Pardee didn't have a real problem with Crowley, why bother to kill him? Everybody was ready to call the professor's death an accident."

"Good question, Joe. I think he saw how easy it was to deal with the professor, and he figured he could make Crowley's death look accidental, too. And don't forget, people saw Crowley saying he had something to tell us. I'm sure that got back to Pardee, and he felt he had to act."

"What about the book about Beauregard?" the sheriff wanted to know.

"Oh, he was working on that one, all right,

but it wasn't the trouble spot. This one was, and this one was finished," Frank said.

"I've heard enough," said the sheriff. "Deputy, take these three men to jail. We'll deal with the charges when I get there." All three men were as silent leaving the room as they had been the past fifteen minutes.

The sheriff turned to Frank and Joe. "I guess I owe you two an apology. And thanks."

"Don't mention it." Frank exchanged an uneasy smile with his brother. "Any time."

Joe was packed and ready to go early the next morning. Their flight left at eight o'clock, and he wanted time for a snack at the airport. As he and Frank loaded their bags into the rental car in front of the mansion, Joe heard Jennifer call.

"Joe, wait!"

Joe flushed, stuffing his garment bag in faster. He had been unable to sleep most of the night, worrying about Jennifer and how she was taking the news about her father—and finally how she felt about the fact that he had helped put her dad behind bars. He had almost called her to say how sorry he was but had held back.

Now he felt as though he had been caught trying to run away. Which, of course, he was.

"Your problem, little brother," Frank said sympathetically. He climbed into the car and closed the door.

Joe turned to face the red-haired girl. "I'm

153

sorry, Jennifer," he said. "It's not the way I wanted things to turn out."

"Me, either." There were tears in her beautiful green eyes. "But you didn't do anything wrong. I know that." She hesitated, blushing. "Will I ever see you again?"

Joe couldn't believe his ears. Had Jennifer forgiven him? "I—I hope so," he stammered.

"I hope so, too," she said. "I mean it." Smiling tearfully at him, she took his hand.

They looked at each other for a moment. Then Joe dropped her hand and closed the lid of the trunk. "I'd better be going," he said.

"Write to me, okay?" said Jennifer, stepping back out of the way.

He grinned and nodded, then climbed into the car.

"You'd better wipe that smile off your face, little brother," Frank said as he pulled the car away.

Joe shot him a questioning look.

"Our job down here may be over, but we still have to write a paper for English, figure out the hit-miss ratio for math, and—"

"Enough, enough!" Joe shouted, putting his hands over his ears.

The brothers laughed. Then Frank turned to look one last time at the green, rolling fields of Shiloh.

THE HARDY BOYS CASEFILES

Simon & Schuster Mail Order
200 Old Tappan Rd., Old Tappan, N.J. 07675

Please send me the books I have checked above. I am enclosing $_____ (please add $0.75 to cover the postage and handling for each order. Please add appropriate sales tax). Send check or money order--no cash or C.O.D.'s please. Allow up to six weeks for delivery. For purchase over $10.00 you may use VISA: card number, expiration date and customer signature must be included.

Name _____

Address _____

City _____ State/Zip _____

VISA Card # _____ Exp.Date _____

Signature _____ 762-43

BUFFY

THE VAMPIRE

SLAYER™

As long as there have been vampires, there has been the Slayer. One girl in all the world, to find them where they gather and to stop the spread of their evil ... the swell of their numbers.

#1 THE HARVEST

#2 HALLOWEEN RAIN

#3 COYOTE MOON

#4 NIGHT OF THE LIVING RERUN

THE ANGEL CHRONICLES, VOL. 1

BLOODED
(Coming in mid-July)

CHILD OF THE HUNT
(Coming in mid-September)

THE WATCHER'S GUIDE
(The Totally Pointy Guide for the Ultimate Fan!)
(Coming in mid-October)

Based on the hit TV series created by Joss Whedon

From Archway Paperbacks
Published by Pocket Books

1399-05